THE SOFTWIRE

THE SOFTWIRE

WORMHOLE PIRATES ON ORBIS 3

PJ HAARSMA

CANDLEWICK PRESS

Copyright © 2009 by PJ Haarsma

First edition 2009

Library of Congresss Cataloging-in-Publication Data
Haarsma, PJ.
The softwire: wormhole pirates on Orbis 3 / PJ Haarsma. — 1st ed.
p. cm. — (The softwire series)
Summary: At the start of their third rotation of service, Johnny Turnbull, his sister, Ketheria, and friends face pirates who seem to know JT and want him to deliver a mysterious message.
ISBN 978-0-7636-2711-9
[1. Computers—Fiction. 2. Pirates—Fiction. 3. Science Fiction.] I. Title.
II. Title: Wormhole pirates on Orbis 3. III. Title: Wormhole pirates
on Orbis three. IV. Series.
PZ7.H11132Sof 2009
[Fic]—dc22   2008029667

2 4 6 8 10 9 7 5 3 1

Printed in the United States of America

This book was typeset in Utopia.

Candlewick Press
99 Dover Street
Somerville, Massachusetts 02144

visit us at www.candlewick.com

In loving memory of
Emma Jane Turnbull
and
Pasquale Fortunato

"Girls," I said, plopping down next to Theodore. *"They're* the aliens!"

"Max again?" he mumbled. His face was pressed against the glass portal that ran the length of the shuttle.

"I don't get what she has against Space Jumpers."

"It's pretty simple, JT. Citizens don't trust them."

"But we're not Citizens," I reminded him.

"We want to be."

I looked up to sneak another glimpse at the Citizens relaxing on the mezzanine above my head. It was just high enough to make me feel inferior. The Citizens dined the entire trip to Orbis 3, reclining on puffy loungers decorated with green and gold Gia silks. *We* sat huddled together on cold aluminum benches and ate only what we brought. There were four other knudniks traveling with us, and they sat obediently near the feet of their respective Guarantors. When ordered, they bolted up the short set of steps to administer whatever mundane or demeaning task was imposed upon them. I hated the Citizens, but Theodore was right; I still wanted to be one.

"What are you looking at?" I turned and asked him.

"I'm trying to see the wormhole. This is the closest any shuttle ever gets. Eight thousand, four hundred, and thirty-three kilometers."

I squeezed next to him and peered out the portal into the stars.

"I see Orbis 3." I gestured to the huge ring hanging in space. "But where is the wormhole?"

Theodore pointed. "Look, there. See how the crystal moon bends a little? The wormhole does that. We must be directly in front of it."

I watched the heavy orange moon Ki pinch and distort as our huge space shuttle lumbered toward our new home. *What will our new Guarantor be like?* I wondered, but I had already resigned myself to the fact that knowing who it was wouldn't make him any nicer.

"Look!" Theodore said, pulling away from the window and holding up both hands in front of his face. It seemed as if some invisible force were tugging at his skin, stretching it toward the wormhole. "It's happening to you, too."

It was happening to *everything*. One of the Citizens above Dalton poured his drink over the edge, and the greenish liquid appeared to smear across the cabin before it splashed onto Dalton's head, much to the delight of the other Citizens.

"Hey!" Dalton protested, but the Citizens only applauded

or stomped their feet. *Would they even notice us missing if the shuttle ripped open and we were all sucked into space? Would they even care?* I wondered. Then the alien ordered Dalton to clean up his mess.

"It's an optical illusion," Theodore said. "The wormhole is bending the light before it reaches our eyes."

I turned my attention back toward the wormhole and immediately noticed that something wasn't right. Directly in front of me, Orbis 3 and the crystal moon were bending and twisting violently. *That's more than an optical illusion,* I thought. Something was coming through the wormhole.

"Is that supposed to happen?" I elbowed Theodore.

"What?"

"That!"

With a crackle of bright blue light, a spaceship pierced the blackness of space. The ship was the color of charred metal and rimmed with flashing red lights. It was much longer than our shuttle and twice as tall. It pushed through the wormhole—straight toward us.

"It's gonna hit us!" I cried, but the huge vessel turned port-side and saddled next to us. Harsh searchlights from the ship splashed through our cabin.

"Wormhole pirates!" one of the Citizens screamed.

"But that's impossible!" another exclaimed.

"What's a wormhole pirate?" Maxine Bennett cried as she clambered next to us.

"I don't know," I said.

"You have to get Theylor," Theodore whispered quickly.

The Keeper Theylor was seated above the Citizens in a small compartment reserved for those who rule the Rings of Orbis. I moved toward the steps, wondering if the Citizens would let me pass, when our shuttle lurched forward and threw me to the ground. I saw Theylor spring from his cabin.

"Get back to your seat, Johnny," Theylor called out to me with his left head. His right head dipped to focus on the ship's portal. He moved so fast that his thick purple robe blurred with his transparent blue skin as he shifted between the Citizens.

I dashed back to my seat and squeezed next to Theodore. My little sister, Ketheria, was there now, too. In fact, everyone had moved to the starboard side to gawk at the mysterious ship that was now upon us. The vessel was so close it filled the entire portal. Painted on the side of the ship was an alien skull posed over gnarled crossbones. I watched three bay doors crack open on the side of the pirates' spaceship and thick mechanical arms unfold from each opening. Once untangled, they clamped onto our shuttle, and the impact knocked even more people to the floor.

"What are wormhole pirates?" Max shouted, pulling herself back up.

But none of us answered. No one knew. Theylor now stood at the top of the steps and faced the hatch. Both of his heads spoke at the same time. "Children, stay where you are."

I asked Theylor, "What's happening?"

"A hostile vessel has emerged from the wormhole. Security will be upon them—"

But heavy pounding on our shuttle door interrupted Theylor's warning.

One Citizen screamed, "You can't let them in!" as she raced to remove her jewelry and hide it in the loungers.

But whoever wanted inside was coming anyway.

WUMP! The shuttle hatch crumpled inward. *WUMP!* And the seal to the metal hatch broke. Ketheria covered her ears as the escaping pressure screeched through the cabin. I swallowed frantically, trying to adjust to the pressure change. One more wallop and the hatch crashed to the floor. Someone screamed.

All the oxygen should have been sucked from the cabin— for that matter, so should I—but besides the pressure change, the atmosphere held. I should have been terrified as well, but my curiosity was stronger than my fear. I had experienced many strange events during my two rotations on the Rings of Orbis, and I wanted to see who (or what) had broken that hatch open. I *wanted* to see a wormhole pirate.

Theodore and I snuck to the far side of the wide metallic stairs. Theylor did not see, as he was now concentrating on the hatch. I had a direct line of sight across the Citizens' area to the gaping hole that now replaced the shuttle door.

"Can you see them?" Theodore whispered.

"No. Just the hole," I replied. "And some sort of green plastic tube that's sealing the opening."

A delicate Citizen with iridescent green skin that spilled off her head like human hair dropped herself behind the closest lounger, blocking my view. The alien shook her hand at us.

"Get away from me," she hissed, and we moved farther along the stairs. I saw more Citizens hiding behind loungers, or anything that would conceal them.

"Isn't anyone going to defend themselves?" Theodore whispered.

"Citizens?" I replied. "They pay people to do that for them."

Max had moved next to us. "Where are your Space Jumpers now?" she said, smiling. I knew that she was referring to our earlier argument.

"Space Jumpers would never show themselves around so many Citizens. It's not allowed," I argued.

"That's convenient. Maybe because there's nothing in it for them."

"Space Jumpers aren't like that. They are protectors. Neewalkers are the ones who do it for money."

"Then who pays for their —"

Theodore cut her off. "Would you two shut up?"

A staunch alien dressed in a black armored suit and heavy boots ducked as he sauntered onto our shuttle. His white skin, stamped with a web of purplish veins, was stretched and pinned to the metal helmet on his head. "What a sorry bunch we have here," he said, and spat on the floor. His skin sparkled as he spoke, his voice thick like radiation gel.

"How dare you boldly . . ."

The wormhole pirate spun toward the voice and hoisted the biggest plasma rifle I had ever seen. He aimed and ignited the weapon all in one motion.

"Keep quiet, Citizen!" the pirate roared.

Theylor, who was as tall as the pirate, stepped forward, speaking calmly. "Security has been alerted."

"We have no quarrel with you, Keeper," the pirate replied. "We're just here for our bounty."

"Rotten thieves," one Citizen hissed, but when the pirate raised his weapon, the alien immediately shrank behind a lounger. We all did, for that matter.

Another pirate peered in from the broken hatch and then skittered next to the first one. He fidgeted with his heavy-looking rifle while repeatedly glancing out the portal.

"Collect their crystals," the large alien ordered.

"Wha—what for?" whispered the nervous one.

The leader struck the pirate on the head with the butt of his plasma rifle. The smaller alien stumbled against the wall but never took his eyes off the portal.

"You know the plan!" spat the big alien.

"They're not going about it very fast, are they?" Theodore whispered.

Max turned to me and said, "Why *aren't* any Space Jumpers showing up? Now would be better than any time I can think of."

"They're too many . . . Oh, forget it," I told her. I was finished arguing about Space Jumpers.

Three more wormhole pirates clambered onto our shuttle. None were as big as their leader, but each was as nervous as the little one, glancing out the portal and whispering to the others. They poked at the Citizens with their plasma rifles and demanded their crystals and jewelry.

"Is it just me, or do they look distracted?" I asked Theodore.

"It's like they're worried about something," he said.

Before we could move away, the small alien was at the top of our steps. "What about these?" he shouted when he spotted us.

"They're knudniks; they have nothing. Leave them be," the leader shouted back.

But then the little alien caught sight of Ketheria. He shuffled down the steps toward her, and I knew instantly what he was after. On my sister's forehead was a large amber crystal set in a silver band that encompassed her head. The Keepers had attached it to her after Madame Lee exposed her telepathic abilities on Orbis 1.

I stepped in front of my sister when I saw him reach for the crystal. "You can't take it," I told the alien.

The alien spun around and shoved the nose of his weapon against my throat. "Who's going to stop me?" he snarled, curling back his lips to expose four rows of yellowed, pointed teeth.

"It's attached to her head," I said. "It can't come off."

"Anything that sparkles is coming with me, even if I have to cut a little knudnik flesh in the process," he threatened me, and turned toward my sister.

Without thinking, I grabbed the alien by the shoulder. He swung around and buried the butt of his rifle in my stomach. I slumped to my knees, gasping for air, but I was glad the alien's attention was concentrated on me now and not my sister.

"JT!" Max screamed.

There were twenty-one other kids on the shuttle with me,

linked together by the debt our dead parents owed the Trading Council. When I fell to the floor, they circled the wormhole pirate. The plasma rifle clattered in his grip as he spun from kid to kid, unable to decide where to hold his aim.

"Enough!" shouted the leader.

"Why is it taking so long?" my attacker shouted back.

Theylor stepped forward and ordered the leader, "Take your trinkets and be gone."

"I was hoping for a Space Jumper or two," the big pirate said, feigning disappointment.

One of the Citizens cried, "They are banished. Orbis does not need those barbarians."

"Banished?" the pirate said, and laughed.

Under his breath, I heard the nervous little pirate say, "Foolish Citizens."

It was then that the shuttle shivered and the cabin glowed blue. Some sort of ectoplasm was seeping through the walls.

"It's about time," the leader scoffed under his breath.

As the transparent blue gel thickened, the security force took shape from the substance leaking into our ship. A host of security-bots, armed with their own weapons, focused on the offenders. Most of the pirates immediately laid their guns down before a single shot was fired.

"Not very brave," Max said.

"Just not stupid," I replied. "Look at all those security-bots."

"Sixty-four of them," Theodore counted quickly. He had a habit of counting things. He counted the fastest when he was nervous.

"Why aren't they fighting back, though?" Max asked.

My sister stood next to me as a security-bot bubbled the nervous little alien in front of me. "I don't think that was their intention," she said.

But then the big pirate lifted his rifle, smiled, and shouted, "Oh, why not?" He squeezed several rounds at the security-bots, striking them with precision. One of the Citizens screamed and cowered under a table. The pirate was now laughing out loud, picking off the robots as they flew closer. He strolled across the Citizens' area as pieces of the shattered machines showered down upon us. Finally the remaining bots tackled the pirate. He hit the floor less than two meters from my face and whispered to me, "Tell him we put on a good show, all right, Softwire?"

2

I was starving by the time the Council officials finished questioning us. Our rendezvous with the wormhole pirates delayed our shuttle trip by a whole spoke as the investigators interrogated everyone.

"He acted like . . . he knew me," I told the official who questioned me inside the spaceport. She was a flimsy alien without a strand of hair on her head.

The passenger who had spilled his drink inside the cabin paraded toward me and shouted at the official, "What did this knudnik just tell you?"

"I didn't . . ." I tried to interject, but the Citizen would have none of it.

"Silence," he ordered, glancing over his shoulder. "You must confine this creature. You must confine him *now*. He may be in collaboration with these bandits. If he claims to know them, then he is a suspect. In fact, I *saw* him communicating with the leader when we brought him down. Yes! I saw that."

"That's ridiculous," exclaimed another passenger, who shoved in front of me. "What's a knudnik going to do?" Then he launched into his own dramatic story depicting his heroic efforts to foil the "vicious" wormhole pirates.

I was glad the attention was off me, and I slipped over to Theylor and the other kids as the two Citizens argued over the accounts of the attack. Standing next to Theodore, I watched more passengers jabbering in small groups — family members, I assumed. A few even waved their arms around, dramatizing their stories for flying camera-bots.

"What are those, Theylor?" I asked him.

"Citizens enjoy a good story," he replied. "They often record or broadcast their adventures for others' amusement."

"But why all the commotion?" Max asked.

"No one has ever seen a wormhole pirate on the rings before this. Most Citizens thought they were a myth, an excuse for disreputable operators who claimed their cargo was confiscated inside the wormhole." Theylor nudged Max forward. "But we need to go now. Everyone over here, please."

The Keeper motioned us away from the crowds. I looked at the Citizens over my shoulder and thought, *Why did that wormhole pirate act like he knew me?* I was just a knudnik. Yes, I was a softwire, but it had served me no good on the Rings of Orbis. The only people who mattered here were Citizens, and they went to great lengths to make sure you knew that. There was no reason in this universe why that wormhole pirate should know me. But I still couldn't get his face out of my mind.

Tell him . . . His order kept repeating in my head. Tell *who*? I answered back.

Theylor guided us into the thick of the spaceport. Orbis 3, he told us, was the ring where most of the Citizens lived. While Orbis 1 was home to the Keepers' city, Magna, and housed most of the government buildings, Orbis 2 handled all of the crystal refineries. But Orbis 3 was exclusive to the Citizens and their powerful Trading Council. Theylor said that the Keepers had little control over the Citizens on Orbis 3.

"That's comforting," Theodore whispered to me.

"Wow, look at that," one of the kids cried out, standing under a crystal sculpture that must have been more than seven meters tall. It was one of eight sculptures posed with outstretched arms and laboring to support the expansive glass ceiling.

"One for each of the First Families," Max pointed out.

"How do you know that?" I said.

"Everyone does," she replied.

"I don't!" Theodore complained.

Theylor saw us gawking at the alien sculptures and said, "The Citizens and their Trading Council profit immensely from the crystal moons."

It was obvious to me that they had spent a fortune on those sculptures, and everything else, too.

"This is unbelievable," Theodore said, staring up through the glass ceiling that framed a spectacular view of the moon Ki, where the Citizens harvested so much of their wealth. Orbis 3 curved up and over our heads, revealing an unending sparkle of lights from more and more buildings.

"There must be a lot of people on this ring," Max exclaimed.

We followed Theylor across tiles laced with metal that seemed to sparkle from some unknown energy source. In the middle of the open foyer, one Citizen stopped abruptly in front of me, glaring. He made a snorting sound and flicked his wrists toward the ground. Another Citizen practically walked over Dalton, unwilling to acknowledge his existence. I straightened my tattered vest, even though I knew the skin was the mark of a knudnik. It was the only thing that visibly separated us from them.

"They certainly have a way of making you feel wanted," Max whispered to me.

"We should just take these things off," Theodore told Max, tugging at his skin.

"Forget the Citizens," she said.

"But I hate being invisible," he replied under his breath.

"I see you," Ketheria said.

I smiled at my sister.

The Citizens on the Rings of Orbis may have been ignorant and self-absorbed, but boy, could they build things. When we stepped out of the spaceport, we were besieged by curving towers of metal and glass, gigantic floating cylinders, and sleek sparkling spires that crowded the sloped horizon. I stood on the steps with Theodore, pointing at objects I'd never seen before, not even in my imagination.

"The Citizens take great pride in their cities. Maybe too much," Theylor announced as he stopped in front of a long transport at the bottom of the metal steps. "It is a shame that they left no sign of the Ancients' buildings." Theylor stared out toward the glimmering buildings with his left head while his right head drooped, looking away.

After a moment, Theylor turned back toward us. "Come, it is time to meet your new Guarantor," he said, and swept his long hand over the shimmering transport. We all piled in.

"Who is it this time?" one of the children asked anxiously.

"Are there any nice Guarantors?" Grace asked. "Will we ever get one of them?"

"We don't need a Guarantor," Dalton grumbled, eerily reminiscent of his friend Switzer, who had died on Orbis 2.

But Theylor only smiled and connected with the craft's navigational computer using his neural implant. He attached the clear cable securely behind the left ear of his right head while his other head turned and said, "Please take any seat. The ride will not be very long. All your questions will be answered when we arrive."

Max and Ketheria sat in front of Theodore and me. Ketheria steadied herself as the transport lifted off the ground and turned 180 degrees in front of the spaceport.

"Whoa!" Max gushed as the craft floated through the city about four meters off the ground. Other crafts sped past, most with only a single passenger.

I hung out the side, looking down at the ground. Only a small metallic rail prevented me from me falling out.

"Theodore, look at that!" I shouted, pointing to small round shuttles scurrying along the precise streets beneath us.

"No, look over there," another kid shouted, and we all strained our necks to catch a glimpse of a huge floating cylinder. The edges were rounded, as if someone had punched the middle out of a security bubble. Inside sat about a hundred aliens watching some sort of performance in the middle of the oddly shaped building. I could not even begin to imagine what job we would have to do on Orbis 3.

"What are we going to do here?" I asked Theylor.

"That will be up to your new Guarantor," he replied.

"Why won't you tell us about him?" Max asked.

Theylor would only say, "Everything will be revealed to you shortly."

My chest tightened with a mix of fear and excitement whenever I thought about our new owner. Our first Guarantor, Joca Krig Weegin, forced us to work on an assembly line sorting his junk. The smell from the radiation gel we used to protect our bodies would be forever burned into my senses. After he tried to sell us in an underground slave ring, we were traded to a far more evil creature on Orbis 2, named Odran. *He* profited from knudniks by selling them illegal passage off the Rings of Orbis. My experience with Guarantors was horrible, to say the least. It frightened me even more to guess why Theylor wasn't telling us anything. Who would we belong to now? I could only wonder.

The glass and metal structures gave way to rolling hills and trees whose branches hung down and rooted into the ground.

Immense compounds dotted the greenery and weaved between small forests. Some buildings were contained in clear domes while others were open-air structures. I saw elaborate fountains, manicured gardens, and stone sculptures. Everything appeared crafted by artistic hands—I was certain they were the hands of knudniks.

"What are these buildings?" I asked Theylor.

"They are the dwellings of Citizens," the Keeper replied.

"We're going to live *inside* the Citizen's home?" Max said.

"We're not going to live in a factory or something?" Theodore asked.

I didn't know what this meant. Was it better or worse? Did this mean we were going to clean up after a Citizen, or would they take us to our workplace later? I wished that Theylor would give us more information.

The shuttle passed three more dwellings before it circled over a sprawling, palatial estate. The building flowed between the shrubbery, winding its dark stone walls in and around the tiny forest of oddly shaped trees. Behind the main structure was a huge glass dome, which evaporated as our shuttle approached.

"Who is it, Theylor? Who lives here?" Max badgered him, but the Keeper simply watched the glass sparkle and dissolve as we descended into the interior.

The shuttle set down on a large circular pad of rough stone that was surrounded by towering bushes with thick leaves of red and purple and blue. The dome re-formed over our heads, and Theylor stepped off first. Ketheria took my hand, and we followed the Keeper out of the shuttle and up one of six paths that led from the landing area. Around every bend, a new kind of plant lined the pathway. A few brandished long spikes while others flowed in the wind so gracefully that they looked like they were floating in water.

Theylor caught Grace reaching out for one of the plants and stopped her. "Be careful," he warned. "They may look pretty, but some are very deadly, especially when they are hungry."

Grace snatched her hand back, and we all huddled a little closer. The garden didn't seem so beautiful anymore. As the path widened, we found ourselves at the bottom of a small rise that led to the Citizen's home. All of the walls were curved, and it was difficult to tell where one ended and another began. A glass wall, or maybe it was a door, began to shimmer at the top of the broad steps. It disappeared the same way the dome had when we landed.

"Who lives here, Theylor?" I said.

"You do," someone replied from the shadows of the darkened interior.

When the figure stepped into the light, I couldn't believe my eyes; in fact, I even blinked once and shook my head.

"Charlie?"

I thought we would never see him again when we were forced to leave him on Orbis 2. But standing proudly in front of us, wearing a long cream-colored robe and a huge smile on his rugged face, was Charlie. Draped around his waist was the ornate belt of a Citizen, flashing the emblem of Orbis.

"Well," he said, his arms outstretched, "what do you think?"

"Nugget!" my sister yelled as the muscular little alien emerged from behind Charlie and leaped toward her on his big-clawed feet. While his thick clumsy hands waved around, my sister scooped him up, and they both fell to the ground laughing.

I didn't know what to think. *Is it true?* I looked at Theylor. Both of his heads smiled and nodded, and we rushed our big friend. The excitement was infectious as each of us hugged Charlie. What a great feeling this was. I stood and watched. I was smiling so hard, my cheeks hurt.

"It's good to see you again," he said. "How's the arm?"

I held up my right arm, the robotic one the Rings of Orbis had given me after Switzer died. "It's good," I said. "I hardly notice the difference anymore."

"That's good. You guys deserve a little fun."

"But how?" I said as he thumped me on the back with his big hand.

"Does it really matter?" he replied.

"Are we gonna live with you?" Max asked.

"If you want," he said, looking at me.

"And Nugget, too?" Ketheria shouted.

Charlie smiled and said, "And Nugget, too."

"Come, Ketheria. Let me show you everything," Nugget said, and pulled Ketheria into the house. The alien was as tall as she was now, and his useless bony wings were beginning to dry up.

"I can take it from here, Theylor," Charlie said. Before the Keeper reached the shuttle, Charlie stopped him. "Theylor?"

"Yes?" the alien replied.

"Thanks. They won't regret this."

But the Keeper only smiled and turned away.

"Regret what?" I asked.

Charlie laughed. "You and your questions. You're as bad as Max."

"You still have a *ton* of things to tell me," I reminded him.

Charlie laughed as Max and Grace dragged him into the house. Most of the others had already followed Nugget and Ketheria inside. There was shouting from every room as we poured through Charlie's house, exploring each curved wall, each new room.

Max grabbed me by my skin and pointed out the wave-like designs on the walls.

"They all have it," she said, and rubbed her hand along the thin channels carved into the polished stone.

"What are they?" I asked.

"They represent the cosmic streams of OIO. I think it's to remind whoever lives here that we are constantly affected by the cosmic energy that flows through the universe."

"You think Charlie did this?"

"I don't think so," she replied. "He doesn't talk about OIO much. I think someone else owned this place before him. Why wouldn't he have mentioned it before?"

"She's right," Charlie said, standing behind us.

"Whose house is this?" Max asked.

"It's our home now," he said.

"But why?" I asked. "What are we going to do here? What about the Trading Council and the debt we owe?"

"Whoa!" Charlie raised his hands to deflect my barrage of questions.

"He gets that from me," Max said matter-of-factly. "But I am curious about where we are going to work," she added.

"Will you be at our workplace?" I said.

Three other kids joined in our assault.

"Where do we sleep?"

"This is a strange factory."

"What do we have to do?"

Charlie closed his eyes and held up his hands again. "Wait, wait," he said. "Stop. It's really simple. All you have to do . . . is be kids. Play. Have fun. Grow up like other children. Just be *kids*."

I must admit that Charlie's words were sweeter than any toonbas I'd ever tasted, but what was he saying? Just be *kids*? We were knudniks. Our job was to pay off our parents' debt. As simple as that. And if we didn't like it . . . well, I had been reminded of the consequences many, many times on the Rings of Orbis.

I had to ask, "But *how*, Charlie?"

Charlie put his hand on my shoulder. He looked at me, but said nothing. His jaw slackened, followed by his shoulders, and his lips tightened, trying to keep a smile. To me the expression said, *Why can't you just accept it?* But I couldn't. I didn't trust very many people on the Rings of Orbis. Everyone had an agenda, and I mean *everyone*—even Charlie. "Soon enough, Johnny," he said. "Don't rush this. Please." The last word was a whisper, and I think it was meant just for me. For a parsec, I wondered if this was how my father would have spoken to me.

Then his tone changed—it got bigger, louder. He shouted to the other kids, "Come on, everyone. I bet you're hungry. Let's eat!"

I couldn't question that. I was starving.

Our new home (I liked those words) was equipped with a chow synth very similar to the one we'd had on the *Renaissance*. No more food tablets or the protein glop Odran forced us to eat. Instead we feasted on peaches, nuts, and heavy chunks of dark bread with something Charlie called peanut butter. He said it was from Earth, and it took him a long time to get the chow synth to replicate the smooth substance. Ketheria devoured it, but then again, she loved every kind of food. I liked it, too, and piled it on my bread as thick as I could. We each took turns trying to talk with the stuff stuck to the roofs of our mouths.

After lunch Charlie handed out new skins to everyone. They were amber yellow and matched the crystal at the center of his belt. He informed us that the new skins would work for this house and the grounds, and then he showed us where we would sleep.

Apparently, the previous tenants didn't care much for sleepers. Charlie said that they had rested inside stimulation tanks of vitamin-fortified liquids. The nurture pods we slept in on the *Renaissance* worked in a similar way, but I could never see myself sleeping in a tank of sludge. The former owners, however, did employ knudniks and therefore had installed sleepers for their slaves' needs. But the Citizens wasted little space on such *luxuries,* and to my disbelief the sleepers were stacked six *inside* the wall. Each sleeper was loaded one at a time and then rotated up and over the next one, disappearing inside the wall. I gave my new sleeping arrangement a try. When the thin sleeper rolled on its side and then tucked back into the wall, it reminded me of the ancient burial rituals humans used on Earth, where they stuck people in the ground after they died. I didn't think this was going to be very popular with the other kids.

"I use one, too," Charlie said, noticing my discomfort. "Maybe we can change them later."

"I doubt it," Dalton whispered to the kid next to him.

Charlie overheard the remark and frowned. Max gave Dalton a shot in the ribs.

"Ow! He's your friend, not mine," Dalton complained.

After examining the sleepers, we followed Charlie out to the garden, where he told us to take seats on the stone benches or on the ground. I sat on a bench under a tall plant that seemed to shy away as I moved closer. Max slipped in front of Grace and sat next to me.

"What do you think?" she whispered.

"About what?" I asked.

"About this."

"I love it. Who wouldn't? It's almost too good to be true. I'm waiting for the catch."

"What catch? Don't you think they might be rewarding us a

little? Think of the work you did with the central computer and with the Samirans. I think this is how they're thanking us."

"I also remember making a lot of Trading Council members very angry. I'm not so sure the Citizens are interested in rewarding a bunch of knudniks. I don't know. Something's wrong. I mean this *is* everything I dreamed about. There *has* to be a catch."

As if on cue, Charlie centered himself in front of us and announced, "There is one small issue we need to discuss."

I knew it! A couple of the kids groaned. I didn't even have to look at Max.

"Now, wait," Charlie said. "It's not that bad. Every human needs to go through this. I did. It won't be hard. You kids are the smartest I've ever met, but you still have to go to school."

"Nooooo!" came a collective groan. Not school!

"There's nothing we can't learn with a simple uplink," Dalton protested.

"Yeah, just give us the files," shouted another kid.

"Really, Charlie?" Max moaned.

"It's important for your future," he said. "If you hope to be a Citizen one cycle, then you have to learn the ways of the Citizens. You must interact with them and, hopefully, discover a way in which you can live here with some sort of purpose."

"What's your purpose?" I said.

Charlie looked away.

Finally he turned back to me and replied, "To take care of you."

I don't know why I put Charlie on the spot like that. In fact,

I don't know what I was feeling at that moment. Something was off. Maybe I wasn't too keen on spending my cycles with a bunch of Citizens. But what did I expect, really? That we would hang out with Charlie in the house all cycle? Even I knew that was dumb. I reminded myself that Charlie was a Citizen now and that I liked hanging around *him*. Maybe they weren't all bad. Maybe it was just the Trading Council that made me dislike the Citizens so much. But then I thought of the Citizens on the shuttle and how they ignored us even after the wormhole pirates attacked. No, they were all bad. School on the Rings of Orbis was not going to be fun.

"Look," Charlie continued. "Don't judge it yet. Wait till you see the school. The Illuminate is an amazing facility."

"Where is it?" one of the other kids asked.

"It's in Tromaine. You get there by chute," Charlie replied.

"What's the city like?" Max asked.

"It's simply amazing, but you must promise to never go there without an authorized escort or clearance by a Citizen — *by me* — for a particular work rule. Knudniks are not allowed to roam the city freely. The vest you're wearing can inform any Citizen if you have been cleared or not. There are serious consequences if you break their rules. Do not challenge them."

Everyone spoke at once, each with a different question.

"See, this is why you have to go to school. To learn all of this and put it into practice."

Max stood up and shouted over everyone, "When do we start?"

"Next cycle," Charlie said, and everyone was quiet.

3

We all waited for Charlie to fall asleep before we piled out of the sleepers and gathered in the farthest corner of the room.

"This feels more like a storage facility than a bedroom," Theodore complained.

"I hate it," Grace said, sitting next to Theodore.

"The rest of the place is golden, though," Max argued, the last to emerge from the wall. In her hands were the workings of the dream enhancement features standard on every sleeper we had ever used on the Rings of Orbis.

"Did you rip that out?" I asked her.

Max nodded. "I just wanted to see how these things work," she mumbled, pulling at the chips and wires.

Ketheria, Nugget, and some of the other kids had brought their pillows with them and were sprawled out on the soft floor. Most of the floors in the house were covered with a cushy, malleable material, much softer than our own sleepers.

"Vairocina?" I called out.

"I hope your trip to Orbis 3 was successful, JT," a voice inside my head said.

"It was, thank you," I told her. "You can show yourself if you like."

The room was dimly lit by warm colors seeping in from a light source buried in a crevice that ran the perimeter of the room. The air in front of me tugged at the light. It gathered and churned and eventually formed a holograph of my friend, Vairocina. She was the girl whose essence I had found inside the central computer. I once saved her from destruction, and now she helped the Keepers protect the immense sentient computer that runs everything on the Rings of Orbis.

The last time I saw her was on Orbis 2. She looked like a little girl then, almost like Ketheria, with brown hair spilling over her shoulders and big bright eyes. Except Vairocina's eyes were darker and without pupils. The image that now floated in front of me was not the same little girl.

"That's not Vairocina," Theodore whispered.

"What do you think?" she said. Her voice sounded slightly electronic.

Variocina looked different, older, more like Max now. Her hair was a little wavier and she was pretty like Max, too, but different. Her clothes were colored pink and white, and her face seemed painted. *Did she change her face?* I couldn't remember. Everyone circled the holograph, admiring the new Vairocina.

"I have made some upgrades," she announced.

"You sure did," one of the boys said.

Even Dalton seemed interested this time. Switzer had never believed Vairocina was real, the same way he never believed I could speak with the computer on the *Renaissance,* and Dalton always followed his lead. This, however, was hard to ignore.

"Why did you do that?" I asked.

"Why, don't you like it?" Vairocina said, frowning.

"I think you're beautiful, Vairocina," my sister gushed.

"No . . . I like it. I mean . . . you know. What was wrong with . . . before? I liked that, too. I mean, not better. I mean, the same," I stumbled.

"I have to grow up sometime," she said. "I am over a million rotations old, you know. Maybe more. I lost count somewhere between an Ysidron war cruiser and a Simgeesian memory chip."

Vairocina had run away from her planet as a child, hiding inside computers.

"I studied images of your human culture and found it very interesting. It's quite similar to my own, you know. I think this new form suits me better," she added.

"I gotta agree," Theodore said.

Grace and Max watched and whispered.

"Did you want to have a conversation?" she asked me, adjusting her pink skirt. *How can a computer code adjust a skirt?* I wondered. Better still, *Why?*

"Actually, I have a couple of questions."

"Ask her about the wormhole pirates," Max whispered.

"I will, but first, is Charlie a Citizen now? Charlie Norton."

Vairocina's gaze drifted away. She was accessing information somewhere inside the central computer. After a moment she replied, "Yes, he is, and a very wealthy Citizen at that. He seems to have acquired a large amount of chits just recently, too."

"Where did he get them from?" I asked. "I always thought Charlie was a knudnik."

"There is no data pertaining to the money's origin. Charlie Norton became very wealthy the same cycle he became a Citizen."

"When did he become a Citizen?" Max asked.

"This cycle," she replied.

"Wow, Charlie became a Citizen the same cycle we arrived on Orbis 3?" Max said.

"The same cycle he became very wealthy," I added. *And the same cycle wormhole pirates attacked the rings,* I thought. "Vairocina, have the wormhole pirates ever attacked a shuttle before?"

"Are you referring to the attack this cycle on the Citizen vessel from Orbis 2?"

"Yeah, the one we were on."

"The bandits you refer to lurk in the dimensions that intersect with the wormhole and other universes. Proprietary technology allows these criminals to remain undetected in space and time, feeding off innocent vessels that pass through the wormhole. No pirate spaceship has ever been caught by Rings of Orbis security, since none has ever ventured outside of the wormhole."

"Until this cycle?" I asked.

"Until this cycle," she replied.

"What are you kids doing up?"

Grace leaped off the floor at the sound of Charlie's voice. He stood at the entrance, dressed in real striped pajamas.

"Is that Vairocina?" Charlie asked before her holograph dispersed.

"Yeah," I said quickly. "She wanted to show us . . . something."

He stifled a yawn with his big hand and said, "Well, back to bed, everyone. You've got school in the morning."

When Charlie turned and lumbered back to his room I whispered, "Vairocina?"

"Yes."

"Can you look around for where Charlie's sudden wealth came from? Something you might have missed."

"Certainly, but it may take a little while," she said.

I spent the remainder of the sleep cycle on the soft, cushy floor. So did everyone else, but while they slept, I could only pretend to be sleeping. I tried, I *really* tried, but my mind was just too busy. *How could that wormhole pirate know who I am? Why did Charlie become our Guarantor?* Nothing fit. *Why don't we have to work anymore? Who gave Charlie all that money?* This wasn't how Orbis worked, at least not during the two rotations I had lived on the rings. My assurance that I was nothing more than a knudnik felt weakened, to say the least. *How did Charlie even become a Citizen?* I turned over and tried to fall asleep again. *And when did Theodore start snoring?*

Charlie was back in our room before I ever shut my eyes.

"Time for school," he bellowed. He paused when he saw all of us out of our sleepers. "What are you doing on the floor?"

No one answered him. Instead we filed past and stumbled toward the bathrooms. It was a sleepy start for the first cycle of a new school.

"I want you to eat before we go!" I heard Charlie shout from some other room in the huge house.

When I was dressed, I headed for the chow synth with Max. In the kitchen Charlie had laid out all sorts of foods. I picked through cereals, fruits, nuts, and even eggs (although I had never heard of any chickens living on the Rings of Orbis before). I was too sleepy to stomach much, or to learn the origins of the eggs, so I settled with more brown bread and peanut butter.

"You're coming with us?" Max asked.

Charlie lifted the belt draped around his waist and stared at the Citizen's emblem for a moment, almost as if he were just as bewildered as I was to see it there.

"This is all new for me, too," he said. "I still don't have clearance for you to ride the chute by yourselves."

The chow synth chimed, and Charlie turned to extract more bread. He fiddled with the controls, pausing to decide which button to hit next. Watching Charlie stumble through his new kitchen and tripping on the fleshy floor, I realized that he was no more accustomed to being here than we were. *I* didn't belong here, and neither did Charlie. Someone (or *something*) had put us here.

I decided right then and there that I was going to find out why. I just didn't know how.

• • •

The chute was a type of light transport that Citizens used to get from floor to floor inside most buildings. I had used chutes many times before, but never like the one installed in our home. In front of me pulsed three purple pillars of light that appeared to be holding up the ceiling inside the front entrance. The iridescent light shimmered as it swam from ceiling to floor. It reminded me of the clear ocean waters on Orbis 2.

Charlie tapped in a code on the small O-dats floating next to each of the light chutes.

"What are you doing?" Max questioned him. "Do we need a code to get back?"

"Don't worry about that. If you do not put in another code, by default, the chip inside your vest will bring you home," he said.

I caught Theodore eyeballing my vest. He ran back to the chow synth to find his.

Charlie pulled me to the front. "JT, you go first and wait for me on the other side. I'll make sure everyone gets through all right." Charlie glanced at us before fumbling with the little notes crumpled in his hands. He double-checked each piece of paper, then checked them a third time.

"We've used a light chute before, Charlie," Ketheria said, trying to calm him.

"Right. Then maybe I should go first in case anyone questions you on the other side."

"I'll make sure everyone goes through," Max assured him,

and pushed Charlie toward the light chute. He disappeared inside the sparkling glow.

Stepping into a light chute is like falling asleep and waking up before you ever knew you were out. It's instantaneous. Using three chutes, we arrived at the Illuminate in no time. Charlie waited patiently, keeping everyone close.

The Illuminate stood directly in front of us at the other end of an open stone plaza. Two glass-and-metal buildings snaked up and around an enormous center spire that poked through the sloping rooftops. There were aliens everywhere. Some arrived through the light chutes, while others landed in the vast plaza on private spacecrafts that whisked away after dumping their passengers. Other students arrived on stilted machines, which they abandoned next to other modes of transportation idling and waiting for their owners to return. I noticed that very few students, if any, walked to school.

"Are they all going in there with us?" I asked.

"Of course," Charlie said, moving toward the building. "Follow me."

"Are they all Citizens?" Max asked.

"So I'm told. I don't think you'll find many non-Citizens like yourselves," he said.

"Oh, great," I said under my breath. There was something to look forward to.

Max nudged Grace, who was frozen in awe under the shadow of the enormous structure. With Ketheria at my side, I followed them toward the Illuminate, stepping around groups of students casually chatting with their friends. The kids clung together in groups and sported clothes far more elaborate than the drab suits and yellowish skins we wore. Often someone's laughter jumped over the din of the crowd, and I searched their faces for the source. I looked away whenever someone caught me staring, until I noticed the strangest thing. Some of the students—in fact, most of them—decorated their neural implants, the small ports everyone used to link with the central computer. Some kids wore devices that wrapped around the backs of their heads, marked or flashing with unfamiliar symbols. Some hung jewelry from their implants, while others transmitted small holographs of flying animals or colorful insects that fluttered around their heads.

Instantly, I wanted one. I wanted to be just like them, even though I knew perfectly well that was impossible. I was a soft-wire. I did not need an implant to connect with the computer. My brain, for a reason no one had told me, evolved to inter-act with any computer device without the aid of hardware or wetware. At that moment, walking into the sea of kids floating toward the Illuminate, I would have given anything for a plain old neural port punched in behind my ear. I did not feel like being different this cycle. I ached to be normal.

Charlie stopped just outside of the main doors.

"Aren't you coming in?" Max asked.

"Not allowed. Children only," he said, and pointed to a couple of robotic sentries standing guard. "They're a little ner-vous since the wormhole pirates attacked. You can't blame them, really." Charlie glanced over his shoulder as if he were looking for someone.

"Why would they come here?" Max asked as Charlie scanned the crowd entering the glass building.

"You kids ask a lot of questions," he said.

"Law of averages. We don't get many answers," I replied, and smiled.

I could tell that Charlie wanted to laugh. I could see it in his eyes, but instead he said, "I'm looking for a person named Riis. I have arranged for another student to show you around on your first cycle. Riis is supposed to meet us here."

"Another student?" Theodore asked.

"Yes, she's nice. You'll like her. She's a Wiicerian."

"A girl?" Grace said, and Charlie nodded.

I had never met a Wiicerian before, so I did not know what to expect. As for *being nice*, I doubted that was possible for a Citizen. Especially when it came to knudniks.

Charlie shouted, "Over here!" and waved over the crowd. He let out a deep breath. *Why is he so nervous?* "We just got here. Kids, meet Riis. Riis, meet the kids."

"Hello," we all mumbled.

Riis was my height. Her smooth skin was so white that it was almost blue, and she was dressed in a sleek green and silver one-piece outfit with iridescent orange kneepads that matched her helmet. She looked like she had just arrived on one of those personal transport devices.

"Hello, everyone," she greeted us. She looked so independent, standing with her helmet casually pressed against her hip. Her thin mouth moved slowly and confidently, and when she talked, she looked at you with big green eyes that were much wider apart than human eyes. They were almost on the sides of her face, yet it didn't look weird. Her oval face was framed with stiff auburn hair that looked as if it belonged on some toy instead of a person's head.

"I apologize for being late. Are you ready to follow me inside?" Riis said.

"They are," Charlie spoke for us. "I'll be here when the spoke is done."

"We can get home ourselves, Charlie. It's all right," I whispered, trying not to let Riis hear.

"Not unless I have authorization for you by then," he said.

"Don't worry. I'll have everyone rounded up and they'll meet you here again when the spoke is finished," Riis assured him.

"Good, then," he said, and clapped his hands. "I'll let you guys be. Take good care of them, Riis."

"I will," she replied.

"*Good-bye*, Charlie," I groaned. Charlie nodded and turned back toward the chutes. Ketheria waved good-bye to him.

Why was Charlie doing this? Suddenly, I felt angry. I didn't need someone to watch out for me and drag me around. I fought Madame Lee! I saved the Samirans and battled with Odran. I could walk through these doors by myself, and for some reason I could not understand, I wanted Riis to know that, too. I *needed* her to know that.

"Everyone ready?" Riis asked.

"You know, we can do this ourselves," I told her. "We have a lot of experience . . . I mean I have . . . well . . ."

"How old are you?" Grace cut me off.

"Well, that depends who's asking," she said. "But I did some calculations, and in Earth years I believe I would be fourteen or fifteen years old. The same as some of you."

It was hard to swallow that she was the same age as me.

"Let's hurry inside. There are some things I need to show you before the spoke begins." Riis slipped through the sparkling energy field guarding the entrance, and we all followed.

The air inside the Illuminate was noticeably cooler. Something else was different, too. I breathed deeply. Were they pumping extra oxygen into this place? I tucked that question away for Vairocina. Hundreds and hundreds of students milled past me, laughing and shouting, moving in packs. My stomach turned over once, maybe twice, and I thought my palms would drip with perspiration. Bad things often happened when I felt this way. The two rotations I had spent on Orbis were never easy. In fact, they were often dangerous. But none of it scared me as much as I was scared now.

Riis stopped in front of a towering glass wall speckled with dozens of little holes about the size of my palm. I saw that each hole was actually the end of a clear tube that snaked up the wall to some unknown destination. Riis held her hand out under the opening and a small oval-shaped device popped out. She took the blue plastic thing and attached it to the port behind her ear. I noticed that Riis did not decorate her port like most of the other kids.

"This is how you get the cycle's announcements, cancellations, test results . . . anything they want you to know. You might as well grab one. You won't understand much of it, but you should get into the practice," she said. "We call it the tap."

Other students were reaching over and grabbing their tap, so each of us followed. Of course, I simply stood there. I had no place to put it.

Max reached out and took the blue device from the tube and inserted it behind her left ear.

"Why don't they just do this wireless?" she said out loud.

"What do you mean?" Riis asked.

"I mean, why all this hardware? Surely with the technology on the rings, this stuff can be sent directly to our implants."

Another Citizen, reaching for a tap, overheard Max and snorted at the comment. Even Riis looked puzzled. "You mean have the information come directly into my brain without asking?"

Max nodded and said, "Yeah, it would be easier."

Riis responded adamantly. "I would never let someone put something into my head without my permission. *Never.*"

"I'm sorry, I didn't mean anything by it," Max tried to apologize.

"My brain. My choice," Riis said, and turned to me. "You need to get one too."

"I can't," I told her.

"He's a softwire," Ketheria said.

"Ugh! You're a Space Jumper!" Riis cried. She sounded just as repulsed as Max on the subject. I thought that Charlie would have told her about me.

"No, I'm just a softwire," I replied. *Why did I sound like I was defending myself?*

"That's weird," Riis said. "Let me see."

Weird. Great. Like I told many before her, "There's nothing to see." But she still reached up and touched me behind my ear anyway. Her fingers were warm and smooth, like glass touching my skin.

"Wow. I don't know what you should do, then," she said.

I reached out to the tap tube and the small device plopped onto my hand. I *pushed* into the chip and uplinked the information by simply willing the file into my mind. The tap was a simple storage device, and the result was instantaneous.

"It says everyone must register for placement testing during this spoke," I said.

Riis smiled. Was she was impressed?

"That's great," she replied.

"What's placement testing?" Theodore asked.

"They need to know what to teach you."

"Why not just a little bit of everything?"

"That's impossible. The amount of knowledge available to an Orbister doubles every three and a half cycles. With the placement test, they can decide what to teach you and when to teach it to you."

"They want to see how smart you are," I said.

"Or how dumb," came a voice from behind me. I turned, almost expecting to see Switzer standing there.

"Go suck on your tap, Dop," Riis snapped.

I turned around and saw a tall greenish alien who reminded me of a plant moving swiftly in the wind. It took everything in me not to roll my eyes. I had met this alien once before on Orbis 1, and I had hoped to never meet him again.

"So you're still here, huh, Softwire? You never took my advice," he said, filling the space between us.

I let out a deep breath. It was too soon for this. I knew Dop's strength from experience, as well as his rotting breath. I turned my face slightly to the side.

"Not so tough anymore?" he taunted me. "I'm glad you've finally learned your place on the rings."

I wanted to ask him if his species had ever invented a toothbrush. I wanted to carve my initials into his green skin. I wanted to crush him with my bare hands and throw him into a compost bin, but I didn't. I couldn't even muster a reply. Maybe it was the new school. Maybe it was all of these Citizens. I didn't know. All I could do was stare at him and hope my knees weren't shaking.

"Well?" Dop pressed on.

"Well, *what*?" I mumbled.

"What are you doing here?"

"Same as you, Dop," Riis said.

"They're attending the Illuminate?" He looked at his two friends standing behind him. "This is the human trash I told you about, orphaned in outer space and left to wean off the nipple of a robot. Losers." Dop turned back to Riis. "When did they start letting knudniks in here? And why are you with them? Did someone force you to show these carbon clumps around?"

A sickly alien with sinewy arms and stiff black hair extending from the back of his head whispered to Dop over his shoulder. He stared at Riis, his eyes widening.

"You volunteered!" Dop flicked his hands out and slapped them together. I had never seen the gesture before, but it looked insulting. Riis leaped toward Dop, grabbing him by his skin as if it were hair. She twisted him around and clamped down on his throat before his friends could intervene, though I don't think they would have even if they were fast enough.

"Golden!" Max cried.

"If you ever do that to me again . . ." Riis breathed into his ear.

"You'll what?" Dop gasped, still defiant.

Riis pushed him away, and Dop rubbed his throat, smiling.

"That's right. You'll do nothing," he shouted at Riis as she stormed away. We followed her up a ramp, glancing back at Dop and his smiling friends.

"It's ridiculous," Dop shouted for everyone to hear. "We have pirates attacking our Citizens, but still we have to care for these freeloaders!"

"Why did you let him go?" Theodore asked Riis, but she didn't respond.

Instead she looked at me and said, "I hope you don't cause this much trouble everywhere you go, Softwire."

Me too, I thought.

Most of the Citizens I had ever encountered shared Dop's beliefs. They presumed that Orbis belonged to them, and they didn't want anyone else here. The younger Citizens seemed especially adamant about this. Somewhere in their history, however, they seemed to have forgotten that *we* did all the work they didn't want to do, or work they considered beneath them. Maybe if they did it themselves, there wouldn't be so many of us here. But Riis said Dop complained simply because he could. That it was his privileged position in life. His grumbling was just an imitation of his own parents' rhetoric. Insults he had heard since he was born.

But Dop had nothing to be worried about. I couldn't wait to get off this ring.

We followed Riis up a curved sloping ramp, past many more students, flying messenger drones, and electrostatic doors. It was going to take a while to learn my way around here—this place was huge, and we tried to soak up every new sight. One group of students circled a tall boy who was projecting an image from a metallic device attached to his neural implant. The wormhole pirates' attack of the last cycle played out in front of them as a 3-D holograph. I slowed and watched this new interpretation of the events. In this version, the Citizens appeared much braver than I remembered, overwhelming the wormhole pirates *before* the security forces ever arrived.

Max saw it, too. "That's not how it happened," she exclaimed.

An alien standing next to the one projecting the fictitious event turned and glared at Max.

"She's right," I said. "Where did *that* version come from?"

A tall alien, the one with the ear projector, glanced at my vest. "Knudniks?" he whispered, and turned his back to me.

Another from the group, a girl who looked identical to the other, with wild carroty hair and skin as white as ceramic heat shields, nudged her twin and pointed at the hologram.

"Isn't that you?" she remarked, pointing at the image of Max.

In the hologram, Max and I were huddled behind a bench, crying. Bawling like the little ones on the *Renaissance*! A Citizen was gallantly defending us from the wormhole pirates.

"That's a lie!" Max snapped.

"I wouldn't want anyone to see this, either, if I were you," the alien said, and the four of them laughed, turning their backs to us.

Max stomped forward, her fists clenched, ready to knock the laughter right out of them, but Riis stopped her and pulled her back. "You can't believe anything from those pob projections," she said. "It's propaganda—that's all that crap is."

"But it's a lie," she protested.

"You were there, right?" Riis asked.

Max nodded, grinding her back teeth and breathing forcefully out her nose.

"Then you know the truth, right?" she added.

Max nodded again.

"Then that's all that matters. Whatever they think means nothing. It's only thought. What they think about you is none of your business."

"But . . ."

"Let it *go*," she said. "You're not going to win this one. They don't know how to lose, anyway—believe me."

The ramp leveled off and opened into a small round foyer.

Along the walls, holographic numbers hovered at eye level. Some were green while most were red. There must have been a hundred of them. Riis walked up to a green one and swiped at the floating numbers. The wall appeared to part, revealing a tall storage bin that slid forward. Riis placed her helmet on one of the shelves. Other students came and went, but none of them acknowledged Riis. *Does she have any friends here?* I wondered. She certainly seemed to know how everything worked, so I assumed she had been here for a while.

"Grab any of the green ones. Remember the number. It should work with those skins you're wearing," she informed us.

I swiped at the number 952, and the storage device slid forward. "Now what?"

"Leave your stuff there," Riis said as she pulled off her green and silver suit and hung it in the locker. She was wearing a crimson outfit that flared at her hips. It covered most of her body except for her long legs. Then she took a small wand from the locker and brushed her hair with it. Riis's auburn hair turned pure white, a striking contrast to the blood-red suit. I just stood and stared. I wasn't the only one.

"I didn't think her hair was real," Grace whispered to Max. "Too stiff."

"Everyone done?" she asked after she put the wand back.

"We don't have anything to put in these things," I told her.

Riis looked at us just standing in front of the open lockers. "Oh," she remarked. "Well, now that you picked one, the Illuminate will leave any notices for you in it—personal notices, test scores, or whatever they like, actually. Anything they can't put in the tap."

"Riis," I said.

"What?"

"Why did you volunteer to show us around?"

Riis checked her hair and outfit in a mirror that hung in her locker, then swiped at the number, closing the storage device.

"That is not your business," she said, and turned up the hallway. "Come, you're late."

I guess Wiicerians don't answer questions, either.

4

We spent the remainder of the school spoke filling out data screens to register for our placement test. Completion of the exam would officially commence our school rotation, I was told. The task was tedious, but proved to be a useful distraction from the sneers and knudnik insults that had been shoved our way all cycle long. It also left no room to think about wormhole pirates. By the time we were finished, the rest of the students had already left. Riis had to go, and she said her good-byes quickly.

Charlie was not outside the Illuminate when the spoke finished.

"Where do you think he is?" Theodore asked.

"Maybe he forgot," Max replied.

"Charlie would not forget," I told them. But I wasn't sure. Charlie often disappeared for a phase or more without even a hint of where he went. Except now he was our Guarantor. He couldn't just leave us, could he?

At the entrance of the Illuminate, the robot sentries remained on guard. A few kids still trickled through the energy field, but most were now gone, finishing their conversations in the plaza or boarding their personal transportation vehicles. One machine, nothing more than a metal wheel with a seat suspended near the center, rolled toward us before lifting off the ground. Max never took her eyes off the thing. *Riis is probably halfway home by now,* I thought.

Max had moved back toward the Illuminate. "Where you going?" Theodore asked her.

"I just want to take a peek at those machines," Max shouted over her shoulder.

"Can you imagine how freaked Charlie will be when he shows up and we're not here?" Theodore replied. "I think we should hang around."

"Then stay there," Max called.

"Think there's any left?" I asked him.

"I don't know."

"Won't hurt to look."

I turned to Ketheria. "Go," she assured me. "Theodore will wait with me."

I bolted toward Max and trailed her to the far side of the Illuminate, where we had seen some of the vehicles land. The metal helmets of the school guards swiveled as we rounded the Illuminate. Only two vehicles remained parked behind the school. One was another of those wheels with the cockpit hanging just below its axis. I could see two gyro jets clinging to a metal fender wrapped two-thirds around the tire. It was impressive, but it was the second vehicle that caught my attention.

"Hold up," I whispered, but Max had seen it, too. We tucked carefully out of sight next to one of the Illuminate's concrete footings.

A stocky alien heaved a heavy-looking pipe over his head before slamming it into the windshield. *CRACK!* His long arms stretched beyond their sockets as he pummeled the machine with the pipe once more. This time the glass shattered into a million little pieces.

"He's going to steal it," I whispered.

"You just figured that out now?" Max teased. "You'd better study for that placement test next cycle."

"Shhh," I warned her as the alien glanced in our direction. He turned back to the vehicle and reached through the busted windshield and released the hatch.

The thief was dressed in a black tattered jumpsuit that gathered at the neck but left his long muscular arms exposed.

And that's when I saw it. That mark on his arm.

I must have been forty meters away, but there was no denying it.

Max saw it too. "How can that be?" she whispered.

Once inside the cockpit of the stilted vehicle, the alien maneuvered the device away from the Illuminate and toward a small forest lining the plaza.

"Max! JT!" Charlie was here.

She looked at me with wide blue eyes. "Should we tell Charlie?"

I peered into the forest, but there was no sign of the alien or the stolen vehicle.

"Maybe we were wrong," I said.

"Both of us?"

It *was* impossible to deny. That creature was marked with the same symbol I spotted when the wormhole pirates attacked: an alien skull sitting over two crossbones.

"Come on, it's not our concern. The Citizens are capable of handling their own problems. At least, that's what they tell everyone," I said. I'd lived on these rings long enough to know they would never believe a knudnik, not even two of them.

"But you know you saw it. We know the truth, JT."

"The truth doesn't matter here," I said, and headed toward Charlie.

When we rejoined the others, Charlie asked, "What were you guys doing back there?"

"Nothing," we both said. Without any further discussion, we had decided to ignore what we saw.

Charlie held our gaze as if I were going to add something. Did he see the wormhole pirate? *No,* I thought, *that's impossible.*

"What?" I said to him. I felt the warmth rising in my cheeks as he stared.

Charlie put his hand on my shoulder and led me away from Max and the other kids. I saw Ketheria smiling.

"I know you and Max . . . are close," he whispered, crouching down while searching for his words. "And there comes a time in a young man's life . . ." These words came even slower.

"What are you talking about, Charlie?"

"My parents were never around to explain things to me, either. And don't misunderstand me; I'm not trying to be your parent. I want to help you, you know, be there for you, the way my parents never could, but . . ." Charlie was sweating. "You kids deserve more. . . . Oh, I'm not very good at this."

What was he talking about? Did he know I was lying to him? Should I tell him about the wormhole pirate? I stared at my feet, covered in my clumsy oversize boots, looking to them for some solution. *Just tell him,* they yelled at me through the rubber. "Charlie, we went to look at the different vehicles the students use to get to school. You know how Max loves machines. Well . . . "

"You were just looking at the fliers?" Charlie almost seemed excited by that.

"Yes," I said.

"You two weren't doing anything?"

"To the fliers?"

"No! Not the fliers. I mean . . . to . . . So you weren't touching the fliers?"

"No, *we* weren't."

Charlie let out a long breath. "Oh, *good,*" he exclaimed, and stood up. The concern on his face washed away; a big smile brightened his eyes. "I'm glad. Yes, they are nice machines." He laughed. "Whew, come on, let's go home. I bet Ketheria's starving."

And just like that, the conversation was over. It was as

if Charlie didn't even want to know about the wormhole pirate.

That's when I decided that adults were very strange.

After dinner I planned to concentrate on the placement exam that awaited us at the Illuminate next cycle. Ketheria acted unconcerned about the exam. She enjoyed her reunion with Nugget and spent every moment playing with him in the garden outside or constructing wild stories that left him on the ground laughing. Ketheria was only retelling the entertainment files Mother had shown us on the *Renaissance,* but Nugget found the actions of humans on Earth to be quite hilarious. I shook my head as I watched him rolling around, snorting and giggling. It was hard to believe that this alien was the spawn of Joca Krig Weegin.

Instead of studying, however, Max and I quietly debated the meaning of the wormhole pirate we discovered after school. We were seated outside, hidden by the alien foliage, but Theodore still managed to find us. He was doubtful, however, that the event had ever happened.

"Are you sure?" Theodore questioned me. "You had to be pretty far away."

"I'm positive," I told him.

Max ignored Theodore's doubts. "JT, do you think there's a connection between the wormhole pirate who stole the transport and the ones who attacked our shuttle?" she said.

"That's impossible. Even if he was a wormhole pirate, why

would there be a connection," he argued, and stood up. "I'm going to study."

"Let him go," Max whispered. "But we should study a little too."

"Do you think the test matters much, you know, for *us*?"

"What do you mean for *us*? You're more than just a knudnik, JT. You're a person, too. What happened to all that talk on the *Renaissance*? You couldn't wait to get here and start your life. You will be a Citizen one cycle, just like them, so you'd better get over this *us* and *them* thing you have."

"Things are different now," I told her.

"Yeah. You're a softwire. And Charlie's our Guarantor. Things are great, JT. Let it go."

"Easy for you to say."

"Uggh!" Max exclaimed, and stomped away.

I went to my sleeper having only glanced at the sample questions Vairocina had found for us from past exams. Max was already in her sleeper when I went to bed.

The next day at the Illuminate, most of the kids were gossiping about the stolen flier, which they called a stridling. It belonged to a young female Voon whose father, Riis said, was a very powerful Citizen. Because of the blatant theft, some kids arrived by escort that cycle and an additional robot stood guard, scanning the kids at the entrance. Riis had arrived with helmet in hand, so I assumed she wasn't worried about anyone stealing her vehicle.

"Did they catch the thief?" Max questioned Riis. We were

standing next to our storage lockers watching Riis adjust her hair color to match her outfit. It was mostly blue this cycle, so she picked a paler shade for her hair.

"She'll deny it, but I'll wager she left the stridling to be stolen. She wanted her father to purchase a newer one," Riis said. "I wouldn't worry too much about it."

"Who would steal it for her?" I asked, interested to hear a Citizen's theory.

"Her neural-net-deficient friends, who else?"

"What if it wasn't her? What if it was . . . a wormhole pirate or something? Could it have been a wormhole pirate?"

Riis stared at me before laughing in my face. "Here? A wormhole pirate? Impossible. How could they ever land on 3 without being detected?"

Her words stung. I had hoped Riis was different, but I could tell she still looked at us as knudniks. And knudniks didn't know anything.

"I've seen stranger things on the Rings of Orbis," I said in my defense.

"So I've heard, Softwire. But there is no way a wormhole pirate stole the Voon's stridling. That's just ridiculous."

I shrugged it off and turned my back to her. I swiped the empty locker closed and reminded myself to bring something to put in these useless things. Anything.

"Really, it's ridiculous," she repeated.

"Aren't we taking the placement test now?" I asked, changing the subject and turning back toward her.

Riis looked at me. "Are you nervous?"

"Does it mean anything?" Max asked. "You know, how well we do, does it mean anything?"

"To some around here, the exam means everything. Their covetous parents reward them with stupid gifts if they place well. Most Guarantors follow the rankings when placing Citizens in cushy jobs, although I would never call them *jobs*. Yes, I guess it does mean *something*."

"What about you?" I said.

"What *about* me?"

"The test?"

"I couldn't care less. But I'll please my parents and do the best I can."

I glanced at her helmet in the locker. She saw me looking.

"I bought that myself," she sneered. "I'm not like these other kids, you know. I don't think this universe *owes* me.

"I didn't say anything."

"It's the way you're looking at me. Who are you to judge me?"

"No, I meant us," Max said, jumping in. "The test. We're not Citizens. What does the test mean for us?"

"That all depends on how you do."

We followed Riis in silence. We stopped in front of four sliding doors on the inner side of a curved hallway.

"Split up," Riis called out. "We take the placement test in the same theater where we have our classes. When the doors open, take the first pod, but only two at a time. The next two must wait for another pod."

The doors opened immediately. Ketheria was standing near the other door.

"Take Max," I told Ketheria, and she did, slipping into the pod and out of sight.

I waited for my turn with Theodore. When the doors opened, I caught a faint medicinal smell as a bright blue light illuminated two narrow seats. I stepped in and sat next to Theodore. The floor tilted slightly, and we pulled our feet back in response. Then the pod closed and the blue light blinked out, encasing us in complete darkness. When the pod shifted to my left, I felt myself pinned to the seat, unable to sit up.

"Hey!" Something tried to connect with the neural port that I did not have. "Theodore, did you just link up?" I asked him.

"Didn't have a choice." His words seemed dampened by the darkness. "I'm not creeped out, though. Kinda reminds me of the nurture pods on the *Renaissance*."

He was right. From the time we were born, until maybe four or five years old, we slept in pods that cleaned us, fed us, and even stimulated our brains, replicating everything any parent could ever hope to give to their new child.

"Do you think they knew about these pods when they designed the *Renaissance*?" he asked.

"What for?"

"So we would be used to this."

"That's ridiculous!" I said, doing a very good impersonation of Riis.

We both laughed out loud in the dark, unafraid of what was coming. We were used to it on Orbis now. Behind every corner was something new, something strange, or something different. I began to expect the unexpected, and it kept me alert. Light soon filled our pod from some unknown source on my left. My mind told me: *Get ready.* Friend or foe, something was around the bend.

At first I was disoriented. I reached out to grab a hold of something, *anything*. What I thought was a door enclosing my pod only reached my knees. The front of the pod remained open, providing me with an unobstructed view of nothing-ness. I looked up and saw white. I looked to my left and I saw more shiny white nothingness. I looked down, I looked right, and saw nothing but an enormous glowing O-dat that encom-passed my entire field of view.

"Awesome!" Theodore said. I saw a thin clear cable attached behind his left ear.

"What do you see?" I said.

"Everything."

I scanned the pod for a computer device located near the linkup behind my head. Once I pushed in, I located the link file addressed with my name and an encrypted access code of twenty-five digits. I didn't know what to do. The access code would not let me into the source of the stream.

"Vairocina!" I shouted out in my mind.

"I was waiting for you to ask," she said inside my head. A small silver file shined inside my mind's eye. "Uplink this before digesting the access code. A key is no good without a lock."

"Why didn't they give this to me during registration?"

"Maybe it's all part of the exam," she said, and then she was gone. I could always tell because I felt a little empty when she ran off to some other part of the central computer. It was like sneezing. Before you sneeze, there is always a sensation that you're about to make a big noise and spray spit all over your friend (if you're lucky), but then you sneeze and the sensation is simply gone. Almost like it was never there. That's the way I felt whenever Vairocina slipped out of my head.

I followed her instructions, and the screen in front of me exploded with colors, ripping me away from the connection I had made with the computer. No matter where I looked, all I could see was the screen. I looked for Theodore, but he was not there. Even the pod was gone. My senses were filled with the image on the screen. All I could do was sit back and enjoy the ride.

That's exactly what it felt like—a free-fall ride through space. I soared over the crystal moons of Ki and Ta. I raced between the Rings of Orbis, whipping through the huge spherical structures I called home. And then I circled the mighty wormhole before launching toward an exaggerated image of the Illuminate on Orbis 3. If this was school, I thought, I was really going to enjoy myself.

The journey settled inside the Illuminate, ran up the sloped hallways, entered the sliding doors, and I ended next to myself inside the pod.

"All journeys begin from here," an authoritative voice bellowed inside my head. "And you alone are the master of your destiny. The children of Citizens *are* the Scions. Chosen to lead this universe and spread freedom and prosperity wherever your journey takes you."

I laughed; I think I even snorted. Who would believe this toilet water? The screen exploded with Citizens strolling through plazas, laughing with each other inside their estates, and watching over knudniks as they mined the profits from the moons. I wondered if the Keepers ever saw this propaganda.

"Now is the time to stand up and be counted. Now is the time to demonstrate your breeding and demand your place in the universe!"

I couldn't see anyone near me, but I could certainly hear the other students. When the announcer inside my head finished the last sentence, the Citizens roared with approval. I forced myself to unlink from the computer, and the screen in front of me went white. I looked at Theodore, who sat back with his mouth slightly open, still taking it all in. I pulled myself away from the soft seat and peered over the edge of my pod. There was another pod next to mine as well as one below me and above me. Wherever I looked, there were pods attached to the gigantic convex wall, filled with students staring at the endless white screen. They each cheered frantically, but then suddenly stopped. As if on cue, they all turned and looked at me—every last one of them. I linked up and glanced at the screen to see an enormous image of myself leaning out of the pod, staring. Who was watching me? How did they know it was me? Worse, why did they care?

I unlinked again. They replaced their cheers with hissing and the sound of people thumping on their pods.

"What are you doing, JT?" Theodore said.

"Nothing. I think."

And then I screamed. The pod had shocked me with an electric charge. "Ow!" It did it again. "Do you feel that?"

"Feel what?"

"Ow! Stop that," I shouted.

"Link up again, JT," Theodore said, and my mind reached back into the computer and took the access code once more. The shocks stopped, and the image on the screen dominated my senses again, isolating me from the rest of the world. I let out a deep breath and told myself never to do that again.

The hissing and the thumping ceased immediately, and the announcer commenced instructions for the exam. I had almost forgotten what we were here for. Almost. I wanted to do well on this exam. I wanted to prove something. I wanted to prove that knudniks weren't second-class Citizens. I didn't care if they thought I wasted a perfectly good home planet. I wasn't even born there. And I didn't care if they were disgusted that I traded my life for their charity. The charity wasn't really that good, anyway, and it wasn't even my choice. I simply wanted to prove that whatever they could do, I could do better.

I quickly discovered that the placement exam wasn't going to be much help.

The scope of the exam was simply beyond my comprehension. There were more than 720,000 questions. We were not expected to answer all of them, however, and I thanked the universe for that. Instead we were supposed to browse through the categories and answer whatever questions we liked, and then the computer would give us another question based on the last one. We were told to keep doing this until we couldn't answer the next question. From there we were simply to browse for another category and begin solving another string of problems. The pods provided an O-dat to work out our answers, and everything appeared on the giant screen in front of me. Some questions involved diagrams; others, equations; and some questions simply asked me to identify objects. I assumed everyone saw something different on the screen, but I was not about to disconnect from the computer to verify my theory.

I browsed through the numerous categories, looking for a place to start: Subdimensional Displacement and Its Effect on Trefaldoorian Biosystems. *Pass.* Economic Indicators of Intergalactic Wormhole Commerce. *Maybe next time.* Effects of Gender-Based Religion on Mythological Symbols. *Who is this test for?* I'd met many people on the Rings of Orbis, and I didn't know anyone who could answer these questions.

I pushed through the different categories, searching for something I recognized, anything, even a word.

Central Computer.

Perfect. I had been inside it many times. Let's see what they were offering.

What best describes the function
of Orbis's central computer?

a. quantum

b. photon

c. black hole

Multiple choices. I liked that. Inside the central computer, information moved on beads of light. I'd seen it myself, so I selected *b.* A new question appeared on the screen.

Does a photon computer ever use binary code?

I thought of the ones and zeros Vairocina carved into the rocks in my dreams on Orbis 1 and the door locks at Weegin's World that I'd manipulated. *Absolutely,* I responded, and gave them examples on the next question.

I continued this way for quite some time, but I never reached many of the more exotic questions. I'm sure a lot of the Citizens could answer them, but I did answer questions about the mass generators I encountered in the city of Magna. I also punched in answers about the creatures inside the crystal-cooling tank on Orbis 2 and their biosystems. I answered many questions about the Keepers, what I knew about the War of 10,000 Rotations, and a few questions about OIO, but only a few of those. By the end of the spoke, I was regurgitating everything I could remember about what Mother had taught us concerning earthly physics, math, and biology, even though I knew whatever they learned on Orbis must be far more advanced than what I understood. When the screen went white, I plopped my head against the back of the pod.

"How many did you answer?" I asked Theodore.

"Four hundred and twenty-five," he said. "You?"

"Maybe a little less."

"How do you think we did?"

"Don't," I said, looking at him and shaking my head. "No more questions, please."

I dragged myself to the light chute in the plaza. The exam had drained me both mentally and physically. The sun pricked at my skin as I crossed the stone circle, staring at my feet the entire time. No one spoke except Dop. I would have walked right into him if he hadn't.

"These knudniks look tired," he joked with his friends. I recognized two of them from the last cycle, but the other was new. Her long face darted about, and her solid black eyes made it impossible to tell where she was looking. "I guess humans don't have what it takes to serve the Citizens of Orbis."

His new friend smiled, stretched open her lipless mouth, and exposed more teeth than necessary for any meat-eating creature I could think of. I was too tired for this. I looked around for Charlie, but then I remembered he wasn't coming. By now he was completely registered as a Citizen and our skins allowed us passage to and from the Illuminate. I really wanted someone else to deal with Dop and his self-important views of Citizenship.

I looked at Max for advice. She was shaking her head, not as a warning but more as a mirroring of my feelings. I simply walked around Dop.

"Do not turn your back to me, knudnik," he growled.

"What do you want, Dop? I know you don't like me—that's obvious. I can't leave here even if I wanted to. I didn't ask to go to the Illuminate. I'm only here because the Citizens of Orbis made it possible."

Dop looked at his friends for an answer. "The Keepers did that," he spat.

"But the Citizens keep using us. *Stop* using knudniks," I told him. "How about that? Do the work yourselves." I turned my back to him once more.

Dop shifted and slid in front of me, blocking the way. I just stared at him. There was nothing more to say.

"I challenge you to *Lyld-den-oo*," Dop declared, as if it were the only option available. The central computer did not translate the last word he said. I could tell because there was no delay through his lips. The delay often happens when the computer translates some of the aliens we meet. The sounds coming out of their mouths do not match the translation I hear in my head.

"I don't understand," I told him.

"I have called you out. You offend me, Softwire. You march through Orbis thinking you don't belong here—not because we force you to work, but because you think you are better than us."

I couldn't disagree with this, especially when it came to Dop.

"In the Labyrinth I will show you who is superior, and you will be forced to carry yourself with the shame suitable to a knudnik."

Challenge? Labyrinth? What was he talking about?

"Whatever you want," I said. "It's your ring."

"And I will make you act like it," he seethed, his rotting-flower breath burning my eyes. "Next phase, after the Arbiter allows the start of the new conclave and filth like you is allowed to play, I will *break* you."

"I'll be there," I said. "May I go now, Mr. Citizen, sir?"

Dop stared at me, his long neck swaying back and forth. His green eyes said, *Is this knudnik mocking me? Yes, I am, you dumb alien.* But then again, I was really tired.

Dop and his friends moved aside, and we walked toward the light chutes.

When we were far enough away, Max said, "What kind of challenge is he talking about?"

"I don't think you should do it, JT," Theodore warned.

Even Dalton asked, "Are you scared?"

I wasn't scared. I could handle Dop. I handled Switzer. But I knew that when I was done with him, there would be another angry Citizen eager to take his place. Pride and ignorance existed everywhere in the universe; I was certain of it.

5

"It's a game," Charlie informed us after we found him in the garden behind our home. "Lots of the kids on Orbis 3 play it. Your Illuminate has a fantastic league. They share the Labyrinth with the professional league; people from all over the ring come to play in that pro league. Citizens can even gamble on the outcome of those matches. It's very, very competitive, but I think you would really enjoy your school league."

"How does the game work?" I asked.

"If I remember correctly, it's modeled after a training course used by Space Jumpers when they lived on the ring."

"Space Jumpers?"

Charlie nodded. "Yeah. Would you like to watch a match?"

"Right now?"

"The Labyrinth is between here and your Illuminate. Someone is always playing," he said. "In fact, I believe they are holding trials for the new pro conclave."

Everyone wanted to go. It was always fun to see something new on Orbis, and since most of the other kids had witnessed my confrontation with Dop, there was a lot of interest in what I would face in his challenge. We gathered quickly around the light chute and Charlie punched the code for the Labyrinth. We were in front of the stadium instantly. The Labyrinth was only a little shorter than the Illuminate and rose to a point on the left side. The gleaming structure curved behind itself, and huge O-dats loomed over the entrance. The walls of light and sound called out to each of us, selling everything from tetrascopes to trips through the wormhole.

Charlie pointed to a list of names scrolling on one of the large O-dats. "During a pro conclave," he informed us, "the contestants play for prize money and prestige, but the school league is simply for fun. A lot of the kids play. Your Illuminate starts a new league next phase, if I'm right. Registration is free to anyone who attends the Illuminate." Charlie put his hand on Ketheria's shoulders. "Let me get some tickets so we can sit up high. Then we can get something to eat."

I know Ketheria liked Charlie because of his kindness, but she *loved* him for his appreciation of food. Even Nugget poked his head up anytime Charlie spoke of eating. The moment we stepped inside the arena, I could smell the food, and it smelled great. It was like the Birth Days Mother celebrated on the *Renaissance*. Every food imaginable was on display for purchase.

"Wait, it's better where we're going," he said.

"You've been here before?" Max asked.

"A couple of times."

Aliens shuffled under 3-D holographs of players simulating the game. The light emanating from the images deflected off metal railings that roped around the balcony we were now standing on.

"Is that the game?" I asked, pointing to the holographs.

Charlie looked up and said, "No, those are just famous matches from last rotation. I think the new professional season has already started."

Past the railing I saw more aliens peddling souvenirs to fans eager to purchase anything and everything. The scores from some of the players flashed on O-dats that floated above the vendors.

"What do they do with all this *stuff*?" Max asked me. "I can't imagine needing any of it."

"I guess Citizens just need more," I replied.

I tried to picture myself waiting to purchase a holographic portrait of my favorite player and bring it back to my home. I couldn't. It just didn't make sense to me. Was this what it meant to be a Citizen? When I was on the *Renaissance,* the Rings of Orbis and their customs were all I would dream about. But watching all of these strange creatures going about their business, laughing and enjoying whatever it was we were about to watch, a familiar feeling flushed through me—I was the alien here, not them.

We followed Charlie through the crowds, past the tiny stations where aliens lined up to wager on the outcome of the game, to an area high above the labyrinth. The huge walls of glass curved around a section in the middle of the arena that was even bigger than the plaza of the Illuminate. The labyrinth was dark, but a pulse of red light revealed the fans standing all around the lower level.

"We should hurry; a new match is going to start," he said.

Charlie purchased twenty-three tickets and explained that we were paying to sit in a better section. I saw the attendant counting us, and he stopped Charlie.

"Why so many of *them*?" the attendant asked.

The alien was not wearing any sort of Citizen insignia. I could only assume he was a knudnik, too. Charlie leaned toward the attendant.

"Who are you to question a Citizen?" Charlie demanded.

The alien shrank back in his seat and quickly accessed his O-dat. It felt strange watching Charlie exert his power over a knudnik. We were knudniks, and he never spoke to us like that. Max smiled at the attendant as we entered the reserved viewing room. It was a *ha-ha* sort of smile, not the *pleasure-to-meet-you* kind.

Charlie found us a large table right at the edge of the glass. The table was covered in purple silk and laid out with sparkling crystal glasses—one for each of us. Four thin aliens dressed in white jumpers waited until everyone was comfortable, then offered Charlie a portable O-dat. They didn't offer any to us.

"What's that for?" I asked.

"So we can order food. I can even place a bet with this, but this time we're just here to watch and maybe eat something," he said, his eyes widening. Ketheria smiled and moved to sit next to him. Max took Ketheria's seat next to me.

There were at least five more rows of aliens sitting behind us, each row a little higher than the one in front of it. Every table was dressed as elegantly as ours.

"There's a lot of people here," Max said.

I looked at Theodore, who was busy counting exactly how many.

"Look at our table," Ketheria exclaimed, pointing.

I stared into the purple silk. The material created a three-dimensional effect, and tiny lights in the cloth twinkled like stars in deep space. I lifted my drinking glass away from the illusion and then placed it back on the table. The crystal goblet looked like it was floating in space.

"This place is amazing," I said to her.

"One hundred and sixty-eight Citizens, two hundred and fourteen knudniks, including us," Theodore said. "I've noticed that a lot."

"Noticed what?" Max asked.

"I always see more knudniks than Citizens."

As I scoped the crowd, my eyes fell upon one alien seated in the row above me, just to my left. The alien was big. Not *Trefaldoor* big, but a lot bigger than Charlie. His skin was a chalky yellow, and he wore a large necklace inscribed with the Citizen insignia. The jewel glittered against the lights as the arena behind me lit up, announcing the next match. The alien snatched a small device off his table and clutched it in his thick fingers. He sat up and pulled the necklace aside to expose a large hole in his chest. The alien covered the hole with the device in his hand and began to speak. The words were raspy and mechanical, but everyone at the table moved. Frail aliens, dressed in soft colors, flittered around as each word emanated from the metal device. Two of them settled against him while another stood patiently in front of him.

"Yes, Athooyi. Your wishes?" the alien whispered, speaking very smoothly.

"I need to place my wager. Quickly," Athooyi said, and thrust a fistful of crystal toward the fragile creature. The alien drifted away with the crystals and the portable O-dat. Another alien took its place at his feet. Athooyi stroked the alien's fine hair and fed it something from the table. There must have been eight of these smaller aliens around Athooyi.

"You're staring," Charlie said, disrupting my trance.

"But . . ." I pointed at the alien.

"Now you're pointing. Turn around; the match is about to start."

Was I the only one staring? The others were all pressed against the glass, waiting for the match to start. Except for Max.

"I know—weird, isn't it?" she whispered.

"Every time I think I'm used to this place, I see something like that."

"Me too. I don't know what I would do if I didn't have you here," she mumbled. "I think I would go crazy."

"Me?"

"Well . . ." Max changed color.

"You look hot all of a sudden," I said.

"I do?" Max touched her cheek. "I am. Sorry. I meant to say, you know, everyone. I'm glad . . . everyone . . . all of us, here. Are here," she corrected herself, sweeping her hand toward the others. "More *humans.*"

"Oh, yeah. I know exactly what you mean."

But I wasn't sure I did. Ketheria glanced at me, smiling.

"What?" I asked her, but then turned my attention to the arena.

What just happened?

Suddenly the lights in our viewing room dimmed. The only lights left were the twinkle from each of the tables and the colored lights illuminating the playing field below. Directly across from me, two enormous O-dats unraveled and draped over the game area. They sparkled to life as images of the gamers sprung from the screens and raced around the arena, larger than life. There were four different gamers, each paired in identical outfits.

The 3-D holographs returned to the screens, and statistics for each of the gamers flashed for everyone to see. The gaming area turned red.

"That means no more bets," Charlie said.

"There are teams?" I asked.

"Yes, in this version of the game, it's two against two. One tracker and one bait," he said. "Here comes the bait now."

Two gamers strolled onto the playing field, waving to the crowd. One was dressed in protective armor of green and silver, while the other sported mostly black. Each wore a large helmet that appeared slightly unbalanced on the left side behind their neural implants. The gaming floor was marked with two semicircles, the flat sides facing each other. The players stepped into a smaller semicircle inside each of the main semicircles. Once the players were in position, an energy field sprang up, surrounding them.

The giant O-dats that floated above the bait, as Charlie called them, displayed two more players as they each waited offstage inside some narrow tunnel. We watched the screens as these gamers stepped onto a flat crystal glowing in the floor, which triggered an O-dat–like energy field to spring up in front of them.

"What's that for?" Max asked.

"That's called the sort. A lot of strategy goes into playing the sort."

"Why can't we see the whole playing area?" I asked.

"Remember the place you stayed on Orbis 1?" Charlie said. "That blue cell?"

Of course, how could I forget that place? That's when they thought I was messing with the central computer and they locked me up.

"That's where I met you," I replied.

Charlie nodded. "Remember how the testing area appeared larger than it should have?"

"Dimensional displacement," I said. "The room appears bigger to the observer than it actually is. Theylor tried to explain it to me, but I never really understood it."

"Well, it's the same thing here. The trackers are playing just beyond that wall," he said, pointing past the semicircles. "For them the playing field appears much larger."

"Oh."

"What are they doing now?" Theodore asked, pointing to the large O-dats overhead.

The screen on the left displayed a close-up of one of the sorts. Three glowing diamond shapes were grouped together over the Orbis insignia. Each diamond displayed a different word: SOLID, LIQUID, and GAS.

The first alien tapped on SOLID, and the crowd cheered, while some pounded their tables out of disgust.

"You can bet on any aspect of the game, including the first round of the sort," Charlie informed us. "Some people just lost a lot of money. But why anyone would bet on the sort is beyond me. Too crooked."

On the right screen, three new diamonds now appeared. These said: MECHANIC, KINETIC, and PSIONIC.

The second alien selected MECHANIC. The effect on the crowd was instant.

"The trackers set the game's parameters with the sort," Charlie said. "If the player is weak in one specific area, he or she may try to force the other tracker to choose around that weakness. They each have one more pick."

"Then what?" I said.

"Then the tracker has to find the bait and bring him back," Charlie replied matter-of-factly.

"What?"

"The tracker. With those parameters selected, he has to work his way through the labyrinth, find his partner, and then they both fight their way back before the other team does," he explained.

I didn't have to look at Max; she was already gawking at me, and so was Theodore. In fact, everyone was surprised by Charlie's statement.

"Are you thinking what I'm thinking?" she said.

"It's Quest-Nest," Theodore exclaimed.

"But how can that be? How could Mother know about a game played on the Rings of Orbis?" I pointed out.

Max shrugged and said, "Maybe she did and didn't tell us."

"What's wrong?" Charlie asked.

"We've played this game before," I informed him, and everyone nodded.

"That's impossible," he remarked.

"Mother set it up for us on the *Renaissance*," Max said.

"Except there was none of that *sort* thing," another kid mumbled.

Charlie shook his head. "This game is only played on the rings. The Citizens make sure of that. It's like a tourist attraction."

"Well, we played it on the *Renaissance*," I replied. "All the time."

"Maybe you're wrong," he tried to assure me. "Let's just watch and see."

But we weren't wrong. The labyrinth was a little fancier, but the concept was the same. The tracker utilized different weapons to destroy 3-D holographs and fight his way to the center before the force field fell. Near the semicircles surrounding the bait, the computer placed several alien monsters waiting to attack the bait if his tracker took too much time. The sort was the only unique part of the game. But then, Mother had randomly changed the parameters of Quest-Nest for us. It was always different.

Charlie pointed to the holographic monsters. "There's a time limit. If the tracker doesn't get here before it—"

"Then the energy shield comes down," I said, finishing his sentence.

"And the labyrinth will begin to shift, too," Max added.

Charlie dropped his shoulders, tilted his head, and closed his mouth.

"I like using the immobility cubes," Ketheria informed him.

"You were the best with them," another kid remarked.

"You found the bait so fast because you could read their minds," Dalton said, and Ketheria only smiled.

"That's cheating!" Grace shrieked.

"Didn't help her get back out, though," someone else pointed out.

Charlie sat in awe while we discussed the game as if we had watched it a million times—and we probably had. I was not worried about Dop's challenge anymore. Actually, I was smiling inside. He wouldn't see me coming. *What a great cycle that will be!*

"But this isn't kids from the Illuminate playing," I said to Charlie.

"No," he said. "This is a like a professional sports league back on Earth. The players are competing right now for entry into the conclave. Citizens own many of the players, and it's very competitive. A lot of money is won and lost on these games. People come from all over to compete. Your school league is separate, but all conclaves are played at the labyrinth."

I figured Vairocina could help me learn about the sort before my match with Dop. And I noticed that some of the weapons the players used in the match were foreign to me, but nothing I couldn't handle.

The alien in green and silver made it to the bait just before the alien in black. When he entered, the energy fields around the bait dropped and the labyrinth shifted. When the shield was down, the alien in black turned, then fired his weapon at the other bait.

"That's cheating," Max shouted, and the crowd seemed to agree. Athooyi stood up, clutched his chest with his speaking box, and screeched raspy insults toward the glass.

"Doesn't do much at this level," Charlie told her. "Only a little sting, but it can disorient the player. There are very few rules. He will not be penalized."

All four aliens fought their way back through the maze. Their plasma rifles obliterated their holographic opponents even though they didn't do much to the other players. The arena transformed below me. The walls faded away, and a purple light chute sprang up from the center of the floor. The room rotated on its axis.

"First team through wins," Charlie said.

"We know, Charlie," one of the kids said, snickering.

I watched on the O-dat as the bait in black covered his tracker from attack. The tracker was much larger than the alien, at least a whole head bigger. They made it through the doors first, but just barely. As they launched themselves into the chute, the crowd behind us roared in disapproval. Instantly, the arena went dark.

The O-dats now displayed the victorious team landing in the winner's chambers. The crowd of spectators mostly jeered and shook different appendages toward the displays. A booming voice announced that this was the team's first victory.

"They beat the favorites," Charlie said.

"They were good," I said.

"Especially the tracker," Max added.

The bait removed his helmet and held it up in victory. I stared at his face.

I knew that face.

I had seen it before, behind the Illuminate, stealing the stridling just the other cycle. There was no mistaking it. Standing with his arms in the air, smiling like a madman, was the thief.

"Look," I whispered to Max, pointing at his enormous image.

"It's him," Max exclaimed.

Charlie turned and asked, "Who is it?"

I blurted it out before thinking. "That alien. The bait. That's the person we saw stealing the stridling the other cycle."

"What!"

I turned to Charlie as the pit of my stomach hit the floor.

I didn't say anything, but I'm sure my eyes told him a thing or two.

"Why didn't you tell me about this before?"

"I . . . I tried," I said weakly. "Then I forgot."

Charlie raised his eyebrows and looked at Theodore and then at Max. "Did you forget, too?" he questioned them.

Max nodded slowly.

"Let's try and remember these things a little more, everyone," Charlie announced. "If you want to be Citizens one day, it's important to fit in and act as if this place is your own. You wouldn't want anyone stealing from *you*, would you?"

"We don't have anything to steal," Dalton spoke up.

"You will, eventually. You won't always be . . ."

"Knudniks?" I said.

"I don't like that word either, but yes—knudniks."

"What are you gonna do?" I asked.

"I'll have to report this," he said. "You should feel proud of yourselves for helping to catch a thief."

But I didn't. Acting like I belonged on Orbis had never done much for my popularity. In fact, it only aggravated Citizens like Dop. Things were better when I kept to myself. I turned to the O-dats and watched the thief celebrate with his tracker. I knew there was more to that thieving alien than just the stolen stridling. The marking I had seen on his arm told me that. He was a wormhole pirate; I was certain of it.

Ketheria, however, wasn't worried about it. "When do we eat?" she asked.

"Right now," Charlie said, and grabbed the portable O-dat.

"What are you hungry for?" Charlie looked up from the O-dat, straight at me. I could feel his disappointment in me. I could see it in his eyes. I didn't like feeling this way.

"I want to be surprised," Ketheria said, relishing the coming meal. "But surprised in a good way."

"Coming right up, young lady."

While we waited for Charlie's surprise, Max and I huddled at the opposite end of the table with Theodore. Dalton, surprisingly, was already there.

"How come you didn't tell *us* about the stridling, Dumbwire?" Dalton hissed, trying his best to act like Switzer.

"Don't call me that," I told him. "I never did anything to you."

"Switzer's gone," Max added. "You don't have to be like him anymore."

No one spoke. We stared at Dalton for an uncomfortably long time.

"You can join us if you want," I said.

Dalton huffed as if he were going to turn and walk away, but instead he sat next to Max.

"I'm sorry," he mumbled.

"Forget about it," I replied.

"How could a wormhole pirate be playing Quest-Nest?" Max whispered.

"A wormhole pirate?" Dalton exclaimed.

"Shhh! We don't know that," Theodore argued.

"I saw the marking," I reminded him.

Dalton seemed confused. "On who?"

Theodore shook his head. "What if you're wrong?"

"I don't think so. I just want to know how he got here."

"Or *why* he's here," Max added.

"Who?" Dalton pleaded, a little too loudly.

"Shhh," Max hushed him. "The alien that stole the stridling is a wormhole pirate. We saw the marking on his arm."

"The skull thing?" he said.

Max cringed. "Yes, but keep it down."

I wasn't listening anymore. Max had asked a good question. Why *was* he here? I couldn't imagine he was here only to play Quest-Nest.

"We should find out," I said.

"How?" Theodore asked.

"I'm gonna join the conclave," I announced.

Dalton almost choked. "Ha! This league?"

"You've got to be kidding," Theodore protested, but that was normal.

"I'm gonna need a partner," I said, looking to Max.

"Wait, you can't be serious." Dalton took Theodore's side.

"I make good bait," Max said, and then she winked at me. *What does that mean?* I felt my face get hot, and I had to look away.

"No, stop. You can't do this." Theodore pleaded. "You don't know how to play the game."

"We're better than these guys," I assured him, recovering myself.

"But you don't know how to play the sort," Dalton argued.

"Vairocina can help him figure it out," Max said.

Our food arrived while we were still talking. Actually, Theodore wasn't saying anything anymore. He just sat there staring at the table and shaking his head. The aliens surrounded our table, carrying four large trays.

"What is it?" Ketheria said with obvious excitement in her voice.

"It's called *pizza*," Charlie told her proudly.

"Why is it round?" Grace asked.

Charlie smiled. "I don't know why exactly. I never thought about that before."

The servers placed the four pizzas on our table. They smelled great.

"What planet are they from?" Max asked.

"Earth," Charlie replied.

"What a crazy place," Ketheria cried. Charlie put a piece of the pizza on her plate, and she picked it up to bite into it.

"Careful, it's hot."

We watched two more matches of Quest-Nest while we ate the earthly concoctions. Ketheria made Charlie order two more pizzas once he explained to her that she could select any type of ingredients she wanted. Anything except toonbas, that is. The restriction gave Ketheria a slight pause before she reordered.

I couldn't eat any more. I was stuffed, and my mind was full of questions. What was the wormhole pirate doing here? Was he the one the bandit on the shuttle was talking about when he said, *"Tell him"*? Watching Ketheria devour the pizzas, I also couldn't help but wonder what other things I've missed from Earth. Things I'd never know about because I hadn't set one foot on my own home planet. Charlie was right. Whether I liked it or not, Orbis was my home now. It's the only home I ever had besides the *Renaissance,* and *that* was only a spaceship.

Ketheria offered Max a bite of her pizza.

"It has pineapple!" Ketheria cried.

I watched Max lean over and take a bite of the pizza. She looked at me out of the corner of her eye, and I quickly looked away. What was the matter with me? Weird.

Even though I felt like my stomach would burst, I absent-mindedly took another chunk of the pizza, or a slice, as Charlie called it, and watched a new tracker select WATER from the sort. The labyrinth filled with liquid. The other tracker selected WEAPONS, and now they fought on boats.

"We never did *that* on the *Renaissance,*" Max said.

She was right. I was definitely going to have to brush up on the Orbisian rules of Quest-Nest before my match with Dop.

6

The next cycle, I was dragged out of my sleeper by Nugget.

"What is it?" I asked him.

"Ketheria. Ketheria's not good," he said, grabbing my feet and swinging them around.

Ketheria was in the corner of the room, curled up in a ball. Her hair was soaking wet, and she was shaking.

"Charlie!" I screamed as I bolted to her side.

Charlie said Ketheria was sick because she had eaten too much pizza. I wasn't so sure. I had never seen her sick before. In fact, I couldn't recall any of us ever being sick. I needed to be patched up a few times, especially when I lost my arm, but none of us ever woke up feeling unwell. Even on the *Renaissance.*

"She'll stay home with me this cycle," Charlie said.

"I stay too!" Nugget yelped, and sat next to her. She was sitting up with a glass of water Charlie had given her. "She'll be fine by the time you get home."

Ketheria didn't smile when we left; she just leaned against the wall, in the corner of the room, curled up in a blanket. Charlie tried to get her into the sleeper, but she wouldn't budge.

"Do you want me to stay?" Grace offered, but Charlie shook his head and nudged us toward the light chute.

"Really, she'll be fine."

"Charlie has his hands full," Theodore said as we emerged from the chute and strolled across the plaza.

"I think he can handle it," I said.

"Handle what?" Riis asked, waiting for us outside the Illuminate.

"Ketheria's at home with Charlie," Max informed her. "She's not feeling well."

"Your Guarantor is looking after her?" she asked, somewhat surprised.

There was that attitude again. Not quite insulting, but passively implying that we were not worth the attention.

"Not big on compassion around here, are you?" Dalton said, walking past Riis and into the Illuminate.

I looked at Max. "Never saw that before," I said.

"Come, we get the placement results this cycle," Riis informed us.

"Don't be disappointed," Theodore said to her as he walked inside. "I think I did really well."

Riis couldn't help but smile. Once inside, I could feel the anticipation in the air. I walked past more than one student projecting sample questions from the exam using their neural port add-ons. They circled the images, frantically debating the answers.

"It's really important to some of these people," I said.

"A lot more than it should be," Riis remarked.

Each of us grabbed a tap and headed for the lockers.

"We went to the Quest-Nest matches last night," I told her.

"The what?" I guessed that the central computer did not translate my word for the game.

"You know, the game in the Labyrinth with the trackers and the baits?"

"You mean *Wor'an'ain*," she said. This time the computer did not translate *her* language.

We stopped in front of the storage lockers, and I called Vairocina.

"Yes?" she said, gathering the light around me and appearing in holographic form.

"The central computer is not translating a word for us," I informed her.

"I could add it to the memory base if you want," she said.

I still wasn't used to Vairocina's "older" form. I missed the little girl I met on Orbis 1.

"Who's that?" Riis wanted to know.

"That's Vairocina," Max told her.

"JT rescued her from the central computer," Theodore added.

Riis was staring. "I thought Vairocina was a program."

"I am a real life force. If I could generate a physical form, you would not say that," Vairocina said defiantly.

Riis ignored her and asked me, "You can talk to her whenever you want?"

I tapped my head and said, "Softwire, remember?"

Riis didn't have a response. She just gawked at Vairocina. It was the usual response.

"What do you call the game?" I asked Riis.

"Wor'an'ian," she said, never taking her eyes off Vairocina.

"We call it Quest-Nest," I told Vairocina. "Could you add that to the translator?"

"Absolutely," she replied. "Done."

I looked at Riis. "What do you call the game again?"

"Quest-Nest," she said. The computer translated it perfectly.

"Thanks, Vairocina. I'll see you later."

Vairocina scattered, sending the light back into the environment. Riis waved her hand through the air where Vairocina had stood.

"Nice pixels, huh?" Theodore remarked.

Max's chin dropped. "She's a hologram!" Max exclaimed.

"Yeah, but she still has nice pixels," he replied.

Max shook her head and walked away.

I caught up with Riis as we headed to the pods. I needed a few questions answered.

"How do you join the conclave?" I asked her.

"You're not thinking of joining, are you? You don't even know how to play the game. The kids here will crush you."

"No, I mean the professional league. The one we saw at the Labyrinth."

"The pro conclave? Are all humans as crazy as you?"

"I'm just asking."

"Why?"

"I enjoyed watching, and I just want to know a few more of the rules."

Riis looked at me. She turned only slightly, since her eyes were already close to the side of her head. "Well, that depends. A Citizen can simply try out, but unless he or *she* belongs to a team, it's pretty hard to place as an individual. Knudniks, on the other hand, can only play if their Guarantor enters them. Any winnings go to the Guarantors. Some Citizens own stables of knudniks they train for the games. Be glad you don't belong to them."

"Why?"

"Just because."

That meant I would have to get Charlie to sign me up. He'd do it; I was sure of it. I just had to ask. *But how could a wormhole pirate enter?* They were neither Citizen nor knudnik. It didn't make any sense.

"Can anyone else enter? I mean someone who is not a Citizen, not even a knudnik?"

"No," she said. "Anyone entering the conclave must have Citizenship or belong to a Citizen."

We paused at the entrance to the pods.

"After the results of the exam are announced, specific programming will be arranged for your . . . level. Chances are we may not even be in the same theater after this," Riis informed us.

"Because knudniks will place poorly," I said.

Riis didn't answer me. She just smiled slightly, trying to be polite. "I didn't say that."

"But that's what you meant."

"Listen to me, Softwire. Dop was correct. I volunteered to show you around the Illuminate. I choose to do that, and my reasons are my own business. But I didn't make the rules on Orbis, and I definitely don't agree with how Citizens care for their knudniks—so quit treating me like I do."

Her words slashed at me, and I felt my face redden. All I could say was, "I'm sorry."

"I'll meet you at the lockers after the spoke," she said quickly, and slipped inside.

You're such a split-screen. I was the one treating her poorly. She didn't treat us like Dop or Weegin, or any other Citizens for that matter. I took out my frustrations on her because she was the only Citizen of Orbis who spoke to me. I used her to get what I wanted and then dismissed her because she was a Citizen. I was doing exactly what the Citizens did to me. She did not deserve that. I felt foolish.

"Good luck," Max hollered, taking a pod with Grace.

Theodore and I took the next one.

"I think I did pretty well," Theodore assured me. "There were 720,000 questions and I answered 425. That's more than half a percent. Pretty good burn rate, if you ask me."

I liked Theodore's optimism. It was rare, but then again, he was always confident when the numbers added up. I hoped I placed well, if only to disprove the theory the Citizens held of us. But the truth was there were too many questions on the exam that I couldn't even understand, and I didn't think half a percent was very much.

The pods drifted into place, and Theodore and I linked up. The white screen exploded with images of Citizens excelling at whatever they tried to do. I watched one alien control a space-port on the moon Ki. Another reclaimed a planet devastated by war. Every image showed Citizens winning against all odds.

The propaganda then faded to some sort of ceremony. An alien, dressed in a black velvet robe similar to the Keepers', with an oversize Citizen's crest mounted on some sort of metal thing that hung from his shoulders, stood up in front of the small crowd sitting in attendance. He looked like he was going to make a speech. I also noticed a telepathic headpiece bolted to his smooth head, just like the one Ketheria wore. The alien drew a deep breath, taking his time. He reeked of confidence. This Citizen was important, and he knew it, or at least he acted like it.

The theater fell silent, eager to hear every word this alien had to say. Floating in front of him were several O-dats from which the alien read to the audience.

"Great Citizens of the Rings of Orbis, your fledglings have labored for placement this phase, and I am . . . privileged to share their results." His tone was far drearier than I had expected.

The students in the theater, however, cheered loudly.

"I guess this guy had a bad cycle, huh?" Theodore whis-pered.

"I think he has better things to do—or at least he thinks he does," I replied.

"Throughout each cycle, our children on the Rings of Orbis have illustrated their excellence using the placement exam. It has primed many for lustrous careers in this universe, and each cycle the students who placed the highest have gone on to noble accomplishments."

The alien paused and consulted another alien near him before continuing. His face scrunched up as if he were filled with anger.

"Show us!" someone shouted from one of the pods.

"Once again your children have excelled," the speaker continued, regaining his composure. "These scores were higher than any cycle before."

The students erupted in response.

"Please don't show our scores," I moaned. I didn't need any more ridicule.

"As an example of our benevolence and understanding of all cultures, and in an agreement with our noble Keepers, this rotation saw the admittance of several children from our labor caste," he announced.

The crowd jeered and thumped on their pods.

"That's a nice way to put it," Theodore remarked.

"Citizens, be proud of your kindness. Be proud of your gracious acceptance of those who can only dream of such stature, for you are the chosen ones."

The students didn't know how to respond to this. Some

cheered while some still thumped on their pods. Obviously this wasn't a normal speech.

"In observance of tradition," the speaker said. "I would like to announce the student who succeeded above all others and placed first in our exam." The alien next to him handed the speaker a small clear screen. "This rotation's honoree is Theodore Malone from our labor caste. Property of Charlie Norton."

Theodore? I couldn't believe it. I knew he was smart, but *Theodore?* Then the other students in the auditorium erupted, screaming and banging on their pods, and I forced myself to concentrate on the huge O-dat in front of me. Walking toward the speaker to accept his honor—*was Theodore!* Larger than life, he stood next to the speaker and took the clear screen scroll the Citizen offered up. Theodore waved it above his head and smiled. The speaker avoided any eye contact with Theodore and immediately departed the podium.

I turned to Theodore and pinched him.

"Ow! What did you do that for?"

"I want to make sure you're not a hologram," I said. "When did you get that award?"

"I didn't!"

"Then how . . ."

"Wow! I'm first." Theodore was glowing. He stared at the screen, watching himself with the biggest smile I had ever seen stretched across his face.

"It's got to be a fake!"

"Who cares? I'm first!"

By now I was forced to shout over the noise of the students. On the screen the placement results scrolled in front of us. Theodore's name was first, and it shot out from the screen.

"Look, there's my name!" he shouted. "Yes! And Max is second! And look, JT, there's yours!"

The air did not move. It was as if a vacuum had sucked it from the auditorium. The entire place was reduced to a point of singularity. *But it can't be!* The third name on the list was *Johnny Turnbull.* Now all of the students were rocking the pods and banging on them in unison. Grace's name was fourth on the list, right behind mine. Dalton was fifth. Every one of us placed before any of the Citizens. Beside our name was our Guarantor's name: Charlie Norton. The crowd continued violently rocking their pods in disgust. I poked my head out, and an angry alien above me threw something. It stuck to my hair.

"What is it?" I turned to Theodore for help.

Theodore scrunched his face and said, "I don't know."

"Get rid of it!"

Gingerly, he swiped at my head, and flung the thing out of the pod.

"This isn't good!" he shouted over the noise.

"Is it ever?"

"We need to get out of here."

"JT!" someone shouted. It was Max.

Cautiously I peered over the edge of my pod and saw Max and Grace defending themselves from an assortment of projectiles being sent their way.

"Get Vairocina!" she shouted.

I could do better. I sat back and accessed the central computer through the pod's uplink. The energetic coolness of the central computer washed over me as I pushed inside it. Without looking, I launched myself down the first corridor of data and accessed the Illuminate. I felt stronger whenever I was inside the central computer. Much more confident than I did on the outside. I located the auditorium on the network grid with my first try. A simple binary code stood guarding the power to the entire room. I reached in with my mind and disconnected the power. I bet that would shut them up.

"Vairocina!" I hollered while still inside the computer.

"This is a nice surprise," she said, floating through a portal. "What's wrong?"

"Can you get the pods moving in the Illuminate and get all of us out of here?"

"Everyone?"

"Just the humans; you'll have to restrict the power flow. Can you locate us by our staining?"

"Absolutely," she said.

I pulled out of the computer.

"Did you do that?" Theodore asked.

"Yeah, hold on!"

The pod jerked sideways. The doors out of the auditorium cracked open, flushing our pod with light. Theodore and I scrambled out and found some of the other kids already waiting.

When Max finally appeared in the doorway, she gasped, "I'm telling everyone now: Don't try so hard next time."

"When did you get that award?" Grace asked Theodore, getting out of her pod as quickly as possible.

"I didn't. That was a fake, but the score still counts," he assured everyone.

"Did you see Ketheria's score, JT?" Max asked.

"No, why?" I replied. I must have been inside the computer when her score came up.

"She placed last."

"Last of us?"

"No, last in the whole Illuminate."

Staying at the Illuminate was not an option. I had no intention of facing anyone from the student body after the way they'd reacted to our placement scores (I especially didn't want to face a mob of them). I also wanted to ask Charlie how Theodore could receive an award without even knowing the event had taken place. Almost immediately, we jumped a chute back home and found Charlie sitting in the garden with Ketheria. She was leaning up against him, wrapped in a blanket, drawing on an O-dat.

Charlie stood up when he saw us. "What's wrong? What happened?"

"They don't like us very much at the Illuminate," Max informed him.

"We're too smart," Dalton added.

"Yeah, I'm sorry, everyone," Theodore moaned, and rolled his eyes, his tone implying that he was the cause of the entire problem. I looked at Max as she bit her bottom lip, trying not to laugh.

Charlie raised his eyebrows and let out a deep breath. "The placement exam."

"You knew?" I questioned him.

Charlie nodded.

"Why didn't you warn us?" The edge on my words was a little too sharp. I tried to soften my tone a bit. "And when did Theodore get that award?"

"The Citizens always honor their own, especially the student who places highest. When Theodore received the best score, the Chancellor refused to acknowledge it. The Keepers made him do it, but he would only perform the staged production you saw."

"The Keepers monitor the test?"

"They wrote it."

My mind was swimming with questions again. I couldn't even fathom what Charlie meant. And I couldn't care less. I really didn't want this attention. Not at the Illuminate.

"Your sister's feeling much better," Charlie said as Max sat next to her.

Ketheria. I forgot. "I'm sorry," I said. "How are you feeling?"

I really wanted to ask her about the test. Did she even answer the questions? How could she place last? It just didn't fit.

I stared at Ketheria, and before I said anything, she said, "The exam means nothing, JT. It only fills their need to label everyone. Forget it. But congratulations just the same, Theodore."

"Thanks," he replied. He was still smiling. In fact, he hadn't stopped smiling the entire way home.

"But . . ." I wanted more from my sister. I wanted an explanation. It infuriated me when she was so passive.

"I just didn't do the test," Ketheria said. "Is that enough? It's better this way."

My little sister could be odd sometimes, and unfortunately, this was one of those times. The device on her head didn't seem to stop her from always knowing what I was thinking, either. I never knew how to reply whenever she blurted out a piece of advice or some sort of warning. I leaned forward, tugging at the O-dat she was writing on.

"What do you have there?" I asked, trying to change the subject.

"Nothing," she replied.

On the screen were lines spiraling around a fixed point like a swirling galaxy. Just kids' stuff. Doodles, really. I ran my hand over her hair, bumping my fingers against the metal bolted to her head.

"You look better."

Ketheria poked her chin up at Charlie and said, "I'm hungry."

"She's better," Max agreed.

From behind me, Theodore called, "JT?" He was now standing at the doorway to the house. "Can you come here?"

I followed Theodore inside. "What is it?"

"I want to show you something."

Theodore stopped outside the room to our sleepers, where we had left Ketheria at the start of the spoke.

"Did you see this?"

I looked in the room, but I didn't enter. "No."

"She's been busy."

I knew Ketheria wasn't feeling well, but I couldn't understand what would make her do this. Drawn on the walls, the floors, and even the sleepers—everywhere Ketheria could reach—were the same spirals she was doodling in the garden. There must have been thousands of them.

"I guess that's why Charlie got her that screen," he mumbled.

Charlie came up behind us and said, "She started right after you left."

"What does it mean?" I asked him worriedly.

"I don't know."

"Is something wrong with her?"

"Nothing. She's as fit as a fiddle."

"What's a fiddle?" Theodore asked.

"For such smart kids, you don't know much about Earth, do you?"

I didn't know much about anything anymore. I just wanted to sit somewhere and turn my brain off. I wanted everything and everyone to go away. What if Ketheria was sick, I mean *really* sick? What if she had picked up some weird alien disease that no one knew would affect humans? I mean, Ketheria ate practically everything she could fit in her mouth. Maybe it was in the food. If Ketheria really *were* sick, would anyone care? Like the Chancellor said, we were the labor caste. I'm sure there was a motto written somewhere on one of their factory walls that read: IF THE MACHINE BREAKS, GET ANOTHER ONE.

I tried to eat, but I wasn't hungry. I tried to read, but all I did was reread the same sentence fourteen times. I gave up and went for a walk.

I had never looked at the plants in the garden before. I had watched Charlie coax some of the more shy plants to come forward, but I never really examined them. The ring was rotating into shadow now, and the fading light was grabbing slivers of purple, red, and bright green. I saw that some plants were spiked, protecting thick flowers blooming under the thistles, while others puffed up their tentacles and wiggled in the breeze. They really were striking.

I rounded a huge tree whose surface was a golden green, its skin as smooth as any metal I'd known. I placed my palm against the trunk. The tree was cool under my touch. It stood there unresponsive to the pressure of my hand. Leaning against the tree, I wondered how long it had stood in the garden, just being a tree. Did it ever try to be a better tree? Did it ever worry about what the other trees thought about it? Was I going crazy?

I didn't want to think that Ketheria was going crazy. I forced the thought from my head. *All she did was draw on the walls,* I told myself. But I knew this wasn't like her. I *knew* she wouldn't care about the exam. I should have seen that coming, but the scribbling—this was something entirely different.

I paused at a curve in the stone path. I saw Max sitting on a crystal bench just five meters in front of me. She was playing with a small plant she must have coaxed out of the bushes.

Max showed no sign of concern about the cycle's events. At least, she didn't appear to—but then, she never did. I liked that about her. Grace could get upset over a tear in her skin, but not Max. She was always looking for more, always ready to try something new. I watched Max brush her brown hair away from her face. That's when she saw me. I felt my skin go hot when her eyes caught mine.

"He's cute, isn't he?" she said. I thanked the Universe that she hadn't noticed I was standing there staring at her. I stepped toward her, and the plant shuffled back into the bushes.

"I don't think it likes me," I murmured.

"Oh, quit thinking the universe is against you." Max made it sound like a joke, and I smiled.

"We'll find out next cycle, won't we?"

"And we'll deal with it then." Max stood up. "You know, I can't believe Theodore beat me. He's much smarter than I give him credit for."

"It doesn't bother you that the entire student body of the Illuminate hates us now?"

"Should it? Maybe now you won't think you're just a knudnik. You can't tell me that you didn't want to place well and show those Citizens a thing or two."

She was right. I did want to beat them; I just hadn't prepared for the consequences. *How does she know that, though?* Sometimes I think Max knows me better than I know myself.

"Were you looking for me?" she asked.

"Huh?" I muttered, distracted.

"We're you *looking* for me?"

"Um, no. I was just going for a walk."

"Oh, good, then, can I join you?"

"Can I say no?" I smiled, and something inside me stirred. "Absolutely not."

We followed the stone path to its end and picked up a dirt path that weaved its way through a patch of wild trees.

"This is a big estate," I remarked, looking back over my shoulder.

"Aren't you curious how Charlie got it?" she wondered. "He doesn't talk much about it."

"Charlie has a lot of secrets."

"That's normal on the Rings of Orbis."

The dirt path came to a dead end, and we stood in front of a thick-looking wall of cut and polished boulders. We both squinted to see the top.

"Typical," I said.

"What is?"

"This wall." I placed my hands on the rock. "It's no different from anywhere else. This place is just bigger and prettier, but it still has the same purpose as every other place on the rings."

"And that is?"

"To keep us here," I said.

"JT, you need to lighten up a little. Seriously."

The next cycle, Ketheria followed us to the Illuminate. She acted as if nothing had happened and didn't show a single sign of the melancholy that seemed to plague her last cycle. Needless to say, I was nervous about our reception. The first anomaly occurred the moment we arrived—Riis was not in the plaza to meet us.

I caught a group of students staring, following our every step. Another group shouted something across the plaza while pointing at us.

"Let's get inside quickly," I whispered.

"They're just jealous," Max replied.

I concentrated on my feet, trying not to look at anyone as we headed straight for the storage lockers. Riis wasn't there, either. Instead, Dop and his misfit friends were waiting for us. Theodore's storage bin was open and Dop was playing with a screen scroll. It was the same one that was given to Theodore in the fake ceremony held with the Chancellor. The Illuminate must have put it in the locker, like Riis said.

"How did you get in there?" Theodore demanded.

"You're knudnik; I'm not," was all he said.

Some of the kids went straight to their lockers in the oval foyer. I stood next to Theodore, along with Ketheria and Max. My anger was quickly connecting the neurons in my brain, igniting them one by one, but Max went first. "Why do you care how we did on that test if you know you're so much better than us?"

Dop tossed the award into the locker and said, "Because you cheated."

"I did not!" she pushed the words through her clenched teeth. Her fists were already balled up.

Dop pointed his willowy finger at me. "He's a softwire. Everyone knows it. He used it to get inside the central computer and change the results. There is no other way."

Theodore's eyes narrowed and he stomped toward Dop, not something you would normally see Theodore do. "I answered every one of those dumb questions! In fact, they were easy. If I had more time, I would have answered them all."

Dop and his friends laughed in Theodore's face.

"Maybe with the help of the Softwire's little friend inside the central computer." Dop motioned his head toward me.

"Who told you about that?" I spoke each word slowly, trying to control my anger.

"Who do you think?"

I blinked as my mind rebooted. Riis? She wouldn't. Why would Riis tell Dop about Vairocina? She didn't like Dop.

"You're lying," I snapped.

Dop shrugged his narrow shoulders and smirked.

"You're a creep, too," Max said.

"What do you want, Dop?" I asked him.

"Admit that you cheated."

"All right."

"Uh, JT? I didn't cheat!" Theodore's eyes flew open.

"If you beat me at Quest-Nest. Then I'll stand up in front of the whole Illuminate and tell everyone I cheated, but you have to win in the arena."

A smile snaked across Dop's face, a devilish smile that made his eyes sparkle. "I like that," he hissed. "I will destroy you."

"But if I win . . ."

"You won't," he boasted.

"But if I do, then you have to leave us alone, and we each want one of those things you guys wear on your neural ports," I said, pointing to the metal device on his friend's ear.

"A *pob*?" There was an edge of scorn to his tone.

"You can afford it."

"Fine, I'm not going to lose."

"One for each of us," I repeated, motioning to everyone in the room.

Dop hesitated for a moment, but then said, "Deal. In three phases you register in the Illuminate league and I will humiliate you at the arena. Then everyone will know the truth."

"I'll be there."

Dop shoved his way between us while his friends slunk behind him. Dop never stopped grinning. It was an over-confident grin, as if his quest was already accomplished. I smiled right back at him. Little did he know that I had been playing Quest-Nest since I was born.

"I don't know about this," Theodore whispered, even though I was sure Dop couldn't hear us.

"He's gonna wish he never made that challenge," Max said.

"Thanks, Max."

"The tap said the Illuminate league starts in three phases. We need to practice before then," she said matter-of-factly.

"You can't make that sort of bet, JT. I didn't cheat," Theodore insisted. He looked at Ketheria. "Are you gonna let him do this?"

"It's not my decision," she replied. "Anyway, Dop *is* nervous."

"Why?" I asked. "Does he know we've played before?"

"No. It's just that no one expected a knudnik to do so well on the placement exam. Maybe he's worried about what else you know."

"Don't you wish you'd taken the test now?" I asked her.

"I'm not the one playing," she answered.

"She's right," Theodore agreed. "Maybe you should use her as a partner. She was always the best at finding the bait."

"Thanks a lot, Theodore," Max protested.

"There's too much at stake here. If Dop wins, everyone will think I cheated. I won't be first anymore," he pointed out to her.

"Dop's not gonna win," I insisted.

"We should practice, though," Max said. "It has been a while."

"That's why we need to join the Citizens' League," I told her. "So we can practice."

Theodore dropped his shoulders, threw his head back, and groaned.

"Out of the question," Charlie said, standing near the chow synth.

"But—"

"No, JT. It's not up for debate. You can play all you want in the school league."

"Why won't you let me play in the Citizens' League?" I protested. I hadn't expected his response. I had assumed Charlie would let us play.

"Because," Charlie said.

"Because why?"

I stared at him incredulously, but the resolve on his face did not wane. "Because I said so."

And that quickly, I had lost. I didn't get it. What was he protecting me from in the Citizens' League? I sulked my way to the sleepers, where Max was waiting with Theodore.

"What did he say?" she asked anxiously.

"He said no," I told them. "You can start breathing again."

Theodore let out a deep breath. His face was warning-light red. Probably from holding his breath since I went to ask Charlie.

"How will we practice?" Max asked, shaking her head.

"We'll ask Vairocina," I said. "She'll help."

Within a few moments, Vairocina displayed holographs of the arena and all procedures for starting a school game. It was almost identical to the one we played on the *Renaissance*.

"Makes you wonder, doesn't it?" Max muttered.

Theodore looked at Max but didn't say anything. It was as if they knew something but didn't want to say it.

"What?" I asked.

"Nothing," they both said.

But I could guess what they were thinking. I was thinking about it, too, but I wouldn't dare say it out loud. If my father was who they said he was, if he really was a Space Jumper, maybe he programmed the game into Mother—but why? Were there more Space Jumpers among the adults on the *Renaissance*? Were they playing Quest-Nest to pass the time? But most of their time would have been spent in their own cryogenic sleepers. Then why would they program an elaborate game into the ship's computer?

"Vairocina, show us the sort. There was no sort in our game. Show us how that works," I told her.

"That's probably because the Citizens added the sort when they began betting on the outcome. It was never part of the original design. The sort is a simple random generator, and each screen offers three selections. There are four screens, two for each tracker," she said.

"That's eighty-one possible game scenarios," Theodore said.

"Not exactly," Vairocina said. "The central computer has its own random generators to decide what to play in each stage. There are 2,554,675,200 game scenarios, to be exact."

"We can't possibly learn every one of those," Max exclaimed.

"You're not supposed to. That's what makes the game so random," I explained. "We only need to learn the strategy of the sort."

"It would help if you knew your opponents' strengths and weaknesses," Vairocina added.

"But we don't have time," Max complained.

"But we do know our own strengths and weaknesses," I pointed out.

"That would help you because I believe, as humans, there are some aspects of the game you may want to avoid. For example, if the final outcome of the sort is SOLID, MECHANIC, TECHNOLOGICAL, and BIOLOGICAL, you might search for your bait in a building using plasma rifles to destroy a group of holographic Neewalkers poised to stop you. But if the sort comes out GAS, PSIONIC, MAGICAL, and MENTAL, you might wind up in space collecting cosmic energy streams to unlock a multidimensional puzzle. I would avoid this, especially if your opponent can survive in outer space and slip through dimensions at will."

"JT, this is a lot different than the *Renaissance*," Theodore whispered.

He was right. Dop was going to have the advantage after all. Suddenly I felt nauseous. My head was swimming with possible outcomes, but I couldn't just give up.

"How can I ever win if my opponent first selects AIR?" I asked Vairocina.

"You must select MECHANIC every time. This will force the central computer to provide you some sort of flying device. Then the playing field is equaled again. That's the purpose of the sort. But be careful. If you do not select properly, the game will be over before you even step into the arena. That's a common amateur's mistake."

The three of us sat with Vairocina while she illustrated as many examples as we could digest. It seemed that the first pick in the sort was the most important. My opponent could force me into a water game if he chose LIQUID. So unless I learned to swim before next phase, I had no choice but to select MECHANIC in the second stage. A selection of PSIONIC could not guarantee that I would be above the water. PSIONIC selections were instruments or weapons that forced you to play in stealth mode—invisibility, sound waves, stuff like that. Only a selection of MECHANIC would give me a tool to keep from drowning.

Theodore fell asleep on the floor long before I was finished. Most of the other kids went to bed after watching for a while, but Max stayed with me the whole time.

"It's all in the sort, JT," she said. "Play the sort properly and we have a chance."

"Vairocina, how can I make sure I get to choose the first stage?" I asked.

"You can't. It's random. Your chance is fifty-fifty, but you may pass."

"Pass! Why would I ever pass on the first stage?"

"It's all strategy," Vairocina instructed. "Some opponents, with certain abilities, may not care where they play, only that they select KINETIC in the second stage of the sort. That is why it's very important to know your opponent. For each professional conclave, volumes of information are published on the players to assist those who wager on the outcome of the game."

This was definitely not the Quest-Nest I knew. There were too many unknowns. I liked the challenge when Mother randomly generated the playing field, but we never had fliers or water or games in space. Dop was going to win after all. I panicked. And how would I live up to my end of the bargain? Theodore would never speak to me again.

"What are you thinking about?" Max whispered.

"Nothing," I mumbled.

"We can still beat him. Just direct the sort to a game we know."

"What if I don't get the sort in the first stage?"

"Vairocina, can you show us as many types of flying devices and water devices the central computer has stored in its game drives?"

"This will take some time," she informed us.

"We'll wait," Max said.

And that's how we lived life for a while, at least Max and I. We avoided most of the Citizens at school and came home to work with Vairocina every single spoke. She demonstrated to us how most of the mechanical devices worked, as well as the alien weapons we didn't know. Theodore and some of the other kids sat for a couple of the training sessions, but none of the others were as determined as I was, except for Max. She was there every cycle, and if I ever glanced her way, she was either watching Vairocina or looking at me.

The rumor that I had cheated on the placement exam spread quickly throughout the Illuminate. "Cheating's typical for a knudnik," I overheard more than one kid mutter. During one spoke, some of the worst kids held a mock ceremony in the plaza where they presented the highest-placing Citizen with Theodore's award. I refused to let their lies bother me anymore. I buried my anger, saving it for the match. That was all that mattered.

On top of it all, Riis was acting strange as well. When she finally showed up at the Illuminate again, she no longer waited for us at the entry. She seemed to make a point of avoiding me and the other kids, usually coming late and leaving early. I tried to stop her once as she slipped into a pod, but all she did was wave, smiling weakly. Her blank eyes told me nothing about her feelings. Did she think I cheated, too? I wanted to know. She was the one Citizen whose opinion I cared about.

When Vairocina finally finished showing us everything she could, I knew there was one thing left for me to do. I went looking for Charlie and found him in the garden.

"Can you teach me to swim?" I asked him.

Charlie looked surprised. "You don't know how to swim?"

I shrugged. "Not a lot of opportunity on the *Renaissance*."

"Well, there's a pool at the Labyrinth. I could show you there. Then we can take in some games. Brush up before your match."

"You know about my match with Dop?"

"Wasn't hard to figure out with all the studying you're doing. I assume the match is in the school league?" It was really more of a question.

I hesitated, dropping my eyes. "Yes, but I still don't know why—"

Charlie cut me off. "That discussion's over, JT." He stood up. "Why don't we go now? Are you ready?"

"Just you and me?"

"Max and Grace make excellent babysitters."

Charlie and I got to the arena before anyone arrived for league play. The air lacked the electricity of the other cycle even though a few aliens were already playing Quest-Nest. Charlie said it was mostly for practice. In the vacant stands he pointed out the most serious gamblers, who sat watching the players' every move. I saw Athooyi sitting high above the glass.

"There's that alien I saw from the other night. He was sitting in our section," I said, pointing.

"That guy? He's a big-time gambler. Bad reputation. Stay away from his kind," Charlie warned, and pushed my hand down. "Come on, the pool is this way."

I walked next to Charlie along the concrete corridors of the arena and down toward the pool. With my other Guarantors, I probably would have walked a few steps behind them, but this was Charlie. Looking at him out of the corner of my eye made me think of the children who were separated from us the first cycle we arrived on the Rings of Orbis. I hadn't thought about the other kids from the *Renaissance* in a long time. *What are they doing right now?* I wondered. *Are they working in factories?* I doubted that any of them were learning how to swim. It was hard to believe life could be this easy, even with Dop's challenge biting at my neck.

The smell of sweat and chlorine grew stronger as we walked deeper under the Labyrinth. "That's where you'll go for your match when you play," Charlie said, pointing at an opening in the dank stone walls splashed with yellow crystal lights. It was not very fancy.

"Citizen players don't go there," I said. "Do they?"

"No, you're right. There's another area for them."

The circular pool where I was going to learn how to swim was lit from below with an enormous blue crystal. The rippled light escaping the water bounced off the low, mirrored ceiling and bathed the whole area in a cool glow. I saw two other aliens in the pool when we arrived. One alien swam the entire perimeter of the pool while remaining underwater. I made a mental note to avoid LIQUID in the sort if he were ever my opponent.

"Go in there and put these on," Charlie said, handing me a pair of short pants. "It's a swimsuit." I took the clothing. "I don't think you want to go naked."

It didn't matter to me. I just wanted to learn how to swim.

"Will these help me?" I said.

"No, you have to do all the swimming yourself. But go

ahead and put them on anyway. I already have mine on. I'll wait here."

"Charlie?"

"What's wrong?"

"Why are you our Guarantor?"

Charlie glanced over his shoulder at the others in the pool. "This is not the time." The other alien stepped out of the pool and was watching us. "Now, get changed. Do as you're told." His voice was low and rough.

I changed quickly. Charlie had never used that tone with me before, but I couldn't blame him. If Charlie did have a secret, he certainly wasn't going to spill it here, not around other Citizens. I felt stupid and embarrassed by my sudden question. *I'm such a split-screen*, I thought.

When I returned to the pool, Charlie was already in the water near the edge. I had never seen Charlie with his shirt off before. He was strong-looking. He didn't have big defined muscles, but his chest and arms looked like they could do some damage. He also had several scars on his body. *Where did he get those?* I wondered.

"C'mon, it's not that deep. You can touch the bottom," he called out.

I waited until the alien, still underwater, swam past me. I stuck my foot in. The water was warm, and I remembered the bio-bots in the crystal-cooling tank on Orbis 2. I also remembered almost drowning.

"Be patient, now. I'm not going to make you an avid swimmer in one cycle, but I can get you started with a dog paddle."

"No tools," I objected. "I need to learn this without any tools."

Charlie laughed; it was more of a snort, really. "It's a swimming style. It's the way dogs swim, very easy."

"I've never seen a dog, so I've never seen one swim."

Charlie laughed again and dipped into the water. "It's like this."

Charlie dug at the water with his hands and kicked his feet. His chin was thrust forward and his lips pursed as he forced his head above the waterline. He was actually moving forward! *I can do that,* I thought, and jumped in. I started to sink, and the water entered my mouth, my eyes—everywhere. I swallowed a mouthful and frantically clawed at the water. I must have been doing a lousy impression of a dog, with or without the paddle.

With a quick thrust, I was above the water coughing and kicking. Charlie had me by the hair. "You've got to hold your breath, kid!"

"You didn't tell me that!" I choked.

"You're gonna drown if you don't."

"I figured that part out," I snapped. "I can't do this, Charlie."

"Yes, you can. I'll help. I'll hold you up while you practice the paddling part."

Charlie held me up in the water and told me to kick my legs, cup my hands, and pull on the water. After a moment he let go, and I sank to the bottom again.

He yanked me back out and ordered, "Faster and harder, c'mon. I know you can do this."

Three more times I sank to the bottom, but at least I didn't swallow any of the water. *I can* do this, I thought. *I have to do this.*

"Let's save some more for another cycle," Charlie offered.

"No, a little more," I pleaded.

I kicked harder and I kicked faster, but I was still sinking.

"One more time," I said. "And this time don't grab me."

When Charlie let go, I sank like piece of iron, but this time I didn't touch the bottom. I kicked and I clawed and I was still underwater, but I was moving forward now. I heard nothing except my own voice screaming in my head for oxygen, but I kept kicking. I opened my eyes and saw the underwater alien swimming toward me. He was so graceful, so confident. Why was this so hard for me? I wanted to swim like that. I reached forward again, hands cupped, and I thrust my legs at the same time. I gave it everything I could, and then I did it again. I broke the surface and heard the shouts and cheers of Charlie.

"That's it! You're swimming, Johnny. Keep going!"

Clumsily, I found a rhythm and paddled my way around the pool. I was snorting through my nose like an animal as I kicked and clawed. I'm sure it wasn't pretty, but at least it wasn't drowning. I did it. I was swimming!

Charlie was still cheering loudly as I lapped the pool. That's when I noticed the one alien frowning at Charlie. Then the alien whispered something to the underwater alien when he surfaced. Charlie caught them staring at him and stopped cheering. I guess his enthusiasm over a knudnik seemed odd for a Citizen.

My match with Dop was only cycles away now. I was confident in my skills using any stage-two MECHANIC from the sort, and I was also swimming pretty well. Charlie decided to teach the other kids how to swim, and soon the lessons were a regular event after school. Charlie began ignoring the reactions of the other Citizens, and for once I had to believe everything was on the up and up. If Charlie was keeping a secret, if he had become a Citizen in some underhanded manner, he certainly wasn't afraid of losing his status. I pushed any further suspicions out of my mind and braced myself for the one final thing I had to do before I faced Dop. I was going to play a match in the Citizens' League.

"You can't, JT," Theodore argued, sitting next to me in the garden.

"I'll remove the registration after I'm done, I promise."

Max stared at the ground. Then she bounced up and announced, "All right, I'm in."

"I'm not going," Theodore protested.

"I'll go," Ketheria said.

Theodore was outnumbered and he knew it. "Fine. I'll go, then, but I'll only watch."

I needed their support. I felt bad for betraying Charlie, especially after the care he took with the swimming lessons, but what would one game hurt? Besides, I desperately needed the experience. I called up Vairocina.

"Wait!" Max hissed. "Maybe you should put the forged registration for the pro league in the computer yourself."

But Vairocina was my friend. "I trust her."

"It's better to be safe," Theodore agreed.

Vairocina was already here. "Hello, everyone," she greeted us.

"Vairocina, how does a Citizen register a player for Quest-Nest, for the pro conclave?" I asked her.

"It's a simple form filed in the arena's archives."

"Thanks, that's great."

Vairocina was looking elsewhere as she spoke to us, probably multitasking some event for the Keepers. "Is that all?"

I looked at Max; the warning was in her eyes. I could do it myself, I thought. It would be cleaner. "Yes, thank you," I said, smiling, and Vairocina disappeared. "At least I know where to start now."

"But when?" Theodore asked.

"I really don't feel like going to school next cycle, do you?"

Theodore rolled off the crystal bench and moaned. "I know we're gonna get in trouble for this."

"If you keep acting like that, we will," Max scowled.

Nugget was a bit of a problem at the start of the spoke as he insisted on going to school this time. Charlie stepped in and smoothed the whole thing over. It only made me feel guiltier for what I was about to do. Once we reached the Illuminate, the four of us lagged behind the other students until we were the only ones left in the plaza.

"You guys ready?" I said.

They each nodded, and we slipped back toward the light chutes.

"The code," Max groaned. "We don't know the code to the arena."

"943-23-555." Theodore shrugged as we gawked. "I like numbers. I watched Charlie punch them in."

"Then you go last and punch in for everyone else," I said.

When we arrived at the arena, we moved quickly toward the lifts that led to the elevated dome.

"We need to stay out of sight until I register us. Any Citizen can read our skins and know we're not supposed to be here," I warned.

"Which way?" Max asked.

"Follow them," Ketheria said, pointing.

Approaching the arena was a sleek, humanoid creature towing four stout and muscular aliens of different heights, each with its own iron collar. The knudniks were dressed in nothing but charcoal-colored hoods, their huge naked bellies sagging in front of them. The Citizen wore a contrasting hood of black material that clung tightly to her head and covered her shoulders. Her Citizen emblem was a jewel pinned to her snug dress, which puddled on the ground around her, dragging as she walked. Her porcelain arms poked out from the material and clutched four rusted chains, one for each of her knudniks.

"Move!" she barked, and yanked the chains.

"Pick someone else," Theodore begged.

"No. She'll take you where you want to go," Ketheria assured us.

There were no light chutes outside the arena to take us to the upper levels. The Citizen dragged her knudniks to a glass pod that navigated one of the arena's slanted exterior supports. There were four supports in total. Each one had its own pod. The alien filled her pod with the hooded creatures and waited for us to board.

"We'll take the next one," Max called out to her, and quickly directed us toward an empty pod.

"I'm not sure about this, JT," Theodore murmured.

"You never are," Max reminded him.

"Don't worry," I said. "Once we're registered, no one will bother us. It will be as if Charlie had set it up by himself."

We tumbled into the pod and sat down. The door materialized, and the pod slid upward. I stared out from the pod and looked out over Orbis 3, growing beneath me. I could see the edge of the ring on both sides and then the blackness of space. Charlie told me once that the atmosphere on each ring was the thinnest at the edges. I wondered if I would ever be free to roam these rings and see it for myself. Before I started feeling sorry for myself again, I reminded myself of the knudniks chained to the Citizen. *This view will do just fine,* I thought.

When we emptied the pod, the alien was already dragging her property toward a circular counter under a low-hanging blue crystal light. Behind the counter stood a tall alien who appeared to be mostly composed of metal, except for the jaundiced skin stretched over his skull. His arms were like metallic bones, but not shiny and new, more old and weathered-looking. Cables jutted out from the back of his head and attached to different places on his spine. The alien wore a thick red apron and was so tall that he bent over even when the tall female approached.

"Hello, Tinker," she called out to him.

"What do you have here?" Tinker said admiringly. When he spoke, wheels and wires in his back began to spin and move.

"I want to register some new players. I think they might have a chance to place in the Chancellor's Challenge this rotation. The big one is quite strong," she boasted.

Tinker stood tall and scrutinized the biggest alien, caressing the yellowed skin on his chin with long metal fingers.

"Ah, this looks like a fine team. I will be sure to make a wager, but just a small one," he replied, smiling. Tinker extended his hand, and I noticed his fingers were really an assembly of metal tools and knives, some at least thirty centimeters long. Deftly, he lifted the knudnik's hood. The alien blinked and turned his head from the light. By accident, his eyes caught mine, and for a brief moment we were both locked in a stare. The knudnik's eyes were filled with fear and remorse. It wasn't the first time I had seen this on the Rings of Orbis: knudniks trying to forget the life they left, or struggling with some command barked at them from an incomprehensible Guarantor. I wondered what the alien saw in my eyes now.

"Do it now, JT. While he's busy," Theodore whispered, snapping me out of my stare.

We slunk to the far side of the counter, and I shuffled as close as I could to Tinker's O-dat. With a push, I was inside his computer searching for the files that would register me in the Citizens' League. I called up the form from the central computer, and it appeared in front of me instantly. The form was simple except for one tiny detail. Every Citizen was assigned a personal data key for their transactions. What was Charlie's code? I had no idea. Was it a number? A genetic ID? What? I called out for Charlie Norton's data key but nothing came. Where would it be? I thought about giving up right there. I didn't want to do this to Charlie, but if I didn't, I would be forced to take on Dop without ever playing here on Orbis. I played a million times on the *Renaissance;* shouldn't that be enough? For me, it wasn't.

"Vairocina?"

She appeared inside the central computer.

"Is something wrong?"

"I need some help. I know I shouldn't be doing this, but I need my Guarantor's data key."

Vairocina just looked at me. "That is not allowed." She frowned. "You would be severely punished."

"I need to play Quest-Nest," I challenged her. "I need to practice."

"Please don't ask me to do this. I know I owe you my life, but I would be taking yours if I fulfilled this request."

She was right. I knew what I was doing was wrong, and now I was trying to involve her.

"I'm sorry," I mumbled. "Please don't tell anyone I asked you."

"I won't," she said, and slipped away through the portal. I pulled out of the computer.

"All set?" Max asked.

"No."

"Why?"

"I need Charlie's data key and I can't get it," I answered honestly.

"Well, that solves everything. Let's go home," Theodore said, his tone full of relief.

I watched the Citizen as she registered her players. *I was so close,* I thought. *I was right there!* Defeated, angry, I turned for the pods.

Standing in front of me was one tough-looking alien. "Where is your Guarantor?" the alien demanded. "Tromaine is restricted to authorized knudniks only."

The alien was the about the same size as Charlie, maybe even a little bigger. His head was bald and scarred, and half of his left ear was missing, like someone had lopped it off with a knife. Over his right eye was a piece of thin crystal, attached by ridged wires that went straight through his skin. I could see flickers of numbers and symbols through the crystal, so I guessed it was some sort of screen.

I couldn't respond.

"Well?" the alien prompted. His eyes, or rather, *eye*, remained fixed on my face.

This *thing* blocking my escape to the pods had me in a trance. I wanted to run, to get back to Charlie, but I couldn't stop staring. Three clumps of hair, wrapped in gold wire and strung with small red rubies, protruded from his jawline. He was dressed in rags of leather and metal, and he carried a helmet. Behind him stood two more aliens, each as terrifying to me.

"We were told to meet our Guarantor here," I blurted out, searching his face to see if he bought my excuse.

"If you're lying, you will be punished. Severely," threatened the alien.

Ketheria came from behind and stood next to me. She cocked her head a little to the side, staring at the humanoid. He mesmerized her, too. I pulled her back, but she held tight.

"You're not a Citizen," she declared. "I can't tell what you are, but you're not a Citizen."

"Ketheria!" Theodore hissed.

The big alien reached his paw slowly toward my sister. Instinctually, I stepped in front of her. The alien grinned. Max tugged at my shirt and I brushed her away. She did it again, and I turned toward her. Max was bulging her eyes and nodding her head to the side. What did she want?

"Behind him," she whispered.

The big alien heard her. "Him?" He reached for the smaller alien. "Buzz, come here."

I recognized Buzz instantly. It was the alien we saw stealing the stridling, the one we saw playing Quest-Nest—the wormhole pirate. That meant the big guy . . . was the tracker. I jerked my head back toward him.

"You recognize us now?" he asked.

"We saw you . . . play," I muttered. I didn't dare mention the stridling.

"You were good," Max added confidently.

"Who are you?" Ketheria asked.

I didn't care. I couldn't take my eyes off Buzz. He was lean and muscular and just as battle-worn as the big guy. *Is the big one a wormhole pirate, too?*

"He is Cap Ceesar," Buzz said. "Best tracker on the rings." Instantly I knew where Buzz got his name. It was as if some sort of electronic vibration amplified Buzz's voice. It was creepy, to say the least. Max even cringed when he spoke.

"You get used to it," Ceesar assured us.

"Hopefully, we won't have the time," Ketheria said. Her voice was icy, full of contempt.

Where did that come from? I wondered. Ketheria was always more passive than this. For some reason, she really didn't like these guys. But these guys played in the pro conclave. I didn't see any Citizen insignia, so I could only assume someone was sponsoring them. Could he help me?

I took my shot and said, "We want to play in the Citizens' League, but my Guarantor won't let me."

"JT!" Max exclaimed.

"Great game, isn't it?" Ceesar said, relishing every word. "You'd like to play, wouldn't you?"

"Absolutely," I replied.

"But we can't, not in this league," Theodore reminded us.

"You can play against us," he offered.

They were good, really good—but even if we lost, who cared?

"You can arrange that?" I asked.

"If you're not afraid. Are you afraid?" Ceesar taunted.

"They're too good, JT," Max whispered, but I shrugged her off. This was my chance to understand my connection to the wormhole pirate and get experience in the game. The answer was obvious—to me, at least.

"We can play now," I suggested.

"Let me see what I can do," Ceesar said, and marched toward Tinker. We all followed.

"Here for some more practice, Ceesar?" Tinker asked.

"Yes, but I need your help."

Tinker did not reply. He waited to see what Ceesar needed first.

"I wanted to play him," he said, pointing to me.

"How is he registered?" Tinker swung an O-dat toward him.

"He's not."

"Knudniks, then? Who's the Guarantor?"

"Not here."

"Citizen?" Tinker's eye lifted suspiciously.

"None," Ceesar replied. "See my problem?"

"It's not allowed. You know that. In fact, they are not allowed to even be here. I could be punished for even speaking with you," he said, turning toward us.

Ceesar reached inside his ragged jacket and pulled out a glowing purple crystal. I had never seen a crystal like that on the Rings of Orbis. Tinker stared at it, then looked at Ceesar. Tinker wanted that crystal; that was obvious. His eyes glowed and followed every twitch of Ceesar's hand. Tinker reached for the crystal and stopped when he saw my sister. He stared at her headpiece.

"A telepath?" he whispered. "Come here, child."

Ketheria did not hesitate and stepped forward. Tinker raised his huge metal hands and gently pushed her hair away from the amber crystal on her forehead. Tinker was so precise with his mechanical hands that he never touched the device, only her hair.

"Beautiful," he admired. "Crafted by an artist. I pray you are worthy of it." Tinker snatched Ceesar's crystal and tucked it into his apron. "I will need a Citizen," he said, returning to the O-dat.

"Inai Gi Athooyi," Ceesar replied. "He will appreciate this."

Athooyi? The Citizen who spoke through the hole in his chest? Charlie had warned me about him. This alien knew Athooyi?

"Shall we register all of you?" Ceesar asked turning toward us.

"No," Theodore gasped.

"Yes," Max said, beaming.

Ketheria said nothing.

Tinker kept glancing at Ketheria until he finished with the registration. Ceesar thanked him when he was done, and we followed our new friends below the labyrinth. Buzz was wearing long sleeves, and I was unable to get a close look at the tattoo I had seen when he stole the stridling. Ceesar's arms were bare, but I could not find any pirate markings.

"JT, are you sure about this?" Theodore whispered, pulling me back behind everyone.

"What? I get to play once before I meet Dop, and we're tracking a thief in the name of Orbis."

"That's not funny," he argued.

"I'm not trying to be. I don't want to lose against Dop—and aren't you even the slightest bit interested in Buzz and that Ceesar guy? What if they *are* wormhole pirates?"

"Then I don't want to be following them anywhere."

"Everything fine back there?" Ceesar called out.

"Great," I yelled back, and turned to Theodore. "Come on, Theodore. Nothing's gonna happen."

We stopped in front of the staging area for knudniks—the same one Charlie showed me when we went for our swimming lessons.

"We know the rules, but we've never played here before," Max informed him.

"Well, who's the bait?" he asked her.

"I am," she replied.

"Then follow Buzz here, and he'll take you to the goal."

Max turned to me and whispered, "Are you ready for this?"

"Absolutely," I told her.

Ceesar scoffed. "Cute."

Max followed Buzz, and Ceesar asked me, "Are you gonna play in that?"

I looked at my clothes. "What's wrong with them?"

"No helmet? Your choice," he said. "Follow the crystal lights along the corridor once you pass the ready area." Ceesar pointed to the hallway slightly to my left.

"Where do you go?"

Ceesar shook his head. "I go that way," he said with a frown, pointing to another narrow hallway to my right.

"What about us?" Theodore asked.

"Follow him," he ordered, pointing to the third alien in their group, a little guy with a lot of teeth. "You can sit with him and watch us beat your friends."

Theodore looked at me and I shrugged. "Unless *you* want to play," I said.

"I've got him," Ketheria replied, taking the lead toward a narrow flight of stairs behind us, away from the players' opening. She stopped and said, "Beat this guy, Johnny."

Ceesar laughed and slipped down the corridor, leaving me poised at the entrance to the labyrinth. *This is it,* I thought. *This is what I wanted.* While I stood there under the stone arch, I wondered if my father ever stood in this place. Whenever any thoughts of my father came into my head, I had always pushed them away, but standing here made all the rumors seem possible for some reason. Who else could have programmed Mother with a training course for Space Jumpers? Still, it was difficult for me to swallow, even after my long discussions with Toll on Orbis 2. Considering the idea, trying it on for size, always resulted in a feeling of despair—as if a big piece of me suddenly disappeared, and I would feel truly alone. If my father were a Space Jumper, would he even have been human?

Am I not human?

Yet now, waiting to step onto the playing field, I was filled with a warm comfort imagining my father standing in this exact spot. The idea was mind-boggling.

The inside of the ready area was moist with steam. Warm water misted from the walls, and a lot of the stone was covered with a light moss. It felt very organic for such a technological structure. I never would have pictured this from the outside of the arena, but then again, it *was* for the knudniks.

At the far end of the ready room, carved in the stone, was a narrow passageway lined with blue crystal lights. I followed the lights down the hall for more than fifty meters. The crystals were mounted closer and closer to the floor the farther I traveled. At the end of the tunnel, a large pulsing crystal was embedded in the floor, beseeching me to step on it.

I walked onto the crystal, and instantly a semicircular energy shield sprang up in front of me. A pulsing light passed from the stone to the shield, quickening its pace as if it were searching for something. *Is this how they decide who gets the sort first?* It was a detail I had overlooked with Vairocina. But the pulsing stopped with a flash, and three diamonds, stacked above and around the Orbis insignia, appeared in the energy field. In the center of each diamond shape was a word: SOLID, LIQUID, or GAS.

I would choose first in the sort.

I immediately selected SOLID, and the shapes spun away. What would Ceesar choose now? What had he chosen when I watched him play? I needed to know these things if I were ever going to be good at this. *How does Dop choose?* I wondered if it was more important to see him play than to play myself.

It was too late now. The diamonds returned to my shield, and this time my choices were TECHNOLOGICAL, INDUSTRIAL, and MAGICAL. I knew this was another weapons parameter. Both the second and third stages of the sort determined the kind of weapons we would use to defend ourselves. If I picked TECHNOLOGICAL and Ceesar had already picked MECHANIC, I might get plasma rifles. I liked those. I had used them a lot on the *Renaissance.* But what if he'd picked PSIONIC? Choosing TECHNOLOGICAL might only give me invisibility cubes. *Nothing wrong with that,* I thought. MAGICAL forced me into a world of OIO and alien mysticism. I wasn't too keen on those, but I knew Max might be good at that on the return run. *You're wasting time!* my mind screamed at me. I needed a strategy. When I had practiced with Vairocina, I saw each stage of the sort and I discussed them at length with Max. This was different, though—very different.

The energy shield began to pulse again, waiting for an answer. Which one? I hesitated and then reached for TECHNOLOGICAL, but I was too late. Before my finger touched the screen, the diamonds disappeared and the word PASS flashed in front of me.

I didn't pass!

"Hey!" I shouted. "I didn't pass! Wait."

But the energy field turned as solid as the stone floor. The game parameters were selected, and I had let Ceesar choose three out of four stages.

I moved back from the energy shield, worried about what was waiting for me on the other side. The crystal on the floor pulsed three times before the wall disappeared. What I saw shocked me. Not because I didn't recognize anything, but because I recognized *everything*. It was as if I had stepped back onto the *Renaissance* right into a game of Quest-Nest. Ceesar had chosen in my favor. He had picked my best game.

On the floor to my right was a plasma rifle, a simple weapon that fires a burst of heated yellow gas at anyone who gets in the holder's way. I even recalled the corridors with their purple lights hidden along the edges of the floor and ceiling. If I remembered correctly, it was a clear run for about twenty meters. But the labyrinth always changed; every time Mother set a game, it was a new course. More important, I needed to remember that Mother wasn't setting *this* game.

I ran up the ramp to a set of closed doors. I was not sure how much time I was allotted to find the bait before the labyrinth shifted. I looked behind me to grab a mental image of where I had just been so I would remember it on my return. Standing in front of the closed doors, I paused and readied my plasma rifle. The door disappeared and I charged in. Too soon. Out of the corner of my eye, I saw a fist coming straight at me. I ducked just in time and then tried to square my shoulders to my attacker. A crazed frontier pilot, his flight suit charred and melted away with most of his skin, was already taking another swing.

As I turned, he cracked me upside my head with a vicious blow. *Holographs aren't supposed to do that,* I thought as I fell to the floor, dazed, the image of the pilot swimming in front of me. The pilot swung again, and I shielded myself with my right arm. I should have shot, but everything was happening too quickly. *This is exactly why I need to practice,* I thought. The pilot hit my mechanical arm, but it registered no pain. I'd turned off the sensors before I started. At least I'd thought of something ahead of time.

I rolled away from the next blow and blasted the demon pilot. His holograph exploded into a haze of yellow light, and I lay back on the ground. *You've got to be smarter than that,* I told myself. *Now, get moving!*

I zapped three more pilots waiting around the next bend. No one was going to get the best of me twice. I also found a long-range scoping device to give me the edge on lengthy open hallways. I only hoped my first encounter with the frontier pilot hadn't cost me the game.

I entered a room with a narrow catwalk and used the scope to search for any challengers lingering below. Through the scope, I caught a glimpse of plasma fire in the far corner. It was Ceesar, and he was moving fast. He took out three pilots with one shot and decked another before he ever saw him coming. Ceesar was good.

I picked up my pace. It was reckless, but if Ceesar was moving that fast, I was already behind. At the end of the catwalk, my only option was a small hole in the ceiling. These were never good. Someone hiding behind a closed door was one thing, but pulling myself blindly through the ceiling was a whole other beating waiting to happen. I took the plasma rifle in my left hand and used my other to grip the ladder. I increased the strength levels in my right arm, hoping to support myself while I fired with my left. I asked the Universe for a little help, too.

I was only halfway out of the tunnel when I saw them. Two pilots charged me from behind. I blasted them both, but the distraction let a third opponent get one shot off, hitting me in the left leg. As I returned fire, I felt my leg go numb. Another stupid mistake. I should have seen it coming; it was a simple trick Mother often used against us. I dragged my bum leg down the corridor and into a clearing. It was like trying to walk when your leg was asleep. It took everything for me not to trip over myself.

Another blast almost took out my good leg. I was caught in the cross fire between the demon pilots and some other alien. Mother only ever gave us one opponent at a time, but I reminded myself this wasn't Mother's game. I returned fire, but a deflected shot hit my right arm. I was doomed without my shooting arm. I waited for my mechanical arm to malfunction from the blast, but nothing happened. The synthetic skin and metallic bones seemed to absorb the blast. A fresh wave of confidence swept over me as I realized my newfound advantage.

I fought my way through all fourteen levels of the labyrinth without ever seeing Ceesar again. I had dumped my plasma rifle after it went dead, and now I was dragging around a heavy tedaado blade. Ceesar might have already reached his bait, but I knew the game wasn't over yet because the labyrinth was still up. When I finally reached the last level, I looked down to the floor below and saw Max locked inside a red energy shield. Four crazed frontier pilots surrounded her, but she was crouched ready to attack them—as soon as I was able to spring her free. I jumped down to Max's level behind one of the pilots, swinging as I landed. I snatched the rifle from my enemy and tossed it to Max as the shield dropped. The other three pilots were taken care of before the first one hit the ground.

"Buzz is already gone!" she shouted.

"Unbelievable!"

"A while ago, too. We've got to hurry!"

After the shield went down, three more corridors opened up and a crew of new enemies charged us. Max took out the first two while I circled wide and got the last ones coming down the corridor. We ran out the way I'd come in. We weren't on the return for more than a parsec before the lights in the floor and the ceiling began to pulsate.

"The labyrinth is going to shift!" she shouted.

Already? This was much faster than what I was used to.

"Get ready!" she cried.

As we ran down the corridor, doors that I had previously passed through morphed into walls, and sections of the walls opened into new passageways.

"Watch out!" Max shrieked as the wall beside me shimmered away. A fast-moving creature, no taller than my waist, charged at me. Its long tentacles flung around its head, sparking as they touched each other. Max blasted him squarely on the back, but the monster did not stop.

"He's got some sort of protection!" she yelled.

"Keep firing," I told her, and released a charge from the blade into the creature as well. Confused about whom to attack first, the alien finally exploded, covering me in its yellow blood. I felt a tiny bit of numbness over my whole body, but it was nothing that would slow me down.

"Thanks," I said, but before Max could respond, the labyrinth went black. The game was over.

We had lost.

Ceesar and the wormhole pirate were standing on a gold crystal, and the huge labyrinth was reduced to the area visible from the stands. It was disorienting. I was never going to get used to dimensional displacement.

"Whatever happened to beginner's luck?" Ceesar boasted from his position on the winner's mark.

"You're just too good," Max told him.

"Yes, I am," Ceesar agreed.

"We only need some more practice," I argued.

"You need more than that," he scoffed.

Buzz, however, was not gloating with his partner. Instead he glanced nervously at the crowd in the stands.

"We need to go, Cap," Buzz hissed, elbowing his partner.

"Let me enjoy my victory," Ceesar snapped, but Buzz would not back down.

"Yes, it was a great victory—but we need to deal with *that,*" he said, pointing to a small commotion growing behind the glass.

"What?" Ceesar moaned.

"Oh, no," Max cried.

It was Charlie. He stood at the edge of the glass with two security drones, and he was pointing at Buzz. Theodore and Ketheria saw him as well, but Charlie had not seen them sitting up in the stands yet. Theodore was trying to pull Ketheria away, but when Ceesar's friend bolted, the ruckus grabbed Charlie's attention. He looked up and spotted them. Charlie's head spun from Buzz to Theodore and finally to us, standing on the playing quad.

"Your friend?" Ceesar asked us.

"Guarantor," Max replied.

"Well." Ceesar raised an eyebrow, surprised. "He wouldn't sign you up to play?"

Charlie and the security drones skirted the playing court, obviously heading to cut us off at the ready room.

"What do we do?" Max said.

But I knew there was nothing *to* do. We were caught. I had disobeyed Charlie. He would be furious.

"Nothing," I replied.

"Well, I don't share the same plan, Softwire," Ceesar hissed, and he and Buzz bolted for the tunnels.

"How does he know you're a softwire?" Max asked, puzzled.

"Doesn't everyone?" I said.

8

"Why would you do that?" Charlie growled, pacing the chow synth. He was certainly angry, but I saw something else I couldn't make out in his eyes.

I was sitting at the table with Max and Theodore while Ketheria nestled herself on the floor. Charlie was rubbing his hands through his hair. Out of the corner of my eyes, I saw Grace and Dalton secretly watching from the hallway. I'm sure a few other kids were doing the same thing. It was embarrassing, and I felt my face grow hot.

"I strictly said no Citizens' League."

"But we saw the alien who stole the stridling," I pleaded in defense.

"And they challenged *us* to play," Max offered.

Charlie wasn't buying any of it, though. "When you saw the alien, you should have come and gotten me or told any Citizen nearby."

"But we weren't allowed to be there to begin with," Theodore reminded him.

"You could have reached out to Vairocina, Johnny," Charlie pointed out. "She could have notified security in an instant, and that thief would have been caught."

"His name is Buzz," Ketheria informed Charlie.

"Probably not his real name, but thank you just the same."

I asked Charlie, "What are they going to do with him?"

"That's security's concern now, and it does not justify your actions."

"What are you gonna do to us?" Theodore asked.

"What do you mean?"

"Our punishment? What's it gonna be?" Max said.

"Odran used to make us sleep standing up," Ketheria told him.

"Or he wouldn't feed us," Theodore added.

"Remember the time Weegin almost pulled Switzer's nose off?" Max said with a tiny giggle.

Charlie was shaking his head and mumbling something to himself while he stared at his feet.

"I'm not like your other Guarantors," Charlie whispered. "I'm not here to punish you. I want to protect you."

"Protect us from what?" I asked.

"From things like joining the Citizens' League!"

"But why?" said Max.

"Yeah, our other Guarantors didn't care what happened to us. Look at JT's arm," Theodore pointed out.

Charlie threw his arms up in frustration and growled.

He paced the floor some more, then stopped in front of me.

"I can't protect you inside the arena," he snapped. "They play by different rules, and Citizens' wagering can lead to cheating, accidents, and even death."

"But we're good, Charlie," Max protested.

"You lost today, did you not?" he reminded her.

There was no denying that. Ceesar and Buzz played incredibly well. That tracker possessed speed I could only dream of. His experience showed, and his skills came naturally to him.

"They were fast. They'd be hard to beat for anyone," I said.

"Not anymore," he hissed.

"Why not?"

"Not until security releases Buzz again, and knowing the Citizens, that could be quite some time."

"They captured Buzz?"

"That's why I was there. I didn't expect to find *you*," Charlie replied. "I trusted you guys."

"Can I talk to him?" I asked

"What! Have you gone stark raving mad? Why would you want to talk to that criminal? What could you possibly have to say to him?"

Charlie was waving his arms in the air. His face was almost purple. My shoulders felt heavy, and it was hard to hold my head up. Charlie's tongue-lashing was worse than any punishment a Guarantor could dish out. The only thing preventing me from feeling total remorse was the fact I hadn't used his personal data key. It didn't help much, though. "I'm sorry, Charlie," I told him.

"Promise me you'll stick to the Illuminate league." His voice was icy.

I nodded. "We'll join the school league." But I couldn't promise him. I hated breaking promises, especially to Charlie.

Next cycle, Theodore did not speak on the way to the Illuminate. In fact, he couldn't even look at me. Trouble was the one thing Theodore tried to avoid most, and I had dragged him straight into it. I was going to have to apologize to him, too.

Max, on the other hand, drilled me on the game, especially the sort. I told her we needed to set a strategy before the next game with Dop. I also decided to ask Riis if she knew which stages he favored, or to point out areas where Dop was strong.

"Unfortunately, I know Dop very well—too well for my liking. Why don't you check out some old scopes?" Riis suggested, standing at her locker and changing the color of her hair to iridescent blue.

"Scope," I said. "You mean a tetrascope?"

"Is there another?"

"They're forbidden to humans."

"Not if you're playing Quest-Nest," she said. "In fact, you can't play without them. Everyone scopes each other to see how they react in the game. Your helmet is fitted so anyone can ride."

"Ride? What do you mean by *ride*?"

"You use the scope to get inside the players' heads," she said, tapping on my skull. "See through their eyes, feel what they feel, practically *be* them." She closed her locker and added, "I hate it when I know someone is scoping me. But, you'd better get used to it if you're gonna play Quest-Nest."

Theodore's mood instantly changed when I told him about the tetrascope. Back on Orbis 2, he had tried to use one during the Festival of the Harvest, but the technician had refused him. *No humans!* I remembered him saying. Now Theodore would get his chance.

Throughout the corridors of the Illuminate, everyone seemed to be talking about my upcoming match with Dop. Kids were huddled in hallways chatting over old games that they projected on their pobs.

"It would be golden to have one of those pobs," I told Max and Ketheria.

Ketheria stopped me in her usual cryptic tone. "It's their *pleasure* you envy, but that's something you already have."

"Huh?" I said, shaking my head.

"You're searching for joy from the trophies those kids can buy. It's not a *real* pleasure," she continued.

"I think you should do as Charlie says, and go be a kid," I told her.

She gave me her usual shrug, as if I were too simple to understand, and wandered up the hall. Inside I knew she was right, but I still wanted a pob.

The cycle of our match against Dop finally arrived. Max and I kept pretty much to ourselves, discussing every possible variation of the sort we could think of. She was eager to try the MAGICAL stage, but I was still hesitant. She gave me a quick rundown on the basic understanding of OIO, but I couldn't figure out how cosmic streams of energy were going to help me get past a crazed frontier pilot or a holographic Neewalker.

It was impossible to concentrate on my studies before the match. Theodore and I were working on the same problem—constructing a triangular-based prime pyramid, and I have to admit that he did all of the work, but I was glad that he was talking to me again. When the spoke finally ended, Theodore disconnected quickly. I could tell he was anxious. "I can't wait to try the tetrascope, but I can't decide whom to ride."

"Scope Dop," I told him. "You already know how I play."

Dop was waiting for me outside the Illuminate. So were another hundred or so kids. "You're going to need this," Dop hissed, and threw a helmet at me. "I don't know a knudnik who can afford one, and I refuse to accept some pathetic excuse to cheat your way out of the beating you're about to receive."

"Crush him, Dop!" someone yelled from the crowd.

"Yeah, bury that stinking knudnik!" was another cry.

The helmet was old and corroded. The visor was cracked, and the back of the neck was much larger than Dop's. I tossed it back at him.

"I don't need your charity," I said. "I can play without one."

But Dop would not take back his offering. He thrust the helmet into my chest.

"You can, but you won't. I paid for that relic, and I plan to make a nice profit letting my friends ride a softwire."

"Just take it," Max whispered, and Dop threw another

helmet at her. That helmet looked like the one Riis wore to school every cycle.

"Let's go," Dop shouted to the crowd. "I've got a taste for humans today."

Some laughed; some rushed to the light chutes. No one was going to miss this.

Once we were at the Labyrinth, I asked Dop, "Who's your bait?"

"That's the best part," he whispered. A huge grin snaked across his face, and Riis stepped out from the crowd, helmet against her hip.

"You!" I couldn't believe it. It didn't seem fair. I looked at her helmet. It *was* the same as Max's. I always thought Riis used the helmet for a stridling or some other transportation device. But this meant she had been playing Quest-Nest every single cycle.

Dop must have caught me staring, and bragged, "Only the best."

I looked at Max. She whispered, "Let it go, JT. Think about our strategy."

"Where do I get the tetrascope?" Theodore asked, obviously unconcerned about the change of events.

"Follow us," another kid said, and Theodore shouted, "Good luck!" over his shoulder as he followed the aliens like old friends.

I pushed past Dop and heard him snicker. It took everything not to smash my helmet against his stupid face. I wanted to beat Dop more than ever now.

Once inside the arena, Max whispered, "Make him pay in the game."

"Oh, he'll pay," I hissed.

"Let's go to the goal, Max," Riis said.

I didn't even try to go to the Citizens' ready room. I went straight to the knudniks' entry crystal. Besides, I needed a moment or two to figure this out. Why did I care that I was playing Riis? It was Dop I wanted to beat. Was that his tactic? Well, it wouldn't work. I was going to do everything in my power to make sure Dop was going to purchase twenty-one pobs when this match was finished.

In the knudniks' ready room I placed the unusual helmet over my head. It smelled funky, like burned cabbage or something, and the metal was corroded from eons of oxidation. *Does it even work?* I wondered. But when I slipped it on, I felt a strange sensation between my ears that wrapped around the base of my skull, as if someone were pulling my hair against the grain of my scalp. The cracked visor fizzled and popped, aborting any attempt to display the data I would never see.

Then I suddenly wondered, *Did my father wear one of these? Did he wear* this *one?* It certainly looked old enough. In an odd way, the possibility was comforting. I was here to do a job, and I planned to do it well. I stepped onto the crystal, and the energy field sprang up in front of me. After a moment it started to pulse, picking up its pace. But when it stopped, it did not land on me. My stomach dropped, taking my confidence with it. I stood and waited while Dop controlled the first stage of the sort.

The wait felt like a light-year. What would he pick? He

couldn't fly, I knew that much. Dop's essence was more plant than bird or aquatic being. And he breathed oxygen just like me, so I knew he wouldn't pick GAS or LIQUID. Or would he?

Finally the diamond shapes faded up on my screen: MECHANIC, KINETIC, and PSIONIC. I instantly reached for MECHANIC. I wasn't taking any chances. The diamonds spun away, and almost immediately they returned with the options: PHYSICAL, MENTAL or BIOLOGICAL. That was *fast*. Did Dop have some sort of plan? I was hesitant to pick BIOLOGICAL this time, since Ceesar had beaten me so easily with it. My gut told me that Dop was dumber than he let on, so I wanted to choose MENTAL. *Never underestimate you opponent*, a voice inside my head said. I needed to play to my strengths, and right now that was my robotic arm. I could control torque, strength, pain threshold. I selected PHYSICAL, and the shield turned to stone.

While I waited, my confidence was beginning to creep back in. *Take it easy—you don't know what's behind that wall.* But I was ready. I wanted this. My head was clear and my mind focused on one thing—victory.

When the wall fell, I was immediately thrust into a smog-filled corridor, so dense I couldn't see my own feet. My throat grew thick, and I could barely swallow. My left nostril plugged up and I gasped for air. What was this stuff? I was standing on solid ground, so Dop must have chosen SOLID, unless GAS carried properties that I had overlooked. A section of my visor flashed red, but the information it was trying to feed me could not make it past the crack in the glass. Nice gift, Dop!

Every gulp of air gave me the minimal amount of oxygen, and I scratched at my throat for more. *I can't lose already!* my mind screamed. *But Dop must be experiencing the same thing,* I thought. I pushed myself blindly into the fog, reaching out with my hands. I fumbled into a wall and groped my way to the left, gulping in short breaths. The game was trying to kill me. *Faster,* I thought. *There must be a solution.*

The corridor turned again. Just ahead of me, two energy fields sliced through the fog, beseeching me to come forward— a purple one to my right and a yellow one to my left. Could one of these reveal the source of the fog? But which one? The familiar blackness crept around my eyes as my brain was starved for oxygen. I knew I was going to pass out. With no more time to think, I dove at the purple force field. My skin tingled as I slipped through a shower of electricity and gasped for fresh air.

There was none.

Instead I sucked in another lungful of the rancid, chemical air. I spotted a large rusted lever on the wall. I shut my eyes, trying to steady myself, and forced my weight down upon the lever. The fog seemed to shift away, but my body still craved oxygen. My brain was swimming. I turned toward the yellow force-field across from me. The fog rolled away, revealing a black trench cut into the floor, about a meter and a half wide, right in front of the energy field. If I had chosen the yellow force-field first, I would have slipped down the trench and the game would have been over.

My ears were crackling, and I could hardly keep my eyes open. There was no time left. I took a step back and then leaped though the field. If this didn't work, the game was over. Dop would have won.

My arm struck another mechanical lever. I pushed on it (or rather lay on it) and closed my eyes. A hissing sound filled my ears. Oxygen! I gulped the air as if I was dying from thirst. I could breathe! My head cleared quickly, and my fingers and toes tingled. I hadn't even noticed that they had been going numb. My vision began to clear, and I stood up. Was Dop already through? I did not have time to think. There were thirteen more obstacles ahead of me.

I tore down the hallway. Around the corner I discovered a maze of metal girders that led to a hallway about four meters above me. I accessed the torque and strength levels in my arm and hoisted myself up, taking the shortest way possible. I went as fast as I could, but I knew Dop would have no trouble keeping up.

I ran and then stopped in front of another opening in the ground. A single chain dangled from the ceiling into the middle of the hole. I instantly thought of the tunnels on Orbis 2 and Max flinging herself onto the metal rope. Without breaking stride, I leaped over the gaping hole and reached for the chain but realized that, like an idiot, I was reaching with my left hand! What was I doing? I caught the chain, but my weak arm could not hold on, and I slid down the chain. With my right hand I quickly clamped onto the chain. My body jolted to a stop, and the rattling chain echoed down the pit. Immediately I jerked my body, getting the chain swinging. I held on with my left hand and reached for the ledge with my right, hoisting myself up.

Faster. You need to go faster, I told myself.

I considered contacting Vairocina. I *was* a softwire. I could easily slip into the central computer and change the game. But that would be cheating. It was not an option. I pushed the thought from my mind and ran faster.

The labyrinth continued to challenge me with more obstacles, each requiring some level of physical prowess. Every detail in the labyrinth reminded me of the manufacturing facilities on Orbis 2, and I guessed that Dop must have chosen INDUSTRIAL in the first stage of the sort. When I rounded the last corridor, I spotted the red energy field of the goal. Max saw me and jumped to her feet, pointing and waving her arms in the air. Circling the goal were two enormous holographic Neewalkers.

How could that be? I'd chosen PHYSICAL in the final stage of the sort.

They towered over Max by a least three quarters of a meter as they patrolled the court, perched on their mechanical stilts. Their massive shoulders bulged under thick metal collars, each sprouting wiry tentacles that circled their bald, painted heads. They carried no weapons. That was unusual for a Neewalker. This would be a physical fight.

Anyone would have panicked at the sight of the Neewalkers, but I smiled. I wasn't going to go into the central computer for help, but I *could* access the computers that ran the Neewalkers' mechanical stilts. I'd done it before, on Orbis 1, with great results.

First, I broke through the goal, dropping the energy bubble that imprisoned Max. Riis was still locked inside of hers. I was ahead of Dop. *Amazing!* By breaking the energy field, I would shorten Dop's time for the return run.

"You were fast," Max squealed as the shield went down. "Where's my weapon?"

"There aren't any. Watch out!" The Neewalker swung at Max and she ducked. "I chose PHYSICAL in the sort. We'll have to fight them by hand."

"Disable them with your softwire."

"I'm already ahead of you; stay behind me."

I circled the first Neewalker. His face was painted with a blue OIO symbol, snaking up from his chin and curving up and around his eyes. His tall stilts whirled and buzzed as he lunged toward us.

"You still smell like fish," I hissed, and pushed into the computer mechanics of the Neewalker's stilts — except there were none! There was nothing to push into. The Neewalker was a hologram created by the central computer. In every way this menace looked and acted like a real Neewalker, very capable of crushing me into the plate metal court. But there were no computers running the stilts of *this* creature. The central computer generated the whole thing.

"It's a holograph!" I shouted.

"So?"

"There's nothing to get my mind into! I don't know what to do!" I yelled.

Max stepped out from behind me and pushed the words through her clenched teeth: "There is something I've always wanted to do."

She charged straight at the Neewalker as it raised its massive fist high above its head, eager to deliver a deadly wallop.

"Don't, Max!"

The alien swung fast and hard, but Max dropped to the ground feet-first and slammed into its stilt. The Neewalker buckled and threw his arms forward, bracing for the fall. Its mangled stilt tore away, revealing a fleshy fin where a foot should be.

"Awesome!" I shouted. That Neewalker was no longer a threat, but there was still one more to go. "Now what?"

"Run!"

We both bolted for the opening. Dop was nowhere in sight. Riis watched the whole thing, still trapped within her own goal. The other Neewalker quickly moved to block the door. I charged at the vile creature, imitating Max's success with the first one. As I dropped to the ground and slid toward the alien's right stilt, it lifted the mechanical support and began to spin on its left leg. *Smart.* But then I reached out for the other stilt with my strong arm, using it as a battering ram. The Neewalker's leg crumpled on impact. As it crashed to the floor, I caught a glimpse of the startled look in its eyes.

Max and I then worked as a team, skillfully maneuvering our way back through the labyrinth. My fresh experience with the obstacles and her cunning gained us valuable time on the return. We were almost near the finish when the labyrinth pulsed red, signaling it was about to shift.

"We're gonna lose the exit!" Max shouted as the energy field where I had begun came into view.

On instinct, we both dove through the field and landed on the winner's crystal.

We had won the match!

We both stood in the glow of the golden winners' circle and looked up at the crowds of students watching our match. My whole body was alive with energy, and Max and I were jumping around like silly little kids. Is this what freedom felt like? Is this what it felt like to be in charge of your own life? I didn't know, but I wanted more of it.

Some of the students watching were applauding out of politeness (a rare action for a Citizen) but Theodore, Ketheria, and the other knudniks were simply ecstatic. They jumped and shouted, punching their fists in the air and hugging each other. It felt good. I had beaten Dop.

Dop and Riis stood at the other side of the court. He was waving his arms as he shouted at her. I could only guess that he was blaming her for their loss. Why was she taking that from him? Especially from Dop. Riis removed her helmet and walked away. This only made him scream louder.

"Let's clean up and find the others," I said, and we raced to the ready room.

The smell of that rancid gas was in my clothes and my hair. The water showers would be a welcome treat, I thought.

"You were so fast, JT," Max cried.

"I couldn't have gotten back so fast without you. You really cut the time down. You were awesome."

Max smiled.

"You're the best, Max," I said matter-of-factly.

In the ready room, I left the helmet on the stone bench and stepped under the water pouring out from the thick gray stones. I pulled my shirt off and let the water soak into my body. It felt good.

"Hmmm," I sighed. "This is great."

I finished undressing, but Max was still standing at the edge of the shower, not moving, just staring at me.

"What's wrong?" I asked. "Don't you want to wash up?"

She just kept looking at me.

Suddenly I felt very naked, seeing Max fully clothed. "What's wrong? I've seen you naked a million times on the *Renaissance*. When did you get so shy?"

But Max was still silent. She dipped her chin, smiled, and walked toward me. She slipped under the water still in her clothes and stood directly in front of me. I'd been close to Max many times, but this was different for some reason. I could see the little sparkles of yellow in her green eyes, and even the tiny little pores in her skin. The water flowed off her hair and a little water bubble collected on her upper lip.

Then Max closed her eyes, releasing the water caught in her eyelashes, and I felt her breath against my skin. Then Max pushed her lips against mine. It was gentle and soft, but not a drop of water was able to pass between us. Something shot up my spine against the direction of the water, and at that moment everything that was Max was now in me. My eyes were still open and as I watched her, she never looked prettier to me than she did at that moment.

When she pulled away, I said, "What did you do that for?"

I could tell immediately that something was wrong. Max's eyes went cold, and I felt a hundred times more naked.

"Oh, Johnny," she breathed, her voice deflated. She dropped her head, but this time she did not smile. Instead she ran from the ready room.

"Max, wait. I didn't mean . . ."

But I was too late. *What just happened? Why do I feel so stupid right now?* The buzz from victory was gone. It was light-years away now. I stood under the water, staring at the spot where Max just stood, trying to focus my eyes on her face, but the water only made everything blurry. I felt awful.

There was nothing in the ready room to dry myself with, so I pulled my clothes over my wet skin. Most of the kids were waiting in the stands after the match finished. Dop was already there when I ran up to Theodore and Ketheria.

"Where's Max?" I asked frantically, searching the crowd.

"That was unbelievable, JT!" Theodore gushed.

"Why is your hair wet?" Ketheria questioned me.

I wasn't listening. "Where's Max?"

"She already left. She was completely wet," Ketheria replied. "Why aren't your clothes wet? Your hair is wet."

"Would you shut up with your questions?" I snapped.

Ketheria dropped her head and stared at the floor in response.

"I'm sorry," I said. "I didn't mean that. Really."

"Don't worry about Max; everything will be fine," she whispered, but I knew it wouldn't. I couldn't do anything right at the moment. I had just won the biggest match of my life, and I felt horrible.

"Way to cheat, knudnik," Dop accused me in front of everyone.

"What?"

His comment seem to rustle up support from his friends

"I know you cheated. Just like on the placement exam. Everyone will agree with me," he continued. "You did something with the central computer, didn't you? You tapped in like some disgusting Space Jumper."

That was too much for me. I had beaten him, and I hadn't cheated. I jumped at Dop, but Theodore stood in the way. "He did not. I scoped him the entire game. He never used the central computer once," Theodore argued.

Dop snorted. "Likely story from another knudnik."

"You were the one who cheated, Dop," called a voice from the crowd. It was Riis. She pushed her way through the crowd and stood next to me. She grabbed my helmet and held it up. "You got him this helmet and busted the visor. I saw you do it. You didn't want him to know what he was up against at the beginning of the match."

"You cheated to beat a knudnik, but you still lost?" someone scoffed. The crowd was turning on Dop.

Riis tossed him the helmet and said, "Maybe it will help *you* next time."

Dop did not catch the helmet, and it hit the ground with a clang. Instead he stepped toward Riis and in a menacing tone growled at her, "Your house will soon be mine, Wiicerian. I will make you pay for this defection."

But Riis did not back down. Instead, she spat in his face. The saliva rolled down his cheek, but he did not move. Dop stuck out his long brownish tongue and slurped the spit off his cheek. I don't care what planet you're from—that is still disgusting.

"Soon," he whispered. "Soon."

Dop spun around and stormed off.

"What is he talking about?" I asked Riis.

"It means nothing," she snapped, watching him leave. "You played a good game, Softwire. You and Max will be very hard to beat." And she left the Labyrinth, too.

"What did Dop mean?" Theodore said. "What *house*?"

"I don't know."

"She really hates him," Ketheria commented.

"I got that much," I said.

A dozen others kids stayed behind, and we discussed the match over and over again. No one had expected us to win, and everyone wanted to know how we did it. I wished Max were there to talk about it; she loved analyzing the game. As the other kids chattered, I glanced around the stands, hoping I would find her, but she was long gone. As we were about to leave, I spotted Ceesar. He was sitting with one of his gang, watching us from high above the glass. Buzz was nowhere to be seen—but sitting next to Ceesar was the Citizen Athooyi.

9

"It was unbelievable, JT. I mean, I really can't describe it. You've just got to try it. I mean, I was *you* during the game. I could see what you were seeing, smell it. I even felt it. It was incredible," Theodore gushed as we sat in the pod at the Illuminate. Theodore had not stopped talking about the tetrascope since the match a few cycles earlier.

"I thought you were going to ride Dop," I said.

"I was. But . . ."

"But?"

Theodore hesitated before saying, "I wanted to know what it was like to be you."

I chuckled. "Not much there, huh?"

"No, honestly, it was the strangest thing I have ever experienced. But in a really good way. While I was scoping you, *I was you.*"

"Wait. What did you see? I mean did you see . . ." *No,* I said to myself. *I wasn't wearing the helmet when Max kissed me.*

"What?"

"Nothing," I said. I thought about Max's kiss. It wasn't the first time since it happened. In fact, I don't think I had stopped thinking about it at all. Max, on the other hand, was acting like nothing had happened, even right after the match when I returned home. I was starting to feel like I'd made the whole thing up in my head.

Theodore was still looking at me, waiting for a response. "You mean about your father? In a way, I'm glad you've accepted what everyone else thinks is true. It's kind of exciting, if you ask me."

"You can hear my thoughts with that thing?" I was shocked.

"Only because you're a softwire. That's what the guys told me."

"What 'guys'?" I wanted to know. "Were they inside my head, too?" Suddenly I felt embarrassed. My thoughts had always been my own. I didn't want people knowing what I was thinking.

"They're my friends, JT. What's wrong?"

"How could they become friends in one cycle?" I didn't like knowing that people could hear what I was thinking with that thing. It made me angry. The spoke was finished, and the pods moved toward the exit. "Well, please don't do it again," I snapped, and stormed out of the pod.

Why was I so mad at Theodore? Did I care what people thought about me? No. But my thoughts of my father were new to me. As if I were trying them on for size, to see if they fit. It was still a lot to swallow. I headed for my locker.

Another student stopped me in the corridor and said, "Hey, Softwire, when you gonna play again?"

"Why?" I asked the alien. He was small and tough-looking. I had never seen him before.

"Never scoped a softwire. Hope it's like riding a Space Jumper. When you gonna play again?"

"I don't know. I'm not," I growled, and added, "I'm not a Space Jumper."

The gruff little alien moved closer and whispered, "Don't worry. Some of us think it's burnin', the whole Space Jumper thing." He looked over his shoulder as if he were telling me a deadly secret. "We aren't like the other Citizens. We'd crap crystals to meet a Space Jumper."

"They're nothing special," I lied.

"You've met one?" The little alien became frantic. "A live one? Where? You've *got* to tell me about it."

He grabbed my arm, but I pulled away. "Let me go," I demanded.

"Sure, sure," he breathed, calming down. "Let me know about the next match," he insisted. "You'll kill 'em. I know you will."

Inside my locker was the pob Dop forfeited for his loss. Grace was at her locker, and she was trying hers on.

"Thanks, JT. These are the best!" she said.

I rolled the tiny device in my hands. Suddenly it didn't seem worth it anymore.

• • •

The next cycle, Charlie informed us that he had to leave to deal with business matters.

"How long will you be gone?" Ketheria asked.

"Only until the following cycle. Max will be in charge, and you are to come straight home from the Illuminate. No Quest-Nest until I get back. JT can contact Vairocina if there is an emergency, and I will be notified immediately."

"Where are you going?" I wanted to know.

"I'm going to the moon Ki," he replied, his eyes darting about the room. "It's Citizen business."

He was lying. I could sense it. But why would he lie?

No one else seemed concerned about Charlie's business trip. Everyone was absorbed with their new pobs. Ketheria was the only one who really didn't care for it. Some of the kids programmed their pobs to display little flowers floating in their hair, while others showed flying creatures or insects. Dalton watched broadcasts from the Citizens on Orbis 3, and Theodore used it to search for uses of the tetrascope. He was so obsessed with the tetrascope that I now understood why humans weren't allowed near the things.

I watched Max from across the room as Grace helped her with her pob. Things were different between us, and I couldn't understand why. I just wanted to go up to her and talk like we always did. I hated this. I wanted my friend back.

"Just go up and talk to her," Ketheria whispered, slipping up next to me.

"Who?" I said coldly, knowing full well she was talking about Max.

Ketheria lifted her eyebrows and frowned.

"I can't," I confessed. "I don't know what to say. I'm just going to say something wrong."

"You don't always have to be right, you know. It's more about the conversation at this point."

"I don't want to. Besides, she's busy. Look at her."

"Light can't enter a closed box, JT."

"Please, would you stop that? Where do you get this stuff, anyway?" I groaned. I didn't want to be mean to her. It just seemed so strange for a little girl to spout these cryptic things. Ketheria laughed.

"Just talk to her," she said, with a sigh.

But I couldn't. I went to Charlie before he left on his trip, looking for some help. I figured he was older so maybe he knew things I didn't. Maybe he knew how girls worked, and what made them do the things they did.

"That's a tough one," he said, packing a small metal case in his room.

"That's why I'm asking."

Charlie looked at the floor and scratched at his ear as if he were trying to pull an answer out. "Well, you've known Max your whole life. You know her better than I do," he said.

"It doesn't seem to be helping much."

"Well, why don't you describe to me a perfect cycle with her. A time when both of you were all right, the way you want it to be again."

"I don't know," I mumbled. "I don't know what she likes."

"Then you're not paying attention. That's the first thing you have to start doing."

I tried to think of a perfect cycle with Max. Before the kiss, they were *all* perfect. Now it was messed up, and I didn't know how I was going to get it back again. Charlie wasn't helping much.

"You have to figure it out first and then make *that* happen," he said. "No one's gonna do it for you."

I was never going to figure that out. I went to my sleeper that night with an even bigger knot in my stomach.

"JT, JT?" It was Max. My sleeper was out of the wall, and she was standing over it. I rubbed my eyes, trying to wake up faster.

"What's wrong?" I asked her.

"It's Theodore. He's not here. I can't find him in the house, either. I think he went out somewhere."

"Without us?" That was strange, especially for Theodore. We always forced our adventures upon him. I couldn't see him going out on his own.

"Did you check the garden?"

"No, only the house."

"Let's look there, then," I offered.

Even though we talked like nothing ever happened at the Labyrinth, I felt it in every word I spoke, like some huge trench carved out between us. I followed her out and into the garden, trying to think of something to say. I wanted to talk about what had happened. It was right there, right on my lips, but the words were tangled around my tongue. I could only talk about Theodore.

"Did he say anything to you?" I asked her.

"About what?"

There it was again. Everything I said held some reference to what now stood between us. "Um . . . you know, about going somewhere?"

"No."

The garden was dark, but several of the plants glowed green and pink, spilling their own light on the path. The top of the ring gleamed brightly, casting an eerie glow over the small forest.

"Theodore!" I called out for him, but I knew he wasn't there.

"Where would he go?" Max asked.

"I have an idea," I said. "I think he went to use the tetra-scope."

"Now? But there's no game."

"I don't think you need a game. Remember the Festival of the Harvest on Orbis 2? I think you can scope whoever lets you."

"Theodore!" Max cried out, but her voice just scared a few plants and they scurried deeper into the garden. "Charlie's gonna be so mad at me."

I was very aware that we were alone again. The silence was excruciating. *Say something!*

"Max, I . . ."

She stopped searching the garden and looked straight into my eyes. She might as well have taken a metal pipe to my knees. *Why is this so hard?*

"What?" she said.

"I . . ."

She raised her eyebrows, waiting for me to speak. My nerve crumpled.

"Should we leave the house and look for him?" That was the best I could come up with.

"Where?"

"I don't know. He mentioned something about friends, Citizens he used the scope with. Maybe he's with them."

"Do you know where to find them?" she asked.

"No."

"Maybe you should tell Vairocina. She could notify Charlie."

No again. "I can't tell on him. But Vairocina could locate him. We're all stained. It shouldn't be that hard."

"*She* might tell on him, though," Max pointed out.

Charlie *did* show up at the Labyrinth after I had spoken to her. I had asked her not to tell anyone, so maybe it was a coincidence. I didn't like doubting my friend.

"I'm going back inside," she moaned. "It's cold."

I wished I had something to give her to keep her warm—a blanket, an extra skin, anything. I looked at her shivering and rubbing her arms as we walked inside. *This is driving me crazy!* I started to say, "Max—" But Theodore came through the light chute at the very same moment.

"Where were you?" Max demanded as if she were his Guarantor.

Theodore did a double take on us when he saw us standing in the hall. "Uh . . . I . . . um . . . What are you doing up?"

"What were you doing out?" I asked him. "Charlie's gonna kill you."

"You can't tell him," he snapped. "I've covered for you a trillion times."

"Where were you?" Max insisted.

"I was with friends," he said coldly.

"I thought *we* were your friends," Max corrected him.

"You were using the tetrascope, weren't you?" I said.

He didn't have to answer. His face went slack, and that told me enough.

"So what?" he challenged.

"*So*, why didn't you tell us?" Max said. "We would have gone with you."

Would we have, though? Illegal things on Orbis have never stopped us before, but the tetrascope must be banned for a reason.

"I didn't think you would come," he confessed.

"Of course we would," Max said.

"You wanna go back?" He pointed eagerly at the light chutes.

"Not now," I told him. "It's late."

"They're still up. I know they are."

"Next time," Max offered. "I can't leave everyone alone, not with Charlie gone. We should go back to sleep."

Theodore fidgeted with his skin. His pupils were dilated,

and his expression was manic. *Could that be from the tetra-scope?* I wondered. I was worried about him, but I must admit that my mind was on Max. Why hadn't I taken the time to say something? By now she had already returned to her sleeper.

At the Illuminate the next cycle, no one spoke of Theodore's late-night excursion. All anyone could talk about was our new pobs. If it weren't for our skins, it would be hard to tell us apart from the other students. Once we were inside, Theodore raised his hand and yelled, "I'll see you at the pods!"

"Where's he going?" I wondered.

"To meet his new friends," Max replied with a shrug.

Theodore never did things on his own, and whenever *we* wanted him to do something, something that he considered risky, we usually had to drag him by his feet. But here he was traipsing off to see whomever to do whatever. It made me feel off-balance in a weird way. This wasn't the way my world usually worked.

I waited behind Max and Ketheria to get my tap.

"Hey, Softwire," someone hissed. "Come here."

I looked around and spotted the burly little alien, the one so intent on meeting a Space Jumper the cycle before, waving at me from under a stairwell. "What do you want?" I said.

"It's me, Nak. Come here!"

I grabbed my tap and walked over to the guy. Out of the corner of my eye I saw Max toss her tap and turn to leave, but Ketheria grabbed her by the elbow and dragged her toward me.

I felt my stomach hollow out. I wished I hadn't seen that. The alien was waiting with a group of three friends.

"Tell them. Tell them what you told me," Nak demanded excitedly.

"Tell them what?" I protested.

"Tell 'em about the Space Jumper. You're a Space Jumper, aren't you?"

"He's not a Space Jumper," Max corrected them.

"No, no, it's all right," he whispered. "It's burnin'. Don't worry. Show 'em, Dass."

Nak elbowed his tall friend to the right. Dass's skin was smooth and thin, like that of an onion. He proceeded to pull his leather collar down and expose a tattoo of the symbol of the wormhole pirates. The marking glowed with different colors, changing from blue to purple to green.

"You're a wormhole pirate?" I gasped.

"No, no, no, no, no, no. But it's burnin', isn't it?" Nak replied.

"Why would you do that? What if you get caught?"

"My brood would skin me alive, but that's half the fun, isn't it?" Dass grinned, exposing an extra row of teeth.

"Tell us about the Space Jumper!" Nak pleaded.

"Space Jumpers are disgusting," Max spat. "They're just as bad as wormhole pirates and just as violent as Neewalkers."

Max grabbed Ketheria and marched off, mumbling something I couldn't hear. I turned to follow her, but Nak grabbed my arm again.

"What?" I said, trying to shake him off.

"Neewalkers are burnin', too!"

"Let go!" I wrenched my arm free and ran after Max.

"When are you gonna play again?" I heard Dass call out.

I was late for study spoke, and so I had to sit in my pod alone. Part of me wondered if Theodore was even there, or off using the tetrascope again. It was impossible to concentrate on the screen in front of me, thinking about Theodore and Max. I was going to have to do something. I knew I *had* to talk to Max about what had happened. She might be able to pretend it was nothing, but I couldn't. I felt like something had changed between us, and I didn't like it. When the spoke ended, I found Ketheria at the locker.

"You ready to go home?" I asked her.

"I'm going to play Quest-Nest with Max," she replied.

"But I thought Charlie said we were supposed to go straight home."

"Max is in charge right now." Ketheria turned to me. "Just talk to her."

"I have been!"

"You've been talking, but you haven't said a word to her about how you feel."

"I don't know what that is!"

Ketheria shook her head and swiped at the numbers of her locker. "Give it time; you will."

Ketheria was now Max's new partner in Quest-Nest. Just like that, too. No comment. No *We'll play later.* Nothing.

It made my brain boil. A few cycles after Charlie got back home, we all went to the Labyrinth to watch Max and Ketheria play.

It didn't help that Max and Ketheria were simply awesome, easily beating their opponents. In fact, they never lost as a team. It was really amazing. Usually only students came to watch the school league matches, but more and more Citizens began coming to watch their matches.

"Your girlfriend's good," Ceesar said one cycle, standing behind me at our usual table.

"She's not my girlfriend," I argued. Ceesar made me feel uneasy. I looked and saw Athooyi. He was watching me, too.

"Why aren't *you* playing?" Ceesar whispered.

"I need a different kind of helmet. Mine's busted."

"Go see Tinker. He's the best. He'll take care of you. Tell him I said I'll pay for it."

"I can pay for it myself."

"No, you can't. Get a helmet," he ordered, and slipped back with Athooyi as Charlie returned.

"Who's that?" Charlie asked. "He looks like the guy from your match."

"He isn't," I lied. "I need to get a helmet if I'm ever gonna play again."

"I thought they had them at school."

"Not for softwires," I informed him.

"But you're only going to play in the school league, right?"

"Yes, Charlie."

• • •

Ketheria went with me to Tinker's. Theodore was nowhere to be found, and Max said she was busy. I knew it was an excuse, but I was beyond making an issue of it now. Charlie made the chits available for my new helmet and programmed my skin to allow us to go. We headed to Tinker's place at the Labyrinth right after our study spoke.

"You and Max play really well together," I told her outside the arena.

Ketheria grabbed one of the glass pods and said, "Not as good as you two."

"Yeah, right."

"Are you going to ever shake this mood?"

"What mood?"

"You've been negative about everything since the kiss at the Labyrinth. I'm sure you're beginning to annoy people."

I spun around in the pod. I felt my face grow hot. "You know?"

Ketheria closed her eyes and shook her head. Of course she knew. If she didn't pick it up from one of us, I was sure Max had said something. And worse still, she was right. The fact was I had started to annoy *myself.* I tried to shake it off, put the incident behind me, but my thoughts wouldn't let me. I kept playing every possible scenario over and over in my head, everything I could have said, and everything I could have done—until my brain was mush.

"Maybe Quest-Nest will help," Ketheria offered.

"I'll try anything right now," I confessed.

We stood in front of the oval counter where Tinker worked,

but no one was there. A different alien, humanoid and female, finally came out to help us.

"We're here to see Tinker about a helmet," I informed her.

"Tinker doesn't make helmets anymore," she said, her voice very soft and frail. Her head was covered in soft silks of white and cream that draped over her shoulders.

Ketheria looked at me, waiting for me to say something. "Don't look at me like that. It was Ceesar's reference," I protested.

Ketheria turned to the girl and asked, "Do you know where we can get one? A helmet for a softwire?"

The girl cocked her head to the side and said, "A softwire?"

"Yes. Ceesar said Tinker would help us."

"Please remain here for just a moment," she said, and slipped through a door at the back of the oval.

"I don't like that guy," Ketheria said with a scowl.

"Who, Tinker?"

"No. Ceesar. He's not a good person. He's hiding something."

"That lumps him in with just about every other Citizen on this ring, Ketheria. You must feel that way about a lot of people you meet."

"Mostly just him," she replied as the young girl returned.

"Tinker will meet with you. Please come this way."

The girl tapped a small device on the counter, and part of it disappeared just like most doors did on Orbis. *Are all the doors on Orbis simply holographs?* I wondered.

My first thought on entering Tinker's workshop was that

Max would have *loved* this place. It was a high-tech electronics lab stuffed with computer parts and alien gadgets. Light spilled into the room through four arched windows behind his workbench. At the far end of the room, Tinker stood over the bench with his back to us. I couldn't tell if the tools fastened to his hands were his actual fingers or not. There was no skin visible on Tinker except for his shiny head. I wondered if that was why he was bald. With those hands, combing his hair seemed like an impossible task.

"I'll be just a moment," he said, his voice deep and creamy.

Shallow lines marked the walls like rolling waves. They were the same designs carved into the walls at our home. *Cosmic streams of energy,* Max called them. *Tinker must also be a believer,* I thought.

"There, that should do it," he announced before turning to us.

Tinker's long blue apron dragged on the littered floor as he moved toward us. His skin was bone white and his crimson mouth cut deeply along his cheeks as he spoke.

"Thank you for your patience. I so hate leaving the flow. It's quite difficult for me to return to it."

I simply stared at him. I didn't have a clue what he was talking about.

"Um . . . I need a helmet," I informed him.

"And I've been told Ceesar's going to pay for it?"

"I'll pay for it myself," I told him coldly. "I have enough chits."

I didn't like the idea that Ceesar had been talking to Tinker behind my back. It immediately made me suspicious. Tinker produced a device to read the chip inside the skin I was wearing and waved it over the vest.

"Yes, you do," he remarked. "But a helmet for a softwire costs much more than that."

Suddenly I wanted to leave. Charlie would have known the price. Why did this guy want more all of a sudden? I took Ketheria's hand and turned for the door. "Sorry to have bothered you," I replied.

The wheels and wires in Tinkers chest whirled and rattled in sync with his laugh.

"Please stop," he called to us when we were at the door. "Not everything has to involve *money.*" The word rolled off his tongue like an insult.

"I just want to buy a helmet," I said.

Tinker turned his attention to Ketheria. "Come here, child," he whispered, sitting on a stool so he was a little more at her height. It was a very short stool, so Tinker's knees almost reached Ketheria's shoulders. He reached out for the metal headpiece wrapped around her head.

"What are you doing?" I objected.

There was a *click*, then a suction sound, and the front of the device, the part with the crystal, fell into Tinker's big metal hands.

"Don't do that," I protested. "You can't have that."

Ketheria closed her eyes and took a deep breath. It looked like her head was filling up with air more than her chest.

"Take it all in," he whispered to her. He smiled and then

turned to me. "This, for example." He cradled the stone in his metal fingers and let it catch the light. A rainbow of colors exploded on the walls. "What do you think the cost of this was?"

"I don't know. The Keepers put it on her."

"To please the Citizens." His voice was icy.

I looked at Tinker closely. There was no Citizen insignia anywhere to be found. "Are you a knudnik?" I asked him.

He closed his eyes at the mention of the word. "I was."

"Then you must be a Citizen now. I thought after your work rule you became a Citizen."

"I chose not to," he replied.

Why would someone stay here if he didn't want to be a Citizen?

"Don't try to figure everything out, Johnny. Just accept it. There is a reason for everything," Ketheria said. She could read my mind again, although I was pretty convinced she had been doing fine even with that thing on.

"You made that, didn't you?" Ketheria asked Tinker.

He moved the metal and crystal device through his fingers with expert ease. "I did," he replied softly. "This is special to me. Everything I make is special to me. But this . . ." He held it up again. "This is very special. This is truly my best work."

In the light I could see an OIO symbol carved into the metal behind the crystal. Tinker touched the symbol with a razor-sharp finger and then touched it to his cheek. This guy really did like his work.

"How much did they pay you for it?" I asked.

"Nothing," he murmured. "Yet it is priceless."

"That doesn't make sense."

"It never does." Tinker attached the piece to Ketheria's head again.

"How much more will my helmet cost?"

"It's not always about money."

Tinker was talking in circles, and I didn't like it. Was I supposed to bargain with him? It was obvious he liked his work, but I just wanted a helmet to play the game.

"Come here," he said.

I followed Tinker to his workbench, and he pulled several helmets off the wall. They, too, possessed the same bulky piece around the collar as the one Dop had given me, and I knew they were for softwires.

"How many softwires have you made helmets for?" I asked him.

"Only one," he answered.

The first helmet fit perfectly, as if it were sculpted for my head. "How did you know this would fit me?" I gasped.

"It's a price *I* may have to pay one day," he said.

More double-talk. He was beginning to sound like Ketheria. I felt a surge of energy around the base of my skull, and the visor blinked on.

"Can people scope me with this?" I asked him.

"Of course."

"Do you have any helmets without that capability?"

Tinker passed the wand over my vest, deducting the amount of chits for the helmet. "That is not the way," he said, and handed Ketheria another helmet. "This will fit better than that bulky one they'll make you wear," he said to her.

Ketheria tried the helmet on and smiled. It fit perfectly over her telepathic blocker.

"Thank you, Tinker," she responded.

Tinker smiled and closed his eyes.

"How much for that one?" I asked.

"A gift." He sighed, placing his hands on our shoulders and moving us toward the door. "You will have to come back and visit me again, won't you?"

"Definitely," Ketheria said, but I was rather glad to be leaving.

At the door I turned to him quickly and said, "Wait. I want to know more about Ceesar. You know him, right? Who is he? Is he a wormhole pirate? What's he doing here?"

Tinker frowned. "Come back and we may talk some more. Right now I have work to do."

"But wait!"

The door reappeared, and we were standing behind the counter with our new helmets.

"I like him," Ketheria said.

"Really? I thought he was strange."

"Wonderfully strange," she replied.

"We should practice with the scope if we're going to play together," Theodore insisted, after I asked him to be my new partner for Quest-Nest. I didn't know if he was excited to play or excited to get on the tetrascope.

"We don't need it," I told him.

"Yes, we do. You don't understand. You can *think* what they think. If you want to know how they choose the sort, scope them. Find out what they are afraid of, what they try to avoid. We need this, JT."

It didn't seem fair knowing that much about your opponent. What good was the sort, then, if you knew what everyone was going to do?

"No," I said. "We can play without it."

Theodore let out a deep breath and dropped his shoulders. His knuckles were almost dragging on the ground, he looked so low. "Fine," he mumbled. "We'll do it your way."

We went to the arena on the very next spoke. Theodore chose to be the bait only after complaining that without scoping our opponents first, he wouldn't know what to do with the sort. I agreed, so I was the tracker. The arena was filled since everyone knew Max and Ketheria were playing right after us and a lot of the Citizens had placed side bets on the girls. Charlie came to watch and said he was impressed with the turnout. He told us that sometimes they didn't get this many spectators at an Illuminate game.

I recognized one of our opponents, a girl, from the Illuminate. The other, a male, I had never seen before. When I slipped my helmet on in the ready room, I worried who was poking around inside my head. I checked every thought twice, worried about what people could see. It was very distracting. I needed to get first choice in the sort because I knew my opponent did not breathe oxygen. She would try to go for GAS, and I wanted to block it. I also wanted to find an easy course because this was Theodore's first game. He chose to scope most matches instead of playing.

As I feared, I did not get to play the sort first and my opponent chose GAS, as I predicted. I then chose MECHANIC, to push the game toward a version of Ring Defender that I knew Theodore was good at. The game began, and I battled opponents in the air using a slick flying machine while trying to defend the bait from attack. It should have been an easy win, but since Theodore had no practice with the real game, he was clumsy and made some beginner mistakes. I couldn't blame him. I had made similar blunders when I first played Ceesar.

Despite my efforts, we still lost.

"I told you we should have scoped them," he complained in the stands after the match.

"You just need practice in the real game," I argued with him.

The match with Max and Ketheria was about to start. A big alien, a Trefaldoor, was trying to bet with the Citizen next to him. Since betting wasn't allowed during the Illuminate league games, he refused. I heard Athooyi, who was seated behind me, offer to take his bet.

"On the humans, on the humans!" I heard him shout as four creatures scurried around him.

That's when I spotted Ceesar and another alien as they came up to Athooyi's table. Ceesar caught me looking and shook his head, as if he were ashamed of my loss. Why should he care? And why were they even watching a student game?

"JT, aren't you listening? That's what makes tetrascopes so good. You don't need to practice. You can get everything you need by scoping," Theodore pleaded, refusing to drop his argument.

"Are you allowed to be on those things?" Charlie asked, eavesdropping on our conversation.

"Yeah, to play the game," Theodore said quickly. "They actually make you do it. You play better."

I leaned toward Theodore and whispered, "Well, it didn't seem to help you."

Theodore just shook his head as if to dismiss me. I had never seen Theodore just flat-out lie like that, especially to Charlie. This was getting serious. I would have talked to Max about it, but I still felt tongue-tied around her. I decided that the next time Theodore wanted to use a tetrascope, I was going with him to find out how much trouble he was really in.

"Well, just be careful and only use them for the game." Charlie frowned. "I've heard some strange stories about those things."

I snuck a glimpse at Ceesar and watched Athooyi throw something on the table and thrust a finger toward the arena. *What is he so mad about?* I wondered. Athooyi waved Ceesar off and turned toward the match. Ceesar, who was almost two heads taller than Athooyi and a lot wider, reached forward and grabbed Athooyi's shoulder. The Citizen spun around, striking Ceesar across the face. He stumbled back, shook it off, and then stepped toward Athooyi as if to challenge him. Before Ceesar could act, the frail creatures that were always around Athooyi sprang toward him. The soft and willowy creatures moved without hesitation, morphing as they positioned themselves to protect Athooyi. Their noses pushed forward as fangs exploded from their upper jaws. Their shoulders heaved up and their forearms mushroomed. They landed in crouching positions as their backs expanded, their fists smacking the ground. These monsters looked ready (and eager) to launch at Ceesar's throat in an instant. Athooyi never once glanced at the commotion. He was focused on the game now. Max was taking her position in the goal, and Nugget squeezed in front of Charlie and pressed his snout against the glass as I gawked at Athooyi's henchmen.

"You're staring again," Charlie whispered.

"Did you see that?" I said.

"I warned you about him. Now, watch the game. His business is none of your business, and it's best to keep it that way."

As Ceesar and his friend slowly backed away from Athooyi, he caught me staring. Ceesar nodded to me, and my eyes darted toward the playing field.

Max and Ketheria won their match easily. Ketheria made a gutsy move: knowing her opponent hated water, she selected LIQUID in the sort, even though she and Max were not the best swimmers. Max must have told her to go for MAGICAL, so they followed colored currents in the water that guided them through the obstacles. It was a perfect example of using one's head over muscle, and their opponents never saw it coming.

"You girls are good," Charlie praised them after the match

as Nugget bounced around the house imitating their best moves.

I had to admit I was jealous. If I had been playing with Max instead of Theodore, Charlie would be praising me right now.

At the Illuminate on the next cycle, Theodore and I were waiting to grab our taps when I said, "I'll go with you before our next match."

"Go where?" he mumbled.

"To the tetrascope place. I don't know, wherever you go to scope people."

"You will?" he cried, his tone much cheerier.

"Yeah. I don't like losing. If you think this will really help us, then I'll do it."

"That's golden, JT!" He grabbed my arm and dragged me to an O-dat near the taps. The screen listed teams looking for a match. Theodore entered our names, and a host of opponents appeared. It wasn't difficult to find someone to play against since we had lost our last game. More and more kids were agreeing with Dop that I had cheated in our match because I hadn't won since, and I think a few also believed that Max was the stronger opponent. Citizens loved to beat up on knudniks, but they didn't like losing to them.

"We got a match," Theodore exclaimed. "I'll get us some time on the scope."

"Why don't we just use the ones the school provides?"

"These are better," he whispered. "Trust me."

• • •

I went to my sleeper early that cycle. I was bored and, quite frankly, a little lonely. No, I was *really* lonely. My worries about wormhole pirates and what they had to do with me paled in comparison to what was happening with Max and, now, with Theodore. I tried to sleep but didn't get much of a chance.

"C'mon," Theodore whispered, shaking me after removing my sleeper from its cave in the wall.

"What are you doing?" I groaned.

"You said we'd use the scope."

"Now?"

He put his index finger to his mouth. "Shhh, you'll wake up Charlie."

Maybe I should, I thought. I dragged myself out of my sleeper and dressed while Theodore checked the hall. This was *so* unlike him. Normally, I was the one coaxing him to do something we shouldn't do. Now here he was trying to sneak out while Charlie was asleep.

"Why can't we go when normal people are awake?"

"These aren't normal people," he replied.

That scared me. Now I wanted to go just out of curiosity. What had Theodore gotten involved in?

Theodore punched a number into the light chute, one he memorized from repeated use. It was a very long number, not a normal destination code.

"How many times have you done this?"

He didn't answer. "You first."

I stepped into the chute and emerged in a part of Orbis 3 I'd never seen before. The Illuminate poked through the dark blue sky to my left, so I knew we were not far from school. But I was still unable to get a bearing on exactly where we were.

"This way." Theodore motioned me to follow him through the chute and away from the Illuminate.

We slogged our way under dripping concrete and steel girders. It was a stark contrast to the slick buildings the Citizens erected in honor of themselves. Despite my misgivings, I was excited. I always enjoyed a good adventure.

Theodore stopped in front of a concrete wall beneath a tall curved structure. The grimy wall was marked with symbols. Unlike the drawings in the tunnels on Orbis 2, though, these symbols were angrier and they slashed at the concrete. Theodore traced a purple one with his fingers. The gesture produced a light chute inside the concrete wall.

"Wow," I exclaimed. "Nice trick."

"Wait," he said, smiling, his eyes widening.

He stepped into the light chute without punching a code. I followed him immediately, and we were both on the other side of the wall before I could blink. In fact, we could have been anywhere on the ring, but it felt like we simply walked through the concrete to the other side. The corridor was cramped, lit only by thin blue crystals dangling from the ceiling. We followed the glow.

"Where are we?" I whispered.

"They call it the shed."

"Who are *they*?"

"My friends."

Even though I'd stood toe to toe with Neewalkers, battled

Sea Dragons, and fought monsters inside the central computer, I had never felt apprehension like I felt now.

The corridor ended at a round metal door. I looked back and noticed that we had just walked through some sort of tube, not a real hallway. Now Theodore was forced to tap an entry code into an archaic keypad on the wall. The wall dilated, and we stepped inside. The first thing I noticed was the sound. A strong thumping filled the air, like a heartbeat. This was broken up with a slight tapping and wailing moans. Not a moan like a person would make, but something mechanical, more high-pitched—like a bot on its last legs. An alien stood in the corner of the messy room, her body jerking violently every time the heartbeat sounded. Covering her face and the top of her head was a tetrascope. It was bigger and bulkier than the one I had seen at the Festival of the Harvest back on Orbis 2. I think about six wires attached the tetrascope to the wall behind her. The wall was covered with different types of connectors and cables. I pushed into it quickly, just out of curiosity, and found a dark, haunting array of computer codecs with more personality than I'd ever felt inside a computer before. Images of masked faces, wires, and knives sparkled on the codecs near the girl's connection points. I pulled out, wondering if Vairocina had ever visited this place. But then I guessed that this place wasn't linked to the central computer. I had heard that Citizens paid a lot of money to block their estates from the probing central computer, and I was sure this place was one of them.

The girl pulled the scope off and said, "What was that? Something just looked at me. Peeked right inside me."

I looked away from the girl, not saying a word. I reminded myself to be careful where I poked around. I didn't know if they would appreciate a softwire in here.

"Who's this?" an alien asked Theodore, getting up from several O-dats. They were taller than normal and hardwired to an assortment of unrecognizable devices. The tangle of wires and machines made Tinker's workshop look very organized. The alien's pale skin glowed blue from a dull sapphire-like crystal perched in the low ceiling. The O-dats provided the only other light source. He twirled a metal tool in his long fingers as he spoke.

"This is JT. He's the one I told you about."

"The Softwire?"

"Yes. This is Sul-sah, JT. He's my friend."

"Hey," I grunted, waving at him as I looked around. There must have been at least eight kids attached to scopes inside the room. Others were too old to be kids, and some looked so frail and emaciated that I wondered if they ever left this place.

"A softwire," Sul-sah said admiringly. "You ever thought of letting people ride you for a living? A lot of freaks would pay plenty to scope a real softwire."

"There are *non-real* softwires?" I asked him. It was a little sarcastic, but I'd never heard it put that way before.

"This big freak came in the other cycle pretending he had the gift, but he was a phony. That's what I meant."

"Thanks, but I'll stick with Quest-Nest," I said.

"No, my friend, really. I mean when you scope someone, it's real. You *are* that person. You see what they see, you feel what they feel, but when you scope a softwire . . . wow, it's so much deeper. I mean you even think what he's thinking. The fears, the joy, the *thoughts*." Sul-sah tapped the side of his head.

"Theodore, can we get this over with?" I groaned.

"Get what over with?" Sul-sah snapped as if coming out of a trance.

"Nothing," Theodore assured him, and pulled me aside, talking under his breath. "Just relax. Don't embarrass me, all right?"

"I'm sorry. I just don't like it here."

"Wait till you try the scope. You'll forget all about this place."

"That's what I'm afraid of," I said.

"I just want to show him the tetrascope, Sul-sah. We're going to play together, and it's going to help our game."

"It's your story," he mumbled, and waved one of those chit verifiers over our skins.

"What's that for?" I asked.

"This isn't a charity organization. If you want to scope for free, I can make a deal with you. I can get a lot of chits for what's inside that head of yours. Otherwise you gotta pay to ride the scope," Sul-sah informed me.

Sul-sah handed us two helmets and pointed to some free space on another wall, away from the girl I had accidentally pushed into.

"It's free to use at school, Theodore," I whispered, even though I was sure Sul-sah couldn't hear me.

"They're not as good as these," he assured me.

The helmet was a blunt oval made from a dull, silver-colored plastic with the face scooped out. That part was a dusty blue. The inside was very soft, softer than anything that had ever touched my face, and the whole thing felt extremely light for its size. Theodore plugged one of the cables into the wall and sat below his connection.

"You're gonna have to interface with it yourself," he told me before placing the helmet over his face. His mouth was the only part left exposed. Two supports gripped the back of his head and one automatically attached to the neural port behind his ear. It was obvious to me that Theodore had done this a bunch of times already.

"Wait," I said. "Aren't we riding the team we're playing?"

Theodore pulled the mask off and looked at me. His face was kind of blank, and I could tell he didn't really care who we were going to ride just as long as he scoped someone. "Yeah," he hesitated, dropping his eyes. "Check to see if they're playing in the lobby. The interface takes you there first."

"At this spoke? They're asleep, Theodore. I thought we were going to watch old games or something."

"Well, let's see what's available. Otherwise just pick someone so you can feel the effect. I know you'll see the benefits of using this in our game," he said quickly, and slipped the scope over his face.

Theodore just wanted to use the tetrascope. He didn't care about the game. What was *wrong* with him?

Reluctantly, I plugged in, placed the device over my face, and pushed into the interface. The effect was instant. I grabbed my seat, feeling like I might fall. The scope was different from a dream. Dreams can be foggy or patchy. This was vivid and real, like when I was inside the central computer. In fact, the effect was a lot like pushing. Using the scope, though, everything seemed heightened for optimal stimulus. Colors, even smells, seemed more pronounced, and I was actually moving around inside the interface. Unlike when I used my softwire, I could see my whole body. This made me feel very small, less in control, like a specimen in a jar.

The "lobby" Theodore had mentioned was a jungle of three-dimensional cubes, each with an alien advertising what he or she had to offer if you scoped that alien. Each screamed at me from one face of the cube, while the other side broadcast examples of what they were doing at that moment. I noticed that many of them were going about mundane activities like eating, and most were simply sleeping. Why would someone want to scope a person when they were sleeping? An alien with shiny skin and puddled black eyes answered my thought by saying, "You can't even imagine what I'm dreaming about."

The cubes were everywhere, strung on top of one another and lined up in rows. *Not very efficient,* I thought, *but then again, I might not be using the interface properly.* Sometimes my softwire took me deeper into a device than I needed to go, and I ended up seeing behind the program rather than just the intended design.

The farther I walked, the darker and more sinister the cubes became. Some offered a chance to ride a tracker, chasing down game on an open frontier. "Feel the thrill of the kill," the cube called out. Another advertised an opportunity to take part in a mugging, where you would actually attack another person and take their belongings! I turned back. *I'll just scope someone eating,* I said to myself, and turned up a different row. I found myself standing in front of a group of ominous black cubes marked with nothing more than slashes. *What are those?* I wondered. My mind wanted to peek inside, but I was too scared. I quickened my pace, but I didn't go too far before I stopped. I stood in front of the cube that caught my eye. It was a Neewalker. The painted face and metallic neck collar were unmistakable, and he was offering the opportunity to ride. *What would that be like?* "Only one way to find out," I said aloud, and touched the cube. All the other cubes in the lobby imploded, and the Neewalker asked me to touch the cube again to accept the link.

I did as prompted, but this time the barren surroundings of the virtual environment collapsed into the cube—with me included. I felt like I was ripped through a cable, my physical self shredded in the process. I tried frantically to maintain my sense of self, but even that was being torn away from my consciousness.

When the feeling subsided, I was a living, breathing, thinking, and stinking Neewalker. I sat down on a cold stone bench and removed my stilt, rubbing my greasy fin. The metal was tearing my flesh. I needed to get that fixed. *Sar Janicj could help me,* I thought. *Who's Sar Janicj?* That thought came from a tiny remote part of my own brain.

I grabbed some paper from the floor and stuffed it into

my stilt. That should help for now. I was hungry, but fighting on a full stomach was never wise. *Just a little something*, I convinced myself, and rummaged through the pile of ice melting in the corner. The last scallit tried to squirm away from me, but I was faster. I snagged the treat from the ice. The creature was frantic now. I grinned at it, showing it my teeth. That drove the scallit crazy. One sniff, and the powerful aroma thickened in the back of my throat. Still fresh; that was good. I smiled. I opened my mouth and squeezed the creature's head into my . . .

"Wow!" I shouted, yanking the helmet off my head and bolting to my feet. "Theodore!" I shook my friend, who was smiling and leaning against the wall. Reluctantly, he pulled his helmet off.

"What?"

"That was incredible. I was Neewalker. A real Neewalker. I was *him*!" I panted.

"I told you; it's amazing. It's just astonishing, isn't it? I knew you would like it."

I instantly wanted more. I wanted to break open every cube in the lobby. I needed it. Theodore was already putting his scope back on when I stopped him.

"And that's why we can't do it anymore," I said.

"What do you mean?"

"Look at you. How many times have you done this?"

"I thought you liked this."

"It has to be banned for humans for this very reason."

"But not for us. We're playing Quest-Nest."

"Not right now. This has nothing to do with the game." My voice was getting louder as I was getting angrier.

"But I *want* to," he confessed, and he meant it. "What does it matter, JT? Really. Think about it. What are we doing here, anyway? Sometimes I think Switzer is better off. I mean, I know we're not risking our lives anymore for our Guarantor, but what kind of life do we have? No one wants us here. With this, I can be anyone I want. Go anywhere. See anything, everything! It's better than the life *I* have."

"At least it's *your* life."

Theodore grunted. "Easy for you to say. You're a softwire. Everyone is interested in you. You're destined for some amazing life. I can see it." Theodore put his helmet on his lap and glanced at Sul-sah. Then he whispered, "Do you really think anyone cares about what happens to me?"

The funny thing was, I couldn't argue with him. He made a very good point, but something told me that life had to be better than *this*. "*I* care, Theodore. This doesn't feel right. You know it, too. It's not real. C'mon, let's go home."

"You go," he mumbled. "I want to stay."

The door to the shed dilated, and another paying customer stepped inside.

"That's the other guy that hangs out with Ceesar," I hissed at Theodore.

"His name is Cala."

"You know him?"

"I sat with him when you played Ceesar, remember? Before they nabbed Buzz."

Cala gestured to Theodore, a simple nod of his head, before he found an open space on the wall.

"I see him every time I come here. It's weird: he always comes in after me. No matter when I come."

It didn't surprise me. The shed seemed like a perfect place for Ceesar and his gang.

"If Charlie finds out, you know you're in big trouble."

Theodore shrugged. "What's he gonna do?"

How did I become the worrier and Theodore the risk taker? I stared at Theodore. He was already back under the scope. I wasn't going to leave him there. I sat next to him and visited the lobby one more time.

We slipped back into the estate as the ring was rotating out of darkness. Charlie was waiting for us. I knew we were gone too long, but it's very hard to judge time when you're riding the scope. In his hand, Charlie held a screen scroll. He pulled on the electronic paper.

"Does this little excursion have anything to do with these charges?" he demanded, holding up the screen scroll.

"What charges?" I asked.

"Computer maintenance, broadcast fees, port repair. What are these for? And twenty-one brand-new pobs?"

"We won those. Dop was supposed to pay for those," I protested.

"And you're gambling? You're not making this easy for me, guys. Everyone is under lockdown. Straight to school and straight home. No exceptions."

"But we have a game to play next cycle!" I cried.

"No exceptions."

"For how long?" Theodore moaned.

"Until I say."

"That's not fair, Charlie," I told him.

"You should have thought of that before you snuck out," he growled, and left us standing by the light chute.

"I've never seen Charlie that mad before," Theodore whispered.

I couldn't look at Theodore. His indifference was infuriating. I didn't get it. Life was supposed to be easier living with Charlie, but everything just felt wrong. I stormed to my sleeper without speaking another word to Theodore. I just wanted some sleep before I had to face the Illuminate.

Ketheria was sick again when we got up. This time she was having trouble standing, and it scared me. She said she was dizzy and her eyes wanted to go black. Charlie called someone to look at her, who told Charlie it was simply growing pains. I could only assume that the guy didn't have a clue about human anatomy. Where would he have gotten the practice? I asked Max to find whatever she could on the central computer.

"Why not? There's nothing else for us to do now that we are *all* in lockdown," she said coldly. Maybe Max was also angry that Theodore and I had gone out without her. I would have asked her if I knew I wasn't just going to freeze up again. The space between us felt wider than the wormhole.

Charlie wasn't taking any chances on our behavior. He changed the exit codes on the light chute, and he added a security program that required his Citizen data key to operate the chute anytime someone wanted to leave the estate. Now I really felt like I was in prison. The only person who didn't seem to care about the lockdown was Nugget. He enjoyed having us around; he just didn't like it when Ketheria was sick. She started doodling again, but I managed to get a screen scroll in front of her before too many walls were marked with her graffiti. Nugget, however, took great pride in letting Ketheria draw all over his big snout.

By the next cycle, Ketheria was her old self again. Just like that, as if nothing had happened. But now *Theodore* was acting strange. Unlike Ketheria, however, it was easy to tell what was wrong with Theodore. One night I caught him tapping different codes into the light chute. He was spewing numbers out loud, tapping faster and faster. His sweat dripped on the floor.

"What are you doing?" I hissed.

"It's not fair. We're not criminals. We should be allowed to leave here whenever we want." Theodore's eyes were on fire.

"We are knudniks," I reminded him. "Would you rather go back to Odran's?"

"Anything's better than this place!" Theodore thumped his fist on the wall and stormed off.

I followed Theodore around school, too. I was worried that he would take off for the shed. Ketheria and Max took turns watching him, and I could tell he was annoyed by all of the attention.

"I'm not going anywhere," he spat.

"Not saying you are," I said.

"Have you tried to buy anything lately?"

I never needed to buy anything at the Illuminate. It provided everything I needed free of charge. At least we shared that privilege with the Citizens. "No, why?"

"Charlie cut that off, too," he said.

Charlie really meant business. At the start of the next phase, I found Grace and a couple other kids crouched by the entrance to the chow synth.

"What are you doing?" I asked.

"Shhh!" one of the kids said, and then pointed at the room.

"How much longer, Charlie?" I heard Max say, and I crowded in with the other kids straining to get a peek inside.

"For what?" Charlie replied.

"The lockdown. How much longer?"

"I didn't put a time limit on it."

"We can't live like this forever."

"Are you the delegate they sent in to negotiate new terms?"

Max looked over her shoulder, and we all ducked out of the way before Charlie followed her gaze.

"I did not like missing my matches at the Labyrinth," Max replied. "It seems like we're all paying for something only a few of us did. It's not fair."

Charlie glanced out into the garden before he said, "So are you offering to keep everyone in line from now on?"

"No," Max said matter-of-factly. "You told us to be kids, Charlie. And one of us is a softwire and another a telepath."

"I certainly have my hands full, don't I?"

Max nodded, waiting for Charlie to speak again.

"If anything happened to you kids, you know, like what happened to . . . Switzer, I couldn't handle that. I don't know what I would do."

"It's not going to happen, Charlie. I'll promise you that."

Charlie stood up and smiled. "You're a good negotiator, Maxine."

"I like Max, just Max."

"All right, Max. But no wandering off at night, no strange purchases, no gambling, and no getting hurt."

Max nodded again, but I noticed she did not promise. *Good job, Max.*

Max turned to leave the chow synth, and we all scrambled. I was afraid Theodore would rush to the shed the moment he heard that Charlie had lifted the lockdown. He just wasn't the old Theodore I knew. The wandering off, the strange charges, even the gambling charges—those were all things Theodore had done. That's how he was hiding payment for the tetrascope. But without chits now, I doubted Sul-sah would let him in.

Theodore let out a deep sigh when he heard the news about the lockdown, but made no mention of the shed or tetra-scopes. He also promised to play Quest-Nest as my partner the first chance we could get a match, and I intended to make him keep his promise. Max and Ketheria got a match right away, and I went to watch them after the spoke.

I went to the Labyrinth and sat by myself in the lower section near the goal. Without a Citizen, knudniks weren't allowed in the fancy section, where we usually sat with Charlie. As I waited for the match to begin, I spotted Riis on the other side of the playing court. I got up to go sit with her, but Dop and his friends beat me to it.

It was obvious to me that Riis did not welcome their company. She moved to another bench, but they simply followed her, tauntingly. Riis finally turned on them. I thought that she was going to strike the closest one, but she stopped. Instead she ran from the Labyrinth. I started to run after her.

"Leave her alone, knudnik," Dop called after me.

"Nice trick with the pobs," I said, turning my back to him.

"Your Guarantor can afford them."

"That wasn't the bet."

Dop grinned, glancing at his accomplices. "When are you going to get it, Softwire? It doesn't matter what *you* want. The sooner you're off this ring, the better it will be for all of us."

"I *will* become a Citizen when I finish my work rule," I warned him, but this only made him laugh out loud.

"So optimistic, these knudniks," he said. "It will never happen; you can count on that. That's why *she's* so upset. Riis likes your kind. She has a soft spot for knudniks—why, I'll never know." His friends laughed again. I turned for the exit.

"You have a nasty habit of turning your back on Citizens, knudnik. It will get you hurt one day."

"Get used to it," I yelled, and ran after Riis. It was time to get some answers.

Riis moved quickly through the narrow streets, away from the Labyrinth toward the center of the city. I knew I was not authorized to wander beyond the Labyrinth or the Illuminate, but I went after her anyway. I was not sure how the roadways functioned, so I kept close to the buildings. Carved paths in the concrete roads channeled some vehicles back and forth while other vehicles moved freely around on the surface. Even more vehicles, fliers and things like stridlings, scurried back and forth in the air. It was a busy place.

I jumped to avoid hitting a Citizen who had her head down, moving very fast. I felt a tug on my skin as the Citizen grabbed me.

"What are you doing here? Where is your Guarantor?" she demanded. The alien's face was painted in soft shades of purple and pink, and her robe glittered in the late light.

"Um . . . I'm sorry, I fell behind. My Guarantor is just ahead of me," I mumbled, trying to think quickly.

"You're lying to me. Security!" the alien screeched, scratching my eardrums. Her jaw seemed to dislocate, and her mouth hung open as she screamed. Her thick purple tongue licked the air.

"He's with me," Riis told the Citizen as she ran up behind me. I was very glad to hear her voice. I didn't know how Charlie would take me getting into trouble again. "I told you to stay close," she reprimanded me. I forced back a smile.

"I was worried it was running free," the Citizen exclaimed. "You can't be too careful anymore, especially with wormhole pirates roaming about and the Chancellor's Challenge so close."

"No, you can't," Riis agreed. "Will you be attending the Challenge?"

"I wouldn't miss it."

"Then I hope to see you there," she said, and ushered me away.

"Thanks," I whispered. "What's the Chancellor's Challenge?"

"A big Quest-Nest tournament for the Citizens."

"Can I play?"

"Not unless your Guarantor signs you up. Otherwise it's Citizens only."

"That will never happen. Charlie only lets me play in the school league."

"It's better that way. You don't want to play in this tournament."

"Can I watch?"

Riis shook her head. "It's in another Labyrinth, deep inside Inner Tromaine. Not even Keepers can go in there."

I had heard of Inner Tromaine before when Theylor told us that it was exclusive to Citizens, and I had no desire to go there. I was quite capable of getting into enough trouble out here.

"Why are you following me, is the question I should be asking," she said.

"I saw you arguing with Dop and his friends."

Riis grunted at the sound of his name.

"What's up with you two?" I asked her.

"Nothing, and it's none of your business," she reminded me.

"So much for liking knudniks."

Riis stopped and grabbed my skin, spinning me toward her. "Is that what he said to you?"

"He said you had a soft spot for knudniks and he didn't know why—but I think he did."

"No one will understand," she said under her breath, and continued walking.

"I'm a pretty good listener," I told her. I ran after her. Riis had long legs, and she could move fast. "Tell me."

Riis let out a heavy sigh. "Dop is a *well-born*."

"And?"

"It means he is a Citizen born on the Rings of Orbis."

"Aren't most Citizens born here now?"

"Many are, but Dop's lineage also makes him a member of the First Families. It was his ancestors who fought for their right to live on Orbis and create the luxuries we have."

I wondered to myself if the Keepers would agree with her statement. "I suppose a lot of people died on both sides of that war," I said.

"Not Citizens," she corrected me. "They spent a lot of money paying others to do it for them. A lot. Much more than most wanted to part with."

"That doesn't seem fair."

"The Citizens don't understand *fair*. We have raped the universe for our own cause. Our power is built upon the forfeited pleasure of others. Others like you."

"Did you say *we*?" I said.

"I am a Citizen, JT. You are a knudnik," she reminded me. "And I've been forced to learn that distinction the hard way."

"What does this have to do with Dop?"

"I, too, am a well-born and a member of the First Families. The power and wealth of our families will be merged through the union of Dop and myself."

"But aren't you two different species?"

"That's trivial. In fact, any argument as to why we should not be together is not even considered." There was venom in her voice as she spoke. She never looked at me once, but I could see her eyes glistening. I didn't think that she'd told me the whole story yet.

We walked in silence. Riis was trying to compose herself, and I was simply trying to understand what she was going through. She stopped next to an open courtyard off the main street. There was a large concave plaza surrounded by square pillars. At one end stood an enormous crystal, maybe five meters tall. It seemed to shimmer off the stars in the sky as it faced the plaza.

"I come here sometimes to think." She spoke softly. "And listen to him."

A diminutive alien walked out in front of the crystal. His back was slightly bent, and he was dressed in nothing more than a dirty rag. His eyes covered a large portion of his face, and his lids looked heavy with worry. On his left hand, attached to his fingers, were three glass bowls of different sizes. The alien held them up to the crystal as if he were letting them absorb whatever gathered at the concave center.

From the rag wrapped tightly to his body, he withdrew a small cream-colored device that looked like a bone, except it was highly polished. He tapped the largest bowl with his fingertip and began rubbing the stick against the glass. Then he began to play.

The sound was a haunting vibration that I felt go straight through my chest. I mean I physically felt the sound, and it wasn't any louder than a regular conversation. Then he struck another bowl, and then another, each layering its own sound on top of the other. I began to see colors and thought I could smell the most amazing flower I could ever imagine. When the alien began to sing, I lost it. I could feel my cheeks now wet with my own tears. My mind wanted to rub them away, embarrassed that I was crying next to Riis, but something in my heart wouldn't let me. Instead, I sucked in every sound, every texture, every feeling this alien gave me, and in return I let out all of my anger, my resentment, and my hatred. I cried like a little one, but I smiled. I was happy, truly happy, and then he stopped.

I quickly wiped away the tears, turning my back from Riis.

"Amazing, isn't it?" she whispered.

"Who is he? What is he?"

"He's an artist," she replied. "And he, too, is a knudnik."

"I can see why the Citizens want to keep him around."

"Most don't even know about him. And those who do are afraid of him."

"How did you find him?"

"He is kin to my love, the one they took away from me after his work rule ended with my family. I begged my family to grant him Citizenship so we could be together. It was all he and

I dreamed about, rotation after rotation, but it did not happen. He was not from a First Family: he was not a well-born."

"And that's why you don't want to be with Dop, isn't it?"

Riis closed her eyes and nodded.

"Where is *he*?"

"They forced him off the ring. When his work rule was done, they sent him to the crystal mines on Ki. It's a horrible, horrible place," she croaked softly.

"He's a knudnik, too?"

Riis could only nod again.

"They have no intention of letting us become Citizens after our work rule is finished, do they?"

"No." She hesitated, dropping her eyes. "Not if the First Families have it their way."

"Then everything I've done was in vain. My parents were tricked."

The Citizens had used us to do the work they were too lazy to do themselves. Their promises were empty. Theodore was right. What kind of life did we have?

"Do the Keepers know about this?" I asked.

"No," she replied. "Many Keepers have been corrupted, too. Most of them, anyway. It feels like there isn't a species in the universe capable of achieving a higher existence."

"What was his name?"

"I'm forbidden to say it ever again. I must obey my family. It is the only way," she said. Her voice was full of sadness. "I do not make the rules."

"But you certainly don't have to live by them," I said. "Especially when the rules are wrong. It's your life, Riis. You only get one."

She looked at me and smiled. Her eyes said *Thank you*, but she was still going to do what she was forced to do. "You are far from home," she whispered. "Come, I'll show you a chute."

10

"What about the attacks on the Borean moon? Thirty thousand people died in one cycle. Survivors said they couldn't tell where their attackers were coming from. They just kept appearing!" Max shouted at me. We were both standing next to the chow synth.

"That could have been anyone!" I cried.

"They were Space Jumpers."

"You sound like a Citizen. Why do you assume that?"

"I'm not assuming anything. Everyone knows it."

"Who's everyone? Everyone who watches those pobs?"

"Not everything is a lie."

This was exhausting. I let out a deep breath. At least Max and I were talking. "Max, you don't find it odd that the moon is now in the hands of the Zinovians? Zinovians and Space Jumpers? They don't make good business partners," I said. "Besides, Space Jumpers aren't like that. They help people."

"Then why don't you just become a Space Jumper?"

Max stormed out of the room. I couldn't understand why Max would say such things, especially when she knew the mystery surrounding my father. It was hard for me not to be mad at her, but I shrugged it off and went to see how Ketheria was doing. I found her sitting in the garden with Nugget. It didn't take my sister long to see that I was troubled by something.

"If it's true who our father is," she said, "have you ever thought of what that means for you?"

"How could I know? No one tells us anything around here."

"You are a softwire, JT. Softwires are usually Space Jumpers, almost always. Citizens despise Space Jumpers. They are not even allowed to live on the Rings of Orbis. If you follow in our father's profession, where do you think you'll live? I don't know the answer to that, but I'm sure it will be far away from us."

I had never looked at it that way before. I had never thought that far ahead. I didn't want to be a Space Jumper. I wanted to stay with my friends. "Is that why she's so upset?"

"I don't know. You have to ask her."

"Or you could tell me. I know that thing on your head doesn't stop you from looking into people's thoughts. Why won't you just tell me?"

"It's more fun this way," she said, and smiled.

"Maybe for you."

"Especially for me, but you're still going to have to talk to her."

Ketheria was right. *Max has to know I don't want to be a*

Space Jumper. Doesn't she? Of course, I couldn't say a word to her on the way to the Illuminate, but I did come up with a plan.

I saw the first advertisement for the Chancellor's Challenge outside the Illuminate that cycle. An enormous floating vid-screen flashed images of trackers and their bait high in the sky above our school. The players looked mean, dressed in ceremonial outfits. They scowled down upon us.

"I would love to see that tournament," I told Theodore.

"We're not allowed," he reminded me. "But I'm sure we could scope it if we got some chits."

"Or we can catch glimpses on the pobs."

"It's not the same thing," he complained. "Especially with *that* tournament."

"Why?"

"You don't know?"

"Obviously not."

"It's real, that tournament. No holographs. You go in with a team and they fight until the death. The last alien standing walks away with the prize, unless he's a knudnik and then his Guarantor gets it."

"Are you sure about that?"

"Sul-sah told me about it. He hacks into other riders and lets his clients scope the players. Some people pay a lot of money to ride anyone in the tournament. The adrenaline rush is crazy. I think we should do it." Theodore said it like it was the most amazing idea he'd ever had, but my mind was elsewhere.

"Huh? We can't enter the tournament," I mumbled.

"I don't mean enter the tournament. I mean scope the players!"

"You're still obsessed with that thing, aren't you? No, Theodore. Please leave it alone."

But he didn't say a word. Maybe I should have been more supportive. Maybe I should have told Charlie, but I didn't. I was distracted by my thoughts of Max and my plan.

After the spoke, I looked for Riis, but I couldn't find her. In fact, I hadn't seen her at the Illuminate the entire spoke. But I did find Max, and she was alone. *This is good*, I thought.

"Can I show you something?" I asked her as she waited for the light chute.

"What is it?"

"Not here. I want to take you somewhere."

"I've got a match to play," she said. She was avoiding me; I could tell by the distant tone in her voice.

"I have one, too. It won't take that long, and then we can get back to the Labyrinth. It's not far from there."

"Fine," she agreed.

"Tuck your vest away, though. We're not allowed to go there without a Citizen."

That got her attention. Max was always one for a good adventure. I wanted to ask Riis for directions, but since she was nowhere to be found, I tried to retrace my steps from the Labyrinth.

Max didn't say much, but then neither did I. I was afraid to say anything stupid, but the silence between us was beginning to worry me. I liked having Max alone again. In fact, I hadn't realized just how much I liked it until now. *Where was this place?*

I stole a quick glance at Max every time I slowed to check my bearings. Her faced remained unchanged, which wasn't good. She only looked annoyed.

"Where are we going, JT?" Max demanded to know.

"It's not far. Riis showed me the place."

Max stopped. "You came here with Riis?"

"Yeah, why?"

Her remark felt like an accusation, as if I had done something wrong.

Max grunted, threw her arms up, and spun on her heels.

"Max! Wait! What's wrong?"

My heart was working faster than my mind, and I felt a surge of anxiety pulse through my body. This was not going as I had planned.

I ran up to her and grabbed her shoulder.

"Max, please. Just a little farther."

"I'm going to be late for my match."

"Just a little farther. Trust me."

Max's gaze darted everywhere but on me. "Fine, but make it quick," she snapped.

I backtracked once more before I finally found the concave plaza with the huge crystal bowl standing on its lip. Silently, I let out a deep breath when I saw the plaza. I knew I could start to breathe again.

"What is this place?" she whispered just as the artist stepped in front of the crystal. The annoyed look on her face was already gone. I knew that Max loved to discover new things, and I was right to assume that this place would intrigue her. I only hoped the music had the same effect on her as it did on me.

"Shhh, it's about to start." I was thrilled that we hadn't missed it.

I stood next to Max, tucked near one of the stone pillars circling the plaza. The alien lifted his hand of glass bowls and struck them softly. The sound echoed off the concave crystal and vibrated right through me again. I instantly knew I had done the right thing. The alien began to sing, a haunting melody layered with smooth tones that breathed wonderment throughout the plaza. I glanced at Max. Her eyes welled up as the sound filled her body. She was close to me, almost touching. I could smell her, and it was intoxicating. I reached down to take her hand, but Max pulled it away. I felt a flush of panic race through my body. *I can't do this,* I thought. My confidence drained quickly. Max lowered her hand again, and I saw it was wet with tears. I took her hand in mine. At first, I was terrified that she would resist, but Max squeezed my hand in return, almost as if she were using me to hold on.

With Max's hand resting safely in mine, I breathed in the music and allowed the sounds to control me. Instead of expelling my emotions of anger and resentment, as had happened the first time I was here, my heart now swelled with unbelievable happiness. I loved everyone and everything. The universe, at that moment, was a perfect place. The music picked me up and held me, caressing my soul and making my insides glow.

I felt Max's fingers locked around mine, and my mind was entangled with perplexing and new emotions. My heart surged against my ribs as if it were trying to escape. I turned to Max and with my other hand I brushed away the tears streaking her face. She was trembling—or was that me? Max opened her eyes. I leaned toward her and met her lips with mine.

The music intensified, swirling around us as Max wrapped her arms around me. The moment lasted an eternity, but it was over long before I wanted it to end. I opened my eyes to look at her.

"I'm *never* going to be a Space Jumper," I told her.

She let out a sob as the tension gushed from her body. "But what if—"

"I'm not. I promise you."

And then she kissed me back, and I let her tears fall on my face. When the music faded, I held her as we watched the artist walk away.

"Who is he?" Max sighed.

"A friend of someone."

Max turned to me. "I'm sorry for being so mean," she whispered.

"I was the split-screen. I didn't know . . . I mean I still don't—" Max cut me off. I wasn't good at saying the right thing.

"I don't want us to *ever* be apart," she said. "And not just you and me, either. I mean everyone, even Nugget. Can't we have it that way?"

"Absolutely," I promised her.

On the walk back, it was as if we wanted to tell each other

everything—all the things we hadn't been talking about for cycles and cycles. Max and I conspired about the wormhole pirates and their attack on our shuttle. We wondered out loud if Buzz was a real wormhole pirate. Max said that she thought he was just another kid looking for attention by pretending to be a criminal. I wasn't so sure. We talked about Theodore and his obsession with the tetrascope, and we even discussed the strange spells Ketheria had been experiencing. It felt like we hadn't seen each other in phases. It was golden to have Max back again. We were still talking by the time we entered the Labyrinth.

My match was scheduled first, but Theodore was nowhere to be found. I could only assume he had wandered back to the shed. Max offered to be my partner, and I quickly accepted. While I was getting ready, though, I wondered if Theodore *had* gone back to the shed. I'd need to enlist others if I was going to help him. Charlie seemed liked a good choice, but I knew Theodore would see my actions as a betrayal.

Max and I won our match easily, working as a team and never missing a beat. Everything felt perfect. I was the same person I had been just the spoke before, but everything had changed.

When Max and I left the ready room, Athooyi stood waiting in the lower arena. He was alone, clutching his speaking device against the hole in his chest. The frail-looking creatures I normally saw around him were absent. *Who is he waiting for?* I wondered.

It surprised me when Athooyi stepped out and spoke to us. "You kids play well, very well." His metallic voice was amplified through the tiny box.

"Thank you," Max said.

"I have a proposition for you," he continued.

That did not sound good. Citizens never spoke of propositions; they only spoke of orders whenever knudniks were concerned.

"I think you should speak with our Guarantor," I offered politely, and swayed slowly to the right of the alien, ready to make our escape.

His thick lips sucked in the arena air, and he bellowed through the hole in his chest. "I am not finished speaking! Be still."

We didn't move.

"I apologize for my outburst. That is not like me," he said, but somehow I doubted that. "My proposition requires your understanding of its magnitude, as I have already spoken to Mr. Norton."

"You *know* our Guarantor?" Max frowned.

The alien closed his eyes and swallowed with difficulty. I elbowed Max. I didn't think talking while he was talking was a wise thing to do.

"I do, and we have conversed, but unfortunately he was unable to see the value in my offer."

"Offer? What offer?"

"I've been watching you play Quest-Nest since you first

started here at the Labyrinth. It is my belief that the two of you have the skills required to win the Chancellor's Challenge. It is a great honor to play in such an esteemed event."

"Don't the players die in that game?" I asked, even though I already knew the answer.

"But with more honor than anyone in your situation can ever attain," he said.

"When did you speak with Charlie . . . I mean Mr. Norton?" I said. Charlie had never mentioned anything to me about this offer. Maybe this was why Charlie didn't want me in the Citizens' League.

"Just this last phase," he said. That was too recent. Charlie forbade me to play in the Citizens' League way before last phase. "But he refused to sell you to me. I was hoping—"

"Sell us!" Max exclaimed.

Athooyi jabbed his thick finger in the air, cutting Max off. "I was hoping I might shed some light on the situation and gain your support in convincing your Guarantor to complete the sale."

Max stood there with her mouth open.

"Never," I said.

"Do not be so hasty. I am willing to offer you a portion of the Chancellor's award. This is unheard of in the history of the Rings of Orbis. You understand I have the right, as a Citizen, to purchase you, and *force* you to play in the Chancellor's Challenge?"

"How kind of you," Max muttered.

Athooyi bowed slightly, closed his eyes, and smiled, oblivious to Max's sarcasm. The image of the Citizen registering her naked knudniks with Tinker flashed in my head. *This one should place well in the Chancellor's match,* she had said. I remembered the look in their eyes when Tinker lifted one of the hoods. I would not want to be that person.

Max put her hands on her hips and said, "You're crazy if you think we would ever convince our Guarantor to let you—" But I clamped my hand over Max's mouth before she made our situation any worse. Despite the severity of the situation, I was acutely aware of Max's lips against the palm of my hand.

"Please excuse her," I said calmly to Athooyi. Athooyi's pupils pulsed as he glared at Max. I could tell when someone was getting angry. I don't think he was used to being spoken to like that, especially by a knudnik. "We are honored that you believe we could win such an event, and I will discuss your proposition with my partner, as well as my Guarantor. Immediately." My hand was still over Max's mouth as I dragged her away from Athooyi.

When we were far enough away, I removed my hand and glanced back at Athooyi.

"Of all the stup—" I shushed Max before she finished and pulled her farther to the side, never taking my eyes off Athooyi.

"Look," I whispered.

I glanced up and saw Ceesar emerging from the shadows. He was shaking his head and arguing with Athooyi. Ceesar must have been listening to our entire conversation.

"What's he doing with Athooyi?" she wondered.

I didn't have a clue, but for some reason it scared me.

"We need to get out of here. When is your match?" I asked her.

"After the next one, I think."

"Let's find Ketheria."

I sat in the lower stands, waiting for their match to start. I was tucked behind a support column and a group of Trefaldoors, and I watched Athooyi's every move up in the Citizen seats. What was Ceesar up to? I needed to know. There was something about Ceesar that rubbed me the wrong way. Ceesar wasn't a Citizen; I knew that much, but he seemed to have a lot of power just the same. *Did he have anything to do with Athooyi's offer?* Of course, Charlie would say no even if Athooyi offered him a lot of money. I was glad that neither Weegin nor Odran were our Guarantors any longer. Either of them would have sold us in a parsec. I made a mental note to be nicer to Charlie when I got home.

I turned back toward the arena and saw that Max and Ketheria were having trouble in their match. I was worried that Max might be distracted, but it was Ketheria who started the game off slow. Was she getting sick again? I couldn't tell, but Max picked up the slack once she was outside the goal. A skilled toss of an immobility cube by Ketheria at the last nanosecond helped them squeak ahead at the finish.

"Good toss," I told Ketheria when she came out.

"Lucky," she mumbled.

"You feel all right?"

"I'm fine now."

"Athooyi still here?" Max whispered.

"Yeah, but Ceesar left when your match started."

"Do you want to stay and watch the other kids play?" Ketheria asked. "I think Grace is up next."

"I want to speak to Charlie," Max replied.

"Me too," I agreed.

"Help! Help me, somebody!"

That was the first thing I heard when I stepped through the light chute. Max and Ketheria were already running toward Theodore's cries.

"Theodore!" I shouted.

"What's wrong?" Max yelled from the front hall.

I hadn't expected him to be home. I thought he was at the shed, scoping someone. I raced through the house, following the sound of his voice.

"Where are you?" I called.

"Out here!"

All three of us tore for the garden.

Theodore was standing on the stone path, leaning over Charlie's body.

"Please, wake up. Wake up," he pleaded.

"Charlie!" Ketheria screamed.

"It wasn't my fault," Theodore wailed, his faced streaked with tears. "I didn't know! I really didn't know!"

"Know what?" Max cried, and knelt next to Charlie.

"No!" Theodore screamed. "Don't touch him!"

Max pushed back from Charlie.

"I'm sorry. I'm so sorry," Theodore sobbed.

Charlie's body convulsed as a small white spot moved out of his nose and across his upper lip. It was followed by another and then another. Soon, every crevice of Charlie's body was filled with these tiny white creatures nestling into any warm spot they could find on our friend.

"Charlie!" Ketheria yelled, but he did not respond. His eyes glowed yellow, and his mouth was now stuffed with the silky creatures. They gathered around his ears, in his armpits, and traveled over his body.

Ketheria looked at me, and I did the only thing I could think of. I called Vairocina.

"Yes, JT?" she said.

"Charlie's hurt. Can you call someone?"

"Absolutely." Vairocina only paused shortly before saying, "Someone will be here shortly."

"What's wrong with him?" Ketheria pleaded.

Vairocina floated over Charlie's body.

"He has been infected with a parasite. I have seen it before. It was quite common in my star system, but the parasite is found only on plants. I do not know the effect it has on humans, but I know it is quite fatal to some plant species," she informed us grimly. "I'll inform Health Services of his condition."

"How did Charlie get it?" I said.

"Cala did it," Theodore confessed.

"Who's Cala?" Max asked.

"He pulled a spike from one of the plants in the garden," Theodore said. "Then he stabbed Charlie with it." There was shame in his voice.

"Theodore, what was Cala doing here?"

"Where's Nugget?" Ketheria cried.

"I'm sorry, Ketheria. He tried to help. He tried to save Charlie, but he got in the way."

"Where is he?" she screamed at him.

Theodore pointed down the path. Nugget's big feet poked out of the bushes.

"Nugget!" Ketheria cried with every muscle in her body, and ran toward him.

"Don't let her touch him, JT," Vairocina warned. "The parasite is very contagious."

I raced toward Ketheria and grabbed her before she flung herself onto Nugget.

"Let me go! He needs me!"

"No, Ketheria. Help is on the way. They'll make him better. You can't touch him."

"Nugget!" she cried, falling limp in my arms. "Nugget! No!"

The dome over the garden crackled and separated to allow a small craft to enter the estate. The wingless vessel hovered a meter above the ground and dispatched a medical lift, which dropped to the ground. Three people emerged, dressed in skintight protective gear, and immediately descended upon Charlie and Nugget. Two other emergency team members exited the craft and corralled the four of us inside the house. We were quarantined while they administered tests on us to see if we, too, were infected.

"Why did you bring Cala to the house, Theodore?" I demanded as the emergency crew removed a plasma censor from my head. I rubbed my fingers in my hair, trying to remove the awful tingling sensation.

"He wanted to see where I lived. I thought he was my friend. I didn't think he would do *this*," he replied.

They pulled the same device off Max's head, and she said, "Well, you thought wrong."

"I said I'm sorry."

I asked the attendant, "What are they going to do with Charlie and Nugget?"

He—or she; I could not tell because the outfit completely molded the alien's body—mumbled through the material that blanked out the attendant's face. "They will be placed in stasis under quarantine as we attempt to remove the parasite."

"How long will it take?" Ketheria croaked.

"That depends on how strong the victim is," the attendant replied, and stuck another sensor in my ear.

"Ow!"

"Sorry."

"But they will survive, right?" Max asked.

"I can't say. This is a very nasty parasite. We should have been notified sooner."

Ketheria swallowed hard, fighting back her tears. Max took her hand, and I glared at Theodore.

"What? We have no way to notify anyone about anything. All this technology, and we can't even contact someone. We're knudniks. What are we supposed to do?" he snapped.

"Where's your pob?" I said, looking for the device.

Theodore covered his ear where the device *should* have been. He wouldn't answer me.

"You sold it, didn't you?"

"I traded it," he argued.

"To whom?"

"To Cala."

"That's how you could go to the shed, isn't it?"

"What's the shed?" Max whispered.

"It's where Theodore goes to use the tetrascope," I informed her.

Theodore held his head in his hands. I was furious with him. He wasn't thinking when he brought Cala home. But something in Theodore's eyes made my heart jump.

"There's more, isn't there?" I said.

Theodore nodded.

Before I could pry him for more information, Theylor stepped into the room.

"They're clean," said the attendant.

"Thank you," Theylor's left head said while his right smiled at us. "Humans do seem to have an affinity for conflict."

"I'm sorry, Theylor," I said.

"No, I am sorry that I have not seen you sooner. We are forced to leave the Citizens to themselves on Orbis 3. They prefer it that way, and unfortunately, it limits my time here."

"Nasty bunch, those Citizens," Max mumbled.

"Not all of them," the Keeper offered in their defense. He looked around the room. "Who was here when the attack happened?"

"I was," Theodore confessed.

"Where were you three?" he asked us.

"At the Labyrinth," Max replied.

"Do you know of anyone who would want to hurt Charlie?" he asked.

We looked at each other, shaking our heads. "Nobody," I said. "Charlie stays at home most of the time."

"Did the central computer see anything?" Max asked.

"Most Citizens use a blocking device—a bubble, if you like—that can prevent the central computer from prying into their affairs. One was activated over this estate when the attack occurred."

"Then a Citizen must have been behind the attack on Charlie," I exclaimed.

"The attacker was not a Citizen," Theylor informed us.

"No, he was a wormhole pirate," Theodore said.

My head spun so fast when Theodore announced that Cala was a wormhole pirate that I hurt my neck.

"How do you know this?" Theylor asked him.

"He told me."

"What?" I yelled.

"Well, he didn't really tell me; it was something he said when he attacked Charlie."

Theylor remained patient and asked, "What did he say?"

"Yeah, what did he say?" Max pushed him.

"He said, 'No one sees a pirate coming.'"

"That's it?" Max said.

"It is an expression," Theylor informed her. "But it does not mean that he's a wormhole pirate. The attack on the shuttle when you came to Orbis 3 was the first time a wormhole pirate ever ventured out of their dimension. I highly doubt that one is roaming freely on this ring."

Max started to say, "But we—"

"Know nothing else," I said, cutting her off. I had a hunch that Cala wasn't the only wormhole pirate roaming Orbis 3. First Buzz and *then* Cala. Ceesar must be a wormhole pirate, too.

"Do you know how to find Cala?" I asked Theylor.

"I am afraid he has disappeared," he replied.

But I knew how to find him.

I would have had to be a split-screen not to see the connection between Buzz, Cala, and Ceesar. Of course they were all wormhole pirates. But what were they doing on the ring? And what was the connection to the shuttle we arrived on? They certainly weren't afraid of getting caught. They played in the Labyrinth right out in the open. Someone must be protecting them. Athooyi? If I was going to find Cala, that's where I would start.

"You're thinking about something, aren't you?" Max whispered.

"How could you tell?"

"You're pulling at your hair. You always pull at your hair when you're about to do something you shouldn't," she said.

"I pull my hair?"

"Always."

I stopped pulling at my hair. Max smiled.

"There is something I want to check out," I whispered.

Once the emergency crew stabilized Charlie and Nugget, they elevated their bodies into the craft still hovering over our garden. We watched as security-bots scrounged the grounds for any evidence left by Cala. There must have been twenty of them combing the immense garden. Ketheria stepped around the bots to reach a small group of Keepers who had come to help tend to the crisis, huddled on the path. She yanked on Theylor's purple robe and pointed up at the craft hovering over the garden. "Can I go with them?" she asked.

"You can visit them in a few cycles, after your classes. I will leave you the coordinates," he said before introducing Ketheria to the other Keepers.

The Keeper Drapling entered the compound with a flourish. "Is everyone all right? Who was hurt?" he demanded. "I came as swiftly as possible." Drapling knelt next to my sister and quickly examined her. When he seemed satisfied, he did the same to me.

"What about us?" Max mumbled.

"You all seem to be fine," he said, casually checking Max's ears. "Who was attacked?"

"It was the adult," Theylor informed him. "Charlie Norton."

After a very long pause, Drapling said, "Oh, I was worried it was the children."

Max spun toward me, stifling a laugh. I swallowed a laugh, too. When we first met Drapling on Orbis 1, the Keeper was always very cold toward us. In fact, I was convinced he hated us. Yet ever since our staining last rotation, Drapling had changed. Now he was nice. Almost too nice, as if he were forcing it, making up for lost time, I guessed. It was something we just couldn't get used to.

"We're fine, Drapling. Thank you," I assured him.

"We will search for the attacker at once," he announced. "I will see to it personally." His robe swooshed as he turned to the other Keepers. "Theylor, may I speak with you?"

Drapling dragged Theylor inside, and we turned to watch the small spacecraft slip through the dome.

"Who's gonna take care of us now?" Ketheria asked.

"We'll take of ourselves," Max assured her. "We've done it before."

I glared at Theodore.

"What?" he said.

"What do you think?"

"Don't worry," he mumbled. "I have no intention of sneaking out. I'm finished with the tetrascope."

"Johnny Turnbull," Theylor called me from the house. "Would you come inside, please?"

I did as I was told and met Theylor at the top of the stairs leading to the house. "I am leaving you in charge," he informed me. "Temporarily, until we assess your Guarantor's condition. If things are not better in a few cycles, I will return to assist your reassignment."

"To a new Guarantor?"

"Of course."

"No! I don't want another Guarantor. I want Charlie."

Theylor's left head looked back outside while his right head focused on me. "You need to prepare, JT."

"Prepare for what?"

"The situation is very severe for Charlie and Nugget. I worry most about Ketheria and how she will respond if Nugget dies. I know about her spells. You do not need to worry, as those are just growing pains, but it will be much harder for her if she loses her friend."

What was he saying? "It was just a plant, Theylor. You can make them better, right?"

Theylor smiled, not a happy smile, but rather a *What-do-you-want-me-to-say?* smile. I felt my stomach drop to my feet.

"I have posted security around the estate and sealed the dome from further entry. You are to contact Vairocina immediately if anything suspicious happens."

If I ever got my hands on Cala, I would make sure he paid for this.

"JT?"

"Sure, Theylor," I assured him. "I can take care of things."

Theylor frowned. "Johnny, I am aware of your history dealing with these matters yourself. I even find it commendable. But this time, it is not necessary. Please leave this to the Citizens. The Keepers are not active on this ring, but I've been informed that the Citizens of Orbis 3 will do everything they can to apprehend this person. I have an added concern for your well-being because Drapling believes that the attacker may have been after you, since you are a softwire. We are simply unaware of the motive at this time."

I didn't say anything to Theylor. I lived on a ring where my status was slightly above that of a broom. Did he really believe a Citizen would spend a single chit trying to solve this, let alone protect a knudnik? No, if I didn't take care of this myself, then no one would. If Drapling was right and Cala attacked Charlie because of me, then I would find Cala and expose his motives myself.

"Whatever you say," I finally told Theylor.

It was getting easier for me to lie.

No one could get to sleep that spoke. Grace spread a rumor that the wormhole pirates were going to attack again. She said that if they could sneak up on a space shuttle, then the security posted by the Keepers was useless to protect us. I tried to convince her that the idea was preposterous, since Cala had had a zillion opportunities to get to me in the past. The logic didn't sway her conclusion one bit.

I found Ketheria balled up in a corner, rocking back and forth.

"No one's coming," I tried to comfort her.

"I know."

"Nugget will be all right."

"You don't know that," she croaked, her eyes filled with tears.

"Yes, I do. That's what brothers are for. We know things like that."

Ketheria lifted her head to show me a smile, and I covered her with my blanket. Every time someone walked past the room, I glanced up to see if it was Max. I wanted to find Max, but I couldn't leave Ketheria, not like this. We all slept there, together, that night on the floor. No one wanted to be alone in their sleepers. I dreamed of Charlie and Nugget. I even dreamed about the wormhole pirates and Quest-Nest. But all I really wanted to dream about was Max.

The next spoke, everyone shuffled around the house like robots. There were no smells from the kitchen since Charlie wasn't cooking, and the sound of Nugget's big feet stomping on the stone floor was noticeably absent. I found Max fussing with the chow synth, and I grabbed an apple. Standing next to her, waiting for everyone to get ready, made me feel that everything was going to be all right.

"I don't think Theodore slept last night," Max whispered as she searched for something to poke at the chow synth.

"You're not taking that apart, are you?"

Max held up a magnetic driver and said, "No. Something is stuck in there."

"Leave it. We'll get something to eat at the Illuminate."

"We're going?"

"Yeah, why not?"

"I thought we'd just go see Charlie," she said. "And then, you know . . ."

I didn't know what *you know* meant. There were two possible explanations. One meant we'd go looking for trouble; the other was very new. My heart rebooted, imagining the latter.

"Uh . . . It's better if we do everything like we always do. We can see Charlie and Nugget after studies. Besides, if Charlie's conscious, he will be upset that we're not at school."

"That's your plan? Last cycle you said you wanted to check something out."

I did want to check something out.

"Spill it, Johnny Turnbull. I want to know what you're up to."

"Spill what?" Theodore yawned, stumbling into the kitchen.

"You don't look too good," Max told him.

Theodore used his hand to force a lump of hair to lie down, but it only sprang up again. "Thanks," he replied. He slunk onto one of the stools. "Are you guys still mad at me?"

"Wouldn't you be?" Max said, but Theodore was looking at me for an answer.

"I wouldn't want to be you when Charlie gets back," I told him. "But I am glad you're off the tetrascope."

Theodore slumped over the counter and nodded slowly.

"We're going to look for Cala," he said. "Aren't we?"

I nodded as I watched Max smile.

To be honest, I didn't have a plan yet. I only had an idea. Really it was just a suspicion, a bunch of images that didn't reveal much, but every one of them included Ceesar. Cala was just the messenger, I had convinced myself, a pawn used by someone with far greater ambition.

I needed more information from Ceesar. The only time I ever saw him was at the Labyrinth, and he was usually with that gambler, Athooyi. I needed to get Ceesar alone. I needed to get into the Labyrinth and challenge Ceesar to another match.

Riis was not at the Illuminate that cycle, either. I didn't think anything of it because she had been missing school a lot lately. At the lockers, Max asked me if I wanted to sit with her in studies, but I reluctantly declined. I had a few questions for Theodore. We found a pod and I waited for the device to slide toward the enormous screen.

"Did Cala say anything to you that seemed unusual?" I asked him.

"Nothing. We were talking about the scope and the Chancellor's Challenge. He said he could get me a ride. I used the pob to hold my place. He was being very nice to me. He was acting like a friend."

"Did he say anything about Ceesar?"

"He never mentioned him. He was always alone when I talked to him. Ceesar only came to the shed once, and Sul-sah wouldn't let him scope."

"Why?"

"I don't know. Sul-sah yelled at him, saying he was a liar or something."

I couldn't imagine anyone yelling at Ceesar. "But Cala stayed?"

"Yeah, Sul-sah never had a problem with him."

"Ow!" I yelled. The pod had sent an electric shock, zapping us for not linking up. Theodore reached for the hardwire while I interfaced with the computer.

"Stupid machine," Theodore mumbled.

"But why did he come to the house?"

"It was weird. We were just talking, walking back to the chute, and he just followed me through."

"But he needed a code," I said.

"He must have watched me punch it in."

"Didn't that seem strange to you?"

"Maybe, but I had been on the scope for a long time. I was tired, and we were having a really interesting conversation about Earth."

"Earth? How does Cala know about Earth?"

"I don't know, but he knew a lot," Theodore said.

It seemed obvious to me that Cala had planned this. Why else would he learn about Earth if not to distract Theodore or gain his confidence? But why did Cala want to hurt Charlie? That's the part I couldn't figure out.

I was still trying to figure it out when the spoke ended and we gathered in front of the Illuminate. Everyone wanted to see Charlie and Nugget. Even Dalton was eager to see our Guarantor.

"Theylor mentioned he would arrange clearance," I told everyone. "But I think we should stay close together anyway. The chute will take us just outside the quarantine building. Once you're through the chute, wait for me and we'll all go in together."

I stood by the light chute and punched the code for each person. I was the last person through.

I arrived at a part of Orbis I had never seen before. It was already in shadow.

"We're on the other side of the ring," Max whispered.

I looked up through the thin atmosphere and squinted to see some recognizable landmark. *We just came from there*, I thought, looking at the sun glinting off things on the other side of the ring.

The building in front of me was an enormous hoop floating in the air. There were no windows, at least none I could see, and the building looked like a miniature ring, only plump and smooth.

"Charlie must be in there," I said, pointing.

We crossed metal walkways, past Citizens who glared at our vests, and reached another chute under the large donut rotating in the sky. Once inside, we were greeted by aliens dressed in brilliant white robes of the same clingy material the emergency crew was wearing when they picked up Charlie. They ushered us into a plain room and closed the door. Before I could ask what we were doing there, a soothing recorded voice informed us that we were being scanned and deloused of parasites, infectious materials, or any other biological microbes that might be along for the ride.

"Don't we get to wear those weird outfits?" Max asked.

"I guess not," I said as an opening appeared in the room that led to a small shuttle. With no other option available to us, we piled in. Effortlessly, the machine pulled away but stopped midway through a bright curved tunnel. There were no markings of any sort along the tube, and it simply stopped against a blank wall that suddenly disappeared. I shuffled into the sterile nothingness with everyone else and fanned out along the curved white walls.

I don't know about everyone else, but I was not prepared for what we saw.

My eyes were glued to the glass container floating at the center of the room. Suspended by thin copper wires in a murky green liquid floated Nugget, inside a square tank. At least a hundred copper wires bore into his skin and every opening of his body. The tiny white creatures that infected him gathered on the wires, crawling in and out of the holes. It was disgusting.

I noticed a sole attendant sitting near a collage of O-dats when he said, "Welcome." No one responded. "Don't be disturbed," he added.

"How long will he be like this?" I croaked weakly.

"Quite some time, I'm afraid. The Sepius parasite is always reluctant to leave such a suitable host, but this one's a fighter. It also helped that the parasite was native to his home planet of Krig."

"Why all the wires?" Theodore asked. "Do you really need eighty-eight of them?"

"The more the better, actually," he said. "Sepius loves copper. It's the only thing they'll eat. Other than their host, of course."

Ketheria let out a cry and nuzzled against me, hiding her face from Nugget.

"I'm sorry," the attendant said. "I don't mean to upset you."

"Can you tell us more?" I asked him.

"As the copper oxidizes, the parasites unknowingly gobble up the by-product. The copper oxide then kills them. It's just a matter of coaxing all the little guys out and having them start feasting on the wire."

"That makes me want to throw up," Ketheria muttered.

"Try not to do that in here, please," the attendant said.

I had to look away from Nugget's ghastly skin, all wrinkled from the water. He was a pale, craggy version of himself, not the little guy I knew. Grace screamed when Nugget's body jerked inside the tank, sloshing the water and straining the copper cables. I admit, I almost screamed, too, but Ketheria moved toward Nugget and put her hands on the tank.

"He's awake?" she asked.

"Just barely. He's definitely a fighter."

"Where's Charlie?" I asked him.

"Who?" he said.

"The human. A big guy. He would have come in with Nugget."

"Oh."

Suddenly, I heard Ketheria scream, "No!"

I turned to my sister as she fell to the ground. Her hands flew up to her telepathy blocker and she yanked down on it with both hands. Little droplets of blood trickled along her temples.

"What's wrong with her, JT?" Max asked, rushing to her side.

"I'm afraid the human passed away," the attendant said. "About half a spoke ago."

Ketheria cried out again.

"I'm sorry, but the parasite was simply too much for the human immune system. No one could have known," the attendant continued.

Ketheria was now grinding her fists into her ears and screaming.

"Please stop thinking about it!" Grace screamed at the attendant.

I stood there frozen between Ketheria and the attendant. *I'm afraid the human passed away.* My body thickened, and I felt the room pull away. The severity of the moment was pushing me into the floor. Charlie's death would forever mark a point in my life. I already heard myself saying, *Before Charlie died,* or *That was after my friend died.* The part of me pulling away was already digesting his death, measuring it against moments yet to come, as if wondering how I would deal with it in a million different situations.

I'm afraid the human has passed away.

You can't go back from a statement like that. The attendant's not going to say, *Sorry, I was joking. Your friend is fine; he's in the other room.* I looked at him anyway, as if hoping he would, bad joke or not, but he had his head down. He was shuffling papers, glancing at us out of the corner of his eye. I'm sure he didn't have a clue what to do with us. Neither did I.

Then the door opened and the room rushed back. Someone was crying. More than one person, I think. Theylor poured into the room, moving swiftly.

"I tried to contact you at the house. I could not get through. I wanted to warn you," he cried, as if apologizing.

It was true. Charlie was dead.

Theylor moved around the room, scooping us together. No one resisted, but he was forced to carry Ketheria. As we shuffled out the door, I turned to the attendant.

"Thank you," I mumbled.

There was something odd about stepping outside with Theylor. Part of me expected to find the ring no longer spinning. Shouldn't everything have stopped on Orbis now that Charlie was dead? Yet when I looked up, I found my environment acting perfectly normal, as it had *before Charlie died.*

I stopped in the open courtyard and watched more Keepers scramble toward the other kids. I watched two Nagool masters rush toward Ketheria and take her from Theylor's arms. She was still sobbing. I turned and watched Theodore drift away and sit under the huge building, which gleamed like a piece of jewelry hanging in the sky.

Shouldn't it fall now? Charlie is dead.

I looked for Max and found her sitting on a concrete ramp. Grace sat next to her and put her arm around Max's shoulder. I stepped toward them, or at least I tried to. My feet would not move. *Is this normal? Why won't my feet work?*

Then, like a delayed reaction, I lifted up my right foot and placed it in front of me. Each step toward the girls required a conscious effort on my part, as if I were knee-deep in radiation gel.

I stopped. I looked up at the ring again. *Still spinning.*

The more steps I took, the more freely my feet moved.

No!

I felt as if I were walking away from the moment of Charlie's death, as if I were leaving Charlie. I didn't want that.

That's how it works.

First one step, then two, then a dozen, then a cycle passes, and then a phase. *Eventually a whole rotation will separate me from this moment,* I realized. Would I forget Charlie completely by then? Does Charlie have to deal with this now that he's dead, or is he just *dead,* no longer aware of *us*?

Is that true?

Suddenly I felt far more worried about people around me dying than dying myself.

"JT?" Max called out. "You all right?"

I looked up at her. I realized I had been staring at my feet.

"Yeah," I mumbled back.

"Come sit with us," Grace offered.

I moved toward them and sat next to Max as she took my hand. It was still wet with her tears. Ketheria was standing now, but Theodore remained alone, sitting under the medical building. Most of the other kids whispered in small groups or explored this side of the ring, but no one ventured very far from the building.

"Why did Cala do it?" I whispered to Max.

Max shook her head. "I bet he's asking the same thing," she said, nodding toward Theodore. "I think he really needs you right now. I think he needs his friend."

"I can't. If Theodore hadn't—"

Max stopped me. "He doesn't need someone pointing fingers at him, JT. Look at him. He knows that what he did was very wrong, but nothing can bring Charlie back, not ever."

"Don't say that," I croaked.

"Go talk to him," Max whispered, and pushed me with her elbow.

I stared at Theodore for a moment before getting up. I made a wide berth of the Keepers and Nagools and slipped under the building from the right. Theodore glanced up at me when I got closer.

"Hey," he mumbled.

I didn't say anything. I just sat down next to him.

"I'm sorry, JT. I'm so sorry."

I still couldn't say anything. I looked up at Max and Grace. They looked away when I caught them watching.

"Are you going to be mad at me forever?" he asked.

I wanted to jump on Theodore and smash him. I wanted to scream at him, *How could you?* I wanted to kick him and punch him, but I didn't. I just looked at him. His eyes were swimming in their sockets, and I knew he didn't want Charlie dead any more than I did. I swallowed hard and felt tears run down my cheeks. I shook my head but didn't speak. Instead I swallowed again.

"I'm sorry," he whispered. Then he reached forward and hugged me. When he put his arms around me, something burst inside me and I cried like a little one. I felt Theodore sobbing, and I hugged him back. After a moment I became aware that others were watching us, and I pulled away. I cleared my throat, wiping the tears out of my eyes.

"I'm not mad at you," I croaked.

"I deserve it, though," he whispered.

After a moment I asked, "Is there anything else you can remember?"

"About what Cala did?"

"Yeah. Did he steal anything? Did he say anything else?"

"No. He headed straight for the chute."

I shook my head, wondering why. What did Charlie do to deserve this?

"What are we going to do?" Theodore asked.

"I don't know," I said, and saw Theylor walking toward the other kids.

He has to assign us to a new Guarantor, I thought. What was that going to be like? It certainly wouldn't be someone as nice as Charlie. In fact, our new Guarantor wouldn't even care that Charlie had died, and he or she certainly wouldn't give us the freedom Charlie had given us. It hit me that I might never find out what happened to my friend. I stood up.

"Where are you going?" Theodore asked.

"I need to ask someone a favor," I replied.

"Yeah, good luck."

I stepped out from under the building and over to the left

side. I let Theylor come to me. I didn't want any of the other Keepers or Nagools to overhear our conversation. When he was in front of me, both heads looked at me while his right one said, "The parasite was too much for Charlie. The plant is foreign to Earth. The same plant often infects Citizens, but they don't die. I worry that Nugget might be too small, but Charlie had no defense. I would not be too hard on Theodore. It may have been an accident, for all we know."

"But we'll never find out, will we?" I said.

"Why do you say that?" he asked.

"You have to reassign us now, don't you? That's why everyone is here, right?"

Theylor glanced back at the other Keepers. "We came to help in your time of grieving," he said.

"But you have to reassign us."

"Yes."

"When?" I asked.

"You will return with us until we examine all of Charlie's requests and follow proper Citizen procedures, but I assume, since Charlie was not a Citizen very long, that you and the others will be put up for auction."

"Auction!"

The others looked over at us, and Theylor frowned. "Please, I know this upsets you, but there are procedures that must be followed."

"Theylor, I've done a lot for you and for the Rings of Orbis, have I not?"

"Yes, this is true."

"Then I would like to ask you a favor, in exchange for what I have done."

"I do not think—"

"Wait, hear me out first. I want you to hold off on the auction. Let us go back to our home, and give me time to find Cala. At least let me give him to you so he can be punished. No one is going to care after we've been reassigned. Charlie's Citizen status was shady already. I don't think very many people will mind that he's dead. That's why I have to do this. If you take us now, that will never happen."

"JT, I cannot—"

"Please, Theylor. I beg you. Please, for me and Ketheria. Let me do this."

Theylor glanced back at the others again.

"There's not a Citizen around right now. We could take the chute back and be gone."

"How long do you require?" Theylor whispered.

"I don't know."

"I will give you two phases," he said.

"Thank you."

Theylor huddled with the other Keepers for some time before they finally left—without us. We were grouped together on the far side of the courtyard as we watched them leave.

"I thought for sure they were here to take us away," Max said.

"They were," I replied, and nudged Max toward the chute.

"What happened?"

"I asked for a favor."

Max smiled. "How long have we got?" she asked.

"Two phases."

Theodore and I were the last to leave the courtyard. I stepped through the light chute to find the estate as black as space.

"Don't move," Max whispered when I bumped into her.

"Where are the lights?"

"Shhh!"

Something moved past the hallway.

"Vairocina?" I hissed, but she didn't answer. "Vairocina?" She wasn't there.

We listened to the silence. And then: "We're in here!" someone called to us.

"Who is that?" Theodore whispered.

"I'm scared," Grace said.

"Don't be," I told her. "It's just the person I want to talk to."

"Who?"

"Ceesar," I said.

"Wait, maybe we should go back, go somewhere else," Grace said.

"The chute won't work," Ketheria said calmly.

I told Theodore to try it.

"She's right," he said.

"We're trapped," Max said.

"Then let's see what our guest wants," I said.

I wasn't afraid of Ceesar. In fact I felt rage toward him. I knew he had something to do with what happened to Charlie and Nugget, and I wanted to know why. If I stayed close to Ceesar, I could reach Vairocina and have her track my location and notify Theylor. This was exactly what I wanted.

Some kids refused to move. The rest, including Max, Theodore, and my sister, followed me as I crept along the walls, past the chow synth, and toward a reddish light glowing from the rec room. Ceesar was waiting inside, sprawled on a lounger. Cala stood to his left, cradling a glowing crystal lamp and holding it over Ceesar. The red light bathed Ceesar in an evil luster but left the corners of the room dark. Something stirred in the shadows.

"You're out rather late, aren't you?" Ceesar said.

"Thanks to him," Max protested, pointing at Cala.

"None of this would have happened if it weren't for *him*," Ceesar said, mocking her and pointing at me.

"Me?"

Ceesar glanced at a metal sculpture on the table in front of him. Then he caressed the lounger with his gnarled hands before speaking. "You've got a nice setup here, especially for a knudnik. I can't imagine how your other Guarantors treated you."

"Horribly," Theodore spat.

Ceesar sat up, waved Cala off, and declared, "I'm bored already." Cala raised the lights and exposed Ceesar's cohorts, who were crouched against the walls or tucked in the corners. We were surrounded.

"There's eleven of them," Theodore whispered.

Ketheria stared at Ceesar, her head slightly tilted with an intense look of concentration contorting her face.

"Why do you care about our setup?" I asked Ceesar. "Besides, it doesn't seem like it's going to last long now, thanks to him." I pointed at Cala.

"Oh, don't give him all the credit," Ceesar said, and hoisted himself up with his muscular arms.

He grinned, shaking his head slightly and turning toward Ketheria. As he did so, Ceesar exposed a pob overwrought with attachments that wrapped around the entire back of his scarred head. He circled the room and stopped in front of my sister, bending slightly and peering at her through some sort of O-dat wired to his face. The device tore at the skin around his left eye.

"Won't work, little girl," he hissed at her. From where I was standing, I could see his eyeball, blank and opaque in its lidless socket.

"Leave her alone," I growled.

Ceesar flicked his long, dirty fingernail against the crystal on her head. Ketheria blinked, but she did not break her concentration on him.

"You can't read my mind because I won't let you," he bellowed, and straightened up. "You can't contact anyone because your sweet little house is bubbled. And as for the security-bots out there," Ceesar said with a laugh, "they don't even know I'm here."

"Why did you kill Charlie?" I asked him.

"Kill?" Ceesar glanced at Cala and then smacked him with his big mitt. Cala doubled over. "Sorry about that: my intention was only to get him out of way."

"Out of the way of what?" Max asked.

Ceesar waved his finger at her and said, "Too soon. Not so fast. Let me enjoy this. This is my monologue. I've practiced it for a very long time."

"Are you a wormhole pirate?" Theodore asked him.

"What do you think?" he scoffed.

"I think you are," I said. "But I don't know how you got on the ring undetected."

"That was the easy part. Even a child could have done it. You provided the perfect diversion."

"Me?"

"Tell him we put on a good show!" Ceesar bellowed, imitating what the alien had said to me on the ring shuttle. "The attack on your shuttle was a brilliant distraction. They waited for the security forces while I quietly slipped onto Orbis 3."

"You sacrificed all of your crew," I said.

"It will be worth it," he replied.

"Who are you?" Ketheria demanded.

"I'm Captain Ceesar, of course."

"The greatest wormhole pirate ever to slip a dimension," the voices in the shadows said in unison.

Ceesar smiled, sucking in the mantra. He plopped onto the lounger again and said, "There's a story I've heard in my travels. It changes, of course: different versions in different galaxies, different players in each version, but there is always one common element. One person. One being. One *weakness*." Ceesar sat up abruptly and said, "Stop me if you've heard this already." He laughed and nestled back into the lounger. We remained still and said nothing. In my mind I was searching for some device to link to the central computer, but every exit from the house's mainframe was blocked, as if nothing existed beyond the local network. "The tale," Ceesar continued, "involves the salvation of the universe. A creature preordained to follow in the footsteps of the Ancients. His arrival has been delayed so long that it has even been forgotten by some civilizations. The story has been reduced to myths and exaggerations, spoken now only to scare little children into behaving. But"—he held up his finger for emphasis—"not here. Not here on the Rings of Orbis! In fact, this is the focal point of our tale. For some here on the rings, particularly those two-headed freaks that everyone loves so much, have been waiting patiently, quietly biding the word of the Ancients and preparing for the arrival of . . ." Ceesar turned to Cala, snapping his fingers, and said, "What's the word they use?"

"Scion," he answered.

"Yes, Scion. That's it."

Theodore yawned, and Ceesar leaped from the lounger and jammed his face against Theodore's. "Don't worry—it gets even better," he spat. "You see, the Scion will travel the universe, growing more and more powerful and enlightening the masses with his brand of consciousness." He paused. "Quaint, isn't it?" he grumbled. "But how can a creature travel the universe and survive? Even if he were able to bend space and time at will, he'd have to eat." He turned to us for an answer. "Anyone?"

"Money?" Max said.

"Yes! Come on, Dumbwire. Don't let your girlfriend get all the answers."

"She's not my girl—" *Dumbwire?* Why did he call me *Dumbwire?* No one called me that anymore. Dalton did once, but he was only imitating . . . It had to be a coincidence, I told myself. It would be impossible. Switzer is dead.

Ceesar stood there smiling. He stretched his arms out and said, "How long is it gonna take, freak?"

"It's impossible," I breathed.

"I knew it," Ketheria exclaimed.

"Knew what?" Theodore asked.

"Switzer?" Dalton said hesitantly.

I searched for some resemblance. There was none. It couldn't be possible.

"This guy thinks he's Switzer?" Max said. "How do you know Switzer?"

Ceesar motioned for the small alien in the corner to come forward. "What's my name?" he ordered the alien.

The toothless alien cried, "Ceesar!" His jaw hardly moved.

"Now say *Switzer.*"

"Ceesar!"

Ceesar looked back at us and said, "He found me. I was almost dead aboard a ship passing through the wormhole. Fortunately, these souls were robbing the thing and took me hostage. My kind of people. I fit in immediately."

"But you're so big," one kid said.

"Switzer was a child when he died," Dalton reminded him.

"Time, my friend. It's not as linear as you would like to think. I've traveled with these guys for over twenty Earth years now. Amazing, isn't it?"

Could it be true? I stared at this creature claiming to be the person who had tormented me for most of my life. I forced myself to look past the scars, his enormous size, and the alien gadgets attached to his body. Could this really be Switzer? I could not connect the two. "I don't believe you," I said. "I think it's a trick."

"I thought you might say that," he said, smirking. "Therefore I brought you a souvenir, something that only I could possess— a witness to my true identity." Ceesar motioned to another pirate lurking in the shadows. "I've lugged this thing around for quite some time, but I'm sure it only feels like a rotation to you."

When the wormhole pirate emerged from the shadows, Ketheria gasped. Max did a double take. "No!" she cried.

The room shrank, shredding everything around me and highlighting what the alien was carrying. My mind reloaded images of the abandoned F.O.R.M. room we had found last rotation, Switzer encased in the blinding light, the scream- ing, and . . .

"Impressive, isn't it?" Ceesar gushed as the alien dropped the glass case on the table with a thunk. It was about a meter tall, and Ceesar tapped the rusted metal lid, illuminating the contents.

Floating inside the container was my old arm.

"Held up pretty well, don't you think?"

I stepped toward the table and peered into the cloudy liquid. The fingers on my hand were still extended, still reaching for Switzer, still pleading for him to stop. The bloated appendage was sliced at the same point I often felt pinches in my new arm. It was mine, all right. I could not deny it.

Ceesar cocked his head and smiled. "No *Welcome home*? No *Good to see you*? No *What have you been up to*?"

"You've been up to thieving and murdering and everything else they say wormhole pirates do," Max spat.

"Rumors. Just rumors," he replied.

"You can take us away now," one kid said.

"If you want," Switzer said, and looked at Dalton.

Is that what he was here for? To take us away? Switzer had returned to rescue us? The concept was not registering.

"I'm not going with him," Theodore said.

"Don't worry, you're not invited, freak," he growled.

"Why *are* you here?" Ketheria demanded. "I doubt you're here as a savior."

"That's what I've been trying to tell you." Switzer stood up, and I stepped back. He was much bigger than me now—that was glaringly obvious. "You see, it all fits," he said. "The Scion, the Softwire, the being from another world, the special treatment our little boy gets from the Keepers. It's you, Mr. Turnbull. You're the Scion. You're the one they've been waiting for."

His words bounced off my brain. *First Charlie and now this?* I needed to sit. I was still trying to swallow his first revelation.

Switzer was dead to me. I would never admit it to anyone, but I had felt safer somehow after I was told he had died. I saw my life slowly becoming better, moving toward the life I always dreamed about. But now the reality of my situation came crashing down upon me, overloading my ability to reason and certainly preventing me from digesting what Switzer was claiming now.

"What?" I mumbled.

"That's stupid. If you're right, then why wouldn't they protect him more?" Max argued.

"Yeah, he's almost died three times," Theodore reminded him.

Ceesar waved his arm in the air, dismissing the objection. "I assure you, I'm right. I've had a lot of time to think about this. Everything adds up. Your little friend is very valuable."

"It still doesn't explain why you're here," Ketheria said. "You're still a knudnik to those on the rings."

"Oh, I'm far worse than that now." He smiled.

If it really was Switzer, there was only one reason he would come back. "Greed," I said. "It has to do with money."

Ceesar held one finger to his nose and pointed at me with the other. "Exactly. They've been saving up for you, Dumbwire. They've built you a nest egg. Why do you think the Ancients did all this work with the crystal mines and building this place? Why did the Keepers defend it so hard? The Ancients' Treasure."

"What?" I said.

"An unfathomable amount of money," Ceesar exclaimed.

"Over a decillion moonstones," Cala added.

The other pirates stirred in anticipation.

"Decillion?" Max said.

"A one with thirty-three zeros," Theodore said. "That's a lot of money."

"Precisely," Ceesar added. "And I plan to take it. I figure I had to go through far worse than you. I deserve that money."

"Then take it. I don't want the money," I told him.

Ceesar clasped his thick hands behind his neck and strolled over to the window looking into the garden where Charlie was attacked. He shook his head and said, "That was my plan, but once again you messed that up. You've always messed things up for me, split-screen, but now you're going to fix it. Now, *you* are going to help *me*."

"How did I mess things up?"

"Buzz."

"Buzz?"

"You see, the treasure is at the center of Tromaine," he informed us.

"You can't go in there," Theodore protested. "Citizens only."

"Except during the Chancellor's Challenge," I said, realizing where this was headed.

Switzer turned. "You've gotten smarter since I left."

"*You* haven't," Max said. "Even if you wanted to play, a Citizen has to sponsor you, and no one is going to let a wormhole pirate inside their precious city."

"Athooyi will," I said. "That's what you're planning."

"Right again! What have they been feeding you here?" Switzer joked, but I wasn't laughing.

"You see, Buzz and I were so good at that foolish little game that I convinced Athooyi we could win, but now that Buzz has been locked away, thanks to you, I need a new team."

"Absolutely not," I told him.

"Never," Ketheria hissed.

"Oh, you will. The Citizens display the treasure at the Champion's Ceremony. The Chancellor loves to show it off, but I plan to take it before the buffoon ever gets the chance," he said, and motioned to the wormhole pirate closest to me. He reached forward and clamped his steel hands on my arms.

"Watch out for the right one," Ceesar snickered.

"What are you doing, Switzer?" Max yelled at him, but Ceesar—or rather, Switzer—only cocked his head, smiling at her in a peculiar way as if he was contemplating something.

Switzer stood up and pointed at Ketheria, Max, and Theodore. "If you three don't play on my team for the Chancellor's Challenge, then he dies," Switzer cried and then pointed at me. "No theatrics. Just a quick death. Right here, right now."

"We'll play," Max said without hesitation.

"I thought so," he replied.

"Why all three of them, Switzer? You only need one. Take me," I yelled.

Switzer turned toward me. "You still are rather stupid, or maybe just ill informed. The Challenge requires *four* players. One bait, one tracker, and two substitutes. More blood for their money. Keeps the matches going longer."

I thought of the Citizen registering her four knudniks with Tinker. He was right. She had used the word *team* and had dragged four players up to Tinker's counter. My body flushed with rage. There was no way I would let him do this. This was a death sentence for my friends and my sister.

"Why, Switzer? I'm the better player; let me play," I begged.

Switzer shook his head dramatically. "Oh, I know you are. You might even have a chance in there, but I want a little payback. *None* of this would have happened to me if you had done what I said on the *Renaissance*. All you had to do was talk to Mother and help me take that ship away from here. We'd probably being living fat on some nice little oxygen-pumping planet right now, but no, you had to do it your way. You had to drag us to this corrupt, maggot-infested Ferris wheel."

"I didn't have a choice," I hissed.

"So you've told me. Well, you don't have a choice now, either. You're gonna watch your friends die. That's *your* punishment for *your* decision. They die, and you get to live with it."

"If you remember, we already had to watch one of our friends die," Dalton spoke up, his voice low and rough. Switzer stared at him but said nothing, then awkwardly turned back to me.

"Switzer, don't," I pleaded with him. "You can win this thing if you use me. Let *me* play."

"I don't need to win! Haven't you figured that out by now? I just need a team that Athooyi *thinks* will win to get me through those gates. Once I'm inside, no one can stop me from snatching the Ancients' Treasure. I'll be gone by the time your little friends are diced up and boiled in this cosmic soup they love to talk so much about."

"You think you're just going to walk away from Athooyi?" I shouted. "If he's financing all of this, don't you think he expects you to win? I've seen him get upset over losing a bet on a student's match. What do you think he's going to do at the Chancellor's Challenge when he discovers you're not there to win? Those creatures that protect him will hunt you down for the rest of your life. I'm *sure* of it."

Switzer paused. The other wormhole pirates began muttering in the shadows.

"Silence! He knows nothing!" Switzer bellowed.

"I can win, Switzer. Take me," I begged.

"Obviously you've never seen a Challenge before. It doesn't matter what combination you put in there; you will lose."

"But I can cheat," I said.

"What?"

"I am a softwire. I can slip into their computer and influence the game. I will make sure we win."

"You're lying," he scoffed.

"No, I'm not. I do it every time. How do you think I win? You need me. I can win the match for you, and you can get the Ancients' Treasure. Athooyi will be happy, and you can leave a free man—well, as free as a wormhole pirate can be."

Switzer's henchmen were getting noisier. Switzer rubbed his bald head, pondering what I had just told him.

"If you're lying . . ."

"I'm not," I insisted.

"Fine, then, who are you going to replace?" he asked me.

I looked at Max. She was shaking her head. Of course she

wanted to play, but *I* didn't want her to play. What would I do if she died? Just thinking about it was like getting punched in the stomach. But then, I couldn't let Ketheria play either. My mind simply would not allow it. She was my flesh and blood, my sister. I couldn't risk either of them. If we were going to win this, Theodore was the obvious choice. He was the weakest. But if I failed, I was sentencing the others to death.

"Do it, JT. Replace me!" he shouted. "I'm the worst player here. You can't win with me. You know that."

"Maybe if you hadn't spent so much time sucking on that scope, you wouldn't be such a failure to your friends now, would you?" Switzer said, sneering.

"Shut up!" Theodore yelled at him.

I was surprised. Switzer sat back as if slapped, his face awash in amazement. It was the first time Theodore had ever stood up to Switzer in his entire life. But Switzer only laughed at Theodore's expense before turning back to me.

"Tough, isn't he?" he said with a smirk. "No matter who you pick, you know the others are going to die. So whom do you let live, Dumbwire? Huh? Your sister, your best friend, or your girl-friend? Please be quick, won't you? I'm getting bored."

I couldn't make that choice. My mind had locked up. Somewhere inside me, something was screaming at me to pick Ketheria, to get her out of harm's way even if it meant the rest of us dying, but I wanted her close to me. That was the safest place for her, and I knew I could win with Max. I just knew I could. Switzer was right; Theodore was a liability, and we would all die if I didn't make him sit out the match.

"JT, pick me," Theodore pleaded.

"Okay, I'll play instead of Theodore," I said.

"I figured you would say that," Ceesar said, and he removed a small crystal device from his belt and pointed it at Max.

"No!" I screamed.

"Be quiet. I'm not going to kill her. Yet," he said.

The air behind Max rippled as if it had turned into water, and two cloaked figures surfaced from somewhere. They clamped their hands around Max. The other pirates, anticipating my response, surrounded her.

"So predictable," Ceesar sighed.

"I said Theodore!"

"Love is the best motivator in the universe," Switzer said, and pushed Theodore aside. He stood close and glared down upon me. "You don't help me, Softwire, you try and think up some stupid little plan to get out of this, and she dies!" He shouted the last words while thrusting his fist toward her. "Something very painful, too." He turned to Cala, smiling. "That just sounds good, doesn't it?"

"You won't do it," Ketheria scoffed.

Switzer turned on Ketheria. "You think I won't kill one little girl? I let them have my entire crew! Look at your Guarantor. We're talking about the Ancients' Treasure here. Don't underestimate me, freak."

Max looked at me and whispered, "Don't do this, JT."

But that was not a choice for me. Of course I would do this.

"What if he dies?" Theodore asked. "How will you get his treasure? I'm sure you need him to open it."

Ceesar held up the glass tomb containing my arm. "I just need a team," he said. "I have everything else I need."

"But why do it this way?" I asked him.

"C'mon. This is so much more fun, don't you think? Besides, Athooyi believes I'm in it to win, and he believes you imbeciles are his only salvation. He has no idea I'm there for the bigger prize."

That's why they wanted Charlie out of the way. He refused to sell us to Athooyi, and now *Charlie* had paid the price.

"When does the Chancellor's Challenge start?" I said.

"No, JT," Max pleaded.

"The last cycle of next phase. If you speak to anyone about this, if you breathe a word to the Keepers, Dumbwire, I swear by all the energy in the Universe that you will never see Maxine Bennett again. Do you understand me?"

No one spoke. I looked at Max. She shook her head at me. How could I not do this? Everyone was here because of me. Everyone was always getting hurt because of me. I needed to fix things once and for all. "Listen, Ceesar, Switzer, whatever you want to be called," I said. "When I do this, we're done. You return Max and you leave the Rings of Orbis. I never want to see you again. I will play your stupid game, but if you do not keep your end of the bargain, I will hunt you down to the end of the universe and I *will* kill you."

Switzer snickered. "It's a big universe," he said. "And such a big threat for a runt."

"Do we have a deal?"

"Don't, JT," Max said.

"Deal," Switzer said.

This was the second time in my life that I had made a deal with Switzer. The first time hadn't gone too well, either.

Switzer waved the crystal again, and Max was gone.

"Max!" Ketheria cried.

The wormhole pirates created a clear passage to the chute for their leader. "Not a word," Ceesar breathed as he passed. "Or she dies."

"What do I do now?" I asked.

"Prepare for your end," Cala hissed as he strolled past.

12

I stared at the empty light chute for a long time after Switzer left. What I felt most was shock, as if I had stood in the center of a meteor shower and I was the only one who hadn't gotten wiped out. I had Cala right in front of me, but now he felt insignificant. How did this happen? How did things get so bad? I did not ask to be the Scion, if what Switzer said was even true. I simply wanted a place for my sister and me to live, a place to call home. *What did my parents do?* The words echoed in my brain. *Did they know? Did they pick this for me? When do I get to choose? When do I get to say what* I *want?*

"What are we going to do?" Theodore mumbled.

"*We're* going to prepare for the toughest Quest-Nest match we've ever played," I told him. "Can you contact Sul-sah about scoping some of the other challengers?"

"Are you sure, JT?"

"I'm very sure."

● ● ●

I wouldn't dare risk telling Theylor about Switzer. I thought about telling Charlie before I corrected myself: *He's dead.* But would I even have told him? I could not risk Max's life in any way. I tried not to think about the outcome of the match—I only thought of rescuing Max. Several of the other kids were glancing at me as if I were already dead. Ketheria told me to ignore them and added, "You don't have to do this."

"Yes, I do," I calmly told her.

"Do you really think he will return Max to us?"

"Why? What are you not telling me? Do you read something in his mind?"

"I didn't read anything. He's using something that won't let me in. It's really more of a feeling I have when I'm around him. It's very difficult to explain, but we don't know him anymore, JT. It's been a long time—for Switzer, anyway."

"I can't forget Max," I told her. "It just isn't an option."

Ketheria smiled. "Then we must prepare. Maybe we can win this."

"Whoa, whoa, there. What's all this *we* stuff? It's just gonna be me and maybe Theodore."

Ketheria shook her head. "You know yourself it's a team, a team of four. That's how they play the Chancellor's Challenge. There are four rounds plus the championship match. Two players could never last that long."

"I'll get someone else, Ketheria. No way."

"You can't win without me," she insisted. "You know that, so contact Vairocina. *We* need all the help we can get."

This was already out of hand, and we weren't even close to the match, but I couldn't think of another way. I agreed with Ketheria (for now, anyway) and contacted Vairocina. I could tell her. I could trust Vairocina. I *needed* to trust her, and I made Vairocina promise not to tell a soul. Max's life was at stake.

"This is very serious," Vairocina said as we whispered in a dark corner of Charlie's room. Everyone was asleep, and I wanted no one to hear us.

"That's why I need your help."

"Tromaine, the area where the Challenge is played, is bubbled from the central computer. I cannot help you once you are inside. In fact, all of the information concerning the Chancellor's Challenge is stored on their computer inside the city."

"Why would such a valuable treasure be located in a city outside the Keepers' control?"

"I can't answer that," she said.

"You can't or you won't?"

Vairocina slumped slightly. "That is unnecessary, JT," she said. "I may function inside the central computer, but I owe my life to you. The central computer has absolutely no contact with the computer of Inner Tromaine. It is a sacred place. That is why the treasure is kept there, outside of the Keepers' reach. I would answer your questions if I could. Always."

"I'm sorry. It's getting very hard for me to trust people on Orbis."

"I understand. That's why I'm coming with you," she said.

"What?"

"There is enough memory space inside your arm for me to fit quite comfortably. I may not have all of the same functions I have inside the central computer, but I can compress myself to fit inside your arm. I will be a valuable asset once inside."

I saw nothing wrong with her idea except for one thing. "What if I don't make it out of there?"

"You will."

"And if I don't?"

"I have traveled from the end of the universe, jumping from computer to computer. Do not worry about me."

"How are you going to get into my arm?"

"Your softwire cannot facilitate the transfer. You must make some sort of hardwire connection."

Max could do it. I knew she could, but she wasn't here.

"Do you have anyone to assist you?" she asked me.

Who could wire my arm so Vairocina could hop in for a ride? I needed someone who wouldn't ask any questions, either.

"What if he won't do it?" Ketheria asked me as I held the pod door open for her.

"That's why I brought you along. I think he likes you."

The pod slid effortlessly up one of the sloped supports beneath the Labyrinth. It was a gamble to seek Tinker's help, and I knew it. But I remembered the way he had helped Ketheria. I needed to exploit every advantage available to me if I was going to survive the Chancellor's Challenge. Losing was not an option.

"Of all the buildings on Orbis, why doesn't the Labyrinth use a light chute?" I asked Ketheria.

"Why do you care?"

I didn't, actually. I was trying to think about anything except Max. I didn't want to think about where they were holding her. I didn't want to think about what Ceesar might be doing to her, or if she was scared. I didn't want to think about any of it, but I realized I wasn't doing a very good job.

"Stop thinking about Max," she said.

"Get out of my head."

"I don't have to read your mind. It's written all over your face," she whispered. "Don't worry—we'll get her."

"And then what?"

"You'll think of something."

I saw two Citizens registering contestants at Tinker's booth. *How many players are there?* I wondered. We lingered behind a sculpture of some nameless Citizen, cautiously waiting for the opportunity to speak with Tinker. A large vid-screen floated past us, flashing an image of the last champion from the Chancellor's Challenge. The thick, fleshy alien with four gold-covered spikes sprouting from his head glared down at us. A large blue emblem scarred his ample belly.

"Was the helmet unsatisfactory?" Tinker called to us from his booth.

"No, it was fine, thank you," Ketheria said, and we ventured out from the shadows.

"Why are you hiding?" he asked.

"Can we talk?" I whispered.

"Aren't we talking now?" He frowned.

"Privately," Ketheria said.

Tinker led us into the same room where he had given us the Quest-Nest helmets. The young female we met before was kneeling before a shallow stone bowl, muttering something I couldn't hear. I saw a thin blue stream of smoke rise from the bowl, illuminated only by the light streaming through the three arched windows cut in the wall. Tinker struck his metal appendages against the stone without warning. The female jumped, gathered her simple cloth robe, and scurried out the door.

"Please sit if you'd like," Tinker offered. "I can tell by the way you're looking at me that this might take a while."

He cleared a bench for us under the windows.

"Thank you," Ketheria said.

But I couldn't sit still. I needed Tinker's help, yet I was troubled by the fact that he knew Ceesar as well. It was essential for me to identify Tinker's loyalties first. I pointed at the etchings on his windows, the ones that were the same as those carved into the walls of our own estate, and said, "Aren't those OIO streams?"

Tinker moved toward the door, glancing at me from the corner of his eye. I continued to admire the glass while he continued to size me up and make sure no one else was near. He tapped a wall control with his cumbersome fingers. The door appeared to lock us in, or everyone else out. It didn't really matter.

"Why do you speak of OIO?" he asked me from the other side of the room.

"Are you a believer, too?" I replied.

For an awkward-looking alien, Tinker moved very fast, towering over me in an instant. "Who are you?" he wanted to know.

"We're knudniks that need your help," Ketheria replied.

Tinker sniffed at the air as if he was hunting for something rotten. "I've already helped you," he said.

"This is different," she told him.

"Trefaldoors refer to them as cosmic winds, and Samirans call them cosmic rivers. Is that right? Or is it the other way around? I can never remember," I said.

"It's all energy," he mumbled.

"So not only are we both knudniks, but we also both like this OIO stuff."

"Stuff!" Tinker shouted, standing tall and stretching out his hands. "A true believer would never refer to it as *stuff*."

"Is Ceesar a believer, like *us*?" I questioned, ignoring his comment.

"Why do you speak of him? Is he paying for this?"

"Have you spoken to him recently?"

"What are these games?" Tinker demanded, and drove the steely point of his index finger into the workbench. "I am no more aware of *his* dealings than I am of yours. He pays for my services and I fulfill his requests, nothing more."

That was enough for me. "I need a hardwire uplink port," I told him. "Capable of transferring a lot of data."

"But you are a softwire. What do you need one for?"

"I just need one."

"Come here," he demanded.

I looked at Ketheria.

"Come here!" he repeated.

With small steps, I moved toward the workbench. Tinker extended a metallic arm toward the wall. "Stand there," he said, and kicked away a small wooden stool. "Assume the Circle of Life."

This was a test, and I was about to fail. *The Circle of Life?* I knew he was talking about OIO, but I did not know the reference.

"Human or Nagool?" Ketheria called out.

Tinker squinted at Ketheria, grinding his teeth together. They were metal, too. "Nagool. Humans are still ignorant," he hissed.

Nagool? Ketheria was sending me a clue. Each time I observed Nagool masters, they were shuffling about with their arms stretched out to their sides. *Floaters,* I remembered someone calling them. I extended my arms, with my feet shoulder-width apart, and raised my chin. I hoped this was the Circle of Life.

Tinker kicked my feet together. "Close the node," he demanded, and then scrounged through his workbench as I glanced at Ketheria. She smiled at me and nodded. Apparently I had passed the test.

Tinker returned with a small device suspended by a chain. It consisted of two concave crystal receptors attached by a spiraling wire. It bore an uncanny resemblance to the doodles Ketheria had been scribbling when she was sick.

Tinker raised the device over my head. Afraid to expose my ignorance, I didn't dare ask what it was. When he moved the gadget out in front of my face, I could see the small crystal scoops begin to rotate around the spiral. Tinker never took his weary eyes off the tool, almost as if he were willing an answer out of it, some sort of signal from the thing. He moved it in front of my chest and it stopped, reversed its motion, and began spinning in the opposite direction. Tinker lifted his head, his eyes widening. He repeated the movement, starting above my head, once more. The device did the same thing. Then Tinker moved it farther out, and it reversed direction once more. He moved it out over each hand and around my body; each time, the tool switched direction.

"What's wrong?" I asked him.

Tinker spun around and cleared his workbench with a swoosh of his mechanical arm. He dragged a thick leather block from the shelf and pried it open. It was a book. I had seen pictures of one on the *Renaissance,* but never a real one. Tinker tore at it, flipping through it, searching manically for something, an answer maybe.

Then he was upon me again, holding the piece of equipment up and repeating the patterns. Each time the device did the same thing.

Tinker slammed the book shut. "You must leave," he said. His weary eyes now glowed red with fear.

"But the port?" I said. "I need the—"

Tinker grabbed a neural implant port from the mess on the

floor and threw it at me, hitting my chest. "Take it, but leave. Leave now."

"What's the matter, Tinker?" Ketheria asked.

"I have done nothing," he hissed, his eyes darting about the room. "I am a faithful follower. I am worthy."

"I can't do this myself," I said, holding up the port.

"I fear your reprisal if I fail," he said, and lowered his head, bending his body in submission.

"Tinker?"

He would not stand up. "Forgive me," he whispered, pointing toward the door.

"Let's go, Johnny," Ketheria whispered. "We'll find another way."

Outside Tinker's room, I asked Ketheria, "What happened to him?"

"I don't know. All I sensed was fear. Enormous amounts of fear."

"What was that thing he had?"

"It's used to read a person's nodes. It's called an Ara."

I shrugged. It was all nonsense to me. "What's wrong with my nodes?"

Tinker's erratic behavior was the least of my worries. I had managed to get a port, but it wouldn't do Vairocina any good if it weren't attached to me. I needed Max. She would have this figured out in no time.

"What are you going to do?" Theodore asked me next cycle as we headed to the Illuminate.

"Tell Vairocina I can't do it, I suppose."

I walked mindlessly across the plaza and into the Illuminate. A cold gray fog had isolated me from the rest of my world. I welcomed it. I could let nothing in. I had to think of a way to save my sister and my friends. I had to get Max back. It actually hurt my head to think about anything else, and I passed on this cycle's tap. I watched while Theodore and Ketheria grabbed theirs. I *was* going to save Max's life, but in order to do that, I would have to risk both of *their* lives.

"There's going to be some sort of presentation," Theodore mentioned after he uplinked the tap.

"In the quad," Ketheria added. "It's for the Challenge."

"We're supposed to wait outside," Theodore instructed, and I followed.

I enjoyed the distraction. There was no way I could concentrate on my studies, anyway. We walked back outside and stood among the other students.

"How many possible outcomes with the sort?" I asked Theodore.

"Eighty-one, but that doesn't take into account the computer interpretation of the selection. That number is incalculable," he said.

"You've tried?"

"I've tried."

"Look," Ketheria exclaimed, pointing across the quad.

A six-wheeled craft dragging some sort of slick metal container maneuvered into the plaza. When it stopped, the container began to swell, branching and forming into a sturdy-looking, multilevel stage equipped with vid-screens and flashing lights. The vehicle backed toward the stage, disappearing underneath it as the Chancellor of Orbis 3 emerged in the center screen— the same Chancellor who had given the fake Theodore his award for the highest test score.

"Noble Citizens," his voiced boomed from the highest point on the platform.

"That's impressive!" Theodore gushed, and I had to agree. The stage was the first thing to actually take my mind off the match.

"It is my esteemed privilege, as the Chancellor's Challenge approaches, to honor those Citizens who celebrate the glory of our great culture through their own sacrifice."

His mention of the Challenge reignited my fears. "What has a Citizen ever sacrificed?" I scoffed. Ketheria shushed me, but Theodore nodded in agreement.

"We must show our gratitude and pay tribute to those among you who have aspired to honor themselves and their families by entering these noblest of games."

"What's so noble about dying?" Theodore mumbled.

"Look upon these fine Citizens and let them feel your joy as they stand proudly in front of you."

My body vibrated from the surge of music that exploded from the stage. The students cheered as each honored Citizen mounted the steps of the stage and stood under the Chancellor's vid-screen. First they waved at the Chancellor and then slowly, as their platforms rotated, they turned to face the admiration of the crowd.

"I don't get this!" Theodore shouted over the music and cheers. "These guys chose to go out and get themselves killed?"

Theodore was right. Why would a Citizen risk his life like this? As far as I figured, the match was just another way the Citizens exploited knudniks. But here were four Citizens willing to die for the *honor* of it. I didn't get it.

Before I could comment, though, a sparkle of gold near the contestant farthest to the right caught the corner of my eye. I leaned on Theodore and stood on my toes to see over the other students. The gold sparkled again, and my eyes traced the origin to the contestant on the farthest platform. Immediately I dropped my head and forced my way through the crowd.

"Johnny! Where are you going?" Ketheria called out.

"This way!" I shouted. "Come on!"

I needed to get closer. I needed to see it clearly, with my own eyes.

The crowd resisted my efforts to get closer to the stage, but I only pushed harder, leaning forward and never letting my feet stop.

"What's wrong, JT?" Theodore yelled, but I just kept pushing.

Something about the fourth Citizen seemed very familiar to me. Maybe it was the slender arm waving to the crowd, or maybe the glowing porcelain skin? But it was the glitter of gold that threw me off. At first I thought it was a reflection of something metallic, maybe armor or something on the stage. But when I stretched up and over the crowd and caught a glimpse of the gold-colored *hair,* I panicked. That could only belong to one person.

When I reached the far side of the quad, I could see Riis standing solemnly on the stage, waving to the crowd.

"Riis, no! What are you doing?" I screamed up at her.

She turned toward the sound of her name. She stopped waving when she saw me.

"Why?" I yelled.

She turned away without a response, but I didn't need one. The look in her eyes was very familiar to me. It held the despair and hopelessness of someone locked in servitude, toiling toward a goal that was not her own. The knudniks on the Rings of Orbis shared that vacant stare, and now Riis did, too.

"Don't do this, Riis!" I shouted, and the platform began to move away from me.

"What is Riis doing up there?" Theodore asked.

I didn't know, but I did know two things. First, I would have to fight Riis in the tournament, and second, she would have to lose. At that moment I hated Switzer more than I would have thought possible. He had put me in this situation for his own gain. He was willing to sacrifice the lives of everyone close to me to satisfy his greed. I made a promise to myself to make him pay for that. And that was a promise I planned to keep.

"They will honor their families in battle," the Chancellor shouted over the cheering crowd. "These are great Citizens. Be proud of them."

The platform Riis stood on shifted, and she sat as the stage hovered higher before reaching a wingless shuttle floating in the air. I shouted at her again, but it was too late now. She was gone. I would not see her again until the Chancellor's Challenge. The next time I saw Riis, I would have to kill her.

13

I did not return to the Illuminate again. I spent every moment preparing for my match. If I wasn't setting strategies or scoping past players, I fantasized about my revenge on Switzer. If I wasn't doing either of those, I thought about my cycle with Max, standing and listening to the music.

Sul-sah, of course, was not interested in letting us scope for free. After I traded my pob, Theodore and I began taking items from the house to barter. The first thing I brought was one of the small crystal sculptures that adorned the house. Sul-sah wasn't impressed, so I collected as many pobs as the other kids would give up, but eventually I began taking larger items: vid-screens, furniture, and computer components that ran the house.

"JT, I think you need to look at this," Theodore said, removing the tetrascope from his head. Theodore had agreed to only scope other players.

"What is it?"

"It's Riis's last game."

I found the interface in the lobby and quickly accessed her cube. Riis was playing recklessly, almost sloppily. Her thoughts screamed louder than her actions, and her emotions filled my own consciousness.

I will not do it. I will not do it! How dare they do this to me? Do they not love their own child? I despise him. Can they not understand this?

In the game, Riis stepped around the corner without hesitation, firing her plasma rifle at anything that moved.

I'll give them honor. They can't refuse me once it's done. First Families. I spit at First Families! The Chancellor's Challenge will be my salvation. There will be no union of profit when I'm done. I will win, and the prize money will take me far away from Dop. Far away from this place.

Despite her erratic behavior, Riis fought extremely well and never missed a shot. She played better than most players I had scoped. I realized that my friend would be my biggest threat in the arena.

I removed the scope and whispered to Theodore, "Her parents are planning to marry her off."

"To Dop, of all people," Theodore replied. "She's going to be hard to beat."

Theodore was right. Not about Riis being a tough opponent—that was a given—but about us *having* to beat her. This was not a match I could lose, and she stood in my way. What else could I do?

"You can't think about it," Theodore said.

But I did anyway.

There were many skilled players entering the Challenge. One player, a creature from a distant star cluster, seemed to have gained mythical status with the Citizens. He played only in these types of death matches, and he never lost. Sul-sah told me he was favored to win.

"Thanks," I replied.

"I'm just telling you the odds." He shrugged.

"What are the odds on us?" Theodore asked.

"You're not registered yet."

"Why?" I asked.

"I don't know—strategy maybe," he replied. "Some Citizens don't reveal who they're entering until the last minute. Keeps people from backing out. More prize money."

"Or someone doesn't want the Keepers to know we're playing," I said.

"Could be."

"So we're gonna meet some players that we haven't scoped," Theodore said.

"Probably."

It just kept getting worse.

"I'm finished," I said. "What happens now, happens. I'm ready for the Chancellor's Challenge."

We returned home to find one of Switzer's flunkies waiting for us in the garden, the one who mispronounced Switzer's name and called him Ceesar.

"Take these," he barked. The words were almost incomprehensible.

"What are they?" I said, but he did not reply. It was obvious what they were. The green and silver costumes were some sort of uniform, reinforced with a thin protective material over the arms, chest, and neck.

"First spoke. Next cycle. These are the chute coordinates." He tossed a small scroll to Theodore. Theodore opened it, and the numbers flashed on the screen, then it disappeared.

"I hoped you memorized it," I said, glad that he had tossed the screen to Theodore and not me.

"I got it," he replied.

The alien was about to leave when I said, "Where's Max?"

"You be there, she be there." Then he left.

His visit made the severity of the situation all the more real for me. If I thought too much, it overwhelmed me, and I couldn't let that happen. Theodore held the uniform up to his chest, checking its size.

"We're really going to do this," he said.

"It's the only way to get Max back."

"But do we actually have to play?"

"What do you mean?"

"Switzer's only using us to get inside. Why can't we slip away before we have to play? Can't Vairocina help us do that?"

It wasn't a bad idea. Switzer said Max would be at the game. We could go along with it right up until the Chancellor's Challenge started and then somehow slip out of the city before

277 ⋅⋅

ever stepping foot in the arena. It was so simple, I don't know why I hadn't thought of it before.

"You're assuming we can get Max and slip away, though," I said.

"If we have her near us, we can make some sort of commotion or something. A distraction. And then take off."

"Athooyi would see that Switzer wasn't even planning on winning."

"And those monsters with him might help."

"That's a lot of assumptions," I said. "I can think of a dozen things that could go wrong."

"Got a better idea?"

"No, but if we're going to use Vairocina, then there's something I need your help with," I told him.

"I can't do this, JT," Theodore said, holding the chow synth knife over my arm. Vairocina floated in the air above us as we attempted to install the neural port into my arm ourselves. Everyone else was asleep.

"The incision should be higher, Theodore. The connectors are located closer to the elbow," Vairocina instructed.

"I can't," he hissed.

"You have to. She'll tell you how to do everything."

Theodore's hand shook as he lowered the knife.

"Wait," I said.

"What?" he complained, pulling away.

"I forgot to turn the pain sensors off," I said, and I interfaced with the controls inside my mind's eye. "There. Cut me."

"Oh, cripes," he moaned.

"And quit shaking; you'll make a horrible scar."

"Actually, if he makes the incision small enough, the skin will knit itself back together by next spoke and you won't notice anything," she said.

"Keep it small, Theodore."

"I can't take this pressure!" he said, placing the knife against my skin.

"A little higher," she said. "A little to your left. Now!"

Theodore pushed the knife into my skin. I didn't feel a thing. It was like watching him cut plastic, except that he was slicing into my arm.

"Now pull the knife ten centimeters away from his elbow," she said. Theodore did as he was told, and a thick stream of yellow fluid followed his blade. "Good. That's enough."

Theodore sat back on the kitchen stool, exhausted. "I can't believe I just did that," he breathed.

"Now put your fingers into his arm and pull the skin apart. Try not to tear it," Vairocina instructed.

"Oh, come on, you're kidding me! Can't you do it?"

"I don't have the same ability as a normal holograph, or I would," she said. "You have to do this, Theodore."

He sat up, scrunching his face, and carefully inserted his thumb and index finger into the hole he had made in my arm, forcing more yellow fluid out.

"Push the synthetic muscle aside and you should see a small chip. Attached to it will be a small blue ribbon. That's what we need. That's where we will make our connection."

"This is disgusting," he said as he nudged the artificial muscle tissue aside. It made a squishing sound.

"There it is," I said.

"You should be able to disconnect it easily," she told him.

Using his other hand, he reached in.

"It's too small," he complained.

"Try," I said.

"I think I'm gonna be sick."

"No, you're not. Just grab the ribbon."

"But I can't."

"Ow," I yelled, and Theodore jerked back, disconnecting the ribbon.

"Why did you do that?" he screamed.

"It worked, didn't it?" I smiled.

"We're almost done," Vairocina said. "JT, can you move your fingers?"

I tried to wriggle them, but they did not respond. My arm was useless. "No," I told her.

"Good," she said. "This is where we must connect the port."

I passed the port to Theodore. Attached to the device was a similar ribbon to the one Theodore had just disconnected inside my arm. Once he attached it, Vairocina said, "We don't have long. Soon a synaptic connection will start to grow and we will not be able to remove it."

"What do we do?" I said, a little panicked.

"We need to attach it to any device linked to the central computer," she said.

I pointed to the counter and said, "How about the chow synth?"

"That will work," she replied.

Theodore shook his head. "We traded it," he reminded me.

"You traded the chow synth?"

"You were there. We had nothing else to give Sul-sah. Besides, we can eat at the Illuminate."

"We need something quickly," Vairocina urged us.

"What about a pob?" I asked.

"No, it needs to be directly linked to the central computer to handle the size of my program."

"The light chute," I said.

We both moved toward the counter, and my arm fell limp to my side, the port swinging wildly.

"Careful," she warned us.

I wished Max were there. She knew how to take anything apart. She may not have always put things back together, but she could have done this. Theodore and I just stared at the chute.

"Remove the keypad," Vairocina instructed.

Theodore ran back to the kitchen and returned with the knife, attacking the panel.

"Just pop the cover; we need to get out of here next cycle," I told him.

With a click, the cover of the keypad fell to the floor.

"Look for the same type of connection," Vairocina said.

"There's too many," he said, panicked.

"It's there," she said forcefully.

"How much longer?" I asked her.

"We need to hurry," she whispered.

"I got it!" Theodore exclaimed. "Put your arm up here."

I held my arm while Theodore pushed his fingers back in and made the connection.

"That will work. I will just be a moment. Do not do anything until you hear from me again. Do not break that connection," she said, and disappeared.

Theodore and I stood there, looking at each other.

"Thanks," I told him.

"Do you think she'll be able to get us out of Inner Tromaine?"

"Once she's inside their computer, she can do anything," I assured him.

"How's *she* gonna get out? Of your arm, I mean."

I'd never thought about that part. "I don't know," I replied. "Maybe we should bring the port with us."

"I'm not doing that again," he said with a grimace.

"JT, is this normal?" Theodore asked, looking at the connection he had made inside my arm.

"What?"

"Those things," he said, pointing. "Is that supposed to happen?"

Thin, snaking tendrils were worming their way from the port and attaching themselves to the connector in my arm. "I don't know," I said. "Vairocina?" But there was no answer.

Theodore reached in to disconnect it. "Don't!" I shrieked.

"Where is she?"

"You can't break the connection yet," I said. "Vairocina!"

"JT, there's more. They're going deeper. What are they gonna do?"

Where was Vairocina? Why wasn't she answering? Theodore was right; the port was making a deeper connection. I could never get it out now.

Suddenly I heard Vairocina call my name inside my head.

"Pull it!" I shouted to Theodore.

He ripped the port away. The tendrils from the foreign device sparked and burrowed into my arm. A sharp pain stabbed my arm and ran up to my head, giving me an instant headache. I felt dizzy, and my arm tingled despite the fact that I had turned off the pain sensors.

"JT?" Vairocina said, louder and clearer than ever before. She felt more present than my own thoughts.

"The port started doing something like it was trying to connect itself," I told her.

"Tell Theodore not to remove it yet," she said.

"Too late."

"Then reconnect your arm."

I reached in myself, fingering the tiny connection, and the ribbon connected with a click.

"Try to move your fingers," she said.

I did, but they hesitated. I moved my thumb, but my index finger wriggled instead. It took two or three tries to get it right. "Something's not right," I told her.

"What's wrong?" Theodore asked.

"We need to repair your arm," Vairocina said.

"We don't have time. The Chancellor's Challenge is the next cycle!" I shouted.

"What's wrong? It doesn't work?" Theodore asked again.

"Get some sleep. I'll see what I can do," Vairocina said. "There's a lot I can do from in here. I just hope I have enough time."

"Me, too," I mumbled.

"Are you going to tell me what's wrong? Are you talking to her now?" Theodore begged.

"Nothing's wrong. Everything's fine. You did great," I told him. "Let's get some sleep. We have a game to win."

But I didn't sleep much. How could I? I might very well be dead next cycle, and so could my friends. If I was the Scion, why was there no protection for me? Why would they throw me into the mix of things on the Rings of Orbis? Was I supposed to protect myself? Was it a test? I hated tests, especially ones where I could die.

I got up before everyone else and sat in the garden near the same spot where Charlie had been killed. For some reason, it comforted me. I was trying to get my arm to respond more quickly before anyone else noticed the damage, but Vairocina said she needed more time. As I flexed my fingers, I followed a comet hanging in the darkened sky and wondered what my father would do. Nothing came to me. How could it? I really didn't know him. All I ever heard of him were stories, rumors, or even lies. His personal files, the ones encrypted on the

Renaissance, were lost to me forever. I could only guess what he would do. It was not a comforting feeling.

I *was* going to save Max, though. That much I knew. Once Switzer released her to me, I would get us out of Inner Tromaine before any of us set foot in their labyrinth. I refused to risk their lives in the Chancellor's Challenge. And when we were safe, I was going straight to the Keepers. I was finished playing their game. If I was the Scion, I wanted answers, all of them. I would use whatever powers were available to me to figure this out. Even if I had to rip them out of the central computer myself. Knudnik or not, I was going to get my way. A voice inside my head—not Vairocina's, not a voice I had ever heard before— told me *that's* what my father would do.

14

I stood between Theodore and Ketheria as we stared up at the extraordinary gates of the Chancellor's Challenge Labyrinth.

"Who are they afraid of?" Theodore said, gawking at the curved steel doors, inlaid with a blue energy field.

"Us," I said.

"Can Vairocina see this?" Ketheria asked.

"I don't know. Vairocina, do you see what I see?" I asked her out loud.

"Somewhat," she said. "I've made a rudimentary connection to your optical nerves, but I need more computer power to get a clearer image."

"What did she say?" Theodore asked.

"She said, 'Kind of.'" It felt like I was on the *Renaissance* again, listening to Mother. I was the only one who could talk to her, and the other kids were always asking me what she said— the ones who believed me, anyway. There weren't many.

I searched for Switzer in the crowd, but it was difficult to see. Blocking the entrance to the Challenge stood a large group of Nagools, their arms outstretched in the Circle of Life. Five or six more aliens scurried about, stopping anyone who would listen to them.

"Stop the Chancellor's Challenge! Stop the Chancellor's Challenge!" they protested.

"Why?" I asked a female dressed in a red robe slashed and torn in different parts.

"They cannot return their cosmic energy to the great Source when they die in this manner. The violent death of each player releases destructive energy. They require cleansing before their source is returned to the Universe," she said, almost begging.

Another alien, eager to have someone listen to his pleas, joined in. "If you do not pay to watch, or gamble on such atrocities, they will stop the games," he added.

"But we're here to play," I informed him, holding my arms out and showing them the fight suit I was wearing.

The effect was the same as if I had kicked each of them in the stomach. After they digested my statement, they laid their hands upon me, moaning and pushing me toward the Nagools.

"Are you enslaved to perform this heinous act?" the male whispered as the female wailed, grabbing the attention of the Nagools.

"No," I said, "Well, yes, we're knudniks, if that's what you mean."

"You're all playing?"

I nodded and said, "We're all dressed the same." It only made them cry out more. Soon all of the protesters circled, nudging us toward the Nagools.

"Let them be!" someone shouted. It was Athooyi. Next to him stood Switzer and Max! Both were dressed in fight suits just like ours. Why? *Do they expect Max to play?* I wondered. The protesters lowered their heads and shuffled behind the Nagools. The Nagools, however, stood proudly and took the positions of the protesters.

"I urge you to release these ill-fated beings," one Nagool said, his voice calm like still water.

"I have the right to enter them in the contest," Athooyi argued, and the Nagool lowered his head, bringing his hands together.

"You do—and I have the right to protect the Universe. Please allow me to cleanse them before they meet their death," he pleaded.

I wanted to tell the Nagool *No thanks.* I wasn't planning on dying just yet.

"Do as you wish," Athooyi said. "But be quick."

Then it hit me. I thought of Tinker's reaction the other cycle. If I *were* the Scion, like Switzer said, wouldn't the Nagools notice it, too? It was the perfect time to make my distraction, and better yet, we weren't even inside the gates yet. I rushed toward the Nagool. The alien, with frozen white skin and the Circle of Life spiral marked across most of his face, reached out to me with long, pale arms.

Switzer saw what I was doing and leaped between us, preventing the Nagool from reaching me.

"There's no time for this, Athooyi. We're late already. They need to be registered. Back off, freak," Switzer ordered the Nagool.

"Let them do it," I protested, stepping toward the Nagool again.

Switzer pulled out a small cylindrical device tapered at booth ends. He squeezed it, and Max fell to her knees and let out a scream.

"Stop it!" Ketheria cried, and the Nagools wailed in unison.

What was that thing Switzer had? Did it work with the suit? What was its range?

"Get inside," he growled, shoving me toward the gate. "Don't even think about running."

"You're making a mistake!" yelled one of the protesters.

"By listening to you!" he shouted back, and hoisted Max up, pushing her toward me.

"Are you all right?" I whispered to her when she was next to me. I squeezed her hand.

"I'm all right now. Do you have a plan?" she whispered.

At that moment, I actually thought about making a run for it. I had not expected to have Max back so soon, but I was worried about the device Switzer had used on her.

"What was that thing he just used?" I whispered, looking across my shoulder. I was searching for an escape route back to the light chutes, but I spotted Cala lurking in the crowd.

"He put something in my neural port. I felt for it, but I couldn't find anything. I think the device works with what they put in my stomach."

Farther to Cala's left was another wormhole pirate and then another. I scanned the plaza. We were surrounded. Switzer was obviously prepared. I hoped that device didn't have a very long range.

"Just get inside," I told her. I needed time to readjust my plan.

I couldn't risk letting Switzer or Athooyi overhear us. Now that they had dropped Max right in my lap, I knew I could slip away once Switzer and his bandits snuck off to steal the Ancients' Treasure. But what if he took Max with him? There were too many holes in my plan, but there was no way I was actually going to let everyone go through with the Challenge.

"This should be a treat for you," Athooyi said, as if he forgot we were here to risk our lives for his gambling pleasures. "Very few knudniks have ever seen this part of Tromaine. It's very special to us."

"I'm sure it's every knudnik's dream to see your city before they're sent to the slaughter," Max replied.

"Do not be afraid," he comforted her, clutching the voice box over the hole in his chest. "I am confident you will win."

We would be gone long before the winner was ever decided.

Two holographic guards sat in elevated booths at the center of the huge gates that opened to Inner Tromaine. Behind them sparkled a blue energy field.

"Citizen?" the guard to my left asked, never looking up.

"Inai Gi Athooyi," he replied, and the other guard scanned an O-dat.

"Four combatants to register," he read, and then looked up, counting the ones wearing the battle suits. "Why the fifth one? You know the rules, Athooyi."

"I am aware of the rules, but apparently, you are not. I am allowed to carry one substitute in case my team cannot pass the weight class. I'm concerned about the smallest one," he said, and nudged Ketheria forward.

The guard took one look at Ketheria and laughed. "You plan to win with this team?" he scoffed.

The other guard joined in and added, "You think you can beat Banar with *them*?"

"Or Turtia?" Now they were both laughing. Athooyi's skin reddened, and the hole in his chest widened as he sucked in as much air as he could.

"How dare you question me?" he bellowed through the voice box. I couldn't believe how loud the thing was. Athooyi's frail-looking bodyguards morphed into the fierce beasts I had seen once before.

The two guards stood up, stumbling for their weapons, with one eye on the snarling creatures.

"Our apologies, noble Citizen."

"Please excuse our ignorance," the other pleaded. "The names of your guests?"

Switzer smiled. He seemed to like Athooyi's power. "The name is Switzer. Randall Switzer," he proclaimed.

The guard to my left searched his O-dat—twice fidgeting with the buttons in front of him. Then he motioned to the other guard to do the same. He was already sweating, even though the temperature outside was perfectly normal.

"What's taking so long?" Athooyi demanded.

The guard hesitated. "Um . . . it says here . . ."

"Well?" Athooyi prompted him.

"It's says he's dead," the other guard finished.

Athooyi glanced at Switzer before turning back to the guards and shouting, "That's ridiculous. Are you mocking me?" The guards cowered under Athooyi's threatening tone and the electronic squelch from his voice box. "Obviously he's not dead. He's standing right in front of you, imbeciles."

"Absolutely, I see that. This is our mistake. I will fix it immediately," the guard stammered. "Please accept our gracious apologies."

"Yes, and welcome to the Chancellor's Challenge," the other one said.

An opening appeared in the energy shield and we followed Athooyi inside the walls of the Labyrinth. It was more than an arena though—it was a city. The entrance was elevated, giving the place a sunken appearance, but impressive nonetheless. Kilometers of towers of bronze and crystal and hematite and gold spiraled toward the center. Artistically arranged spheres rested on enormous cradles like giant soap bubbles on spoons.

"That's the actual labyrinth," Athooyi said, pointing to a

stadium elevated among the spheres and domed in sparkling blue glass.

"It's the most beautiful thing I've ever seen," Theodore whispered.

"Let's just hope it's easy to get out of," I said.

Athooyi directed us to small pods located just beneath the curved platform. Once inside, we darted across the sky, straight to the labyrinth. I could not find a single remnant of the Ancients' architecture anywhere inside the city. Unlike other parts of the ring, where some of the Ancients' timeworn buildings still remained, every sign or symbol of the previous owners had been paved over with glittering displays of wealth. Layers of elevated trams sparkled below and webbed their way around cold structures of metal and glass. Max gawked as if intoxicated by the city, but I kept making mental notes of the landscape so we could find our way back. I only hoped Vairocina was doing the same.

"When do we play?" I asked Switzer.

"Soon," Athooyi interrupted.

"Next spoke," Switzer said. "We have time to prepare and get something to eat before round one."

And plan, I said to myself. The pod moved in a straight line from the entrance. *Is that automatic?* I wondered. I had not seen Athooyi program any destination into the pod. *If I jumped on one of these, would it take me right back to the gate?* Once inside the labyrinth, Vairocina could find that out for me, but I didn't dare ask her that now.

"Yes, they will," she responded inside my head,

"You can read my thoughts?" I asked her silently.

"Yes. I was unaware of how much you liked Max."

I didn't respond, but I did detect a note of coldness in Vairocina's tone. I hoped it was the result of our new method of communications. She wasn't jealous, was she?

The pod slipped through a crack in the lip of the Citizens' labyrinth. It nestled on a landing cradle, and the whole thing rotated clockwise and then tilted slightly, forcing us to disembark.

"Everyone, right hands out," Athooyi yelled, and produced a bag of crystals, just like the ones Weegin used to rope us together when he tried to sell us on Orbis 2.

"What's this for?" I asked.

"Knudniks are not allowed to run free in the Labyrinth," he informed us.

That was fine by me. It kept us together. I planned to leave here with everyone, anyway. Athooyi gave each of us a crystal, and we kept our hands stretched out in front of us.

"You too, Ceesar," Athooyi said.

"Me? Why me?" Switzer protested, and I agreed. I did not want Switzer tied to us. This was disastrous.

"That's the way it is. You're not a Citizen. Put your hand out," he ordered.

Switzer hesitated. He looked at us and then back at Athooyi, who stood there waiting. Switzer hadn't planned for this. Neither had I.

"Now," Athooyi demanded.

Switzer held out his hand and accepted the crystal. Athooyi then clipped the last link somewhere onto his body. The effect was instant, and a bright red electrical rope now bound us together with Switzer and Athooyi.

"Follow me," Athooyi ordered.

We stepped out from the pod port and into the thick and unmistakable alien perfume of the Labyrinth. The glass dome polarized the thin atmosphere and bathed the throngs of aliens in a cool, clean shine.

"Wow," Max exclaimed.

The festive atmosphere reminded me of the harvest on Orbis 2. We walked under huge floating O-dats that displayed the odds for different matches, and groups of aliens cheered as their favorite players splashed across the screens.

"It's the most popular event on Orbis 3, and it only happens every other rotation," Athooyi said, his voice full of pride.

"Takes them that long to scrounge up more split-screens willing to play," Theodore whispered.

"Just count everything you can, Theodore. Remember, I don't plan on staying here that long," I whispered back. I tried desperately to remember every landmark, but the place was huge and crowded with aliens.

"Planning strategies?" Switzer called out.

"Absolutely," I said.

"For the game, I trust."

"Of course," I replied.

"You'll play fantastically," Athooyi bragged. "I have a lot of money placed on your success."

You should have bet on someone else, then, I answered silently.

We pushed through the boisterous crowds, and I found myself walking behind the same female I saw register her knudniks with Tinker. Still hooded and naked, her knudniks fidgeted with their chains, their shoulders bulging under the fresh metal armor now embedded in their skin.

"JT!" I heard a voice call out. "JT!"

Laboring toward me through the crowd of fans was a human. *Who is that?* I wondered, but I could not recognize the face. Reddened and puffy, with the whites of his eyes yellowed in a sickly fashion, I could not place him.

"JT, it's me. Daniel," he said, standing before us.

I had known a Daniel on the *Renaissance,* but this bloated human reminded me more of a Trefaldoor than of the Daniel I knew.

"Daniel?" Max said.

"I know it doesn't look like me. I'm hosting a Citizen," he said, and pulled back the charcoal shirt that draped over half his body. His stomach contorted and shifted, as if it were alive.

"Why?" Max cried in horror.

Daniel leaned in and whispered, "One less rotation on Orbis for me — not bad, huh?"

"Let's go," Athooyi growled, and Switzer yanked the light chain.

Theodore stared at him, slack-jawed. "It's inside you?"

"Um, that's great, Daniel," I mumbled.

"Does it hurt?" Max asked.

"Only if I get him mad," Daniel replied, smiling. "Are you here to watch the Challenge? Maybe we can sit together."

"We're here to play," I told him.

Even under Daniel's strained skin, I could see his face go pale. "Oh," he replied, and took a step back as if *we* were the ones who were diseased-looking. "I guess, good luck, then," he muttered as Switzer yanked the light chain toward him.

"I never liked that guy," Switzer said.

Seeing the effect on Daniel's body broke my concentration. I had never once imagined us as vessels for some alien back when we lived on the *Renaissance. What has happened to us? How did it get like this?* I remembered dreaming about coming to the Rings of Orbis. It was all I ever thought about. But now . . . my fists were clenched tightly, squeezing the blood from my hands as my fingernails dug deeply into my skin. I hated this place. I refused to die for these people.

I needed to get Switzer off this chain.

"Right here!" Athooyi announced.

He stopped us in front of another energy shield guarded by two enormous aliens with tiny heads and arms thicker than a Trefaldoor's.

"Out of our way!" Athooyi shouted, but the crowd parted only slightly.

"But Banar has arrived!" someone protested. Just then the crowd roared.

The group of onlookers swept to the side in one huge wave of bodies, taking us with them. Athooyi became disoriented. He wobbled on his thin legs, dropping the light rope. As we quickly became separated from him, I realized this was our chance to run.

"We need to break away from this chain," I whispered to Max.

"But that thing he has. I can't leave," she said. "Besides, Switzer's still attached to us."

"Vairocina, can you do anything about this light rope?" I asked her.

"I'm searching for something right now," she stalled inside my head.

Someone yelled, "There he is!" and the crowd heaved once more.

I looked over the crowd to see a gleaming black creature strutting toward the shield—not as tall as a Keeper, but daunting still the same. It was as if the creature were encased in a glossy metal cast with sections that shifted and spun as he walked.

"We have to fight that?" Theodore exclaimed.

"We're not going to fight," I hissed.

"You won't get the chance to refuse if he gets his hands on you," Switzer remarked.

Banar slipped through the energy field, and the crowd thinned out, pressing up against the glass near the shield to catch one more glimpse of their hero.

"Hold your hands up," Athooyi demanded, stomping toward us. We held our hands out. "Inside the shield first."

We moved past the guards and through the shield. Athooyi cracked the crystal, and our hands dropped, except for Max. Athooyi gave her another crystal and tied Max to himself.

"Wait," I said. "Ketheria hasn't passed the weight class."

"I waived it," he replied. "She'll do well in there. I want to see her fight."

Then he pulled on the light rope and slipped back through the shield, dragging Max with him. She turned, and I caught one last glimpse of her before she was gone.

"What now?" Theodore whispered.

"I think we *are* going to have to fight," I said.

15

Each team was given its own holding cell, a small metal room with running water, something that looked liked a first-aid kit, and several large O-dats. On one side were four plastic bunks and a food dispenser.

Ketheria leaned against the far wall near the only exit. I figured that it led to the labyrinth. Her arms were folded, and she was staring at Switzer.

"What are you looking at, freak?" he spat.

"What happened to you?" she said softly.

Switzer turned his helmet in his hand, thinking. "More than you can even imagine, little girl. And much more than you can probably stomach."

"You don't have to be this way, you know. There is time for you to change. There is still time for you to do good."

Switzer jumped up, laughing. "Would you get a load of her?" He towered over my sister. "You don't get it, do you? It doesn't get any better than this. You're only going to have what you take. No one in this universe is going to give you anything, no matter how *good* you are. This universe is crammed with creatures that think nothing of your suffering, as long as their needs are met first. You can obey all the rules you want, but remember something: they made the rules to benefit *them*, not you.

Ketheria turned away without responding and sat on one of the bunks.

"Leave her alone, Switzer. Save your angst for the match."

"How long do we have to wait?" Theodore asked.

I was wondering the same thing. But I was waiting for Switzer to make his next move. Max was with Athooyi in a public area. I wasn't worried about her right now. She could handle herself out there. Did Switzer plan to fight? That was good, actually. I just had to make sure I went with him. But when was he going to go after the Ancients' Treasure?

"So what's your plan?" I asked him.

"My plan? Exactly. It's *my* plan. You just sit there and contemplate your fate. You don't need to know my plan."

"Switzer, I told you that I don't care about the treasure. It's yours. Take it. I'm just worried about us. If I knew what you were doing, then maybe I could save everyone here."

"And your little girlfriend?"

I moaned. "Oh, would you let that go?"

The room pulsed. Everything went green for a moment, and a soft chime filled the air.

"*That's* my plan," Switzer said, motioning to the signal. "To watch one of you die right now." Switzer stood up and put his helmet on. "So who's ready to meet the Source?"

I jumped up. "I'm going," I said as the room pulsed red and the chime was replaced with a clang. The O-dats displayed our opponent. It was the Citizen I'd seen with Tinker and her four hooded knudniks.

"It's those big guys," Theodore said, pointing at the screen.

"The bigger, the better," Switzer remarked, and headed for the exit.

"Be careful, JT," Theodore whispered.

Ketheria moved toward me. "You don't have to kill anyone," she said softly. "There are other ways. Use those first, all right?"

"I'll try," I said, but I couldn't promise.

"C'mon!" Switzer shouted from down the hall. "Everyone has to come!"

"Why everyone?" I yelled after him.

"C'mon!"

The three of us followed Switzer down the corridor. I thought it led to the labyrinth, but instead we found ourselves standing in another antechamber. This one was completely white, with two sloped seats clinging to the wall.

"Subs go there," Switzer grunted, pointing to the seats.

"Listen, Switzer, you may not care about winning, but at least let us have a fair chance. Tell me what else is different."

The antechamber pulsed like the other waiting room.

"Nothing's different. The subs wait in these chairs. They can watch the match from here. Along the way you'll find gold crystals throughout the maze. If you're hurt, hit one of those and these split-screens will appear. If you die, don't worry; the game will do it for you. Now let's go. You're the bait."

"What? I track. I don't bait. *You* have to be the bait."

"Forget about it, Dumbwire," he said. The section of the antechamber closest to him crackled and disappeared, exposing two corridors. Switzer grabbed my uniform and thrust me down the hall closest to me. He turned and took off down the other. The hallway sealed behind him.

"Be careful, JT," Ketheria said. "Remember your promise."

I jammed the helmet onto my head and ran down the corridor. *I never promised,* I muttered to myself. I wouldn't think twice about killing Switzer if I were given the chance. But I needed to push those thoughts out of my mind. I was about to enter the Chancellor's Challenge, and I needed to concentrate on surviving. It made me very anxious that Switzer was playing the sort. We had never once discussed strategy for our match. For all I knew, I could end up fighting in outer space, collecting cosmic streams of energy while trying to unlock a multidimensional puzzle. Then it hit me. What if I lose? What if I purposely play poorly and simply lose the match? We would be eliminated and no one would die.

"I already thought about that," Vairocina said inside my head. "But a survey of the last 2,800 matches in the Chancellor's Challenge revealed that their computer is not as random as the one you normally play with. Of the millions and millions of possible game scenarios, it seems the Citizens have weighted their computer to choose the games that have the most . . . blood."

"But it's possible, right?"

"I wouldn't count on that as a strategy, JT. Be prepared to fight. I took the liberty of adjusting the parameters of your right arm to maximize its abilities, and I have linked to the helmet's visor through your optical nerve. If you would like, I can monitor the visor while you concentrate on the game."

"I would like that," I replied as I stepped out into the labyrinth to take my place in the bait box.

My opponent was doing the same, and from where I stood, I could tell that he was just as amazed as I was at the spectacle above us. Towering over my head, circling the playing field, were rows and rows of spectators. They went so high that I couldn't see where they ended. Bots of different sizes and shapes skittered from level to level, attending to the crowds, while enormous O-dats lumbered through the air, flashing statistics, game shots, and even pictures of me as I entered. Other screens advertised food and clothing just like in the Trading Chambers. The sound from the spectators was deafening. It was as if all the noise was concentrated in one single wave that crashed down upon us as we stepped into our individual waiting areas.

I tried to search for Max and Athooyi, but that was impossible. *Everyone from every ring must be here,* I thought. Surely someone would recognize me. Wouldn't they tell the Keepers? But who? None of the Citizens I knew would rat out another Citizen, and Charlie was dead.

The floor sparkled, and an energy field shot up around me. The match had begun. *What did Switzer choose?* my mind screamed out.

The light in the arena faded. Then the floor slipped away, almost as if it had never been there to begin with. The crowd roared in response. I glimpsed across at my opponent and saw him crouched upon a glowing disc. A narrow metal pole rose up out of the nothingness now surrounding us and supported his platform. The stars around him blinked on, and I stared out into the vastness of space. That meant that whoever picked first from the sort had chosen GAS. We would be fighting in space. *Please, please, please, let Switzer have been smart enough to choose* MECHANIC *in the second round.*

"I detect an atmosphere with oxygen," Vairocina informed.

"How?" I asked her.

"There are a lot of features in your arm I don't think you've ever accessed. At least you will not have to worry about the air."

I looked up, straining to see the match on one of the O-dats floating in front of the spectators. I knew they could no longer see us on the playing field. They would be watching Switzer and the other guy working their way through the labyrinth. Not until one of them reached the bait would this part of the field be revealed again.

As one of the huge O-dats swung near me, I caught a glimpse of an explosion. Good! That meant someone chose TECHNOLOGICAL in the third round. I couldn't see INDUSTRIAL or MAGICAL creating that sort of explosion.

"You cannot assume that," Vairocina said.

"I'm trying to be positive."

Then, from out of nowhere, the wall to my right burst apart and Switzer barreled through underneath the spectators.

"He's good," Vairocina said.

"I know."

Switzer was piloting a strange flier called a rattle basket: two circular discs, each supporting a tall, thin cage for each of the pilots. Switzer stood on the largest, navigating the machine from controls mounted near his wrists. From the way Switzer was crouching, I could tell that this machine was not designed for a human. The second disc swung erratically around him, flinging back and forth whenever he turned the flier. That's where I was going to sit. I had seen this device before when I was studying the game with Max and Vairocina.

"Can you believe this piece of crap? Jump on!" Switzer screamed, and then maneuvered the flier in front of me. The back cage flung around, and I caught it with my right arm. Mounted directly behind Switzer was a plasma turret.

"You were fast!" I shouted.

"Maybe not fast enough," he yelled as our opponent stormed the arena, too. The light in the labyrinth grew brighter, and with it came the deafening roar of the crowd.

"I created a link between you and Switzer through your helmets. You can talk normally," Vairocina said.

"Now, please!" Switzer said, still yelling.

I threw myself into the cage, unhooked the turret, and slid it around in front of me. The huge weapon locked into place with a clank and instantly hummed to life. The glow emanating from the massive gun ignited everything in a blue inferno.

"You know how to use that thing?" Switzer screamed.

"Yes."

"Then use it now!" he yelled as four more fliers, each manned with two aliens, broke through the wall, firing.

Switzer swung the flier around, making a wide arc of the arena. Two of the fliers gave chase while one concentrated on our opponent and the other stood guard at the only exit.

I pumped four blasts at the aliens chasing us. They were Garins, tall monkey-like creatures who must have felt just as uncomfortable as we did with these fliers. None of my shots hit its mark.

"I thought you knew how to use that thing," Switzer shouted over his shoulder.

"I do!"

"Then kill them!"

I remembered Ketheria's request, but I saw no way to appease her. Switzer slowed the flier, and the Garins charged the gap between us.

"What are you doing?" I screamed at him.

"Maybe you need to be a little closer."

I pumped the turret once more, but the first Garin dodged to his left, avoiding the blast with little effort. Then he jerked the flier to the right, and the back of the flier spun around and locked in front. The pilot aimed his turret right at me.

I pumped three times in succession. Each shot struck the weakest parts of the flier, shattering it to pieces.

"Nice shooting!" Switzer cheered.

The one pilot was still gripping the turret as he spun off into space. *I didn't kill them,* I told myself, but I didn't see much difference.

The crowd cheered with the explosion and cheered even louder as the other crew took the place of the one I'd just blown up. Switzer cut sharp, turning back toward the opening in the wall and directly in line with the aliens guarding the passage back. The other flier copied Switzer's maneuver.

"What are you doing now, Switzer?" I growled.

"Just shut up, keep your head down, and squeeze that trigger!"

When I fired, the aliens giving chase returned my favor. With great skill, Switzer dropped the rattle basket twenty meters and my stomach lurched into my mouth. It took everything not to vomit on my visor. The blast from the Garins sailed over my head and directly into the flier of Garins guarding the hole in the wall. The bits and pieces of their unintended target rained down on us as Switzer beelined for the now unguarded opening.

"Don't fire at that one," he ordered. "When they see us reach the opening, they'll turn on our opponent. We'll use them to slow those guys down."

I could not deny it: Switzer was good—really good, in fact. *Why didn't Switzer just stay and try to win this thing?* I wondered. *He might even turn into a hero or something if he won. I'm sure he would enjoy that.*

Switzer's skilled flying and fearless fighting placed us in the winners' circle for our first match. The other knudniks were nowhere to be seen. I couldn't help but wonder if our opponents were dead. I felt some remorse, but a very big part of me was glad I was standing in the winners' circle with Switzer, hearing the crowd cheer for us. Switzer turned and waved to the spectators (more than once), soaking up every drop of their affection. Even if I did feel guilty about my opponents' deaths, though, I would have to get used to standing under the adulation of this crowd if I was going to survive. I needed to be here at the end of every match, no matter what the consequences.

Back in our holding cell, Switzer strutted about as if he had just been chosen Chancellor of Orbis 2.

"You won! Can't you enjoy that?" he cried, slapping me on the back.

"I call it *surviving*," I muttered.

"That's your problem, Dumbwire. You're not enjoying the ride. That wall behind you could drop on us and kill you right now. Stop waiting for your life to start. This is it; you'd better have a little fun."

"Let's go see Max," I sighed, ignoring his comment.

"Shoulda said good-bye to your girlfriend when you had the chance. No leaving here until the Chancellor's Challenge is done, but I doubt you'll be leaving here anyway."

"What do you mean, we can't leave?" That was not going to be the last time I ever saw Max!

"Try it. Door's locked from the outside." Switzer strolled over to the chow synth. "You hungry?"

"Did you keep your promise?" my sister whispered.

"No, I didn't, Ketheria! What am I supposed to do out there? Do I need to remind you they're trying to kill *me*?" I yelled at her.

Ketheria recoiled, and Theodore slid over to comfort her.

"JT, stop it. That was unnecessary," Theodore said.

"You're right," I mumbled, and sat by myself. It was obvious I shouldn't have done that. I couldn't even look at Switzer because I knew he would be smiling right now.

"I'm sorry, Ketheria," I apologized. "I tried my best, but we were fighting in space. I don't think they all survived."

"*I'm sorry baby-malf, I don't think they all survived,*" Switzer mimicked me in a high, whiny voice while cramming his mouth with a powdery cake-like substance, showering me with little pieces of food.

"Shut up," I told him, but he only laughed at me.

"This is so much fun," he gushed, licking his fingers. "You guys havin' fun?"

I turned my back to Switzer and stared up at the festivities displayed on the O-dats. The other people in the Labyrinth certainly seemed to be enjoying themselves out there. I wondered where Max was. I hoped she was safe.

"You guys did really well," Theodore whispered, sitting next to me. "Keep this up, and Ketheria and I won't even have to go near the match."

"I just wish I knew what his plans were," I replied, glancing over at Switzer.

"The Ancients' Treasure is held temporarily *underneath* the Labyrinth. The Chancellor raises it up for the whole audience to view after the championship round," Vairocina informed me. "If he is going after the treasure, I can't see him waiting until the Challenge is over. It would be best to do it now."

Her logic worried me, but Switzer was locked in here with us. How was he planning to get to the treasure? He must have thought of another way. Something I just couldn't see.

Theodore started to say, "Maybe we can—"

But Switzer cut him off. "Maybe we can what? Maybe we can get ready for the next match?"

"Get ready? You don't even discuss strategy with me. What about the sort? Don't you even want to plan it out?" I complained.

"No. You did fine without any discussion."

"Suit yourself," I replied.

The room pulsed green again.

"Already?" I moaned.

"Don't want to keep the fans waiting," Switzer remarked, jumping up and grabbing his helmet. The three of us followed him down the corridor. Switzer didn't say a word to us as he headed off to the sort. Ketheria was silent, too, as she took her seat on the wall.

"I'll try my best. You know, not to kill anyone," I whispered to her.

"Do what you have to do," she mumbled.

I wanted to be mad at Ketheria. I wanted to scream at her, ask her what I was supposed to do. We could all be dead shortly! It wasn't fair to put that pressure on me. But I didn't. I wouldn't. I placed the helmet over my head and turned down the hall.

"Good luck!" Theodore yelled after me.

The hallway pulsed red just before I stepped into the labyrinth. The crowd looked even bigger than before, although I didn't know how that could be possible. It had been packed the last time I'd stood in the bait box.

My opponent was already waiting. Every point on her body was tapered as if she were built for speed. I wondered if her tracker would use it to their advantage. I didn't think I could beat her in a foot race.

I scanned the audience in vain, searching for Max. It was hard to concentrate. I had no plan except to do what Switzer wanted, even though that meant I could be dead at any moment.

"You can't think like that," Vairocina said to me. "I'm working on finding a way out of here, although my resources are limited. I've managed to link to their computer through your softwire, but I can't maintain the connection. Maybe if you made the connection, I would have better access. When this match is finished, we should attempt to do that in the holding cell."

"*If* I make it through this match," I reminded her.

"If you don't, then your sister will have to fight."

She was right. What was I doing feeling sorry for myself? My plan (if I really called it a plan) was to win this contest. I had the experience and the skills to pull it off, and Switzer was a good partner. Let him do what he wanted. I just had to survive and win the Chancellor's Challenge. That was the only plan I had, and the only one I could control.

"I agree," Vairocina said.

The labyrinth dimmed, the crowd roared, and my heart hit the floor as the stadium filled with water. Any control I thought

I had just dissolved. One of the trackers must have chosen LIQ-
UID in the first round of the sort. I glanced at my opponent;
she was smiling! Then I saw it—my opponent wasn't built for
speed; she was a swimmer! The alien unfolded her hand, exposing the webbed skin between her fingers.

This was horrible!

The alien rolled her head and stretched out a small fin that
ran down the back of her neck. I could see gill slits crack open and
expose the red tender flesh that would help her breath underwater. I hoped that Switzer had learned how to swim during all
those years he was plundering spaceships in the wormhole.

The water kept rising until it reached the edge of my platform. Turquoise lights banding the arena illuminated the water
from below. It would have looked beautiful if it weren't for the
shadows crisscrossing the lights. Something was moving in the
water. Something fast. I could not imagine that it was Switzer
who had chosen LIQUID in the first round, but why would he
choose BIOLOGICAL in the last round? What was he thinking?

I had no clue what to do. I simply stood there tracking the
shadows hunting in the small ocean now lapping at my feet.
My opponent stretched as if she were getting ready for a casual
swim in the pool.

"What should I do?"

"I do not know," Vairocina said.

The alien dove into the water like a comet streaking across
the sky. The shadows changed direction, tracking her, and then
she broke the surface of the water. She landed back on the platform in one graceful swoop.

I groaned. I was sunk. Worse, I was dead.

The shadows turned again, away from my opponents, and gathered to my right. Another shadow, much faster, darted through the water and across the arena. It rose quickly and then broke the surface with a roar.

"Switzer!"

Switzer shot through the air, dragged by some sort of propulsion system that he held with one hand.

"Want to give me a little help here?" he yelled, and flung a weapon at me with his free hand.

The weapon was a Zinovian Grand Talon, a light device that fired poisoned blades. Switzer dove back into the water, skimming the surface while three creatures in the water chased him. Our opponent was pacing on her platform now, searching the water. *She must be looking for her tracker,* I thought. I aimed the talon at the water, and the crowd above me cheered.

"I'm sorry, Ketheria," I said, and fired into the water as the last creature passed. The creature recoiled when the talon struck and sank out of sight. There were still two creatures chasing Switzer.

Switzer broke the water again. "You might want to go a little faster," he yelled, and dove back in, close to the platform. I fired two more times, taking out both creatures, and Switzer surfaced at my feet.

"Finally!"

"Where's the other tracker?" I asked him.

"Don't worry about him; just get on."

"On your back?"

"I don't think you can swim, now, can you?"

"I can swim," I said, cringing at the whiny sound of my voice.

"Fine, see you back there."

"Wait!" Before Switzer could leave, I jumped into the water and landed on Switzer. Switzer passed me a breathing tube from the propulsion device and took one himself. When he dove into the water, I could see our opponent still on her platform.

The ride back was quick and uneventful. The bottom of the underwater maze was littered with the creatures like the ones I had killed from the platform. When we had almost reached the winners' circle, I spotted the lifeless body of the other tracker slumped on the floor, a talon sticking out of his back. Switzer had killed him.

Inside the winners' circle, Switzer basked in the glory while I tried to figure out what to tell Ketheria. Maybe I just wouldn't tell her anything. That was the easiest. In reality, if Switzer hadn't done what he did, that could have been me lying on the maze floor. Because of Switzer's ruthlessness, I just might make it out of here alive.

I followed Switzer back on a small catwalk. The water from our match still filled most of the playing area, even up to our ready room. Switzer sat down outside our door to ring out some of his wet clothes.

"You're really good at this," I told him.

"Don't get so comfortable, Dumbwire."

"What do you mean?"

"I told you that you were going to watch your friends die. That wasn't an idle threat."

"I don't get it. We're doing great, Switzer. I mean, it's been all you. You're really good. Let's keep going. I really think we can win it. If we can control the sort, you know, so we don't get stuck with LIQUID, like we just did . . ."

"I chose LIQUID in the sort."

"What?"

Switzer shook his head. "You always were an idiot," he scoffed. "You never think for yourself, do you? That's how you can live here. It's the only thing I can figure. Why else would you put up it? With *them*? Is that what you want, though? To be their little dog for the rest of your life?"

"What, and have your life instead?

"Well, at least it's *my* life."

"But . . ." I really couldn't say anything. He was right. Switzer did have his own life. He did only what he chose, not what others made him do. I stared at him. Underneath all those scars and contraptions bolted to his face, I found the kid I once knew, rummaging around Orbis 2, simply trying to survive.

"You could come with me," he said. "Everyone, if you want."

"What?"

"I'm not going to beg you. There is a better life out there, you know."

"But . . ." Could I leave with Switzer? What would that be like?

"Forget it, split-screen. Stay here and rot."

Then Switzer took his helmet and smashed it against the floor. The helmet cracked.

"Wait! What are you doing?"

"Can't have anyone along for the *ride,* know what I mean?"

He put his helmet on, took off his boot, and pulled a small knife from his pant leg.

"Put your helmet on."

"Why, what are you doing, Switzer?"

"PUT IT ON! Hurry! The water is receding."

Before I put my helmet on, Switzer swiped the blade along his foot, slicing his skin just enough to make it bleed, but not very deep. He squeezed the blood out and smeared it everywhere.

"Now, look at me."

I was already looking, but once I had the helmet on, Switzer began screaming and flailing about.

"Ah! The poison. Ah! The pain!"

Switzer's acting skills were no match for his Quest-Nest skills. I took the helmet off.

"Switzer, what the hell are you doing?" I cried.

"I had to make sure everyone saw I was hurt," he said, pointing at my helmet. "Whoever's riding you will see that." He stood up.

"Where are you going?"

"That water drains out underneath the Labyrinth. Those tunnels will take me straight to the treasure. Well, close enough, anyway."

Switzer had planned this the whole time. He wanted a water event to get underneath the Labyrinth.

"Switzer, don't. Please. Let's finish this. I need you," I pleaded.

He looked at me for a second and then said, "Too late for that. Have fun dying."

Switzer dove into the water.

I thrust my helmet over my head to record him leaving, but it was too late. Switzer was gone. And I had to choose between Theodore and Ketheria to fight with me in the next round.

16

"Why didn't you go after him?" Theodore cried.

"And do what? I don't care about the treasure. Let him have it. Besides, that would have left you two to fight in the match," I reminded him. I did not mention Switzer's offer to leave. I don't know why. I guess I sort of felt guilty that I had turned down a way out of here.

Theodore glanced over at Ketheria and moved under the O-dat.

"There are eight teams left," he mumbled, reading off the screen. "Riis is still playing. We could get her next, you know."

I stared at my sister. What was she now, eleven years old? This wasn't what eleven-year-olds were supposed to be doing. She should be playing or going to school, anything else but this. How could I make her go into the labyrinth? How could I force her to take the life of another living creature merely for the sport of it? It's not that she couldn't stomach it; she just wouldn't do it, even if it meant letting them take her life.

"You're not much older," Vairocina whispered inside my head.

"That's different," I replied, forgetting that Vairocina could read my thoughts.

But was it different? How come I could kill so easily? Why wasn't I repulsed when I shot the talon at a creature I didn't even know? Or when I blew up those rattle baskets with the Garins still inside? I felt nothing. Zero. Had I become some sort of monster? Is this what the Rings of Orbis had turned me into?

The room pulsed green.

"Oh, no!" Theodore cried, still staring at the O-dat.

"What is it?" I said.

"We're fighting Banar!"

"So?"

"If survival is our goal, I'd much rather be fighting Riis," Theodore replied.

"He's just another opponent."

"JT, you don't understand. I've scoped this guy. He doesn't just play the field. He plays the opponent. He'll kill you just because he can. This is *bad*."

I thought of the opponent slumped at the bottom of the waterway. Switzer had played his opponent. I would have to do the same.

Ketheria stood up and put her helmet on.

"No, Ketheria," Theodore said. "I'm going to do this."

"Theodore, no offense, but I play better than you," she told him.

"Yeah, but I've scoped this guy. I know Banar's weaknesses. I know how to beat him."

Ketheria took her helmet off as the room pulsed once more.

"Then let's go," I said.

We headed down the hall with Ketheria trailing.

"How did they beat him last time?" I whispered to Theodore.

Theodore glanced back at Ketheria and murmured, "They didn't. Banar has never lost."

"Never?"

"Ever."

I hesitated before stepping into the sort. Despite the fact that I felt more comfortable playing as the tracker, Theodore's ominous warning made it hard to concentrate.

"Push those thoughts away," Vairocina whispered.

"I'm trying," I said.

"You must try harder."

I stepped onto the crystal embedded in the floor and I was instantly encased in an energy shield.

"Play to your strengths; don't try to play your opponent," she said, but it was more of an order.

What if I don't get to choose first in the sort? What would

Banar choose? Why didn't I ask Theodore? I was doing a very poor job of concentrating when the sort flashed in front of me. I would choose first!

I immediately stabbed my finger at the SOLID triangle floating in front of me. I wasn't taking any chances. I was good at any of the selections in stage two of the sort. While I waited for Banar to choose, my confidence was beginning to flow back. I was relieved that I wouldn't have to face LIQUID or GAS in the match.

Banar was taking his time choosing the second stage. That was odd, I thought. Then the sort flashed red with the information: YOUR OPPONENT HAS PASSED.

Passed?

Why would Banar pass? I was instantly worried. What sort of strategy was he using? Did he want to pick in the third stage? Why? What was so important in the third stage?

"You're panicking," Vairocina whispered.

"Of course I am!"

"This is good. You are in complete control now."

"But why did Banar pass? Who passes?"

The words PLEASE CHOOSE THE 2ND STAGE, flashed in front of me.

"You're assuming he did this on purpose. Maybe he's just as upset that he missed his choice."

I doubted that. Banar was up to something, and it was freaking me out. I reached out to choose MECHANIC.

"I wouldn't do that," Vairocina warned.

I withdrew my hand. "Why?" I cried.

"Banar has been playing Quest-Nest for quite some time, and his conquests are legendary. I'm sure he's proficient in every weapon imaginable, and some more than others. If he's aware of your playing habits, he will know that you choose MECHANIC 90 percent of the time. He's assuming you will do it now and therefore he'll choose a style of weapon in the third stage that he is extremely skilled with. Remember, Banar plays his opponents."

"I thought you said it might have been an accident that he passed!" I reminded her.

"It might have been that, too, but I still wouldn't choose MECHANIC. I would choose something that allows you some sort of stealth advantage. You might make it through the match without ever confronting Banar."

The sort flashed again, and I selected PSIONIC.

Almost instantly, the fourth stage selection came back to me.

"He knows you will choose PHYSICAL," Vairocina warned me.

"And he's right. You said play to my strengths, and this is my strength," I told her, holding up my right arm, and then punched the PHYSICAL diamond floating in front of me.

"Here we go," I mumbled.

"Good luck."

"They used that expression on your planet?"

"No. They don't believe in luck."

"Neither do I."

The force field dropped away and left me standing in a

shining round chamber. Some sort of metallic-colored force field wound around the floor. All around me, thick chrome support beams reflected the cobalt-colored floor. The beams angled outward and were placed close enough together to lock me in. The only visible exit was a black hole placed at the center of the chamber.

Standing over that hole was my opponent, Banar.

He hesitated, as if he was just as shocked to find me standing there as I was to see him. His upper body spun toward me, and he lunged over the hole. Two huge pieces of his shoulder armor clicked into place as he readied to attack me.

Only one thought entered my mind. *Survive!*

I lunged at Banar. I had no intentions of engaging him. I simply wanted to make it into that hole before he crushed me. Hoping for the best (or at least a soft landing), I dove headfirst into the darkness. Banar howled in anger. His acrid breath stung the back of my neck as I dropped underneath him.

I curled into a ball, ready for the impact, but there was none. Some sort of invisible gravity field had caught hold of me and was slowing my descent. After a moment, I found myself floating, suspended in another, larger room. A dim golden light streaked the glossy walls.

"The room you just left may be the first of the fourteen chambers of the labyrinth," Vairocina said. "If you can simply make your way through each chamber ahead of Banar, you might have a chance to leave this match unscathed."

"I like that plan," I whispered in reply.

I looked up, expecting to see Banar drifting down the cylindrical chamber behind me, but he wasn't. That's when I realized, though, that I was drifting *downward*.

"The exit might be on the wall," I cried. "If we pass it, we may have no way of reaching it again."

"Maybe that's a good thing," Vairocina said. "You would be out of the match and Banar could go on to win. No one would get hurt."

"What if they put in Ketheria to take my place? I can't take that chance. We have to find the way out of here."

I flailed my arms, forcing my body to spin around, and searched the walls for some evidence of a door or a lock, anything.

Below me I saw some sort of marking—four circles that protruded from the wall, each with an iris made of three triangular sheaths of etched metal. One of the circles was quite large—large enough for someone to slip through. I began flailing my arms again to try to move toward the shapes, but I was dropping too fast.

Then I heard Banar. The chamber echoed with his roar, and I looked up to find him diving headfirst toward me.

"You have to get out of his way!" Vairocina cried.

"I'm trying!"

Banar reached toward me with both arms—thick battering rams of jointed black metal. I was directly across from the circles on the wall now. *That must be the way out of here,* I thought, and flailed my arms once more.

"I'm not gonna reach it!"

I looked up at Banar. He swept the air with his right arm, as if testing it. *If he hits me*, I thought . . . *That's it! If he hits me, I might just make it to the wall!*

"This is going to hurt," I said.

"JT . . ." Vairocina asked.

"Turn off the pain sensors in my arm, please."

I reached up, trying to get closer to Banar. He was moving quickly now, grinning wildly and swinging his right arm faster and harder. I needed him to knock me toward the hatch.

"This isn't going to work," Vairocina cried. "What if he crushes you?"

"He won't!"

I raised my right arm to protect myself.

"Prepare to die, Softwire," Banar growled.

I made myself as tall as possible, and Banar reached back with his right arm. He grunted as he swung at me.

"Now, JT!"

I curled into a ball, and Banar's metal-plated arm swished over my head.

"Stay still, coward!" Banar cried as I stretched out again. He was so close now that I could see his large steely eyes and fiery red pupils. Banar bit down and swung at me with his backhand. I held my arm out and prepared for impact.

Banar's crushing blow split the skin along my arm on contact. My fingers flexed backward in a grotesque and unnatural position. I'm certain real bones would have snapped off from the convulsion that ravaged my arm. I slammed into the wall almost instantly. The air gushed from my flattened lungs, and my helmet slammed against the bottom of the metal hatch. I pawed at my throat, trying to breathe. Every bone in my body cried out in anguish, but I flipped over and scrambled for the hatch. It was now about two meters above me. As the air seeped back into my lungs, I looked over my shoulder and tried to focus my eyes on Banar. He scrambled frantically, trying to swim back up the chamber, but he was only descending faster.

"JT, you're slipping!" Vairocina warned. The impact with the wall had ignited a siren in my head that blurred my vision. The circular opening was nearly three meters above me now. I tried to flex my fingers, but my arm refused to obey.

"My arm! Can you fix my arm? Something's wrong!"

"Try now!"

My arm surged with a tingling sensation. I adjusted the settings for maximum force and drove my fist into the metal wall. A bolt of pain struck my brain, and the wall buckled, not a lot, but enough for my fingers to grip on to the edge of each indentation. I pulled myself up and smashed my fist into the wall again, and then again, until I had built a ladder of holes back up to the escape hatch.

"You did it!" Vairocina cried.

"It's not over yet," I breathed. "This is just the beginning."

Each level of the labyrinth presented a different obstacle course for me to negotiate. Vairocina worked on my arm as I raced through each task. On one level, I stumbled upon three Neewalkers sleeping near the entrance to the next level. A dimension cube that I had found in the previous level allowed me to move unencumbered past the fetid beasts.

I reached Theodore without ever spying Banar again. I couldn't help but wonder if he was stuck at the bottom of the second level of the labyrinth. Theodore cried out when he saw me. The crowd, however, reacted with a mixture of cheers and hisses. I guess they wanted to see their hero more than a human softwire.

Banar's bait was still locked behind the energy field waiting for his famous tracker to release him.

When Theodore's energy field dropped, he leaped out and gasped, "You made it here first!"

"C'mon, there's a lot of ground to cover before the labyrinth shifts," I yelled, and turned for the exit.

"What's wrong with your hand?"

I held my hand up. My fingers were bending backward again.

"That's just a little glitch. Vairocina is working on it. C'mon!"

Banar's bait banged on his electronic cage, igniting a shower of sparks to which the crowd erupted in approval. We didn't stick around for his next act.

I wanted to retrace my steps through the labyrinth as quickly as possible, since I already knew what lay waiting for me. Theodore could simply follow my lead without ever having to navigate a new obstacle. But if the labyrinth shifted on us, then it was a whole new game.

We passed the first three stages of our return with minimal effort. Theodore began counting the escape buttons: large gold crystals embedded in the walls that would allow you to swap out players on your own team. I think he did it to keep his mind off Banar. There was one for each level, and each button we passed meant we were one stage closer to the finish. For me, those escape buttons did not exist. I knew that if I pressed one of those crystals, Ketheria would be there, waiting—forced to play against the monster, Banar. I was trying to ignore the buttons.

On the fourth level, Theodore had trouble scaling the slanted cubes we needed to navigate in order to get to the exit. I was forced to backtrack to help him.

"It's my shoes!" he cried. "I can't get a grip."

I stretched out from the top of the last cube and extended my arm. "Just grab hold. I'll pull you up!"

Each stalled moment eroded my confidence and allowed my anxieties to seep out. I watched Theodore struggle over the top of the last cube.

"Hurry, Theodore," I breathed. "We're almost out of ti—"

The labyrinth shifted, cutting off my last sentence.

The corridor in front of me sealed shut while the wall to my left disappeared. I spun around to find Theodore lagging behind.

"Theodore! Move!"

If we were separated, I could spend the rest of the match looking for him. Theodore leaped toward me just as a new wall formed behind him. He was lying on the ground when the wall to his left disappeared.

Behind the wall stood Banar's bait. He lunged toward Theodore and stepped on his leg with a large four-taloned foot. Theodore never had a chance. His leg buckled under the weight of the alien. Even over my friend's screams, I could hear the bone in his thigh snap. Theodore cried out, and the alien smiled, raising his arm to strike.

Instinctually, I ran at the attacker. Leading with my good arm, I dove and thrust myself into his soft, exposed underbelly. With the wind knocked out of him, the alien reeled backward, tripping over Theodore's other leg. He crashed onto his backside, his plated armor clanking on the metal floor. Then the final part of the maze shifted and a new wall formed between the alien and us.

"JT, my leg! Look at my leg!"

I lifted myself off the ground and turned to see Theodore. My stomach wrenched as I saw Theodore's left leg lying useless, twisted at a grotesque angle.

"What are we going to do?" he cried. "I don't want to die. Not like this."

"You're not going to die," I told him, and grabbed him by his underarms.

"Agh!" he screamed.

"I'm sorry, but this is going to hurt."

I dragged Theodore toward the exit and past the escape button.

"Where are you going?" he protested.

"To the exit!"

"JT, I can't! It's killing me. Please."

He didn't ask me to push the escape button. I don't know if he would actually say the words. Theodore knew how I felt.

"You can't drag me for ten more levels. Banar will finish both of us off," he breathed.

"I have to!"

"No, you don't," Vairocina whispered. "Replace Theodore with your sister. Do it quickly."

"I can't," I hissed. My brain refused to turn my need into action.

"Now, JT," Vairocina urged. "Please."

Breaking my trance, I punched the crystal button and the wall disappeared. Ketheria was sitting there waiting, her helmet already on. She jumped out and helped me put Theodore into the chair. Then she gently placed her hands on Theodore's leg as he cringed.

"It's okay now," she whispered. "Everything's going to be all right." Then she tapped the escape button. The wall swallowed him up.

"Stay close," I told my sister. "This is it."

The game felt different now. I felt different. I wasn't concentrating on the labyrinth anymore. Instead I was constantly watching Ketheria. Was she too far behind? Too close to that opening? To that channel?

"What's wrong with you?" she yelled out.

"Nothing," I cried.

"Concentrate! Grab that immobility cube. I can use that. Let me take the lead, too."

With Ketheria in front of me, I actually felt a little better. I could see her and I could see the path ahead of us. This calmed me somewhat. We had cleared three more levels and were almost halfway home. On our return, we found the Neewalkers again, still frozen near the level's exit. They were no longer sleeping, though. Someone had killed them. By the position of their bodies, it looked as if someone had killed them in their sleep.

Ketheria saw them first and stopped, peering over the lifeless corpses.

"Did Banar do that?" she croaked softly.

"Don't look at that," I told her. "C'mon, we're almost there."

I pushed Ketheria toward the only exit. The shift in the labyrinth had placed it on the other side of the room now. I paused and took one last look at the dead Neewalkers. *Could I do that?* I asked.

The room pulsed.

"Ketheria!" I screamed at my sister, but she slipped through the exit just as the labyrinth shifted. The wall swallowed her up. I leaped to the wall and pounded on the metal. "Ketheria!"

A thunderbolt of pure anxiety struck my mind and body. I spun on my heels looking for the new exit, but there was none.

"Shift!"

A hole opened in the floor and I dove in. *This could lead to anywhere,* I thought, but I didn't care. I had to keep moving. I had to find Ketheria. Blindly, I leaped over each obstacle, looking only for the next opening. I didn't know if I was going forward or backward, but at least I was moving.

"Ketheria!"

"You'll find her, JT," Vairocina assured me, her words just a whisper.

"Ketheria!"

I slid down a steep chute and into a smoky passageway. About four meters above my head was a thick ledge that lined each side of the corridor. I don't know why, but something told me I had to get up there. I sprinted down the length of the hallway and spotted a ladder. Then I saw him.

I couldn't tell if it was Banar or his bait, since they both carried the bulbous, black armor on their backs.

"Hey!" I yelled at him, but he did not turn. "Hey, split-screen!"

I scrambled up the chrome bars embedded in the opposite wall and onto a broad, square landing. I could see both of them. Banar *and* his bait. Ketheria was there, too. They had her cornered on the landing.

"Ketheria!"

But she couldn't hear me, either. I hadn't been able to see it from below, but a glass wall sealed up their side.

"I'm gonna jump!"

"You don't know how thick that wall is! You don't even know if it will break," Vairocina protested.

I didn't know if I could jump across the corridor, either, but that wasn't going to stop me. I took a good run at it, put my good arm forward, and jumped.

The glass exploded on impact, bursting into a million pieces. I landed on the floor, rolling.

"JT!"

I scrambled to my feet. Banar's frozen expression told me that Ketheria had used her immobility cube on him, but the bait was moving fast. His battering ram of an arm was pulled back and poised to strike. I reached the alien just as he swung at my sister. She crumpled under the impact, her body flailing against the wall, blood already escaping her mouth.

My mind went blank. It was as if a switch flipped and erased every bit of fear from my body. Neither sight nor sound registered with my senses. My mind was more focused than I had ever experienced in my life.

Banar's bait spun toward me. The blackened metal plates on his back whirled and then locked in front of him, protecting his vulnerable underbelly.

By some means that I could not explain, I knew that with his armor now locked in front, the alien's back was exposed. I just needed to get around him. To do this, I simply visualized the location within the room and in a blink, *I was there.* A faint smell of dirty socks lingered in the air.

As if by reflex, I thrust my hand forward and into the warm flesh of his back. My fingers clamped around his spine and with a quick snap, I rotated my hand counterclockwise. The alien did not scream or cry out in pain; he simply slumped to his knees and fell forward. A chunk of his spine was still clutched in my fist when his face hit the floor.

"No!" I heard someone scream. It was Banar. The immobility cube had worn off while he helplessly watched his partner die. I wasn't afraid of Banar anymore. He was simply another obstacle I needed to dispose of. I turned and prepared to deal with him, but before either of us moved, the light in the room shifted—bent, if you will—and four hulking Space Jumpers stepped into our dimension. They brushed past Banar and gathered around me. Two of them scoped the room, while the other two took hold of my arms. I wrenched my body, looking for my sister.

"Ketheria!"

Then nothing.

17

"Ketheria!"

I was still calling her name when I woke. In my dream I had cradled Ketheria's broken body in my arms, screaming at her to open her eyes. *Did that happen? Where am I? Is Ketheria with me?* One part of my mind told me I had just been sleeping, but another part told me I had been fighting in the match less than a nanosecond ago. I was confused. I had no clue where I was, but I definitely wasn't in the labyrinth anymore.

I lifted myself up, but my right arm refused to participate. It clung to my side, held in place by thin, transparent wires. *Who did that?* I fell back onto the misty blue sleeper. It reminded me of the conveyor belts on Weegin's World.

"Hello?" I called out, and waited for a response. There was none. I was alone, locked in a room that looked like someone had scooped it out of a rock, then placed some sort of weird sleeper in it and sealed the whole thing up with a crude-looking force field.

"Vairocina," I whispered. "Vairocina?"

She was gone, too. I tried to access the controls in my arm through my softwire, but those, too, were unavailable. It felt as if someone had turned off my arm and taken Vairocina with them. *Who? Who did this?*

I stood up. *How long have I been here?* I peered through the force field, but I couldn't see anything. I paced the perimeter of the small room, searching for clues to where I was.

All the while, a question that I didn't want to ask—that I couldn't ask—was hovering at the edge of my consciousness. I turned on my heels and searched the room again as if it were my only distraction. *Don't ask it,* I told myself. *Don't!* But I couldn't stop myself.

Is Ketheria dead?

"Ketheria!" I cried out loud, falling to my knees.

I know what I had seen. Ketheria was crushed by Banar's bait. She was unconscious before she even hit the wall. I saw blood, too, *her* blood. But the last thing I saw before the Space Jumpers took me, the thing that frightened me the most was Banar's hulking form lunging toward my sister.

My head throbbed. *Oh, what have I done? Please, let her be all right!* Who was I talking to? Who would answer me? No one. I felt empty and alone. I had failed my sister.

Then something stirred beyond the door.

"Who's there?"

I stood up and slunk toward the transparent force field,

approaching it from the side. I peered into the darkness. Something darted past again, and I jumped back. Whatever was out there was big and fast.

"Hello?"

"Hello," someone blurted from the darkness. My heart thumped in my chest. It sounded like a kid.

"Hey, kid, can you help me? Can you help me get out of here? I need to get out of here!"

Suddenly I realized I was shouting. I didn't know who could hear me, but I shouldn't be attracting any attention.

"Please," I whispered. "Can you help me?"

"Can't," the kid replied, mimicking my whisper.

"Why not?"

"You bad."

"Bad? I'm not bad. I didn't do anything," I said. "I have to find my sister. Bad things are going to happen to her if I don't get out of here." Maybe they had already happened, but I couldn't stand waiting here and doing nothing.

I put my face as close as I could to the force field.

"Hey! Are you still there?"

"You bad."

"I'm not bad!"

Whatever was out there shot past me again. *That's an awfully big kid,* I thought. I didn't even try to call after him. I knew I had scared him away. *What a split-screen I am.*

I had been sitting on my sleeper for what seemed like an eternity when the force field opened. I immediately sprang to my feet. Before I could make it to the door, though, a small cream-colored ball floated into the room. I kept my distance. I was well aware of the surprises things like this could hold. As the orb moved toward me, it flattened out and began to elongate. Something pushed at my mind, forcing me to turn around, as if I'd been ordered to, yet no one had spoken to me. The bands holding my arm at my side slipped off. Instantly I felt the energy fill my arm and Vairocina's voice flood my head.

"What happened?" she cried. "Where are we? Oh, that was horrible! It was as if I was locked in a box, unable to move, unable to see. I was going crazy. Johnny, what happened?"

But I couldn't answer her. Something else was controlling me now. I think it was that weird orb.

"JT?"

I was raising my arms as the thing snuggled up against my back. The transparent wires that held my arm in place returned. This time, though, they wrapped around my legs, my forehead, my arms, and even my waist. I think I heard Vairocina scream before my body became completely paralyzed. I felt the orb lift me off the ground and then tilt me forward. Now I was face-down about half a meter off the ground, my arms stretched out to my sides and my feet together. Finally, something reached over the top of my head and blocked my sight.

I felt the device gliding in the direction of my door. *No! I need to find Ketheria!* But I could tell we had slipped outside my room, as the air was much warmer on my skin. I began to hear things moving around me, or moving out of the way; I couldn't tell which.

"You bad," I heard the kid whisper in my ear. Was I being

paraded around in front of my captors like some prized possession? Where were they taking me?

Hey! I tried to scream, but even my mouth was paralyzed.

The sounds of people shuffling around me dropped off, and the air grew very cold. The device stopped, and my ears became plugged as if the air pressure had suddenly changed. Then the thing I was strapped to released me. Instinctually I thrust my arms forward to cushion my fall. As I hit the stone floor, Vairocina's voice came rushing back into my head.

"Stop doing that to me! What's happening?"

"Quiet, Vairocina," I whispered to her. "I think we're about to find out."

I paused for a moment, my hands and knees connected firmly with the cold, damp floor. Its rough texture sparkled from a shivery blue light glowing all around me. I would not look up. Some part of me was waiting for Ketheria to call out my name, waiting for her to rush over and tell me not to worry, that they had grabbed her, too.

"Get up," ordered a frigid and passionless voice.

I waited one more second for Ketheria, and then I looked up in the direction of the voice.

"Oh!" Vairocina gasped.

I was kneeling at the center of a vast, cavernous room. I think the entire room was constructed from stone, but I could also see metal, glass, and *flesh*. Directly in front of me, about three meters above the ground, were five glowing alcoves carved from the rock. Four of the chambers were occupied. The center one was empty and casting most of the icy blue light that filled the room. The *creatures* inside each chamber looked almost human, except that parts of their bodies were indistinguishable from the rocky surroundings. An arm would disappear into the wall and surface a meter away at an unnatural angle. Piping of all sizes emanated from the rock, into the chamber, and right through its occupant. It was as if these things were part of the room, each highlighted by the glowing light inside their chambers. That's when I noticed more people in the rock; I counted fourteen altogether, except the lights in their chambers were turned off. Only the center chamber was lit and empty.

"Who are you people?" I croaked softly.

"We are the Trust."

I stood up. My eyes darted across the four glowing members of the Trust. I did not see any lips move, but it was as if each of them were speaking to me.

"I have heard of you, but you have to let me go. I have to get back to my sister."

"There are matters that need to be discussed."

"I have to get back!"

Every bone in my body flexed at once, igniting a pyre of pain. It was short but effective. *Okay, so don't yell at them.*

"Yes, please don't do that again," Vairocina breathed in my ear.

"Listen to me," I told them. "I know you think I'm some sort of savior, this Scion thing of yours, but I'm not. I'm just a kid. I just want to *be* a kid. I want to take care of my sister and figure out how to live on those stupid rings. My sister needs me right now. For all I know, it might be too late. Please just put me back—"

"You are not the Scion," the Trust interrupted.

"What?"

"You are not the Scion."

It felt like someone had slapped me across the face.

I recalled snippets of conversation I had heard on Orbis 2 when they had replaced my arm: talk of the Scion and the Trust and their fear of my death. I should have felt relief, but a tiny part of me felt disappointed.

"Then why am I here?" I mumbled.

"Your jump."

"It was an unauthorized space jump."

"Where is the *burak*?"

"Yes, where is the belt?"

They all seemed to be talking to me at once. Their different body parts flinched as their eyes darted about. Even the ones in the dark seemed to be listening, as if waiting for my answer.

I did jump, didn't I? One moment I was standing in front of Banar's bait, and the very next instant I was on the other side, thrusting my fist into his back.

"How *did* you do that?" Vairocina asked.

"Quiet," I replied. "I don't have a Space Jumper's belt," I told them.

One member of the Trust twitched so hard that she dislodged her right arm from the rock with a sickening snap.

"That's impossible!" she cried out (or one of them did, anyway). Her arm shriveled like dead moss on a rock while tubes and wires slipped through the black stone and attended to the fresh wound. The improbable combination of rock, metal, and flesh made it difficult for me to understand what was happening.

"He hit my sister. I don't know how it happened. One moment I was here, and the next moment I was there."

The lights that illuminated each berth flickered in response like some broken control panel button. Their eyes, black and vacant, darted back and forth but never rested on anything. It seemed to me that they were talking to each other, but I wasn't sure. The silence was unnerving and painfully long. Another member shifted in the rock, and I flinched at the obscene sound of mutilating flesh and bone that cracked the dead air.

"Space Jumpers cannot jump without a belt," Vairocina whispered. "It's never been done. The belt works with the jumper's softwire ability to bend space and time, but the way I understand it, the belt does most of the work."

"This has set a new precedent," one of them interrupted.

"You must be observed."

"This is another augury."

"Can you demonstrate this ability now?" they asked me.

"No . . ."

My bones ignited as a fiery bolt of pain convulsed my body once again.

"I'm telling you the truth! Please!"

The pain stopped as quickly as it had come.

"Please. Can I go back? I won't do it again. I know things

have happened in the past, things like this, that make people think I'm the Scion guy, but—"

"You are not the Scion."

"Tell me who he is so the next time I see him I can thank him," I said.

"That knowledge must be restricted."

"Forbidden."

"Why?" I asked them.

"History has recorded its most tumultuous events upon the awakening of a Scion."

"I'm taking that to mean that bad things are going to happen, then. So where are the other Scions?"

"There are no others. Throughout the history of the universe, every last Scion has been killed by the very people who seek its enlightenment."

"Or so they claim," one of them mumbled. This set off a flurry of assertions by the rest of the Trust.

"They know not what they ask."

"That's why no one can know the identity of the Scion."

"If the Scion's identity is revealed . . ."

"If the Scion blossoms before the revelation . . . "

"The Scion will surely be killed."

Suddenly I felt very relieved that I wasn't the Scion.

"Your home planet has murdered several Scions."

"If the Scion does not succeed, then the universe will succumb to forces that feed on the fear and negativity generated by its masses."

"Then why aren't you protecting the Scion?" I asked them.

"We cannot intervene. The auguries have warned us not to interfere. Free will must choose the path of enlightenment, not force."

"But you," the Trust whispered, every member hanging on the last word, as still as the stone that encased them.

"What about me?"

For the first time, the eyes of the Trust focused on mine. Their stares linked to something inside me, something so deep I couldn't breathe.

"You can be trained to protect the Scion, for you are the Tonat."

"I'm the what?"

"The Protector."

"A champion."

"Some will worship you."

"A seraph."

"Others will fear you."

"A devil."

"Stop! You're all talking too fast."

My head felt heavy, crammed full with information that I could not decipher. *Vairocina, are you getting all of this?* I whispered inside my head.

Most of it, she replied.

"Does anyone know about this? Do they know about this Tonat thing?" I asked.

"Several Keepers have had suspicions since your staining."

"The event was seen as a favorable augury."

"An omen outlined by the prophecy."

"The genetic identity of the Scion is hidden."

"Until you are trained."

"It is safe."

"No one will look where we hid it."

"They will protect it with their lives."

"Who will?" I asked.

"The Citizens."

"Greed serves them well for this task."

"Everyone protects a treasure."

I held my hands up. "Please stop with this double-talk. It's too confusing. What do you mean a *treasure*? The Ancients' Treasure? What does that have to do with it?"

"You know of the Ancients' Treasure?" one asked me.

"Unnecessary information."

"The identity is safe."

Did the Trust hide the identity of the Scion near the Ancients' Treasure? Switzer was going after the treasure. I didn't care about the treasure. I told him to have it. Did he know? But I didn't care about the identity of the Scion. At least it wasn't me. Some poor split-screen was going to have the destiny of the universe thrust upon him. *Does* anyone *get to pick what they want to be around here?*

The Trust was waiting, but for what, I didn't know. I did, however, see an opportunity to get back to my sister. If I told them I would help, maybe they would let me go.

"Send me back now and I'll help protect this guy," I said.

"He knows too much," one of them replied.

"He has not yet chosen."

"Just tell me where it's hidden," I asked them.

"You do not need this information."

"If I'm going to protect this Scion guy, I will."

"You have not chosen."

"Chosen what?" This was frustrating. Every second I was here was one more second Ketheria was left with Banar.

"To become what you were created to do."

"Created? What do you mean *created*?" I asked.

"You are special."

"You are a success."

"You can be a Space Jumper."

"What if I don't want to be a Space Jumper?"

"That choice is also yours," they replied.

"But I doubt you can make that choice," someone whispered, close to me. I spun around, but no one was there.

"What do you mean? You said it's my choice."

"Technically."

I held my head in my hands. I didn't even try to figure out what that meant. What was happening to Ketheria? I thought about my promise to Max. I told her I would never become a Space Jumper. Would she understand? Would she accept the responsibility if she were in my shoes? I told her we would all stay together. Could I keep my promise to Max if I chose to be the Tonat—to be a Space Jumper?

"What if I say no?" I asked them.

"The fate of the Scion lies in the cosmic streams that flow through this universe."

The universe? That only means he'll be left to deal with the likes of Weegin or Odran, or Madame Lee. Even the Switzers of the universe!

"You would just let him die, then?" I said.

"We cannot interfere with the prophecy," they argued.

"I think you broke that rule a long time ago."

"The Universe will decide," they replied matter-of-factly.

"I can't believe you're willing to take that chance," I said.

"Then you accept."

"You choose your destiny."

"Your fate."

"No, I will not be a Space Jumper," I told them. I had made a promise to Max. I was not going to break it.

"An unwise decision," replied the Trust.

"It is not honorable."

"Quirin was wrong."

"This is a bad augury."

"Take him back to his cell."

"Maybe he will change his mind."

"Wait! Who is this Quirin guy? I've heard his name before. You have to put me back."

"No, we must understand your gift."

"To jump without a belt."

"Extraordinary!"

"Look," I pleaded. "My sister is in danger right now. Let me help her, and then I'll think about it. She's playing in the Chancellor's Challenge! You have to put me back!"

I crumpled to the floor, not because I was pleading with them but because my body had exploded with pain.

"You will obey us!" their collective voices rang out. It was more than sound; their voices were the very air I struggled to pull into my lungs.

"Put me back!"

More pain. I clutched my arms in fear that my bones were about to rip from my body. I thought about Ketheria lying on the ground—her broken body vulnerable to Banar. I was so tired of this. Tired of playing *their* games, following *their* rules. I was tired of being a knudnik.

"Put me back!"

JT, stop this. They're going to break every bone in your body, Vairocina pleaded in my head.

"I don't care. Put me back. I demand it!"

I pictured Banar standing over my sister while the Trust tried to snap my spine.

"Now!" I screamed at them.

And then I was gone. Wherever I had been, I wasn't there anymore. The pain was gone, too, and I was kneeling on the floor inside the labyrinth. Just like I had pictured, Banar was standing in front me, looming over Ketheria, his arm raised to strike. The faint smell of sweaty feet lingered in the air.

"Banar!"

The alien spun around and laughed when he saw me.

"Wait your turn!" he cried.

I stood up. "There won't be any more turns," I said. "This is enough. The game ends now."

A champion? A seraph? A devil? I'll show them. From where I stood, I pushed into the Labyrinth's computer through the escape button to my left. I willed my mind through the massive computer simply by thinking about where I wanted to go, almost as if I were *jumping* through it. I settled over the programs controlling the stadium. The data flashed through the virtual metropolis, exposed and vulnerable. I reached out with my mind and trashed whatever was in my path, without discretion.

"What are you doing, JT?" Vairocina questioned.

"I'm *choosing*—that's what I'm doing. I'm choosing not to play their game anymore. I'm choosing to protect my sister. I'm choosing . . . I'm choosing for *me* now."

"Oh."

I pulled out of the computer to find the labyrinth exposed and barren. Gone were the holographic walls, the obstacles, and even the lights. Banar and I stood at the center of an enormous circular pad comprised of concrete, circuits, and metal. It oddly reminded me of the Trust. Ketheria was still unconscious on the floor.

"What have you done?" Banar roared.

The crowd was on its feet, high above us. The aliens were screaming and pointing at me. I ignored them. The facade was gone. It was just Banar and me now.

"You want the same punishment I dealt your bait?" I asked him.

"Ha!" Banar's armor spun forward, locking in place as the monstrous alien lunged toward me. I *jumped* as he reached forward, or at least I tried to. Nothing happened. I remained exactly where I was. No smell of stinking feet. No pitted feeling in my stomach as if I were falling. Only Banar moving swiftly, arm raised ready to strike.

"JT?" My sister mumbled from the other side of the labyrinth. Ketheria was alive! I glanced past Banar to see Ketheria struggling to sit up. Every cell in my body wanted to be next to my sister. I jumped again, and this time I slipped through space and time as easily as if I were blinking. I was kneeling next to my sister as Banar stumbled over my previous location, reeling about. I heard the crowd gasp.

"Space Jumper!" someone screamed.

"Ketheria, Ketheria, are you all right?" I said, tapping my sister's cheek. The blood had not yet dried on her mouth.

"Ketheria!"

Her eyes were closed again, but then they flickered open. She *was* alive. I let out a breath I had been holding for a very long time.

"Where are we?" she croaked, looking around.

"We're still in the labyrinth. Can you walk?"

"I think so."

Ketheria stood up, a little wobbly at first, but she assured me she would be all right. Banar was just as cautious. Everyone had heard stories about Space Jumpers, and I'm sure he was no different.

"It's your choice," I told him. "You can let us pass or you can die here. You might even find that honorable. The task will be nothing more than an annoyance for me."

"JT?" Ketheria whispered.

Four security drones, larger than any I had ever seen before, drifted into the vacant playing field and splashed us with their incriminating searchlights.

"Remain where you are," they demanded in unison.

"Nope," I said, and pushed into each device simultaneously. I corrupted any functioning code I could find. The machines, disoriented and useless, crashed into the wall before hitting the ground.

"Well, Banar?" I said.

Banar did not speak. He simply stepped aside.

"Where are we going?" Ketheria asked.

"Down there," I said, pointing to the drain at the center of the labyrinth.

18

A new and invigorating sense of myself streamed through my body as I dragged Ketheria through the drainage system of the labyrinth. It felt like someone had cracked open my skull and rewired my brain. The new data screamed at me, *Can you see it now? Do you get it?*

I did. The Trust had awakened something inside me. I could even see Switzer's point of view, if just a little. Whatever my parents had planned for us on the Rings of Orbis, it was not for me to find out, and I didn't care anymore.

Ketheria and I were forced to squeeze together as the tubes narrowed. They were much smaller than the tunnels that led to Toll Town on Orbis 2. I was very aware, however, that the Trust might come after me. I had jumped again, and this time right in front of them. I didn't have a clue if they could track my movements or if they simply focused on the point of my jump. The Trust *did* mention that they were aware of my staining, so

I had to assume that they could track me as easily as my last Guarantor had. If that were the case, then where were they? They should have caught me the moment I jumped. Whatever technique they used, though, I was planning to make it very difficult for them to find me.

I stopped when the tunnel split. This new part of me felt very alien. This fresh sense of myself, of my own identity, pushed me, but I was still unaware of what it actually meant. My feelings kept giving me pause as I looked at each decision with this new filter. I knew I was no longer going to wait for people to tell me what to do. I was living for myself now. For the very first time, I felt like my choices were my own. Right now I wanted to find Switzer. I needed his help.

"You can't possibly be considering that," Ketheria said, reading my thoughts as I chose the tunnel to my right.

"Why not? I should have listened to him a long time ago. Besides, he's only a means to an end."

"You can't trust him."

"I don't plan to."

I knew Switzer was going after the Ancients' Treasure. I was counting on the idea that the Citizens would make it quite difficult for him to get at it.

"What if he's already gone?" Ketheria said.

"He's not."

Something inside me told me that he was still on his quest; that Switzer was still on the Rings of Orbis. It was all I had to go on.

Ketheria and I waded knee-deep through a small pool that

gathered in front of another grate. The metal bars had been cut and pushed apart. Switzer had come this way. "What about the others?" Ketheria said.

"Once you're safe, I'll come back and get them. I'll jump if I have to."

Ketheria did not reply.

"Even Nugget," I added to reassure her, but Ketheria simply waited in front of the grate.

"There's a drop," she said, peering through the gnarled metal. She was hesitating, but I sensed that it had nothing to do with the drop.

"If Switzer can do it, then so can we."

"You're assuming he survived," she argued.

"He did."

Ketheria jumped into the tunnel and disappeared. All I heard was her scream.

"Ketheria!"

I dove in after her, only to discover that the tunnel dumped into a large reservoir. It was a five-meter drop before I hit the water, barely missing my sister.

"This has to recycle back into the labyrinth," I cried. "Switzer is close."

I swam to the edge of the pool and then helped Ketheria out of the water. There was only one exit from the room, and the door was already pried open. A pinkish light seeped through the forced entry. From where we stood, I could hear the sounds of a struggle on the other side of the door.

"He's in there," I told her.

"JT, wait. Let him go. Don't go in there," she pleaded, wiping the water from her face, but leaving a look of worry.

"What are you *not* telling me?" I asked her.

"Nothing. We don't need Switzer."

"Yes, we do," I said. "Now, stay close."

We stepped through the door and under a huge dome. The pink light emanated from something suspended in the center of the room. It looked like some sort of kid's toy—a bouncing ball covered in rubber knobs or something. The details were hard to distinguish as beads of golden light zipped around the strange artifact, obscuring it from my view. *Is that the Ancients' Treasure?* I wondered. It couldn't be; it seemed so insignificant. On the far side of the object stood Switzer. He was under attack from four heavily armed security bots. I saw two more robots lying lifeless on the metal walkway that circled the room. Switzer was no match for the remaining bots. He was already bleeding from a gash to his head, and his back was up against the wall, literally.

"Switzer!" I called out to him.

"Just in time!" he shouted casually as one of the bots blew a hole in the wall close to his face. I moved around the weird thing in the center of the room and pushed into the bot, disabling it. The flying machine exploded when it hit the ground.

"Where were you earlier? Stop the others," he ordered me.

"I want to make a deal first."

"You're in no position to make a deal!" Another bot managed to zap Switzer in the shoulder.

"Fine. See you later," I said.

"Wait! Stop them and we'll talk."

"No, we talk now. Besides, I don't think you have much longer."

"What could you possibly want? I am not giving you back your arm. I've kind of grown attached to the thing."

"Keep the arm. Do you have some sort of plan to get off the ring when you get the treasure?"

"No, I thought I would hang out on the rings, see if I could get my old job back. Of course I do, Dumbwire!"

"Then I want you to take us with you, away from the Rings of Orbis. I want out of here."

"No, JT!" Ketheria cried. "You know the consequences."

Switzer swung a chain at the closest bot, but his effort was in vain. The thing didn't even budge. "I think you should listen to baby-malf," he shouted. "You don't want to go where I go. You couldn't handle it."

"Let me decide that."

The three bots had Switzer cornered. One moved in and fired some sort of wire that bolted Switzer to the wall. Switzer struggled, but he could not remove the wire.

"I changed my mind," he cried. "You can come with me. Just get these filthy adding machines off me!"

I pushed into the remaining bots and wiped them clean. The bots crashed to the ground. Entering a computer component was getting easier for me. I didn't even feel it this time.

"There will be more," I said.

"You can count on it," he replied.

I walked over to Switzer and, using my good arm, ripped out the wire pinning him to the wall.

"What's wrong with her?" he asked.

I spun around to find Ketheria leaning against the wall, her eyes closed.

"Ketheria, what's wrong?"

"Nothing," she mumbled, and tried to straighten up. I grabbed her arm to help her up.

"What is it?"

"Nothing. We have to leave here."

"We're going, but not until I have that treasure," Switzer said.

"Hurry, then. Where is it?"

"Right behind you," he replied.

"That?" I said, pointing to the device hovering at the center of the room. The treasure was suspended over a metal craft comprised of five tapered spokes. Each spoke, or arm, ended with some sort of small propulsion engine, and the whole device floated over a huge void at the center of the room. I followed a trail of light that descended into the nothingness and out of sight. I assumed they used this to raise the device up and through the ceiling.

"It almost looks alive, doesn't it?" Switzer beamed. There was admiration in his voice.

"How do you plan on getting it?" I asked.

"Walk across those spokes and take it."

"Are you nuts?"

"I've done it once already. That's what triggered those flying chow synths. I even had the treasure in my hands, but it simply floated back to where it is now."

"Don't you think more people are going to come?" Ketheria questioned him.

"Of course they will," Switzer mimicked in a high, whiny voice. "So let's get moving."

"How? Where?" I said.

Switzer stepped on the closest engine, and the strange flier teetered before readjusting to his weight. He moved quickly along the spoke to the machine's center, where the treasure hovered.

"When the final match of the Chancellor's Challenge is completed, the silicon gray matter in this sweet little thing sparks to life and lifts my treasure up and onto the labyrinth floor."

"Right into their hands," I pointed out.

"Quit interrupting," he snapped. "The flier doesn't stop. It can't. It's hardwired to continue up and past the audience, through the roof of the Labyrinth, and into an awaiting ship that collects their prized bauble and whisks it off to safety."

"So you're going to swipe the treasure on the roof? How are you going to get off the Labyrinth? This building is enormous."

Switzer shook his head. "You're going to make a lousy wormhole pirate."

"Trust me, I don't plan to stick around long enough to follow in your footsteps."

Switzer snickered. "My men are pirating the craft assigned

to retrieve the Ancients' Treasure as we speak. Once we're on the roof, this device, with us and the treasure on it, will tuck itself into the spacecraft and we'll be back inside the wormhole before these space monkeys even know what happened."

"You're forgetting that many thousands of fans are about to watch you do this," Ketheria reminded him.

"You give them too much credit. Now hurry and get on this thing."

I took Ketheria's hand and stepped onto the spoked flier.

"Don't look down," I whispered, and gingerly moved to the platform. Switzer knelt down and removed a long metal panel. He took a small device from his trouser pocket and attached it to something within the flier before replacing the panel.

"Wakey, wakey," he ordered, and the five engines of the craft hummed to life. I looked up to see the iris in the ceiling crack open.

Switzer stood up, swiped at some of the dry blood puddled on the metal embedded in his forehead, and stared at the treasure. "I can't wait to see what's in there," he mumbled.

"How do you plan to open it?" Ketheria asked.

"Only the Scion can open it," he replied.

"The Scion won't open it for you," she said.

"I have his arm, remember? I have his fingerprints, his DNA. Hell, I even have tissue samples. I figured any one of those little trinkets would do the trick, but now that he's here—"

"I'm not the Scion," I interrupted.

"Yes, you are," he insisted.

"I'm not."

But Switzer wasn't listening. I shook my head.

"I honestly thought it would be bigger. Folklore whispers that the treasure can buy a trillion starships, but I'm sure that's an exaggeration. It doesn't look big enough. What do you think's in there, yornaling crystals?"

I didn't answer Switzer. Something felt wrong. I couldn't stop thinking about the Trust's warning. I glanced down at the chamber shrinking away from me. Nothing in the room looked special now that the treasure and its craft were headed out. Maybe the Trust had hidden the Scion's identity somewhere deep within the abyss that was slowly consuming the vacant room. The metal carcasses of the broken bots seemed like such a weak defense for their prized secret. I breathed deeply and consoled myself with the idea that we were leaving this place without exposing the identity of the Scion. It was no longer my concern, I told myself. Instead I needed to concentrate on getting off the Rings of Orbis, since Switzer's plan was a fantasy at best.

Despite my doubts in Switzer's revelations, the craft drifted up and through the iris as promised, arriving at some sort of auditorium. I instantly recognized the Chancellor, and he immediately noticed us. Armed guards jumped into position upon our arrival.

"I thought no one knew you were doing this, Switzer," I said, motioning to the guards. I had never seen live security aliens like this on the rings, only security-bots.

The Chancellor's private army raised their weapons and rested their aim upon us. Switzer seemed prepared for his virulent reception and grabbed the treasure, pulling it close.

"Wouldn't want to hit this, now, would you, Chancellor?"

"Do not fire!" the Chancellor called out, wildly swinging his arms above the heads of two aliens hunched over a bunch of O-dats. The small aliens tapped furiously on the O-dats, stopping only to glance at the craft as we rose steadily within the auditorium.

"Hurry!" the Chancellor shouted at them. "Why can't you stop them?"

"We're trying," one of them pleaded.

"They've taken control of the flier somehow," the other complained.

"It's the Softwire!" yelled one of the Citizens.

"Kill the Softwire!" someone else hollered.

"Better get closer to me," Switzer said as a volley of blistering plasma screeched past our heads.

"Stop! Stop! You'll damage the treasure!" the Chancellor yelled.

Ketheria caught Switzer grinning. "You're enjoying this, aren't you?" she said to him.

"Of course I am. Look at them—they're pathetic."

"I would still like to know how they knew you were coming."

"Me, too," Switzer mumbled under his breath.

More and more Citizens scrambled into the auditorium, then stopped the moment they spotted us. One of the aliens, dressed in some sort of transparent armor, toppled over two other Citizens trying to enter the room

"Get to the roof!" he shouted at them. "They're going for the roof!"

"Shoot the flier, then!" the Chancellor barked.

"But sir, the engines will explode."

The Chancellor grunted so loud that spit flew from his puckered mouth. His eyes, bulging with rage, searched each Citizen in the room, frantic to find a solution. When none of them spoke, the Chancellor turned to Switzer and snarled, "You won't live to enjoy that treasure."

But Switzer only laughed at him. His confidence was high now, and it surprised me. Switzer actually planned to walk (or, rather, fly) right out of here.

"JT, several traces have been placed on your staining," Vairocina whispered in my mind. "I think we should call the Keepers."

"Don't," I told her. "I think we might actually be leaving."

The ceiling began to peel back, revealing the distant stars. *Which one will we head for?* I wondered. It was actually happening. I could feel it. Secretly I had hoped that Max and Theodore were on the roof, but I knew they wouldn't be. I'd never convince Switzer to come back for them, but I would jump back to the ring in order to get Max.

"It's too easy," Ketheria said.

"What do you mean?" I replied

"Something as valuable as the treasure, and he just walks up and takes it?"

"He hasn't left the ring yet," I reminded her.

"That's the easy part," Switzer interrupted.

But I didn't see anything easy about it. At least forty more armed aliens were now waiting on the roof. I saw Switzer searching the horizon for something. Seemingly unsatisfied, he began searching the sky.

"Where are they?" he grunted.

"Who? Who's not here?"

"His ship," Ketheria said. "Have your goons let you down, Switzer?"

"Shut up," Switzer barked. "They'll be here. Or else."

"Or else what? If we don't have a way out of here, I don't think you'll have much of an opportunity to punish any of them," I said.

"Shut up!" Switzer said, and swung at me, knocking me to the floor.

"Stop it!" Ketheria screamed. She knelt next to me and whispered, "How can you want to do this now? How can you even think of leaving the others—to go with him? The brother I knew would never do that."

"I can *jump*," I whispered back. "I've done it already. I can come back and get them."

"How? Without a belt?"

"Yes."

"And you are absolutely sure you can do this?"

"Yes!"

But could I? *Was* I absolutely sure? I had tried to jump when Banar came at me and nothing happened. It wasn't until . . . *Ketheria*. It wasn't until I thought about *her*. How could my ability to jump be attached to my sister? It had to be a coincidence. All I needed to do was concentrate more. The moment Ketheria was safe, I would jump back and grab Max and Theodore.

Ketheria was staring at me, her big brown eyes scanning my mind.

"Don't do that," I told her. "I don't know what I'm thinking, so don't trust everything you read."

"It's what I don't see that worries me the most."

"There they are!" Switzer shouted. "Get ready to board ship, everyone. We are cleared for departure."

There was a ship coming, a shallow but broad flier, ample enough for us—and anyone else on the roof, for that matter. *We are actually getting out of here.* The ship was moving quickly. Three armed fliers chased the craft, and all four of them were exchanging fire.

"Be quick! The boys are bringin' her in hot!" Switzer called out.

Once I was on that ship, could I jump back to Orbis? Could I actually do it? I was suddenly mad at Ketheria for making me doubt myself. I *would* do it. There was no choice for me. I sprang to my feet.

"What do we have to do, Switzer?" I asked.

"You can start by opening that treasure. I don't need the damned case, just what's inside it."

"Switzer, I told you I'm not the Scion."

"I've done my homework, little man. You are the Scion, whether you want to believe it or not."

"I'm *not.*"

"Listen to me, Dumbwire. We're not kids anymore. At least, I'm not. This is not the time to get *tricky.* Open the treasure, and I'll get you off this revolving hunk of junk."

"You're getting me off the ring because I stopped those bots. That was the deal."

"Open the treasure!"

I reached out and grabbed the treasure to prove to Switzer I was not the Scion. The golden lights orbiting it sparked and gathered speed. The colored knobs changed from a pinkish-purple to a deep amber shade as the treasure vibrated in my hands.

"But . . ." *The Trust told me that I wasn't the Scion. They told me I was the Protector. Was it all a ruse?*

"See! What did I tell you? It didn't do that for me," Switzer exclaimed.

The treasure began to distort and elongate. I looked at Ketheria; her eyes were closed and she was mumbling, or moaning, I couldn't tell. Above her in the sky, I saw a dozen large wheels spinning vertically in the air. One by one they landed on the roof ahead of our spacecraft, which was now under fire from the guards on the roof. Each circular flier carried a Keeper, and as they came to a rest on the roof, the aliens disembarked and moved toward us.

The treasure vibrated erratically in my hands, and I struggled with it to keep my grip. It was bright red now, and I could feel the energy from the thing spreading into my body. If this thing was going to open, I wished it would hurry up and do it.

I'm the Scion? It was more of a question than a statement. I wondered what it meant. What was going to happen now? Surely people could see me. I saw more and more Citizens gathering on the roof. *So much for keeping the Scion's identity a secret,* I thought.

Switzer's escape craft settled over us, and three wormhole pirates descended from the belly of the ship using thin black ropes. The one closest to Switzer tossed him a plasma rifle, and Switzer immediately began picking off the guards on the roof.

"They're not firing at you!" Ketheria yelled.

"They would if they could, little girl."

"Move back!" a Keeper shouted. "Do not return fire!"

The Keeper was Theylor. He was moving quickly. The Chancellor was behind him. Then I saw Athooyi with Max. Athooyi's guards were with them, but it didn't matter. Seeing Max made me feel like everything was going to be all right. She looked worried, almost panicked, but then her face drifted out of focus. Her image blurred with that of the Keepers. In fact, everything seemed to soften and smudge together.

"JT, the treasure has somehow penetrated your nervous system," Vairocina warned.

She was right. The energy from the treasure had taken over my body. My hands appeared to have melted into the casing. My head was spinning, and my knees felt weak, like I was going to fall.

Then the treasure exploded from my hands and shot into the air toward the ship. "Now!" I heard someone scream.

Switzer yelled to his men, "Grab the treasure!"

Everyone began firing at once. The blood came rushing back into my head, but my eyes were now blackening around the edges.

"Move!" Switzer shouted, and shoved me out of the way.

A burst of plasma, a shot meant for me, hit Switzer squarely in the shoulder. He stumbled back, dropping to one knee as I fell from the flier and hit the ground.

"JT!" Ketheria screamed.

Switzer growled in pain. With his left arm useless, he shifted all his weight to his right leg and hoisted the heavy gun against his hip. He returned fire with such viciousness that the flier was set aglow by an explosion of purple plasma that rained down from his firearm.

"Do not hit the girl!" Theylor shouted.

More Citizens were moving toward me, and I scrambled to my feet, searching for the treasure. Ketheria was standing behind Switzer when the Ancients' Treasure descended upon her. My sister lifted her arms to accept the object of so much attention. When the vessel touched her fingertips, it hovered for a moment before convulsing into a deluge of brilliant white light. The shock wave knocked Switzer from the flier, and the entire night sky lit up as if someone had fired a magnesium burner. Ketheria, her arms reaching up, stood motionless under the rapturous glow. The sparkles of gold light that had once circled the treasure now danced around Ketheria's fingertips, displaying the same little spirals Ketheria had drawn when she was sick. The golden lights flickered from her fingertips and enmeshed inside her cupped hands as the playful lights began to build within the white glow. One by one the golden sparkles converged to assemble a chain—a DNA chain. The double helix spiraled in my sister's grasp, rising up toward the ship before morphing into the shape of a little girl. The image was undeniable.

The image was Ketheria.

The crowd on the roof stood motionless. Even Switzer stopped and watched the miraculous event. The mirror image descended upon her and merged with Ketheria's physical form. She did not fight it; in fact, she breathed deeply and smiled as the transformation completed.

Ketheria was the Scion, *not me*. The Ancients' Treasure was the identity of the Scion. Of course the treasure could buy a million starships. The look on the faces of those watching told you that they had just witnessed the event of the millennium.

Ketheria looked up and smiled. Then the very physics that held the stars in the sky seemed to fail—in other words, all hell broke loose.

Switzer grabbed Ketheria with his bad arm, and the crowd gasped.

"Put her down," Theylor demanded.

"I came here for a treasure and I plan on taking one," he replied.

"Switzer, don't," I pleaded.

Switzer looked at me. "If you're coming, then I advise you to come now."

Theylor was near me. "You are the Tonat, Johnny Turnbull. You must help her. The Scion must stay with us."

"You knew?"

"I know now. You must believe me. Do not let her get on that ship. Now that her identity has been revealed, she is at tremendous risk. Your sister is not even of age yet—she must still experience her awakening."

I didn't know what Theylor was talking about, but my desire to leave Orbis had weakened enormously.

"Switzer . . ." I turned to reason with Switzer, and everything around me went silent. I had been bubbled. I turned inside the green fog to see the Chancellor running toward me, his right arm outstretched. Theylor was arguing with him, but the Chancellor now had his sights set on Switzer.

Max had broken free from Athooyi and ran toward me. She banged her fists on the security bubble, her face streaked with tears. She turned and grabbed one of the Chancellor's aides, but he pushed her away.

Switzer hoisted Ketheria in his arms, her feet dangling just below his knees. She did not resist. Another wormhole pirate swung a rope to Switzer. He grabbed it while firing at the Chancellor. He hit the Chancellor's aide on the first shot.

If Switzer got on that ship, I would never see either of them again. Why wasn't Ketheria resisting? The thought of Ketheria leaving without me ignited that feeling inside me once again. It was as if a rope had been tethered between the two of us and something had pulled it very taut. The closer Switzer got to the ship, the tighter the rope felt, only now it was ripping my skin with each tug.

I jumped out of the bubble.

I pictured myself behind Switzer, and then I was there. Only, Switzer was on one of the ropes, halfway up to the ship. I scrambled to grab on to something and caught Switzer around the neck.

"What the . . .?" Switzer cried out.

He strained to see who was on his back.

"Nice trick," Switzer said when he saw me. "Couldn't you have waited until we were inside?"

"Don't drop her," I warned him.

"Then grab the rope and get off me!"

Theylor was watching me. That new sense of myself, the one that had brought me to this point, was screaming at me not to get on that ship with Switzer. I stared at my friend and nodded. I hoped he understood. I hoped he was right.

"I'm sorry, Switzer. It's different now. There are things I need to understand first, and I believe people around here are going to start answering my questions."

"Don't be a fool, split-screen. They just want to use you!"

"We're not getting on that ship."

With one motion, I kicked the gun from Switzer's hand and latched on to Ketheria. Then I jumped. Instantly we were next to Theylor. The Keeper was already ready, reaching out with his right arm, and Switzer was bubbled before he even realized we were gone. With Ketheria out of the way, the guards fired upon those remaining, and the wormhole pirates were subdued before Switzer's new green cell hit the ground.

But those now on the roof were more interested in the Scion than in a captured wormhole pirate. They rushed toward Ketheria. Athooyi was shoving the other Citizens and ordering his guards to do the same. I shielded my sister from Athooyi, waiting for a barrage of insults from him. Then Athooyi's guards circled Ketheria and turned to face Athooyi and the mob. The creatures began to morph, but instead of turning into fierce beasts, their bodies stretched upward and thick silky robes replaced their flashy garments. Soon four Nagool masters were protecting my sister and me from Athooyi and the mob that was now on the roof. Throughout the crowd, some were screaming; some dropped to their knees and shielded their gaze from the Nagool masters. Athooyi suddenly turned to run. Before he was able to take a single step, he was bubbled.

"What is the meaning of this?" demanded the Chancellor. "Where is the treasure?"

"The treasure belongs to the Universe," Theylor replied.

"Security! Take everyone into custody," the Chancellor ordered.

The guards rushed the Nagool masters, and Theylor motioned toward the device on his wrist. Instantly a half-dozen Space Jumpers appeared in the crowd. The Citizens on the roof screamed and shrank back from the Space Jumpers as they moved toward us.

"Have you gone mad, Keeper? Do you want another war?" the Chancellor spat.

"Right now I only want some room," Theylor said calmly.

"No one is leaving here until I am satisfied."

"I am not interfering with the efforts of the Trading Council. You may prosecute the wormhole pirates as you see fit."

"It's him I want!" the Chancellor bellowed, pointing at me.

I felt someone's hand slip into mine. It was Max. She was at my side.

"I must protect the Scion," Theylor said. "I offer that we move these individuals to a private chamber where we can satisfy the needs of the Trading Council."

The Chancellor glanced at the Space Jumpers before mumbling, "I doubt that's possible now."

"For the sake of the rings, I ask you to try," Theylor said.

19

Nugget was released while Ketheria and I were in the custody of the Trading Council. Ketheria was ecstatic to see him. It only reminded me that Charlie was gone. Despite every effort by Theylor, the Council refused to hand us over to the Keepers to bear witness to the ceremony planned by Rose and Albert, Charlie's two closest friends on Orbis. My only consolation was that Cala would now face the Council for the murder since Charlie was a Citizen.

It was difficult for me to comprehend Charlie's death. I think my mind simply believed I would see Charlie again, but it wouldn't happen. At least Ketheria had Nugget. Secretly, I worried that I had become some cold, hardened machine, since Charlie's death hadn't affected me as deeply as it did the others; at least, I felt that way. I loved Charlie, but the emotions I felt over his death were eerily similar to the way I felt when I had learned of Switzer's supposed death. Was that what it meant to be the Tonat?

Theylor told me that Switzer was being held in the Center for Science and Research and that many Citizens wanted to see the wormhole pirate dead, especially when they learned that he had once been a knudnik. I didn't know how to feel about that. During the Chancellor's Challenge, I had somehow grown to respect him in a weird way. Switzer had taken control of his life. He was living the life of a free man, but then again, that had only landed him in one of those pale blue cells somewhere on Orbis 1. I often thought about the moment I had jumped with Ketheria and left Switzer to be bubbled. What if I had crawled into the ship with him and then jumped to safety with Ketheria? If I could do it all over again, I think I would have done it that way. I don't know why I wanted Switzer to be free, especially since he was partly responsible for Charlie's death. Somehow I felt that a part of me, a part of all of us, was locked inside that cell with Switzer. If he were free to roam the stars, then that part of me would be out there with him. Instead, he was in prison, and I was still a knudnik. That concept and my actions were slowly eating away at something inside me. The feelings kept me awake at night in my sleeper while we waited for the Trading Council's decision. It was worse than thinking about Charlie's death.

The Nagool masters had come to visit me with Theylor to inform me about the Council's decision. Theylor explained that they had been working with the Keepers for many rotations.

"You mean you're a spy?" I asked.

"You might say that," he replied.

"Monitoring Athooyi was necessary for us to see if anyone

was ever getting close to the Ancients' Treasure. We always knew what was in there."

"Did you know it was Ketheria?"

"We had our suspicions after the staining. That is why we placed you in Charlie's custody."

"It was you who gave him all that wealth?"

"With the help of the Nagools," Theylor said.

"The Citizens are very secretive on Orbis 3. This was the only way to stay close. I was scoping your entire match. Because you were a softwire, it made it very easy for me to know what Captain Ceesar, or rather Switzer, was up to. He would never have gotten off that roof. The fact that you and Ketheria were with him only slowed us down a little. We did not want to hurt either of you."

I tried to accept his statement. I told myself that Switzer would not have gotten off that roof no matter what I did, but my reasoning rang false.

"What's going to happen to us now?" I asked.

"The Chancellor is not a believer. He is also extremely upset about his match. A lot of money was lost, and the Chancellor is partial to his chits," Theylor informed us. "They disqualified you, and since you left the labyrinth unusable, they had to disqualify Banar's team, too. That left the only remaining team victorious."

"Riis's team?" I said.

"How did you know?"

"Just a guess," I said.

At least someone is free now, I thought. Riis got her wish. A dangerous way to go about it, but I was very glad I never had to face my friend in the labyrinth. At least something had worked out for the best.

"The Trust told me that it was very dangerous for the Scion if her identity was revealed."

"This is very true," Theylor agreed.

"But the auguries are very clear. We cannot intervene in the life of the Scion prior to the awakening," one of the Nagool masters added.

"And when is that supposed to happen?" I asked.

"Soon."

"Until then, the Council demands that you and your sister finish out your work rule," he said. "And we must abide."

"Are you kidding me? That's impossible."

"But she has her Tonat," Theylor said, resting his arm on my shoulder.

"But I never accepted that. I never chose," I told Theylor.

"There is still time," he whispered.

"Never chose what?" Max said as she entered my room with Ketheria. Theodore was with them. He was limping, with a strange contraption around his leg, but at least he was smiling. At least he was still alive.

"He means that we have not yet chosen your new Guarantor, I'm afraid," Theylor interrupted.

"Oh," Max said, and sat next to me. "We still have to do that stuff?"

"I'm afraid so," Theylor said. "It is the only way they will release JT and Ketheria. The Trading Council wants things to remain the same."

I looked at my sister, and she said, "I doubt things can ever be the same around here now."